Margaret Tufts Yardley

The New Jersey Scrap Book of Women Writers

Vol. 1

Margaret Tufts Yardley

The New Jersey Scrap Book of Women Writers
Vol. 1

ISBN/EAN: 9783337386306

Printed in Europe, USA, Canada, Australia, Japan

Cover: Foto ©Andreas Hilbeck / pixelio.de

More available books at **www.hansebooks.com**

THE

NEW JERSEY SCRAP BOOK

OF

WOMEN WRITERS

PUBLISHED BY THE BOARD OF LADY MANAGERS FOR NEW JERSEY TO
REPRESENT THE MANY WRITERS WHO ARE NOT
BOOKMAKERS AT THE

WORLD'S COLUMBIAN EXPOSITION.

COLLECTED AND ARRANGED BY

MARGARET TUFTS YARDLEY.

—

VOL. I.

NEWARK, N. J.
ADVERTISER PRINTING HOUSE,
1893

PRESS OF

ADVERTISER PRINTING HOUSE.

NEWARK, N. J.

BINDERY OF

WILLIAM KOCH,

NEWARK, N. J.

PREFACE.

THE last article for THE NEW JERSEY SCRAP BOOK has been placed in the hands of the printer. The index arranged, the title-page provided, a little history of the work of the Board of Women Managers prepared by our Secretary, Mrs. Roebling, the preface only is needed. Perhaps it is as well to answer for the last time the question that has been most frequently asked : " What is THE NEW JERSEY SCRAP BOOK for ?" When the Commission appointed the Board of Women Managers last June, each member was asked to attend to a certain line of work, and that of collecting a library of the writings of the women of New Jersey was given to the compiler. This work was begun in October last. Several complications arose. It was found that, though many writers lived and wrote in New Jersey, their works were published in New York. There also appeared to be a number of women writers who had never written books, yet were constant contributors to the magazines and newspapers of the day. With the hope of collecting their names and some short articles from their pens between the two covers of a book, THE NEW JERSEY SCRAP BOOK was thought of, and the writers appealed to. Two hundred and seventy have responded favorably; a few have preferred to be identified with New York. The time was too short and the work too arduous to use the influence that might have inspired them with a little more loyalty to our wave-beaten State.

The articles sent have generally been too long, and the very trying duty of "cutting down" has had to be done, so that all long articles are extracts. Almost every article has been published in some magazine or newspaper.

THE SCRAP BOOK has grown to a two-volumed one, and might easily have filled three volumes, had it been prudent to undertake so much. Five hundred copies only are to be printed of the two volumes; that, and the fact that it is the first collective work of the women writers of New Jersey, will give the book its value. The interest shown by the members of the Literary Committee all over the State, the many pleasant incidents connected with the voluminous correspondence with the contributors, and the feeling that the work has been a liberal education, are the compiler's reward.

MARGARET T. YARDLEY,

Chairman of Committee of Literature
for New Jersey.

MARCH 8TH, 1893.

History of the Board of Women Managers for the State of New Jersey.

By the authority of the Legislature the Board of Lady Managers were appointed by Governor Leon Abbett, in June, 1892. This Board consisted of Mrs. Robert Adrain, New Brunswick; Miss Mary S. Clark, Belvidere; Mrs. Thomas T. Kinney, Newark; Mrs Washington A. Roebling, Trenton; Mrs. Edwin A. Stevens, Hoboken; Mrs. Sarah G. Ware, Salem; Mrs. Charles B. Yardley, East Orange; Mrs. John Watts Kearny, Kearny. Mrs. Kearny having tendered her resignation Mrs. Michael T. Barrett was appointed in her place.

Governor Abbett, in his message, says: "This Board has organized by the election of Mrs. Edwin A. Stevens as Chairman, Mrs. Thomas T. Kinney as Vice-Chairman and Mrs. Emily Warren Roebling as Secretary, and has entered heartily into the spirit of its work, and will undoubtedly succeed in making such a display of the handiwork of the women of New Jersey as shall be creditable alike to their sex and to the State."

The work to be done was divided among the nine members of the Board as follows:

Mrs. Stevens became Chairman of the Committee to Aid in the Collection of a Loan Exhibit.

Mrs. Thomas T. Kinney, Chairman of the Art and Decorative Art Committee.

Mrs. Roebling, Chairman of the Statistics as the Amount of Woman's Work in the Manufactories of the State, the Number of Women in Industrial Pursuits and the Patents Obtained by Women.

Mrs. Adrain, Chairman of the Committee on the Charitable Work of Women.

Miss Murray, Chairman of the Committee on Philanthropic and Church Work.

Mrs. Ware, Chairman of the Educational Statistics of Women.

Miss Clark, Chairman of the Committee to Collect and Exhibit the Colonial and Revolutionary Relics in the State.

Mrs. Yardley, Chairman of the Literature Committee, whose duty was to collect two copies of every book in the State written by women, and to compile and arrange the NEW JERSEY SCRAP BOOK, which should contain at least one article of every female contributor to periodicals or newspapers. One set of the books collected will be placed in the Library of the Women's Building, and at the close of the Fair presented to the State Library in the State House, Trenton. The second copy will be placed in a bookcase in the Reception Room of the Board of Lady Managers in the New Jersey Building, Jackson Park. Many of the duplicate copies being only loans will be returned to their owners at the close of the Fair.

In addition to these duties as Chairman of special committees each lady member of the Board took charge of all the work of all kinds that was intended for Chicago from the Congressional District from which she was appointed. This work consisted in selecting chairmen to take charge of the work in each County, and then to work with this County Chairman in selecting chairmen for sub-committees, rousing an interest in the work—furnishing them with all the information they needed—and taking a general supervision of everything in their district, which concerned woman's work or woman's welfare. It was no easy task to visit cities where all were strangers, organize and conduct a meeting, address an audience that felt but little interest in the work and showed no enthusiasm. But this work was finally accomplished in every part of the State ; in some places we must own not very well, but then there were many earnest, zealous workers who have done so well they have made up for the shortcomings of the few who have failed us.

Mrs. Ware represented Camden, Cumberland, Cape May, Gloucester and Salem Counties.

Mrs. Roebling—Atlantic, Burlington, Mercer and Ocean Counties.

Mrs. Adrain—Somerset, Middlesex and Monmouth Counties.

Miss Clark—Sussex, Warren and Hunterdon Counties.

Miss Murray—Bergen and Passaic Counties.

Mrs. Kinney—The City of Newark.

Mrs. Barrett—Harrison and Kearny.

Mrs. Stevens—Jersey City and Hoboken.

Mrs. Yardley—Union, Morris and Essex Counties, outside the City of Newark.

It is to be feared that history will not chronicle the great deeds and patient efforts of this little band who have endeavored, to the best of their talents and abilities, to aid in the great work now being carried on all over the civilized world to show the advancement of woman, her needs and her talents, and to help to lighten the burden of the many women who have to earn their daily bread. If we have aided or encouraged even one woman who, without our encouragement and advice might have failed, then our work has not been in vain. Doubtless we might have done much more and done much better the little we have undertaken, but we hope the people of New Jersey will feel as Governor Abbett expressed it, "That our work has at least been creditable to woman and to the State."

EMILY WARREN ROEBLING,

Secretary.

Index to Writers.

THE NEW JERSEY SCRAP BOOK.

THE ADVANTAGES OF A COLLEGE EDUCATION FOR GIRLS.

BY LUCILLE ANDREWS.

There was a young woman who knew
Greek, Latin, perhaps Sanscrit, too;
But in making of pies she was not very wise,
And baking she never could do.

She could construe, could parse, and could phrase,
She had studied the stars in their maze;
But to know if a chicken for broiling was " fittin' "—
That subject to her seemed a haze.

At length this young woman did wed
A youth whom we will call Ned;
She loved him, 'tis true, but what could love do
Towards keeping him even well fed?

If you think I'm going to tell
All the scrapes which this maiden befell,
You will find you are wrong, for that's not my song,
As she got along tolerably well.

For she did the most sensible thing—
She caught her fine thoughts on the wing,
And set them to work, without letting them shirk,
On the duties that dinners will bring.

And so, before very long, Ned
Was the happiest Benedict wed;
For his wife was so bright, and her muffins were light,
Her coffee was good and her bread.

Mistakes she did make the first week—
For perfection on earth who would seek?
For I'm sure we'd make more, by a dozen or score,
If you and I tackled her Greek.

RECREATION.

BY MRS. IRVING ANGELL.

Recreation, wholesome and judicious, is the watchword of the hour. We live in a curiously active world with its whirl-pool of excitement and press of duties, and perhaps it is well that we are beginning to realize how much is involved in this constant desire to follow the outflowing tide of pleasure. In every age, from the days of the Spartans down to the present time, games and athletic sports have been among the institutions of the country. Men must and will have amusement of some kind. It is the irresistible law of their nature to seek relief and recreation from toil, and it is right that they should amuse themselves by passing away the tediousness of a winter's evening or the occasional leisure of a summer's day. Recreation is the outgrowth of a necessity. Health and strength must be maintained against the wearisome monotony of life. In this busy-day world men and women are continually sighing, "O, for the luxury of time "—time for rest, time for pleasure, time to recuperate both mental and physical forces. True, we seem to be in a vortex of activity from the varied experiences of life, a vortex from which it is hard to extricate one's self, even if it were wise, for it teaches us human sympathy, and from the various forms of work we draw our conclusions as to the kind of rest needed by each individual. It is the testimony of ninety-nine out of every hundred that the busiest people are the happiest and the best in health ; and it is equally true that to elevating sports, systematically and wisely indulged in, depends in some considerable degree the activity of the brain and the longevity of life.

Recreation is as much of a necessity as the air that we breathe and should fall into the plan of a well regulated life as a religious duty and a part of religious instruction. There are a thousand games as harmless as a rippling brook over its pebbled bed. No one would check the stream as it laughs and plays in its winding course, but the watchful eye guards with proper care and guidance its rightful flow, bringing joy to the joyous and refreshment to the weary. So with our sports of to-day, within the moral limit of health, pleasure and recreation, they are desirable and essential. As the dignity of labor brings men into a higher standard of living and the nobler avenues of experience, so the play-day of our people is a needed comfort from the wear of continued occupation whether it be that of literary pursuit or the toil for daily bread.

Every life needs a margin for play; to think otherwise would be to dwarf our self-development and the needs of the human race. Good, wholesome, elevating, refining and educational sports, with pure thought as the motive force, is a question which should be borne to every thinking-mind of the day, since many are easily influenced by what they most enjoy. Amusements have a charm to both old and young which nothing else can equal, therefore, it is well and wise to bestow some time and thought in that direction which shall solve the modern problem of the desire within and give to all that freedom of bodily rest which is more thoroughly appreciated than ever before. Special training, special knowledge, special experience in details, are valuable conditions in the discipline of life, but he who has failed and still fails to take his needed recreation robs nature of her rights and falls prematurely in his career. The human frame must have rest and daily contribution from the great reservoir of life. Recreation in thought, recreation in sports and the full free exercise of human faculties, with frequent change in usual conditions, is the constant need of the individual, and the part of the wise philosopher. This is a busy world, but let us remember that relaxation and pleasure are the demands of weary brains and hands.

> For he who adds to work a little play,
> Makes life the sweeter every day.

CASTLE BUILDING.

BY M. WINCHESTER ADAMS.

What becomes of all the castles
   That we build from day to day?
Do they stand in all their beauty
   In some country far away.

Shall we find the tiny cottage
   With its keepings all so plain;
Which we built when first we ventured
   In that castle-land of Spain?

Do we not recall the pleasure
   As we furnished each wee room?
Oh, the sweet air from the windows
   When the lilacs were in bloom!

And the dear, loved friends who often
   Came to share our simple fare,
In the structures since we've builded,
   Only one or two are there.

All the rest have journeyed onward
   For a brighter land than Spain;
To the house of many mansions
   Where the heart shall know no pain.

Yet we go on building castles
   Which we think are very fair;
What if they are never dwelt in,
   And are frail and light as air.

Build away. Who knows but somewhere
   For us in the Better Land,
Angels build our home eternal
   From some castle we have planned.

PRESIDENT CARNOT.

BY MARY JOSEPHINE ATKINSON.

No financial complication of the present century compares with the Panama scandal in far-reaching political importance. Our own Credit Mobilier, disgraceful enough, had no effect upon the stability of our institutions, while France seems again upon the verge of general disorganization. This disastrous affair will rank in the pages of history with the famous Mississippi Scheme and the South Sea Bubble. One of the saddest features is, that the deserved infamy of the guilty throws its shade over many honored names, including those of Carnot and the elder De Lesseps.

The French have been appalled by the charges against their President, but it is supposed he will be able to prove his innocence.

Marie Francois Sadi-Carnot, who has been President of the French Republic since near the end of 1887, was born at Limoges in 1837. He was educated at the Polytechnic School and the School of Bridges, and after his graduation was made engineer in charge of Annecy. In 1871 he became Prefect of the Lower Seine, and Commissioner Extraordinary to organize the national defense of the three departments of the Lower Seine, L'Eure, and Calvados. In the general elections of February, 1876, he was elected to the Chamber of Deputies from Beaune and became its Secretary. Carnot was appointed Under Secretary of Public Works in 1878, and, in 1880, Minister of Public Works. He held this portfolio until 1882, when he was made Minister of Finance, a position to which he was reappointed January 7, 1886, in the DeFreycinet Cabinet. He held this until the Goblet Ministry came into power, December, 1886. About a year after he was elected President.

KRYLAND.

BY MISS ANNIE E. ATKINSON.

Once upon a time, long, long ago, before all the fairy god-mothers died and left poor mothers to take care of their own children, there lived in a beautiful palace a little princess named Belinda. Her beauty would have been perfect but for a dis-agreeable look about her mouth, caused by a dreadful habit of crying over every little trouble. She not only made herself un-happy, but all her friends and relatives as well.

The first thing heard in the morning was Boo-hoo-hoo, " I don't want to be bathed in cold water?" Then " Boo-hoo-hoo— you are pulling my hair." In fact, all day could be heard the weeping and wailing of the miserable little princess. If nurse was not near just when Belinda called her, or if mamma could not give her everything she wished, she would cry and cry until mamma was nearly heartbroken to think what an unhappy woman her little daughter must become, if not cured of this fault. Belinda was blessed with a fairy godmother, and one day, just when mamma was nearly distracted by the constant flood of tears, the fairy godmother appeared; for fairy godmother's always used to come when very much needed. " Why this sad-ness?" she asked. Mamma told her how badly she felt that Belinda should fret and cry over trifles, and not be happy and contented. The fairy thought for a moment, then said : " Kry-land might cure her, but it is a severe remedy, and you will have to let me take her away for some time." " Anything," answered mamma, " would be better than to have her ruin her disposition by crying all the time." Such crying and screaming as Belinda indulged in when told that she was to leave home, had never been heard in the palace before. The fairy paid no attention to it, but took a pair of silken wings from her pocket, fastened them to her shoulders, and lifting Belinda in her arms flew out of the window. The little princess was so surprised at its that she actually forgot to cry.

Away they flew over land and sea until they came to a small island, over which a heavy mist hung, caused by the warm streams of tears constantly flowing from the eyes of the inhabitants.

"This," said the fairy, "is Kryland. Here all the people who love to cry, may stay and cry to their heart's content without troubling any one else, or they may climb the Mountain of Cheerfulness, just as they choose."

In the center of Kryland stood a high mountain up which Belinda could see many people climbing, each by a different path; but its top was hidden from view by heavy clouds of mist.

"Now," said the fairy, "if you ever want to go home again you must climb to the top of this mountain ; but I warn you that every time you cry you will slip back a day's journey."

She then pointed out the path Belinda was to take, and left her. For hours the princess cried and cried, but at last, remembering what the fairy had told her, she started on her journey.

That first day of climbing was the most difficult task Belinda had ever undertaken. The path was wet and slippery. When she put her hands on the rocks to help herself she found them damp and mouldy.

At night ugly brownies brought her a supper of black bread and muddy water, at the sight of which her ready tears fell, and down she slipped to the foot of the mountain. The next morning she started up again, and after some days of climbing, with occasional back-slidings, grew so much interested in her journey that she felt no desire to cry. She kept steadily on and there was no more slipping back. The wet slippery mud gave place to firmer ground and flowers began to spring up beside the path—primroses and violets.

To her surprise, as she climbed, the path became easier. Through the breaking mist a rainbow appeared over which bright fairies came, instead of ugly brownies, to attend to her needs. At last, one day she reached the top, where all was sun-shine and gladness, a happy, cheerful child.

Then the godmother again appeared, and they flew over land and sea, back to her delighted mother; and for the rest of her life Belinda was a joy and blessing to all about her.

———— —

LITTLE BOY BLUE.

BY LUCILLE ANDREWS.

Little Boy Blue has forgotten his horn,
Little Boy Blue cares naught for the corn,
The cows they are in it; and eating their fill,
But the Little Boy cares not, nor can he until
The trim little figure that's disappearing
Is gone from his sight and out of all hearing;
The trim little figure belongs to Miss Muffet,
(Perhaps it was she who once sat on a tuffet),
Now she is dairymaid up at the farm,
While he is the cowherd—but just now his arm
Was circling around that dear little waist
And kisses in plenty of bliss gave a taste
The Little boy heeds not, he cares not for cows
That wander in cornfield and eagerly browse
On the tender green stalks, so juicy and sweet;
Ah no, he is thinking of when he shall meet
That dear little maiden, so loving and true
Who will soon, I am thinking, be " Mrs. Boy Blue."

PRACTICAL PHYSICAL CULTURE.

BY CLARA ALLEN.

We hear with feelings very much the same as those inspired by tales of the Inquisition of "ye olden time," when men, as well as women, incased themselves in steel corselets, in order (as they thought) to enhance the beauty of the form. Later on in the days of our grandmothers, the lacing board was a regular institution of the ladies' toilet. We cannot sin to ourselves alone ; the sins of the fathers are visited on the children. We, the posterity, are far short of what we should be physically and mentally, and the habits and fashions of our time have not done much to counteract the frailty entailed on us. God surely sent man (his noblest work) into the world a perfect animal. You rarely see one of the brute creation that is not strong and healthy, unless it be by man's interference, and certainly we, who are "a little lower than the angels," would not have been less favored.

Generation after generation have disregarded the body, until now a great portion of the people cannot combat with the cares and responsibilities of life ; cases of heart failure, nervous prostration, and general debility are so common they scarcely excite comment.

That mind and body are very closely related no one will dispute. The healthy person is capable of more and better brain work than another who has the same mental capacity, but a weak body. The ancient Greeks understood this and they gave as careful a physical education as intellectual. What a rich heritage of philosophy, poetry, art and diversified learning we have from them. As soon as Greece became luxurious and slothful, the physical being was neglected, and soon "the glory of Greece had departed." If you recall the facts of the rise and fall of the Roman Empire, you will find them the same.

The Germans have for a number of years had a system of physical culture, and there is no nation on the face of the globe that furnishes more scholars to the world. Of course we have had great men among us, and if you will take the pains to investigate you will find nine times out of ten they were men who gave attention to the care and development of the body. All that the mind contains, has but one way of making itself manifest, and that is through the medium of the body. If the mind is cultivated so far in advance of the body, the latter will be an imperfect means of interpretation of the former. The body should be under complete control of the mind, every joint and muscle a willing or obedient servant. An example of want of control is often seen in a person doing some muscular work with the hands and at the same time clinching the teeth, contracting the brows, and at the same time holding other parts of the body tense, and thus using a great deal of nervous energy that might better be kept in reserve. These persons have no desire to use brows, jaws, chest, muscles, etc., to do a piece of work the brain has commanded the hands alone to perform, but they lack the nervous control of the body, and so the useless waste of energy goes on.

There is a great deal of physical training that some one aptly says had better be called " physical straining." Exercise should be taken for health. Muscular strength such as enables one to perform acrobatic feats, and violent exercises that cause an unnatural beating of the heart, should be avoided, as there is danger of injury to that organ.

We want enough muscular strength for health and all parts evenly and carefully developed. Excessive muscular strength takes from vital strength. Pugilists and acrobats are short lived men.

The foundation of physical culture is good deep breathing. The blood after circulating through the body is returned to the heart loaded with refuse and dead matter from the tissues, and carbonic acid gas, which is injurious to the system after its work has been done. The heart sends this blood to the lungs where it gives off its impure cargo, and we expel it from the lungs in expiration or the outward breath. The blood then takes on a load of oxygen, which we supply in the air we breathe. Now the better we breathe the more completely will this work be done, and the life-giving oxygen is sent dancing to all parts of the body laden with health and beauty. With sunken chest and drooping shoulders one cannot get the benefit of good breathing, for the reason that the lungs are cramped and their full capacity cannot be used. Children are bending over school desks, contracting curvature of the spine, cramping the lungs, etc., without any counteracting influences being brought to bear on the body. I think, however, the day is not far distant when we will understand and obey the physiological conditions of our being.

TO THE CONNECTICUT RIVER.

BY ELSIE ST. JOHN ADAMS.

Flow on—although thy way be long to reach the sea,
While trees that fringe thy banks thy sentinels shall be,
Let lads and lassies row and rock upon thy breast,
But sing thy song of Life when e'er they pause to rest.
Though in thy midst are rocks and currents deep and strong,
Yet on thou glidest with thy never-ending song.
Let us, as we pass on, should trials hard appear
To stop our progress, and no seeming help be near—
Recall the lessons of the song we learned of thee.
Patience! the way is long to reach the mighty sea—
But yet by patient journeying from day to day
The distance that now seems so great shall pass away.
So we must patience learn, must bravely work and climb,
Look up, not down, and with God's help and in good time,
Through earnest thought and prayer, at last will reach the
　　height
We sought, as thou hast reached the sea of thy delight.

APPLE BLOSSOMS.

BY LOUISA C. AARON.

Saw you ever aught so fair,
As these flowers of beauty rare?
Some have petals white as snow,
Others tinged with sunset's glow.
Pink and crimson colors dwell,
Delicate as the sea-shell,
In these blossoms sweet and pure,
Far too lovely to endure.

Kissed by golden sunbeams bright,
Bathed in crystal dews at night,
Rocked by merry winds at play,
They grow fairer day by day.
Crimson buds once folded tight,
Open slowly to the light ;
Oh, what beauty they disclose,
Fragrance sweeter than the rose

Hidden in their hearts of gold,
Lies the perfume none behold ;
Carried by the winds afar,
'Neath the light of sun and star.
Nestling 'mong the leaves so green,
Fairer flowers were never seen ;
Every branch is loaded down,
Lovelier far than jeweled crown.

CONYNGHAM'S CHRISTMAS GIFT.

BY ALICE BALCH ABBOTT.

It was Christmas night, seventeen hundred and seventy-six. The candles flickered, as the wind shook the walls of Denton Green's cosy farm-house; the fire burned with fitful flashes, the tall clock in the corner ticked solemnly, and the short rockers of two high-backed chairs moved rythmically backwards and forwards as two pairs of high-heeled slippers rose and fell, with gentle clicks, on the polished floor.

Christmas night, but the girlish faces were sad and sober, as were many others in the war-torn State of New Jersey.

Denton Green's farm-house stood on an unfrequented road, about ten miles from the town of Trenton. When its owner had joined the army, he had tried to pursuade his young wife to take refuge at her uncle's home, in the Orange hills, three miles to the north of Newark. But Hetty Green came of a fearless stock, and looking around the cosy little home the thought of leaving it to be desecrated by rough hands proved too much for her housewifely soul, and so, with calm determination, she announced her decision. Her husband had finally yielded, after insisting on her having two of the farm hands sleep under the roof.

In his last flying visit, early in this month of December, he he had found two fearless women instead of one.

"Well, Cousin Dorothy, what brings you to this dangerous part of the country?" had been his first words on beholding the sprightly figure which tripped hither and thither behind his wife. "To see if I could get one chance to fight a redcoat. It seems to me, Master Cousin, that his excellency, Mr. Washington, is serving the king's troops to a fine dish of Jersey fare, with 'running' sauce to make it easy of digestion." "Hist, Dorothy," Denton's wife broke in, "blame not his excellency;

when the chance comes he will surely make a stand, and then the British will see that buff and blue, though ragged and torn, can make the red and gold turn and flee," and Hetty laid a caressing hand on the faded sleeve beside her.

But Dorothy Griswold had only shaken her wilful head. " How about the chances of the last month ? Ted Oldton dashed by the house shouting ' Washington's in Newark, and Cornwallis is at his heels,' and I mounted Bess and galloped to the mountain to that rock where one can see even to New York, and I waited till I was chilled, and my eyes were weary, and then to think they retreated to New Brunswick, where, I am sure, we had another fine chance to give them a lesson, for father heard that the British had to ford the Raritan right in the face of our troops, and Washington retreated again. H'm, I think I would like giving his excellency a piece of my mind."

" A valuable acquisition he would find it, I doubt not," Denton said, with a low laugh. " If ever you have the chance, I hope I may be present. Meanwhile, I am convinced that were Mistress Dorothy Griswold in command of the army, the regulars would be crossing the ocean ere this."

" I would not promise that ; but I trow I would not let the new year in without one hard blow, be assured."

" Look here, friend Dorothy ! I cannot abide even a woman's talking against my chief."

Wicked Dolly smiled at the proud tone in the young captain's voice as he spoke those last words.

" His excellency will do what is best. Surely, if ever a man were in a desperate strait, he is the one," and Denton looked sober, as he thought of the fast thinning ranks of the militia, the half-clothed, half-famished troops, and worst of all the rumors which had begun to creep through the camp, rumors of dissatisfaction with the commander. Dorothy, watching his face, had refrained from further vehemence.

All this had occurred early in the month of December. Since then, albeit the army had been cheered by the arrival of the Pennsylvania militia, still the British had followed them to the bank of the Delaware, and would have crossed had not

Washington removed all the boats to the further side. Aye, Washington had crossed the Delaware, and apparently had left New Jersey to her fate ; for Cornwallis held New Brunswick, and Rahl and his Hessians were at Trenton, only waiting favorable weather to cross the river and annihilate the weary troops on the other side.

    *   *   *   *   *   *   *   *

The two pairs of rockers went steadily to and fro ; but the thoughts of Mistress Green and her companion went farther and faster.

Sadly disappointed was the lady of the house, for her husband had promised to spend Christmas (their wedding day), with her, if he had to row himself over the Delaware. Ten o'clock had come and the anxious wife gave a long sigh as the sleet rattled against the windows, while in the lulls between the gusts could be heard a distant creaking and rumbling, which she knew must be the floating ice in the river, barely two miles away. " God grant that Denton may not attempt the crossing," she murmured to herself.

In spite of the mournful outlook, early in the day, Dorothy had insisted on their dressing in honor of the double anniversary.

" For who knows but Denton may come," she had said. Hetty Green, being a wife of but two years, had submitted to being arrayed in the violet folds of her silken wedding dress. She had offered her friend a dress, saying : " Here, Dolly, this will be charming. Red was always your color ; how well I remember that famous habit of yours."

But her offer had been met with flashing eyes.

" Well, Hetty Green, I should think you knew better than to offer me anything of that color, I have never worn a scrap of it since the battle of Lexington."

Mistress Green smiled at the recollection of the scene, as her eyes took in the vision on the other side of the chimney place. In spite of the fact that she had chosen a blue gown, Dolly Griswold was a fair sight as she leaned the high mass of chestnut curls and puffs against the back of her chair and gazed

into the fire, with eyes that surely saw visions far beyond the
burning embers. Yes! to the shame of her ardent patriotism,
be it told, her thoughts had left the sad state of her country and
its troops and traveled back on the road of memory to a gay
June day, two years before. And all the bright picture that replaced the slowly curling smoke on which her bright eyes were
fixed had been summoned by those idle words of Hetty's, "Remember that famous habit of yours." Remember it, aye, could
she ever forget it and the last time she wore it, that summer
day, when she had stood in the porch of her home in the Orange
hills and watched the clouds of dust on the Morristown road grow
into the figures of a gay riding party, who drew rein before her
father's door, and with many a laugh and gay greeting, entered
its hospitable portal to partake of the bountiful luncheon served
by the stately lady of the house and her seventeen-year-old
daughter. And here a new light came into the black eyes and
the curling smoke shut out all else but a maiden, clad in a flowing habit of scarlet cloth, pouring tea into a cup held by a handsome cavalier.

Then came the scene of the merry mounting, and the gay
party set out for the highest point in the Orange hills. "For,"
laughed dashing Kitty Livingston, "I have promised Master
Conyngham one look at New York to fill his heart with envy ere
he returns to Philadelphia."

As the bright troop had cantered on in the soft June sunshine, Dolly Griswold had found the stranger at her side. He
had been presented as "Master Morris Conyngham, from Philadelphia, one of Mr. Ogden's classmates at Princeton, and we are
trying to prove to him that New Jersey is somewhat beside
sand-flats," Lady Mary Sterling had said.

As they drew in their horses on the rocky platform, Dorothy, with cheeks flushed by the mountain breeze, had turned to
her companion with a wave of her whip, as she proudly pointed
to the broad view before them.

"That, sir, is Newark, in the valley, with the Passaic river
just beyond, and in the horizon, where the smoke is rising, is
New York."

" I thank you," was the reply, " with such a sight before me
I can well plead vanquished, and hereafter will never doubt
aught that can be said in praise of the beauties of New Jersey,"
·but Master Conyngham turned from the beautiful panorama
and concluded his sentence with his laughing eyes fixed upon
the New Jersey girl, who sat her black mare so fearlessly, albeit
the rocky platform ended a few feet in front of them in an almost perpendicular descent.

Suppose we leave Dorothy for a moment and let me tell
you of the riding party gathered on that rock that day in
" seventy-four." There were the hostesses, the ladies Mary and
Kitty Sterling, for most of the company were staying at their
home in Baskingridge, that famous place of Lord Sterling's,
tales of whose hospitality have come down to the present day.
Then there were the two cousins of these maidens, the daughters
of William Livingston, of " Liberty Hall," Elizabeth. One of
them had been married but two months—Sarah Livingston Jay
—who in a short time was to take Madrid and Paris by storm,
with her beauty and piquant American charm. Between these
sisters rode Alexander Hamilton, a youth of seventeen, who
darted the keen glances of his flashing blue eyes hither and
thither, and kept all lively with his witty sallies. He was on
most brotherly terms with his fair companions, as it was to their
father he had been sent on his arrival from the West Indies, and
" Liberty Hall " had been almost a second home to him, the
year he had spent in Elizabeth. Having failed in his desire for
a special course at Princeton, he had entered Columbia, and
many were the battles to be fought for his Alma Mater that
day, in the Orange hills, for his three companions were ardent
Princetonians. They were Aaron Ogden of Elizabeth, who had
graduated the year before, his classmate, Conynham, and Aaron
Burr, a member of the class of " seventy-two." The latter had
been paying a visit to Newark, and riding over to Elizabeth to
visit Ogden, had found him about starting for Baskingridge.
Ogden, knowing the hospitality of the Sterlings, insisting on his
joining the party, rightly judging that with his courtly grace

and fascinating manners, Burr would form an addition to any company. Ah! little could that laughing set of young people forsee that just thirty years from the next month two of its members would stand as rivals on another New Jersey height almost in sight of their present station, and fight that fatal duel, which has thrown a lasting shadow over the fair heights of Weehawken.

But to return to the picture in the fire.

After another short stay at Mr. Griswold's the riding party had galloped on its way to Morristown, but in those few brief hours a certain wicked little God had been hard at work in a certain little damsel's heart. As the last cavalier to mount bowed low in his saddle, a voice said in Dolly's ear: "Would that Philadelphia might possess some of the beauties of New Jersey!" The pictures faded away and Dorothy awoke with a shiver to the gruesome present; for the wind still moaned, the candles were low and the fire was in its last stages, while Mistress Hetty was quietly napping. The clock struck the half after eleven as Dorothy woke her friend, saying:

"Surely Denton will not come, now."

"I am not so sure, Dolly ; I have a feeling in my bones."

"So have I, and its a very chilly one. Suppose we are extravagant and have a cup of coffee and then to bed."

In a moment the fire was burning merrily and the kettle singing on the crane. But suddenly the cousins gave a quick start. Surely that is the sound of horses feet. One instant, and a clear low whistle sends the glad light into Hetty's eyes, as the door bursts open, and with a soft cry she runs into her husband's arms. Two tall figures follow. She hears the proud ring in Denton's voice as he says: " His Excellency." She is so astonished that the other name is lost. Turning to present her cousin, she stops short, for there stands that maiden with cheeks and eyes aflame, as with head erect she receives the stranger's low salute, while she says in icy tones: " I have met Master Conyngham before."

" His excellency has broken his spurs, Hetty, can you find that large pair of mine," were Denton's first words after a hurried explanation of their presence. Washington had resolved to strike an offensive blow at last, and the colonial troops were slowly crossing the river a mile or two away, and by daybreak Trenton was to be attacked.

Green and his wife retired to find the spurs. Washington sat by the fire, with his head on his hand, thinking of the risk he was running that night, and what depended upon it. A fresh burst of the wind made him turn toward the window. Even in the midst of his trials he smiled at the sight that met his eyes.

It surely is wonderful what can happen in fifteen minutes. It this case it had proved sufficient time to turn two people from a very uncomfortable position to a very comfortable one. It was the old story; a falsely reported engagement, vain endeavors for forgetfulness on either side, when a happy chance clears up the mystery, and happiness ensues. Visions of Greenaway Court and his own young wooing passed before Washington's mind as he saw the sturdy young captain of his Pennsylvania militia bending low over the pair of fair hands he held.

A few moments later the three officers stood ready to depart. Dorothy suddenly remembered her coffee.

"See," she said, "there is just time to wish a 'Merry Christmas.' Let us each give a toast." All eyes turned to Washington for the first. Not one moment did he hesitate. It was always his first thought, in war and peace—"Our Country. May God preserve her." Then came Dorothy's turn, and with eyes filled with awe and reverence, forgetful of all her former antagonism, she softly spoke "His Excellency." Hetty gave "The Army," while Denton, not to be outdone in gallantry, pledged "The Army's Wives and Sweethearts." Conyngham came last, and if Dorothy had blushed before, her cheeks turned their reddest at "The Beauties of New Jersey."

Washington had passed out of the door, when Denton, as if forgetting something, turned to his cousin. "By the by, did you give his excellency that promised piece of your mind?"

As quick as a flash the answer came: "No, I gave him a piece of my heart, instead," and then, with a glance at Conyngham, who still stood at her side, "what there was left of it."

History can tell you the rest of the story of that Christmas night, for history, as far as this country is concerned, would have been vastly different had it not been for the capture of Trenton, the battle that proved to his enemies and the world that George Washington could take his place in the foremost ranks of the world's commanders.   *   *   *   *

Five months later there was a festal gathering at the house of Edward Griswold. Over the Jersey hills came many a stately cortege; the Sterlings from Baskingridge, the Ogdens and Livingstones from Elizabeth, and many a gallant officer from the Continental army. But there was one guest, whose presence fair Dorothy esteemed more highly than all others. Though life held many a happy hour for her in the years to come, she was wont to say that the proudest moment was that in which, George Washington, bending low, touched her hand with his lips, and turning to her husband, said: "Ah Conyngham, that dark night last winter surely brought you the best of Christmas Gifts."

LOVE'S PHANTASY.

BY ALICE I'ANSON.

Thou smilest, and I seem to hear thee speak,
 And yet so surely did I see thee dead !
I watched beside thee when thy pulse grew weak,
 I helped to place thee in thy narrow bed,
And smoothed the mother earth above thy head.
 Yet there thou standest ! Love, whom dost thou seek ?
 Thou smilest, and I seem to hear thee speak,
And yet so surely did I see thee dead !

O, thou dear Presence, most serene and meek !
 Draw nearer still, and thus allay my dread ;
Since thou wert lost the days have been so bleak !
 O, Love, recall the rapture that is fled !
Thou smilest, and I seem to hear thee speak.
 And yet so surely did I see thee dead.

A NATAL MORN.

BY ADALAIDE BUCKLEY.

The morning has come, my darling!
  It is sixty years this day
Since God, in his goodness, set thy feet
  In life's gray and gold pathway.

Dawn lay in the shadow, my darling ;
  And at noon there were clouds in the sky ;
But the afternoon is bright and clear,
  All storms have drifted by.

It is not years, my darling,
  That makes a man grow old ;
But a worn-out brain, a weary soul ;
  And a heart grown faint and cold.

Thy brain is strong, my darling ;
  Thy soul is glad and bold ;
And the heart on which I lean my love
  Is neither faint nor cold.

What matters it, my darling,
  How many years are spent ?
There's time enough for joy and peace
  In the days which still are lent.

Then open thine arms, my darling,
  A birthday greeting I bring ;
Let me kiss the eyes and lips so dear,
  While a *Deum laudamus* we sing.

A TOUR ON WHEELS.

BY CLARISSA ADAMS BOOKHOUT.

Summer was near, foretelling its approach by the soft carpet of grass peeping forth from old mother earth, and the cheerful twitter of birds.

My home was situated in a pretty little village near the banks of a peaceful river, which wound itself in and out like a ribbon, terminating in a beautiful falls. We had boats, and I used to enjoy myself sailing or drifting about or practising for a race. But before this came my wheel, rides by moonlight, rides by day and rides when the first faint streaks of dawn o'erspread the sky, when the sun peeped over the distant horizon, nodding a cheerful and glad good morning to all. These rides always remained a bright spot in my early days to be looked back upon with pleasure.

It was about this time of the year when my father suggested a tour on wheels. Nothing could have suited me better. So after a careful study of maps and guide books we decided to go to New York and try to reach Delaware Water Gap. We started from Central Park, stoping to see the curiosities and paintings in the Metropolitan Museum of Art. We then went along the Riverside drive, stopping now and then to rest and to admire the beautiful scenery. We passed a curious little house with thatched roof, which, if either of us had been an artist, would have made a charming picture, and being tired and thirsty we stopped and inquired if the inmates would be kind enough to give us a glass of water. An old woman came out and said she had some milk if that would do, and as it was near twelve we bought a pitcher of milk, and walked a short distance till we came to a pine grove. Unstrapping our frugal repast from our wheels we sat down to a most enjoyable meal, though it was not.

quite so elaborate a dinner as one served at Delmonico's. I must not forget to mention the old well-sweep which graced the cottage.

But before this we had stopped to admire Grant's tomb, which many of you know is just opposite the Palisades. He has indeed, or will have, a fitting monument for all his deeds of bravory and valor.

We next reached Tarrytown, an old historic place, and as it was late we decided to spend the night there. Procuring rooms in a house where it is said Washington stayed, we left our wheels and wandered about the town; we had no use for narcotics that night. Next morning we took the boat across the Hudson to Nyack and stopped to gaze at the monument built by Cyrus Field to commemorate the capture of Major Andre.

We next descended to the Ramapo Valley, which is filled with beautifnl scenery, high mountains on one side, while on the other, the Ramapo river rushes along breaking out in little gurgling streams, sparkling and flashing in the sunlight.

Night fell and my father finding no town near, and as it was warm and sultry, we decided to spend the night in the woods. He built a bed of boughs in a little glen on the side of the mountain, and I think I spent as restful a night as if I had been at home in my own bed.

After passing through several small towns we reached Port Jervis. Hearing from the townspeople that there was to be a country dance we decided to remain and see it. We had to ride about eight miles out of the city, until in the distance we caught sight of a brilliantly-illuminated barn, and taking the general advice followed the crowd. We at last reached our destination, and by paying a quarter at the door we were admitted. Soon the music struck up, consisting of a fiddle, very much out of tune, banjo and accordeon. The couples began to get places for a "Virginia Reel." The men were attired in rough flannel shirts, with their pantaloons tucked into cowhide boots.

The girls shown forth in purples, reds, yellows and blues, in fact every color of the rainbow. Soon I was assailed by a rough country lad "to hev a swing." Very much taken back, I retired behind the safe protection of my father's back, while he said "I was tired."

We soon left them and as we rode away we could hear them call out "twirl your huckleberries," "cheat or swing," and like phrases. The next morning we started and traveled over hill and dale ; the scenery was magnificent. We gathered laurel and dogwood and bedecked our wheels. Beautiful falls and picturesque nooks greeted us on every side. Not a sound broke the stillness as we bowled rapidly along ; at one point as we were going at the rate of ten miles an hour, my father (who is an expert rider, by the way), rode over a "thank you, ma'am," and very suddenly parted company from his wheel. I hurried to his assistance, but found him not at all injured, only "well shaken up." We next reached Stroudsburg, and before that we crossed Dingman's Ferry. The ferry-boat differed slightly from our own Albany day boats and Sound steamers. It was a rough scow large enough to hold thirty or forty people, while a man pushed it over with a pole. Delaware Water Gap was next reached, and spending the night at the Kittatinny House we enjoyed ourselves at a hop, very different from the one we attended the night before.

Next morning we started for home on the train, getting off at Plainfield. Soon we were joined by some members of the Cranford Cycling Club who greeted us with their cry, and then rode home, both thoroughly pleased with our week's tour.

MORAL TRAINING IN OUR PUBLIC SCHOOLS.

BY EMMA L. BALLOU.

In looking back over the various educational systems of the world, we find that everywhere, and in all ages, the youth were trained in those characteristics which they were expected to possess when grown to manhood. Herodotus tells us that Persian boys were taught "to ride, to shoot, and to speak the truth." The Persians wanted warriors; they believed themselves destined to be the conquerors of the world and they wanted men who would be formidable in battle. They believed also, unlike other nations, that truth-speaking was a virtue. They trained for what they wanted and they succeded in getting in. Their soldiery fought with reckless valor, their people spoke and acted the truth, in that early time when the people of other nations blushed not at the practice of the deepest perfidy.

The Greeks, in their system of education which is so justly noted, made everything subservient to bringing out in their boys the qualities needed in manhood. For the purpose of developing desired traits of character, the writings of Homer were put into the hands of every Greek schoolboy, and he was given poems, telling of the deeds of famous men, to learn and to set to music. Viewed in the light of our modern civilization, the moral teachings of the Iliad and the Odyssey seem hard to find, but if the heroes of these tales possessed few virtues and many vices, they were brave soldiers, enduring suffering and hardship without flinching. The education of the Roman boy was much the same as that of the Greek boy, in fact was founded upon it. Perhaps his body was more thoroughly developed and less attention given to his mental training.

In Greece the education of the Spartans differed from that of the Athenians, inasmuch as the aim of the two States differed.

In Sparta the individual was entirely lost sight of ; the boy was to be trained for the use of the State and for that alone. He was taught obedience, for obedience was what was wanted. His body was developed and hardened. He was compelled to endure the most intense suffering without complaint. He must know how to be hungry, and thirsty, and cold, and to smile. He was, like the Athenian boy, taught music, but the lyre was his only instrument and stirring battle peans his only songs. He was not prepared, in any way to think for himself ; his superiors were to think for him and he was to obey ; not to live for himself, he was to live for the State. The Spartan girl was educated much like her brother, for when grown to womanhood was she not expected to give up her tender babe to be devoured by wild beasts on the mountains without a murmur ? And the children that she was allowed to keep were not her's but the State's. If she were not to be a soldier, she was to be the mother of soldiers. In Athens, where more freedom was allowed and the people were expected to take some part in the government, the training was less rigorous. But Greece and Rome, like Persia, wanted soldiers and to this end the training of the schools was subordinated.

If we examine modern school systems we shall find much the same thing. The nations of Europe to-day are training with the end in view of making intelligent citizens, obedient subjects, or unthinking, unquestioning machines, according to the genus of their institutions. Now the question comes : What do we in America want ? What are we training for ? What are we expected to make of these children, good and bad, who are placed under our care ? Not soldiers, for fighting is no longer the chief business of mankind even in other countries, and in our country it does not enter into the problem at all. We know, moreover, that should any dire fortune plunge us into war in the future, soldiers, brave soldiers too, will be ready to serve our country in her need. What, then, is to be our aim ? I take it that we are to train for citizenship. We are to make men and women strong, wise and good. We want strong bodies, practical, cultured brains, and good characters. These are requsite for a perfect manhood and womanhood. The mind, at the expense of body and soul, has for too long a time received our principal attention. It will no longer do to neglect character training. It must take its place with mind training.

Of late years, together with many of the best, most intelligent and industrious of other countries, immense numbers of illiterate, and oftentimes vicious people, have been poured out upon our shores, increasing the difficulties of solving the problem of self-government a thousand fold. Self-government by the people without this constant invasion might be more easily managed, but with it, it becomes a serious matter. There are several influences working together toward solving the problem in the right way.

Free air to breathe, the chance to work with the surety of making a fairly comfortable living, a little broader life to live, these do their part. The press, bringing, as it constantly and persistently does, the needs of the people before the public, the Church with its many branches of work, Sunday-schools, city missions, etc., etc., these also do their part.

But let them all do what they may, we have still a most important work to perform if our Republic is to stand. The second generation must be a vast improvement on the first. They must be prepared in the schools for a more intelligent citizenship. We import about as much ignorance and vice as we can well bear at any one time. All this increases the necessity, which without it would still be a necessity, of the three-fold development. We are to take these little human beings, many of them the slaves of selfishness, passion and heredity, and try to make of them—no, help them to make of themselves, free men and women, fit to govern themselves and the nation.

We do not need to go down to them. They are brought to our hands. Perhaps I may seem to exaggerate the importance of this part of our work, but it seems to me that he spoke truth who said: "If you would lift humanity you must lift from the bottom."

But this is not, by any means, all that we have to do. There are the sons and daughters of better parentage. They must not be allowed to lag in the battle of life. The strong must be prepared to be leaders ; they must be trained to high thinking and noble action. They must be inspired with the desire to make the most of themselves that they may be prepared to do the most for others.

Such is our aim. Now the question comes : How shall we seek to reach it? How can we shape our school work so as to accomplish these ends? That is a broad question and many-sided. A complete answer can never be given. There is so much that I do not know, that I feel abashed at the thought of trying to give even a few hints in answer. A few hints, and those not new, are all that I can pretend to give you. I am here not to instruct, for I know no more than you, probably much less than some of you, simply to rouse an interest in a subject that is too often neglected.

First, we can see to it that we ourselves are cheerful, honest, true men and women. I am aware that this involves the personality of the teacher. It is an old subject? I grant it ! And threadbare? Perhaps. And yet, isn't it all-important ! Doesn't personality enter into every business under the sun? What is the press without the personality of the editor, the pulpit without the personality of the preacher, Christianity without the personality of the Christ—that wonderful personality that through nineteen hundred years has kept it alive and glowing with love to God and love to man. You cannot help your personality entering as a factor into whatever work you do. If you are weak or cowardly, if you are rude in your conduct, rough or slangy in your speech, if you are slothful, ill-tempered or untruthful, do you suppose for an instant that you can help having these characteristics tell in your schoolroom work? If, on the other hand, you are strong and brave, gentle and energetic, cheerful and true, will this not as surely have its influence ? We may not possess in perfection the virtues that we wish our pupils to acquire, indeed none of us can, but before we begin work for the children should we not see to it that the virtues have at least "kept school" in our hearts ?

Closely allied to personality, is love for the work. Another old and threadbare subject! Yet, this too, enters into all the practical affairs of life. Work for love, not money? No, work for love and money. Many, like Socrates, have done most noble work who have taught for love alone; but it can hardly be expected of the rank and file. Most of us need the incentive of necessity to get from us our best work. Most of us are born more or less "tired," and are always too "tired" to do much worth doing in the world unless we are driven to it. Sometimes I feel quite thankful to the kindly people who have not died and left me heir to a half million dollars, more or less, for fear my love of teaching should not survive the shock, and I should find myself, like many another, lazily drifting on the tide of prosperity. It is only occasionally, however, that I feel that way. As a general thing I should be quite willing to take the risk.

Again, what is considered good discipline, may or may not be moral training. Discipline that aims at obedience as an end, seems to me not to be moral training. We certainly want obedient children and law-abiding citizens, but only when the rules laid down for the children, the laws for the citizens command right actions. Obedience should be a means to an end. Says the hero of one of Wilkie Collins's novels: "My father taught me never to obey him, because he told me to do a thing, but because the thing that he told me to do was right." I used quite often to say to a boy who hesitated about obeying, "Won't you do it because I wish you to?" or "Don't you see that you are making me trouble?" The appeal was nearly always successful. Few boys could resist it; but I seldom use it now, never when a question of right or wrong is at stake. What! ask a boy to be honest, or truthful, or just because I wish it! If he do right simply to please me where will he be when that pressure is removed. If he do right simply to evade punishment it is much the same thing. If his conscience and the law of right have nothing to do with the matter it might about as well be left undone as far as he himself is concerned.

The kind of discipline that requires, not a healthful self-control, which is, perhaps, one of the most important lessons of childhood, but an unnatural, unhealthy self-repression, preventing all independent moral action, is not moral but immoral training.

"Our new teacher makes us sit perfectly still with our hands clasped," said a gentle little fellow who had just been promoted. "She treats us like prisoners. Oh, I can do it," he added with a sigh, "but I hate her." I know his teacher, knew her to be more than ordinarily faithful and conscientious. She had a mistaken notion of what constituted good discipline, that was all. She, I am sure, hadn't an idea that any child in her class felt as if he were being treated like a prisoner.

I once asked a little brother of mine, what he would do if he if he were being very good. "Sit down and keep perfectly still," was the answer. Poor, restless, fun-loving little lad. He had been told to "keep still," so often, that his ideal of goodness was sadly awry and one that he surely could never have begun to reach.

Discipline that is cold and hard and unloving, discipline that makes a hope of reward or a fear of punishment the principal incentive to right action, discipline that exaggerates into crimes, actions that are simply inconvenient, discipline that does not take into account the child nature, all these are immoral not moral in their tendency.

Each little child naturally feels his own personality intensely, and he should be allowed to keep the feeling. I hold that it is one of the inalienable rights of childhood to be educated as an individual human being. He should have his place, his work and his duty that belong to him and to no other. His rights too, should be respected. How else can he be made to feel that he ought to respect the rights of others.

In our country he is not to be prepared to be an obedient subject only. His labor of hand or head will give him power in the business world, his vote power in the political world. He must be taught to use that power as a responsible individual, responsible to his conscience, his country and his Maker. He must think and act for himself, and not go with the mass, regardless of duty.

Individual training means a great deal. It means that we are to know and take a personal interest in each one of our pupils. To know each one's faults and try to eradicate them, each one's weak points and try to strengthen them, each one's strong points and try to make them most useful to himself and to his fellows.

Again, definite moral instructions should be carefully and systematically given. I think this is very seldom done, and I know that many do not believe in it, but it seems to me most effective. Many a child knows that lying is wrong who does not know that deception is wrong. Many grown people do not know that punctuality is a duty. Many a person would scorn to beg or steal who, nevertheless, will not pay his debts, and does not realize that he is on the same level as the beggar or the thief. Children should be taught these things. Strikes and labor troubles would be less frequent if boys were taught that it is wrong not to pay labor what it earns, and for labor not to earn what it gets. How many boys or girls, think you, begin work with any definite idea of the duties they owe their employers? I imagine that most of them, never for one moment think, that they are doing wrong when they shirk work that they are paid for doing.

I repeat it, definite moral instruction should be carefully and systematically given, so that our future citizen may know the right from the wrong, and understand the duties and responsibilities of life. What a pity that some of our politicians hadn't received a few such lessons in their youth?

Surely as we look over the work that we have to do, we must decide that ours is a high calling, one that requires constant, earnest, prayerful effort, effort for which dollars and cents, be they few or many, can never repay us. Often, too, we shall not be repaid by the results that we crave. Frequently our work will seem to be a failure, seldom perhaps, an assured success. Yet we must never be discouraged ; we must keep right on, trying, again and again, with our ever changing material, thinking not of reward, anxious only to do the best possible work for each and every one of the little immortal human beings that we must, perforce, influence for good or for evil.

Let us, then, with brain alert, and hearts filled with sympathy, devote ourselves to the work of helping each child to build up for himself a goodly character, a palace for his soul to dwell within, fair, stately and beautiful, with solid virtues for the foundation, truth for the chief corner-stone, its pure walls garnished with jewels, the precious stones of the graces of life, such as frankness, modesty, courage, cheerfulness, and courtesy.

A JUNE HOLIDAY.

BY MRS. ANNIE DOUGLAS BELL.

Over the meadow of clover blooms
Butterflies idling in summer noons ;
    Delicate fairy things !
    Dazzle of golden wings,
    Now nearer, now far.
Rainbow tinting of every hue
Rosy windows for fairies to look through.
    Mingling of colors rich,
    Scarcely can we tell which
The butterflies are !

Through the fields where strawberries grow,
Two small maidens hand-in-hand go
    Searching for berries sweet ;
    Robins and bluebirds meet
    All care free are they !
Gayly dancing the June day through,
Ever finding some pleasure new ;
    What though the shadows fall ;
    Blue sky is over all ;
And thus ends the day.

TESTS ON WOMEN OF THE RED COLOR-
ING MATTER OF THE BLOOD.

BY ETHEL BLACKWELL, S. B.

For some time past physicians have been testing weak patients to see whether they were anæmic—*i. e.*, whether their blood contained an insufficient amount of hæmoglobin or red coloring matter. It was with special interest in the tests on women that I took up the hæmoglobin experiments. The work was done at Bryn Mawr College under the supervision of Dr. Joseph W. Warren. I will give the subject more or less in detail and in about the order of the practical treatment, so that the connections of the experiments may be best seen and the suggestions possibly help other investigators. The results of the experiments are given without reference to others' work.

The method of testing was practically that of Fleischl. The instrument used was Fleischl's hæmatometer. The locality tested was the ball, generally of the third or fourth finger, this locality being taken simply because it was by far the most convenient. In the early work corroborative tests were made, and in all tests the mean of five readings was taken. (Tenths may, of course, be neglected.) Most of the tests were made at about 7 P. M.

Testing forty of the college girls without discrimination, I found 10, or 25 per cent., to be above 90 on the Fleischl scale ; 18, or 45 per cent., between 80 and 90 ; 11, or 27·5 per cent., between 70 and 80 ; and 1, or 2·5 per cent., at 51 ; or, putting it another way. 2·5 per cent., at 51 ; 5 per cent. between 70 and 75 ; 22·5 per cent. between 75 and 80 ; 30 per cent. between 80 and 85 ; 15 per cent. between 85 and 90 ; 12·5 per cent. between 90 and 95 ; and 12.5 per cent. between 95 and 100. It will be seen

4

that nearly half were in the eighties, and the rest about equally divided between the seventies and nineties.

These figures I have called the " normals."　They are deter-

NORMALS.

1.	97·2			
2.	97			
3.	97	5, or 12·5 per cent.		
4.	96·2			
5.	95·8		10, or 25 per cent.	
6.	94·4			
7.	93			
8.	92	5, or 12·5 per cent.		
9.	91·8			
10.	90·6			
11.	89·2			
12.	89·2			
13.	86·9	6, or 15 per cent.		
14.	86·3			
15.	86			
16.	85			
17.	84·4		18, or 45 per cent.	
18.	84			
19.	83·6			
20.	83·2			
21.	83			
22.	82·4	12 or 30 per cent.		
23.	82			
24.	81·6			
25.	80·8			
26.	80·4			
27.	80·2			
28.	80			
29.	79			
30.	78·9			
31.	78·3			
32.	78·3			
33.	77	9, or 22·5 per cent.		
34.	76			
35.	76		11, or 27·5 per cent.	
36.	75·5			
37.	75			
38.	74·3	2, or 5 per cent.		
39.	73			
40.	51	1, or 2·5 per cent.		

mined by averaging *all* of the 7 P. M. tests made on the individual.

On examination, twelve of the above forty were seen to be first-year students averaging twenty years in age ; thirteen were undergraduate students, other than first year, averaging twenty-three years in age ; and fifteen were graduate students averaging twenty-six years in age. It must be remembered that in no cases are these tests on the *same* students, taken three years apart ; but in all cases they are tests upon different students taken in the same year. Therefore from these nothing can be *proved*, but perhaps a *tendency* may be seen. It suggests that in the beginning of college work we have college girls in a good deal the same general hæmoglobic condition ; that in the succeeding two or three years an evolutionary process goes on, and those best suited to a student life show an improvement in their hæmoglobic condition, while those not so well suited show a falling off ; finally, that with prolonged study, the student able then to work more wisely, there is a general improvement.

TESTS ON WOMEN.

	Twelve first year Average age, 20.		Twelve undergraduates other than first year. Average age, 23.		Sixteen graduates. Average age, 26.	
90+	2	17 per ct.	4	33 per ct.	5	31 per ct.
80 to 90	9	75 "	3	25 "	6	38 "
70 to 80	1	8 "	5	42 "	5	31 "

WHAT MARIAR DIED OF.

BY MME. JULIE BERJOIR.

"Wimmen is the most curiousest thing I ever seed! even the best on 'em, as I make no doubt poor Mariar was," groaned the bereaved husband.

"What did she die of?" I asked.

"Wal, if you don't mind a-steppin' in a minit, I'll show you what she died of. You see that there winder by the chimbly? Wal, that's what she died of."

"Died of a window?"

"Yes, ma'am; and if you don't mind a-settin' down a minit, I guess I'll tell you how't was.

"Yer see, when we fust came to live here—nigh onto ten year ago—there wan't no winder there, and Mariar she looks around and sez she, quick as flash, sez she: 'I wish there was a winder on that side o' the room,' sez she. Wimmen is allus a-lookin' for suthin' as ain't there; and the more it ain't there, the more they hanker arter it.

"Wal, Mariar she began to hanker arter that winder. She must have that winder. She couldn't live without that winder. She wanted more light and more fresh air, and it would be so kinder cheerful a-settin' by the stove and a-seein' what was a-goin' on outside, she said. For it's just like a woman to want to be hot and cold at the same time.

"Wal, she kep' a-wishin' and a-talkin' about that there winder, till I got kinder tired a-hearin' on't. So sez I to her, sez I: 'If you wait a spell, I'll put in that there winder for you,' says I. And I meant to do it, too, seein' as we'd one to spare, and I am kinder handy-like; but we'd been a-livin' here nigh onto seven year without that there winder, and we wa'nt dead yet, so I waited a while. For it ain't my way to rush inter things kinder mad-like.

"But wimmen haint no faculty for waitin'. Leastways Mariar hadn't.

"Yer see, I'm kinder easy to live with, and that's what's spiled her temper. Mariar allus had her own way; there's no woman ever had her own way more nor what Mariar had. When she wanted anythin' she'd ask an ask for it, and she kinder jawed me about it a while, then she'd go and do it herself. She allus did, and I allus let her, for't ain't my way to counteract a woman. And then—laws-a-massy!—it wan't no easy thing to counteract Mariar.

"Wal, one mornin', that's about three weeks ago, she got up awful cross.

"'Air you goin' to put in that winder, or air you not? that's what I wanter know,' sez she, kinder scornful-like.

"'Not on sich a cold day as this,' sez I.

"'Yes,' sez she, 'it's allus too hot or too cold, or too suthin' or other for you,' sez she. Which no one can say it's my fault if our climate ain't reg'lar.

"Wal, she went on a-talkin' and a-raking up things as was past and gone and hadn't nothin' to do with it, as wimmen allus do—its their way. 'I'll have that there winder afore I die,' sez she, 'if I put it in myself,' sez she, kinder sarcastical.

"'I bet yer can't do it,' sez I kinder mild.

"'I bet I can.' sez she, 'I've had to do wus nor this, sez she.

"Wal, she went on a-talkin', you know, and as it wan't just kinder peaceful enough to hum to suit me, I went down to Jim's place,—Jim ain't married, yer see, so its kinder soothin'-like to a man as is.

"It was an awful cold day and the wind a-blowin' like mad, but when I came hum at night, what do yer think I found? no supper, nor nothin' ready for me, but—I declare for it—if that there winder wasn't in! It was put in crooked and it wa'nt much of a winder, but it was sorter convenient for all that.

"Wal, I felt kinder provoked at fust, but the old woman was took sick that night, and I kinder forgive her afore she died. Of course, if I'd a-knowed as she was a-going to die for it, I'd a-let her done it without so much jawin' about it. Tho' I ain't so sure

as she'd like that either, for she was the jawingest woman as
ever I heerd on.

"Yer see, Mariar allus had her way, so she couldn't give up
for anything ; but she was a real smart woman, too, and I feel
kinder lonesome without her. And I know it ain't good for a
man to be alone, especial about his vittles and things ; but,—I
ain't so sure as it's allus good for him to be married neither.

"Yer see, it's mighty hard work ter please a woman—woman
is the most uneasy, and unsarten critters I ever knowed.

"Things don't never suit them ; so there ain't never no
pleasing them clear through.

"Leastways that's been my experience and it's a doubt in
my mind if its good for a woman either : yet I allus was kinder
easy to live with.

"Wal, that's what poor Mariar died of."

TEMPERANCE LESSON.—THIRST.

BY MRS. M. G. BALDWIN.

Were you ever thirsty or did you ever want for drink ? In
eastern countries like Persia and Arabia they suffer very much
for drink. Often they have to bring it from wells and rivers a
long distance off. Men go about with great sacks or bags of
water on their backs and sell it as they go singing, Ho, every
one that thirsteth, come buy—just as men go through our streets
calling out Brooms, brooms, come buy my brooms, or kindling-
wood, kindling-wood. Sometimes travellers are not permitted
to give drink to their animals in those places unless they buy the
water, because it is so scarce.—Livingston in his travels said the
poor animals would low pitifully at the sound of water, and when
they came to a river would wade in till the water was even with
their mouths and suck it in till their sides would stand out from

drinking so much and if suddenly surprised after coming out of the water would throw it out of their mouths. Water pure, water bright, how should we do without it. How thankful we should be it is not sold in our country, but is found everywhere, even on our streets, free to all. But are men satisfied with this drink God made? Oh, no. There are many kinds of drink men have made, and everywhere we see the signs up saying, Come, come, buy. And those who have learned to love these drinks and thirst after them are NEVER SATISFIED. They will lie and steal and abuse their dearest friends to satisfy this terrible thirst. It will make a proud father forget his own wife and little children.

What will a man not do to gratify this thirst? and it only increases as men keep taking these fiery drinks. Listen children to a true story.

A man, and a gentleman he was too, a kind husband and father, a friend to the poor—had even risked his life to save a poor child who sold matches from drowning; began to drink, not water, but wine. He had a beautiful home, a dear wife and little children. But as this thirst grew npon him he was obliged to give up one after another of what was once his dearest treasures. Only the thraldom of a wife remained and one little girl named Nellie. He still loved this little eight year old child and when sober was very kind to her. But when drunk he would beat her, and abuse his poor sick wife whom he once loved and called his dear Ellen. They had a miserable home now, one poor little dingy room with only a bit to eat now and then, and fire when Nellie could find coal to pick up. Poor Nellie's life was very dark as she listened to her mother's wrenching cough or the hard words of her drunken father. But she had one comfort as the darkness fell upon that little room—only lighted by the cinder fire. It was a dolly some kind lady had given her at Christmas-time, and it often kept her from crying when hungry and cold as she rocked it in her arms. She would watch for her father some nights until midnight before the saloon door.

One very stormy night she waited and watched, cold and hungry, to see him safe home. He reached their miserable home before her and closing the door locked it. She was afraid to call lest he might kill her, and there she stood. It was midnight dark and cold ; at last she ventured to call, Father, father, let me in! its me, its Nellie—please let me in. She heard the poor mother cough who dare not speak a word for her little girl. Then the father's voice, not to say come in Nellie, but "Be off ! I'll teach you to come watching me. Be quiet or I'll break every bone in your body!" Poor Nellie ! her hands dropped and she fell upon the cold floor. She knew it was no use until he was sober, and only for the kindness of a neighbor must have frozen to death. Morning came ; the poisoned and MADDENED BRAIN began to do its work again, and he thought of his child. Where was she? What had he done? The poor mother was asleep, but where was Nellie? He did not dare to ask ; he would get no pity. He went into the street and looked into every place where he thought she might have crept. He passed the saloon easily now ; he was looking for his child—for the little form dearer than all the world to him when sober. How could he go home to his poor wife? At last he dragged his poor weary feet up the miserable stairs. There was the poor child trying to start a fire. She only raised her head and said, Hush ! mother's asleep ; come in and get warm. Then she rubbed his cold hands and said it wasn't you, father, it was the drink. Nellie, he said, Do you love your poor old father? To be sure I do. When mother is gone there'll only be me left to take care of you ; kiss me and its a bargain—I'll never get drunk again. She covered him with kisses and told her mother as soon as she awoke.

But this terrible thirst—the drunkard's thirst—makes men forget even their promises. All day he remembered and cared for them. Night came and with it this terrible thirst. He had no money. Every moment his agony increased and he felt he must have it, but where would he get the price of a drink. Poor Nellie had rocked her doll till she fell asleep on the hearth, her treasure in her arms.—The father looked about, nothing was left he could sell, till his eyes rested upon the blue dress and scarlet sash of Nellie's doll and in a moment he thought, I could sell that. He was ashamed of himself ; but that awful thirst was upon him. He thought, I will buy it back again. He went to her and said, Nellie, would you mind lending me your dollie? I'll bring it back. She began to cry, Oh, I cannot let her go. Running to the bed she gave it to her mother, crying all the time. But while the mother said The Lord have mercy on you, he took the doll and went out into the street and into the saloon. What made him forget all his promises and dear ones? Yes, DRUNK-ARD'S THIRST. Days passed; only now and then did he come home.

One day, weary and wretched he climbed the narrow stairs. All was still and he went and looked about and thought it empty. But looking again he saw something and went up to a coffin and beside it lay the poor wasted body of his once fond wife Ellen. He sank on his knees. She looked more like herself in death than in life. He thought of her as she was twenty years before when he took her as his bride; and he said can it be this is the end, and I have done it all? He thought of his beautiful home, his children gone, only poor Nellie, and he had robbed her for the gratification of this terrible thirst. And he said, God if not man, will charge me with her murder. The night came. She looked whiter as the darkness increased. There she lay still. He caught the perfume of the violets some kind hand had placed there. His head ached. His brain was racked with remorse and the thirst came again. I must have it, but where shall I get the money. He looked about. Not the coffin—no, but the flowers. Saloon keepers like flowers. Even the poor drunkard shuddered to think of robbing the dead wife. But the thirst must be quenched, so he thought how he should get them without touching the cold fingers. The thirst gathered force every minute; so he stretched out his hand and got the violets and rushed to the saloon and gave them for drink. This terrible thirst which is never satisfied is robbing men of honesty, truthfulness and HEAVEN.

THE NAMING DAY

Of the Priscilla Braislin School, Bordentown, N. J.

BY ALICE G. BRAISLIN.

Join we now our song of gladness,
  With the spring tide hope allied,
To the opening buds and blossoms
  Of the swelling April-tide.
To the flowing of the river,
  Pushing onward glad and free ;
To the glowing, deepening sunset
  Full of hope and mystery.

Sing we too in happy measures
  One who loved the true and good ;
One who, in life's stress and battle,
  Nobly and heroic stood.
All life stronger, sweeter, purer,
  For one life which strove and won,
All life grander, better, truer,
  For the things which she has done.

Each good word, when gently spoken,
  Each good deed, when truly done,
Lives in love and strength unbroken,
  Clear as day or light of sun.
And each echoes from the cloudland
  All the music of the spheres,
Sweeter growing, softer flowing,
  With the passing of the years.

Crown we now in stately measure
  All the hopes her soul imbued,
Counting it our greatest pleasure
  To fulfill her meed of good,
To be brave in simple duty,
  To be women, loyal, true,
Doing with a will and earnest,
  What the heart may find to do.

Gathering here from wood and river,
  From the great heart of the West,
Out of books and hopes and teachers,
  All there is, of finest, best.
In the moulding, in the holding
  To the path which she has trod,
We shall find the future for us,
  Waiting in the heart of God.

THE CHILDREN'S QUEST.

BY SARAH M. BONHAM.

Hans and Gretchen, hand in hand, set out one morning toward the greenwood which lay over against the sunrise, for where the sun rises one may find all things which they seek. These children were wishing to hear the fern seeds grow, to see the dew grow in the heart of the white rose, and to find the jewel in the toad's head.

They wandered far into the leafy wood : silver-throated birds sang in the tall trees and violets and buttercups spangled the emerald grass. When they had walked a long way and were very tired, Hans and Gretchen sat down by the side of a pearly brook, which rippled over a bed of smooth white stones, and drank the sparkling water from tiny acorn cups, and ate May apples to appease their hunger.

" Oh! see! " said Gretchen, "there is a spotted lizard."

" Let me kill it," said Hans, picking up a stone and carefully taking aim.

" Ah, no ! " and Gretchen laid her chubby hand upon his brown fist. "Let it live ; it is so happy sporting in the bright sunshine.

" Pshaw ! I will show you how quickly it will fall off the log when the stone hits it."

But the tall trees bent their heads and whispered together, and the voice of the rill was no longer pleasant, and a cloud came over the sun, and the trees, and the rill, and the cloud, all whispered, " Cruel, cruel."

Hans let the stone fall slowly to the ground, and the lizard stretched himself on the mossy log and went to sleep in the sunshine, for the cloud disappeared when the stone fell from the little boy's hand. The children journeyed on, for the sun was high in the heavens, and they had not yet heard the fern seed grow, nor seen the dew distil in the white rose's heart, nor found the jewel in the toad's head. Further on they saw a honey bee sipping sweets in the cup of a scarlet lily which hung its head in the passing breeze. Hans ran up and closed the petals of the lily; the struggling bee buzzed in vain. Hans shouted aloud in glee over the useless efforts of his captive to free itself.

" Buzz away, old fellow ! You can't get out ; I've got you fast."

" Let him go, dear Hans," said Gretchen. " Liberty is sweet."

" I shall pull off its wings and see how funny it will look when it tries to fly."

" No, no ! " and the blue-eyed little girl tore a slit in the calyx of the lily. " it is much pleasanter to make him happy than to cause him pain."

The waxen bells of the lilies of the valley rang their silver chimes, and the thistledown fairies floating in the air rested gently on her neck and hair with their caressing touch, for all creation is glad when little children are good.

Down in a shady dell where the star mosses grow, and the

partridge berries trail in the verdant sod, a flower fairy sat on a pink mushroom, holding her foot in her hand and sobbing aloud.

"Come on," said Hans, taking his sister's hand, "we have no time to tarry here."

"Let us ask." said the little Gretchen, "why the fairy is sad."

She knelt by the mushroom and laid the radient flower fairy's foot in her little moist palm; it was pierced with a brier thorn. Carefully Gretchen drew out the mischievous little thorn, so small she could scarcely see it, and running to the spring, bandaged the foot with buttercup leaves wet in the cool water. The fairy dried her tears on her handkerchief, just one square of lace which the black and yellow spider had woven for her, and flew away in haste, for the flower fairies have no time to be idle.

When they are gone the bugs and snails and bats all find it out, and then they sting the beautiful flowers which droop and die ; but when the fairies are at home this cannot happen.

"Let us go on faster," said Hans, when the fairy was gone. But Gretchen sighed.

"Perhaps if we had asked the fairy she could have shown us how the dew grows, but it is too late now."

From a hollow stump a striped snake reared its head, and fixing its beady eyes upon the children, hissed almost in Gretchen's face Hans ran for a stick.

"Do not hurt him," said Gretchen ; "see, there is no poison in his fangs, and even those that we cannot love have a right to live if they are harmless."

The children walked all day, and when the sun was setting they followed the butterflies home, for they knew that so far away from the sunrise they could not expect to find the things they sought. They passed out of the wood by a small brown house, and a little bent old woman with a white cap, and leaning on a broomstick, stood in the open door. The children looked up and smiled.

"Where have you been, my dears ?"

"Over toward the sunrise," answered Gretchen in her little tired voice, "to hear the fern seeds grow, to see the dew grow in the white rose's heart, and to find the jewel in the head of the toad."

"And did you find all these things?"

"Ah, no!" said the children sadly; "we only found a lizard playing in the sunshine, a bee in a lilycup, a fairy and a snake."

"I know," said the old woman nodding her head.

"How did you know?" asked Hans, a little ashamed.

"The trees told me. and the brook, and the thistledown. I know the language of all these things, and when they speak I understand."

"Oh! tell us then," said the children, "shall we ever find the things we seek?"

"You have found them to-day," said the old woman, laying her wrinkled hands on the little flaxen heads.

Kindness and justice and mercy are sweeter and more precious far than the music of the growing fern seeds, the perfume of the dew in the heart of the rose, or the sparkle of the jewel in the head of the toad.

THE PRINCIPLE OF THINGS.

BY MRS. A. C. BRISTOL.

In a previous discourse I spoke to you of a principle arranging inorganic and organic phenomena, dealing with nebulous matter, condensing it into worlds, setting these worlds in moving balance in the heavens, and regulating not only the forms of vegetable and animal life, but the social system itself, and even the moral and spiritual nature of man. This principle we designate by different terms according to the class of phenomena we are considering. In the planetary system we speak of it as counter-balance, or centripetal and centrifugal forces; in society and government as centralization and decentralization; in the moral and spiritual nature as self and other self, or in philosophic terms as egotism and altruism. It is the principle which in the planetary system secures harmony of movement ; in society, order and progress ; in human character, moral equipoise.

Preachers, teachers and authors are prolific in illustrations and analogies taken from nature, when they wish to emphasize a moral lesson, and confirm it with infinite seal and sanction. By a kind of instinct or intuition they move in a direction of argument, which is sure to reveal itself some day under the light of science, as demonstrable. Just as scientific philosophy now reveals that the religious instinct under the theological régime, has, during the last eighteen centuries, been moving in the true and valid direction. however erroneous it may have been in method or detail. This philosophy reveals that the motive for conduct which the religious sentiment exalts as the superior motive, is identical with that which science also reveals as the superior motive according to the principles of evolution. Motives for conduct, as they pass from an inferior to a superior grade, involve more numerous considerations. They do not relate simply to one's self and what is near, but involve considerations of others, and results to which are more or less remote. Science pronounces such motives superior because they are more complex, and are therefore a higher evolution. Religion pronounces them superior because they put by immediate personal gratifications in view of larger and more blessed result in the future. Thus science and religion point in the same direction in reference to motives for conduct, but with a difference of terminology.

There are not such barriers and divisions existing between different classes of thinkers and believers as these same thinkers and believers imagine. It is mostly a war of words, the combatants on either side being so intent on their own methods that they fail to perceive they are but champions of one cause clad in different armor. We should come to recognize the fact that the cause lying nearest our hearts may often find assistance from those whose interpretations of life and the universe are quite unlike our own. Interpretations are words ; let us get at the soul of things and of one another. I will go by what I find in your face despite all you may say. I will go by what I read in your eye and what I discover in your voice despite all I may be informed about you. I do not need the symbols of words to stand between you and me to secure your acceptance or rejection at my hands as a coworker in the cause I espouse. If you are noble and sincere in yourself I defy calumny to blind my perception to the fact. If you are pretentious, personal, and selfish, and less wise and noble than you assume, though you should come with a flourish of trumpets and the spreading of palms before your feet, yet will I note you as a fraud by the very cadences of your voice. Those who live in the spirit are not limited by the symbols of language. Let us make up our minds to discern the reality of things, and build upon it with infinite courage and infinite trust. I who say this am weak. I am as the blade of grass in the wind. But that in which I rest ; that which not only shapes the sphere and holds the heavens in balance, but rounds the character also ; that which working up through inorganic to organic life, ultimates in moral expression in the relations of men—that is strong and mighty. I will not quarrel with you about its name, whether it be one that belongs to the department of science, or philosophy, or religion ; if so it be you recognize that it is the invincible, that which is ultimately never to be balked or evaded, that to ignore it is to insure failure in yourself and your undertakings, that all external prosperity, whether individual or social, that is not built upon this principle, which radiates from the heart of the universal, holds the germs of decay and disaster, the principle of attraction and balance in matter, of order and progress in society, of liberty and justice in government, of moral equipoise in character.

The truths of science which we may discover must be wrought into the minutia of our lives, must regulate our eating, drinking, sleeping, dressing, housekeeping. If we are conscienciously loyal to the truth in the matter of the senses, we shall find sense opening into spirit like one triumphal procedure. We cannot steal a march on eternal life here nor hereafter. If we would set the inner spiritual nature to the poise and harmony of the heavens above us, we must try to perfect this instrument, the body, through which alone the soul can utter its music to the world. This is the gospel of life which science, religion and philosophy blend in one trinity of authority.

We cannot pursue the course and development of science in any comprehensive manner without becoming impressed with our insignificance as separate fractions, and our almost infinite importance as parts of one great whole. This revelation both of our littleness and our greatness, forms the source both of humility and aspiration, and impresses us as never before with the consequences of conduct. For we see that those consequences are unvarying, and that they do not cease with our own good or evil fortune, but affect in some way the whole unity with which we are involved. Repentance cannot call back the note of discord our conduct may set afloat in the life around us. But repentance may tune the spirit to such harmony, that it will send abroad a strain of sweetness that shall even take this note of discord and drown it in music. So let us not fail to repent the evil, science itself revealing the validity of repentance, and laying a broad foundation of reason under all the superstructure of emotion and sentiment.

If we venture to set at naught the revelations of science in any department of our being, whether in the realm of sense or spirit, we shall find that we do it at an immense cost. It does not pay to be otherwise than loyal to our inmost truth. It will never pay, in shaping our conduct, to keep an eye and ear so out for the world that our inmost truth is held in abeyance. For believe me, it is only those who are courageous to put the reins of their conduct in the hands of this inmost and invincible, who compel the world and human destiny to follow the train of their white royalty, for the whole economy of the universe is behind them. But if in gathering up the reins of our conduct for guidance, we find two voices within us, let us see to it that we do not confound the voice of inmost truth with the voice of inmost desire, since this is the fatal error which has wrecked many a consciencious soul. The universe does not pardon such mistakes. If we take a by-path for the open way, we must contend with the jungle and the thicket.

5

AT EVEN-TIDE.

BY MRS. GERTRUDE S. BOWEN.

A rare and beautiful picture
  On the canvass of memory glows,
And brings to my weary spirit
  A calm and sweet repose.

Away in the far New England,
  In a quiet, peaceful home,
By the glow of the evening fire-light,
  A grandmother sits alone.

In the chamber above sleeps the baby,
  The darling and youngest of three
Wee boys—the joy of the household,
  With their pranks and innocent glee,

Grandmother herself is a picture,
  With her cheeks so fresh and fair,
And the light so brightly shining
  On the waves of her silvery hair;

Her folded hands rest lightly
  On the page of an open book,
While her eyes so calm and restful
  Have a far-off, dreamy look.

But list! through the open door-way,
  And down the winding stair,
Comes the cry of the wakened baby,
  Who misses his mother's care.

Grandmother, aroused from her dreaming.
  Ascends the darkened flight,
But pauses above on the threshold
  To gaze on a wondrous sight.

'O pure and heavenly vision!
   'Tis rarely to mortals given
To look thro' the gathering tear-mist
   Into the gates of heaven:

The shadows of the pale blue drap'ries,
   And the drifts of filmy net,
Took shape, in the fairy lamp-light,
   Like white wings above our pet.

A tiny, night-gowned figure
   Kneels close to the cradle-side,
And a little voice croons softly
   A song of the even-tide.

For baby's elder brother,
   Loving and manly and true,
Had heard the little one's moaning,
   And did "as mother would do."

To and fro swung the cradle,
   And the "Hush, my dear," was sung,
While fast to the hand of the singer
   The baby fingers clung.

Still the soft voice sweetly chanted,
   "Angels, holy, guard thy bed;"
And the sigh of the little sleeper
   Told that he was comforted.

Then the cradle ceased its swaying,
   And the happy singer fled
Back to the warmth and comfort
Of his own trundle-bed.

   *   *   *   *   *   *   *

O, Christ! dear elder brother,
   Like babies, we moan and cry,
Till by the touch of faith sublime
   We feel that Thou art nigh.

RAINETTE.

A Letter to the Children.

BY MRS. JAMES B BEAUMONT.

My dear little friends, what do you suppose we have for a pet in our cozy home? I wonder if you can guess if I tell you something about it first? It was less than half an inch long: last autumn, but now is an inch and a half in length, with small bright eyes, and has four fingers and five toes, and it lives in our parlor in the winter-garden with the vines and plants. Its skin is smooth and the color of lichen which grows on the north side of trees and on fences and stone walls, with blotches of greenish brown, with white lines outlining them; but then it is not always of the same color. When on the ground it is dark like the earth, and when on the yellow earthen jar is yellow, or when suspended from the under part of leaves is of a greenish hue, sometimes it seems to be very white, and *at will* can change color (which no doubt is a provision to enable them to elude their various enemies). When our garden needs water the little creature makes a great chirping noise, and seems quiet content after a good shower.

It comes every day from its hiding-place under the leaves, and sits in the sun, and waits for its dinner, which we give, of flies, and it takes them from our fingers with its tongue. It will not touch them if they are not alive; it is fresh and not stale food it craves—our dainty pet—and not a dead thing will it touch. I guess it finds its own supper and breakfast; for never were the plants so free from insects before.

Have you guessed what it is? I am sure you have. A tree-toad? Yes. The French boys and girls call them "rainettes."' Now I want to tell you a story about our pet "Rainette."

While at breakfast the other morning, our neighbor from over the way came running in with a little green tin pail, saying, "Melissa, I have come to borrow your toad to eat up our bugs."

We heard the little prattler in the next room, and called her in. Yes she was in earnest, and had a note from her mamma begging the loan of our toad for a few days' visit in their conservatory, promising good live fare of the choicest larvæ. Rainette must have heard us talk; for it hid, and we could not find it until two hours later, when it was enticed into its novel carriage, and transplanted to a new home of flowers and beauty.

We missed the wee pet, and it seemed lonesome without his chirp, and every stray fly on the window-pane we felt was a loss to our toad. But the visit was not long. After the second day little May brought it back saying, "He hid away, or just sit still all the time. He is lazy, and didn't catch any bugs; so I bringed him back."

No wonder! It was used to the quiet, plain way of the parsonage; and the strong light, varied foliage, and bright flowers dazzled it—so it cried; and just before a shower it cried so loud, May's brother said "That toad makes my heart shake!"

So Rainette has come back to the old home of its infancy, and seems content.

> ' Be it ever so humble,
> There is no place like home."

So thinks your loving friend.

THE ROMANCE OF WAR.

BY EMMA FRANCES BENEDICT.

To many of the thoughtless of that day the early tidings of the first attack upon a Southern fort were regarded as a mere bit of exciting news from a far off country, until the call of the President for volunteers electrified the land and brought the matter face to face with every man. It is the old story, told and re-told with a thousand variations to younger generations, by those who shared in the excitements of the time.

Memory recalls a company of young people idling away the sunny days of April in a delightful old mansion on the banks of the Hudson, happy in their ignorance of politics and careless of the approach of the intruder, Mars.

Amidst this peace, how harshly clanged, into their untrained ears the loud alarm of war! The new subject was gravely discussed by their wiser elders, who concluded that it was a trouble which would quickly clear away. Great was their astonishment and dismay when they beheld their leader, the joy and life of the party, arrayed in the uniform of a Sergeant-Major, a real soldier, enlisted in the volunteer army of the United States, ready for active service, chevroned, and girded with an enormous cavalry sword which curved about his legs, and threatened, when unsheathed, to cut them off. In fact, he was to be regarded as a soft of Fourth of July soldier about to start on a mammoth picnic. How often after, amid the deafening roar of battle fury, came ringing through his brain the cry of one in jest, "Don't you get shot in the back, boy!"

*   *   *   *   *   *   *

It was the winter of 1863. The army of the Potomac was sunk ingloriously in the mud. It was mired to the hubs of its artillery wheels. Taking advantage of their opportunities, its soldiers swarmed the North on brief visits to home and friends. Upon the eve of his return to duty, it occurred to the aforesaid young warrior, that the present was a most convenient season in which to solemnize a marriage engagement; an idea quickly acted upon. Bidding adieu to his newly made wife, the youthful benedict, returning, reported in camp, in a state of combined joy and misery. It was an anomalous wedding journey, taken in sections, the bride following a fortnight later, under the escoit of a brother officer, rejoining her soldier-husband in camp, near Falmouth, Va.

The city of Washington, then so incomparable to the Washington of to-day, was thronged with the blue coats daily growing familiar throughout the land.

The passes necessary to enter the army lines being secured, she found herself upon a busy steamer *en route* for that glorified land, the South, adown the broad Potomac.

Now began their initiation into military life. The air itself grew soft and balmy and laden with sweeter odors. But everything visible betokened the near presence of the war, which at home seemed almost mythical.

There were stacks of arms, glittering in their newness, suspicous looking kegs, barrels of beans, sacks of government coffee, salted meats—loads and loads of supplies.

Aboard was a nondescript, mysteriously appareled, whose costume suggested a compromise between the freedom of masculineness and the grace of feminety. Her peculiar attire was composed in part of a short skirted tightly fitting gown, buttoned *à la militaire* over a large-boned figure, and in part, by a baggy, bifurcated, Bloomerish garment of navy blue merino.

This Amazon became known as the Daughter of a Vermont regiment, and had been to Washington executing small commissions for its officers. What added to her appearance a greater military air, was an officer's sword which she had been purchasing and which she carried at her side. Instead of the charming little *vivandière*, gold-laced and scarlet-capped, with a silver cup and a bright canteen pendant from the graceful shoulders—this heroine was tall, strong, somewhat masculine and more practically useful, judging from the condition of the ungloved hands, which betokened a familiarity with the coarser duties of life. She was good naturedly communicative regarding her army experiences, and with a loud voice entertained her fellow passengers with her opinions of camp life, and expressed her contempt of that early education which neglects teaching a man to sew on his buttons and to darn his stockings. "La, they jest squeeze up the edges in a little hard bunch and wind and twist a string around. Then they lay it upon the ground and pound down the lump with a stone. My, my, how they do take to a woman's mending."

The drive in an army ambulance was the first experience of camp life. Fancy a long, rude, canvas-topped wagon, devoid of springs, or perhaps use had rendered them useless, with narrow side benches covered with enameled leather on which the mangled brave were presumed to repose as on the oft quoted "bed of roses," and be carried to that home of luxury, the hospital. Over a worn out corduroy the ambulance chopped and jolted in a break-neck fashion. The road was composed of logs laid closely side by side, except where they had slipped apart or been crushed by heavy wheels, leaving an aperture like a trap where the leg of many a valuable horse was broken.

It was the twilight of a winter's day, when she arrived at Boscobel, the manor house, where comfortable quarters had been assigned. It was claimed by some lovers of American history stationed here, that Boscobel was the plantation on which the youthful Washington was reared, and many were the jests over the supposititious discovery of the famous cherry tree.

The house, for the present occupied by Major-General Sickles and a part of his staff, was an excellent type of an old Virginian mansion, with looming chimneys outside, and immense fire-place within, where bulky walnut logs flamed cheerily. The tide of war had swept over its roof, sparing little, save its bare walls, its staircase and its great veranda, the living room, in pleasant weather, of the Southern people. The room was carpetless, of course, and sparely furnished. But there was a heap of heavy gray and scarlet army blankets on which to lie, luxuriously, in dreamy Eastern fashion, before the illusion-weaving fire.

Johighphus entered, announcing supper, provided from the mess. Johighphus—a waiter of hardly the Saratoga type—had adorned himself with a sprig of evergreen stuck in his button hole in token of the unusual honor accorded him in serving a lady. The repast consisted of an oily liquid contained in two yellow earthern bowls, "desiccated soup," to be partaken of with the aid of two heavy metal spoons. There was a chunk of bread on a tin plate, some baked beans, "hard tack" and army coffee. 'Twas thus the newly united pair began life as one, supping together from the only empty plate, and sipping together from the one tin cup provided.

Existence in an ordinary farm house soon palled upon the fancies of the soldier's wife and she naturally longed for the romance and experience of life in a tent. As her "liege lord" had now been commissioned a captain and chief of division staff, with headquarters at a considerable distance, it was determined to remove thither, and accordingly, they, with their small stock of chattels, were transferred to a new scene.

Two wall tents had been placed end to end, with the intervening canvas rolled up in curtain fashion and then laced together, thus forming two convenient, comfortable apartments. Officers and privates had scoured the country around in their efforts so secure comforts for their unusual visitor. Sutlers contributed their precious packing-cases, invaluable for flooring, two or three gallant men brought a cherry table from some Southern home, and had transported it with difficulty a distance of twenty miles. A Jersey General presented his compliments with a luxurious chair, ingeniously sawed from a barrel and supplied with a covered hay cushion. A chivalrous soul denied his body the comfort of a little round sheet-iron stove, which he donated to the cause, a stove with a pipe which pierced the side of the tent, and, it must be confessed, wheezed and whirled back the smoke, distressingly, on a windy day. A hospital-surgeon tendered neat little iron bedsteads with comfortable mattresses. Indeed, it seemed a revival of the old-fashioned game of " What

will you give an old bachelor to go to keeping house with?" A
traveling trunk covered with a gayly hued shawl was transformed
into a *tete a tete*, and a strip of rag carpeting begged or bought
from an impoverished F. F. V. furnished comfort underfoot.

There seemed to be no end to the recitals of thrilling escapes from grim death upon the battle field. Three or four
sociable surgeons were accustomed to bring along their own
camp-stools and loved to rehearse their blood curdling experiences, which are still shiveringly remembered. At night there
was always the music of glee clubs, or the sad solo of some home-
sick soldier, pouring out his sorrow in the war songs of the day—
"We're Tenting To-night on the Old Camp Ground," "When
this Cruel War is Over" and "John Brown's Body" being the
favorites. Occasionally, substantial dinners were exchanged,
the tables well supplied with "flannel" cakes, camp hash, hot
biscuit, apple tarts, mince pie, and once in a while a fresh
beef-steak. But luxurious edibles were regarded as a sacrifice
of romance to a common gratification of the appetite.

There were excursions made to Falmouth town, opposite
Fredericksburg, on the banks of the Rappahannock. On the
opposite bank of this historic river, in plain sight, was the dreadful enemy. He certainly did not look then "as bad as he was
painted." The boys in gray were cheerfully shouting and jest-
ing with the boys in blue like so many school urchins let loose
for a recess; the pickets on either side being for the nonce on
most amicable terms. During a favorable breeze, a tiny boat
would cross to Dixie laden with newspapers, perhaps, and at
change of wind, would return to Yankee-land with a small cargo
of tobacco. And every day the formidable earth-works of the
enemy were rising before the eye.

Upon the "sacred soil" there fell a heavy snow of veritable
Northern birth, which, however, had not come to stay. The
captain's wife sat close to the little stove, disenchanted. Was
this a promise of mocking birds and oleander blossoms? The
captain himself lay on his back, dislodging with his heels the
mass of snow which had accumulated and sagged down the canvas roof of their domicile, when up to the entrance of their tented

village jauntily pranced a quartette of spirited horses attached to
a rude sled, formed of the box of a supply-wagon, its wheels replaced with smooth runners fashioned from the branches of trees,
its rough boards gaily lined with blankets. The improvised
sled was occupied by a few of the merriest, fun-loving officers
who had called to induce the captain and his wife to join them
on their "lark." "They hoped," they said, "to call upon every
lady within visiting distance and treat her to a good old-fashioned Yankee sleigh-ride."

The party started, the fun and laughter and songs began ;
the horses entered into the spirit of the hour and capered threat-
ingly. One more experience with being rudely upset in a
yawning mudhole. and the feminine element of the party, resolved to wait at a neighboring farm house until a wheeled
vehicle could be secured for her return. This dwelling was
occupied by a tall, gaunt woman with her two pale, gaunt
children. But on this lonely being, so long debarred from companionship with her sex, becoming assured of a sympathetic ear,
she told with some reserve her pitiful story of deprivation and
woe.

Stripped of her small possessions, first by one advancing
army and then by the other, she feared each morning what the
day might bring forth.

"No," she confessed. "I can't say that you 'uns trouble me
much now, 'less to tote off my chickens ! Hev' to keep a right
good eye on my pies 'n cakes, though ! Some o' them soldiers I
ain't got no use fer ! General, up there, said he'd gi' me a heap
f I'd take the oath o' 'legiance, but I ain't never goin' to do that.
never, never, never !" and the determined patriot stood her
ground, proudly erect, with a rising scion of an F. F. V. at either
hand She made no attempt to conceal the fact that the masculine members of her family were enrolled in the army of the
Confederacy, and one could not resist a feeling of admiration
for the bravery which kept this woman at her post, supporting
herself and children with the pittance received from the soldiers
by the sale of her home-made "pies 'n cakes." And here an
awful discovery was made ! The young Northerner, lately brev-

eted major by the commanding general of a division, thereby outranking her husband, the captain, was found guilty of affording sympathy and aid to the enemy by patting the heads of the two small rebels nestled so comfortably in the warm fur of her victorine, while she distributed between them dainty *bon-bons* fresh from Washington.

*　　*　　*　　*　　*　　*　　*

A daintily inscribed card of invitation was received to a tea-party to be given at the headquarters of the courtly General Sickles, for the purpose of meeting, socially, with General Joseph Hooker, who had recently assumed command of the Army of the Potomac. In camp the days of the week seem to disappear from the calendar, so when it was discovered that the day appointed fell upon Sunday, it was quite too late to recall the invitations, for tea may be drunk as well upon Sunday as on another day.

The tea, which assumed the importance of a banquet, was prepared in the mess kitchen, and was served by deft-handed soldiers. The late General Hooker, "Fighting Joe," the idol of the army, was, though a bachelor, one who might be styled a "ladies' man," when occasion required. In the eyes of the women he was a particularly handsome man of magnificent proportions, tall, erect, with hair and whiskers tinged with that becoming gray that softens the complexion, with cheeks as rosy as a child's and with fine, sparkling blue eyes. Added to these endowments his hearty friendliness and care for the least of his men, his singular good humor and his abundant stock of animation, no wonder that wherever he rode along the lines he was greeted with wild hurrahs. The event of the evening was when the ladies beguiled the popular General into a remote corner and remorselessly robbed him of his hair, which was afterwards converted into miniature drums and dangled from their watch-chains, or was woven into finger and ear-rings and proudly preserved as mementoes of a famous man.

It was this impassable condition of the roads that kept the army of sixty thousand troops imprisoned for months, and it was this "slough of despond" which enabled a newly-wedded couple to enjoy their novel honeymoon. But the wind had now subsided and had apparently performed a service in drying up the mud. The friendly moon was shining gloriously, illuminating the way. The ambulance was ready to take the party to camp. Alas for the witchery of the deceitful moon! There was a plunge and a sensation as of sinking into a fathomless ocean. In vain! The beasts and the vehicle were momentarily sinking deeper and deeper into the shining, yielding mire. The travelers were obliged to confess themselves stranded. The horses were detached, and the driver was instructed to make his way to camp and report for assistance.

Abandoned in the dead of night in the midst of a wide, unhabitable desert of mud! Already wearied by the excitement of the day and evening, the young woman suffered from alarm. In this weird and lonely place she began acutely to realize the proximity of the enemy and her fears invested him with the ghoulishness of a nightmare.

Now this predicament, so alarming to the poor wife, was simply one of annoyance to her husband. He bore the delay with philosophic composure. He pulled down the leathern curtains at the sides of the wagon, piled the wraps and shawls by way of making themselves more comfortable, and then he, the imperturbable, fell fast asleep in the easy, aggravating way of a man accustomed to more appalling dangers.

No sound, no light of camp, no sign of life—not even the sight of a friendly tree nor the rail of a fence. What perils excited her imagination! She clung to the side of her unconscious husband for protection from she knew not what! At last, after what seemed an interminable period, there was the distant sound of a slowly approaching horde. Friends or foes? Then was heard the encouraging shout of a hearty Hibernian returning to the rescue with a pair of fresh horses and another conveyance.

Again the hospitality of General Sickles was extended—on this occasion to meet and lunch with the President and Mrs. Lincoln, the President being at the front to confer with his generals and to review his army. A great disappointment to the handful of ladies present was the decision of Mrs. Lincoln to

recall her acceptance of the invitation. But the President himself rode into view. A tall, awkward man, with protruding cheek
bones in his large, thin face, bearing that well-known sad and
tired expression. He wore a "stove-pipe" hat—the only one in
the army—that alone making him conspicuous in a crowd of
dashing military men, and sat his horse in a particularly slouchy,
ungainly fashion. He received his visitors with an earnest
friendliness which captured their hearts. It is a memory
preciously cherished that the gentle, fatherly feeling overflowing the heart of this great man, caused him for a moment to
drop the affairs of state to interest himself in the happiness of
an obscure, unimportant woman. And she never forgot the day
when she "ate salt" with President Lincoln.

It was the dusk of that same day when she, accompanied by
her husband, was quietly proceeding homeward. A deep gulch
separated the camp from the main road, through which flowed a
lazy stream, where the horses regularly expected a drink. Laying the bridle on the neck of her steed she rested indolently in
her saddle, reviewing the events of the day. They had just
descended one precipitous bank while another equally steep rose
before them. Bucephalus stood knee-deep in the water, when
suddenly from the rear came a frightful roar—a rushing tramp
as of the approach of the whole Confederate army. Ah, what a
moment of consternation ; one to test the spirit and bravery of
a Northern woman, a would-be heroine, a soldier's wife ! She
had not even time to collect her bridle reins when the sharp
sound of horses feet clattered about her, a whirl of blinding
dust enveloped her, a confused mass of flying cavalry surrounded
her, and she was conscious that this was the most trying moment
of her life.

At this moment a strong hand caught at the curb of the
animal, there was a firm and powerful grasp about her waist,
while a voice in trumpet tones shouted closely in her ear the
awful, awful command, "Surrender !" She had not a moment
to think more than that she would sell her freedom as dearly as
possible—her life was at stake, and, having about her no other
weapon of defense, with her slender riding-whip she struck one

noble, terrible blow at rebellion, and then cowardly burst into tears. Next, she felt her feet upon the ground, her husband's arm supporting her, the enormous body of calvary vanquished and vanished, save for one peaceful orderly soothing her stamping charger, while a fun-loving, tender-hearted General, big and impulsive, stood before her, overwhelming her with apologies. He explained that, returning with his mounted staff to his quarters, at their usual break-neck speed, he had jestingly thought to lift her from her saddle, transfer her to his own and bear her captive to camp.

A grand review of the Army of the Potomac followed the President's reception. There were Generals and their imposing staffs, changing importantly from one point to another ; processions of artillery, with gun-carriages supporting formidable cannon now rolling peacefully along, the bright sunlight gleaming on their polished surfaces, their masters sitting above them with arms patiently folded, as if awaiting future labor. There were immense bodies of cavalry, with fierce clatter of iron-shod feet, terrifying to meet even in this moment of transient peace. There was music everywhere. Flying over the fields was the young Captain upon a cream-white horse—a conspicuous mark for the rebel sharpshooter on those future battle-grounds. The presentiment of its fate was subsequently verified in the fierce fight of Chancellorsville, where the poor animal fell, pierced through the breast. The nerve of the heroic young woman who *would* go to the wars, was often sorely tested, fulfilling prediction of the "I told you so's" of home prophets. The Captain explained to his wife:

"The dispatches report the enemy approaching in full force. I must go to the General. Don't worry over whatever may happen. If there is any serious trouble you can find shelter in the cellar of the General's headquarters. *But don't worry.*"

Did ever a woman cease from "worry" because she was bidden not to? Then she discerned the slow, measured tread of the sentry as he paced upon his beat before her tents. She sharpened her hearing for the noise of distant attack. There came a rumbling sound, a low muttering at first. She knew its meaning, the "long roll" which summoned an army to its feet. In a moment the camp had aroused from its lethargy. It was alive! Tramp, tramp went the resolute feet outside. Now she could distinguish the voice of her own husband. Why, what was she, a soldier's wife? and then he himself came in—to buckle on his sword? No—to yawn stupidly and go to bed.

At daylight a second dispatch announced "All quiet on the picket line." And all this disturbance had been produced by the meanderings of some stray cow, mistaken in the darkness for the enemy by the disordered vision of a picket. Notwithstanding these frequently groundless fears, there were occasions when real danger impeded and was unconsciously experienced, as, for instance, when the p-i-ng, p-i-ng of bullets whizzed closely by and over her tents, where she sat unconcernedly reading while the air was filled with their shrill shrieks. There ever lurked within her comparative safety that possibility of danger which gave a zest to her position. The season was still further enlivened by a most unusual event in the annals of military life—the celebration of a wedding in the camp of the Seventh New Jersey Regiment. Leaves of absence being now more sparingly granted, the application of a certain officer was "returned, disapproved." His nuptial arrangements in Washington were thus interrupted. The sympathies of his Colonel and brother officers becoming aroused, an invitation was extended by them to the bride-elect and her friends to solemnize the union appropriately within the Union lines, and to accept the hospitalities of the regimental camp. To everybody's delight, the invitation was accepted, and immediately the camp was alive with preparation, in which the soldiers of every rank participated. The village of tents was transformed into a bower of beauty. As the hour arrived for the performance of the ceremony, the regiment was drawn up in a hollow square, in the centre of which an altar had been majestically formed of drums and cannon-balls and draped with the beautiful American colors. The visiting ladies, accompanied by their escorts, and followed by prominent officers, preceded the bridal retinue and arranged themselves before the improvised altar. A band of music burst into the inspiring strains of "Hail to the Chief," as General Hooker, head of the army, approached and was adroitly changed to Mendelssohn's March when the wedding party assumed position before the regimental chaplain. Amid this pomp and ceremony of the occasion there was something absurdly incongruous. A southern sun shining brightly, suggesting warmth, a northern wind blowing viciously and cold. A shivering bride in robes of fleecy, transparent white, and a party of guests in dark woolens and warm furs. It was a symbol of future unity between the North and South.

A wedding breakfast was hospitably tendered by the regiment, and the following day the festivities were continued at Boscobel, with General Sickles once more as host. There the General displayed a miraculous skill in entertainment, in a place and at a time when entertainment might seem impossible. The chandeliers were ingeniously constructed of evergreen branches, on which cunning hands had fastened the glistening points of bayonets, which pierced and supported illuminating candles. The ladies had contributed most of the gay ribbons in their possession, red, blue and an occasional green one, undistinguishable from the blue by candlelight.

Then there was a wonderful supper, presided over by French artists, who had transported a supply of delicacies from Washington, to which every one was welcome, and, later, in the gray of the early morning, a second banquet of game and wine to the ladies and to favored officers. Dancing was indulged in upon the broad veranda of the old mansion, and never was the old Virginia reel more heartily enjoyed.

Then there were the officers of every grade in brilliant epaulets, gold lace and rows of buttons. There were illustrious persons present whose names have since grown even more famous. Prominent among these were the foreign Prince and Princess Salm-Salm. The prince, with a sympathy alike to that of Lafayette, becoming fired with admiration for the cause of the Union, crossed the seas, accompanied by his wife, to offer his services in time of need. Had the tongue of the noble Prussian

6

more fluently spoken the English language, it is said that he would have been offered an important command. Being a man of military experience, he accepted the position of a Colonel and won honors upon the field. The name of his vivacious wife has since passed into history.

But there was wisdom overlooking all, as was confessed when it was subsequently understood that in that very hour an attack from the enemy was anticipated. The Commander-in-chief congratulated himself that his officers were assembled where they might receive his immediate orders, and he expressed satisfaction that the ladies were so congregated that they might be sent without delay to a place of comparative safety.

As the spring approached and the condition of the roads improved, a suspicion grew that the army was about to emerge from its winter quarters. Leaves of absence grew more and more infrequent. It became even impossible for a brigade or a division commander to obtain leave for a day's run up to Washington. The ladies were summoned and requested to elect an escort to accompany them beyond the army lines, and to prevent all favoritism, the escort must not be a married man. Sagacious General!

A special steamer had been prepared to convey the party up the river. A day or so later, the train which was to bear them to the landing, carried away from Falmouth station a sorrowful little company of wives.

It was a dreary morning, the rain splashed upon their faces and disguised the tears which they heroically strove to conceal. There was a flutter of white handkerchiefs, a waving of blue caps, and the winter's experience of one woman in the Army of the Potomac was ended.

Immediately after, the army crossed the narrow Rappahannock on pontoon bridges. Then followed death and destruction at the battle of Chancellorsville, where the many gallants of the camp, by their heroic sacrifices, proved themselves the most chivalric of the field.

A GROUP OF FOSSILS,

Found in East Somerville.

BY MRS. ANTOINETTE BROWN BLACKWELL.

Do you call them lightly "fossils!"
  They grew old when earth was young;
Curious, ancient, graven gospels;
  Older songs than lips have sung.

Fair of form as tiny roses,
  They are music set in stone;
Time-worn some, like fading posies,
  Richly dight when they were grown.

Fine and small, the dainty treasures,
  Nothing coarse, and nothing large,
Almost microscopic measures
  Used, when Time had these in charge.

Piles of fairy columns rising
  Rank on rank, in beaded lines;
Honeycombs; all forms surprising,
  Buried half in stony mines.

Little fluted shells: and creatures
  That in life must half repel,
Glorified in meanest features;
  Purified and saved as well.

Crowns of jewels set about them,
  They have gained the second birth;
Gemmed within, and gems without them,
  Apotheosized on earth.

All these grew in mighty waters;
 Stranded here beneath our feet,
Green earth's bright hued floral daughters,
 Overran them fresh and sweet.

But *they* faded as our dreaming,
 When the night its course has run;
Ages more will watch the gleaming
 Still of these, beneath the sun.

They are older now than Adam;
 Brief his day, from dust to dust;
These of firmer clay, dear madam,
 Take their rank as upper crust.

Law and order strong as duty,
 Governed in that ancient sea,
Wrought with care each type of beauty,
 Formed each line of symmetry.

Over law, and under order,
 Trace the guiding impetus,
Binding actions ever broader,
 All to all, from them to us.

Once, long since, *life's* surge of gladness
 Overflowed their ancient rest;
Almost joy, and almost sadness,
 Something worst, and something best.

Overladen thick with glory,
 Every tale of life must be;
Stranger yet the later story;
 Long and full the history.

Cradled in the brooding ocean;
 Slowly raised with mountain heights;
Tossed, mayhap, in wild commotion
 Upward, mid volcanic lights.

Onward borne by glacial river,
  Solid, mighty type of power,
Yet by sunshine's flash and quiver
  Vanquished, leaving these for dower.

These, to watch the rise of ages,
  Slowly moulding history;
All of life from clams to sages,
  Moving onward wistfully.

Old and curious group of corals!
  Many kinds, but close akin:
Older than all codes of morals;
  Older than all human sin!

A–LO–HA.

BY MISS M. BUXTON.

On the bosom of the placid Pacific lie the fair Hawaiian Islands, whose equable climate is one long, sweet summer. A sort of half-way resting place for vessels of all nations plying to and fro across the vast ocean, they are the resort of a motley crowd of Europeans, Asiatics and Americans, who mingle and intermarry with the gentle, but fast diminishing, native inhabitants. Occidental and Oriental tongues of all varieties blend with the liquid syllables of the natives, who are unable to pronounce two consonants together. Among such a varied and fluctuating population there is need for some word of wide and diverse meanings, which all may use and understand. Such a word is the musical *A-lo-ha* heard from every lip on these fair, sunny islands. It means everything that is sweet, gentle and touching. It is the word of greeting from friend to friend, from parent to child. The lover whispers it low in his sweetheart's

ear, and with it the husband cheers his wife and fondles his
child. It is the word of welcome to the new-born, and the last
farewell of the dying. It expresses love, esteem, gratitude
and blessing. Every joy of life or nature awakens a cheerful
A-lo-ha, every grief and sorrow deepens into a sad and wailing
A-lo-ha. Sailors shout it from shore to ship, from boat to boat.
No stranger visiting these shores fails to hear this sweet soft
word ; no native wandering thence ever forgets it. A gentle
maiden graduating, after pursuing her education in this country
for nine long years, retained it as the one remembered word of
her tongue. It is the morning's glad salutation and the evening's
sweet good night. It is the word of peaceful benediction, and
the vehicle of tenderest ejaculatory prayer.

Perhaps under no circumstances is the deep pathos of the
word, with its varied significations, displayed so strongly as when
the poor stricken leper is conveyed from family, friends and home
to his distant island prison. To that lazaretto all are immediately conveyed who show any symptoms of the dread disease,
unhappily so prevalent among the simple and affectionate natives,
and thence there is no return in life or death. The parting is
final and complete, and oh! the agony of such a farewell! The
faint, despairing *A-lo-ha* floats along the waves to and from the
fast receding ship, and the doomed one is torn forever from all
his heart's treasures. Thenceforth, be his life long or short, he
dwells only with other lepers, snatched like himself from friends
and home to pass as best they may, the wretched remnants of
their earthly lives. Let us trust that in the blessed Hereafter a
glad *A-lo-ha* may re-unite the severed ties, and welcome each
broken heart to Paradise.

A CHRISTMAS LETTER.

BY MARY C. BARRY.

Dear Children—I must keep my promise and tell you about Christmas in Christ Hospital and your Daisy Ward. That Holy season has come and gone, leaving with our sick people its blessings of "Peace on earth and good will to men." Let us go back to Christmas Eve. Come with me in thought to Christ Hospital.

On the Tuesday after Christmas at three o'clock we had our Christmas tree in the Daisy Ward. The tree was given by two dear little girls named Hattie and Eva, who live in Jersey City, and it was very tall and full and had great spreading branches. It was full of toys and ornaments and dollies, who looked over the branches at the sick people and daisies and girls and boys who stood around it. The four cots in which there were four little sick children were moved very near the tree ; the others sat in the little Daisy chairs all around it. The sick daisies in the cots were Heinrich, our little German boy, who does not speak one word of English ; Tommy, a bright little fellow who has a broken arm. He was getting up early on Christmas morning when he fell and broke his arm. We said to him, "Tommy, were you looking for Santa Claus?" He said that he did not know anything about him or Christmas until he came to the Daisy Ward. His mother said : "We are too poor to know much about Christmas." Tommy had never seen a Christmas tree. Our dear little Henry, who has hip disease, was in bed, and Harry, another little sick boy. Henry had his rag doll in his arms. We said : "Your doll is a little boy ; name it Jack." He said : "My doll's name is Nelly." I said : "I wonder who made these wonderful rag dolls?" when I heard Henry's voice from his cot : "I know." "Who, Henry !" I said. "God made them." We told him "that God made the beautiful Tree." "Well, then," he said, "I suppose Santa Claus must have made the dolls." After the four cots had been moved near the Christmas tree and the daisies seated in their little chairs, and a long row of girls and boys, poor children who had been invited, our little ex-daisies and brothers and sisters of those who were sick in the ward, the service commenced. There were sick men and women around the tree as well as children, and besides the four sick children in the cots there were Minnie and Christie, Annette and James, and Walter and Jessie, and seated there looking bright and well was little Bridgie, the poor little girl who was so fearfully burned. You would never believe her to be the poor suffering child of a few weeks ago.

You remember Cisto, the Spanish boy. His mother works in the hospital, and Cisto comes every year to spend Christmas in your Daisy Ward, for he used to be in the ward himself. He is a big boy now.

This is a sort of a Christmas letter, and I will end it by telling you a story I read of a little fellow who had read "The Christmas Carol." On Saturday evening, December 17th, a little fellow about ten years of age was seen to enter Westminster Abbey shortly before Evening prayers. Going straight up the main aisle toward Poet's corner with a directness that showed that his knowledge of the position by custom, he stood bareheaded and reverently over the grave of Charles Dickens. Then looking around in evident doubt as to whether his action might give offence to the authorities, he produced a tiny bunch of violets, with an envelope attached, and kneeling down, placed his tribute tenderly upon the tombstone. The little fellow hovered affectionately around the spot for a few moments, and glancing around to see that his tribute remained undisturbed, went with a happy, satisfied look and took his place for the service. Curiosity led one of our representatives, who happened to be present at the time, to examine the childish offering, and this was what he found written in half-formed characters on the envelope attached to the unassuming violets: "For it is good to be children sometimes and never better than at Christmas when the Mighty Founder was a child himself." Dickens' Christmas Carol.

Your dear little sick daisies said I must wish you all, for them, "A Happy New Year," and Heinrich's voice was heard from his little cot in the corner sending to you his greeting in German : "Gluckliches Neu Jahr."

RETROSPECT.

BY GRACE BROWN BLACKWELL.

'Twas early morn, the grass was wet,
And spiders' wheels were sparkling yet
With dew-drops on each filmy net.

Slow, up the hill an old man went,
His hair was white, his form was bent,
Yet from his eyey outshone *content*.

He stopped and smiled at th' hill's wide crown,
And turned about ; then, gazing down
Beyond his homestead to the town.

With factory chimneys reaching high,
And steeples pointing to the sky,
The old man breathed a weary sigh.

"Yet wherefore sigh ?" he softly said,
"Would I call back the time that's sped ?
' Let th' dead past bury its dead. "

I clear recall when, looking down,
The place was bare ; there was no town,
A broad green stretch one looked adown.

And I recall a later date
When still within fair childhood's gate
Longing to enter youth's estate.

Homesteads dotted the green space then,
Homesteads owned by tillage men,
And Kate dwelt there, a girl of ten.

'Twas there, years since, I claimed her hand
Right on the spot where solid stand
Those great stone houses, tall and grand.

She came to me, their farm was sold ;
Blessings she brought me manifold ;
Our love, dear wife, has not grown old.

Oft' down this hill I strode at night ;
You met me then with step so light,
A sweet smile on your young face bright.

We met half way the hill's ascent
And with clasped hands, in calm content,
Down towards our own new house we went.

And years went by with sun and sleet ;
Our children came with restless feet,
And pleading voices soft and sweet.

The children came to meet me then,
Children ! Now they're gray-haired men
Save one, Helen ; she died since then.

The child God took—Is she old now ?
To me youth still is on her brow,
No lines of age her sweet face show.

Our boys have gone from th' old home nest ;
Young John, the doctor, lives out West ;
And scattered around are all the rest.

And Kate and I have th' house alone ;
We will not grieve our birds have flown,
For each a well-spent life has known.

Wife's been a cripple for nigh a year,
And yet she smiles with old-time cheer ;
Oh, that *again* she might stand here,

And view with me, as oft of yore,
This stretch of varied country o'er,
If thou, swift Time, could'st turn once more !

What are the sounds that greet my ear?
I hear a cry, 'tis " Father dear ! "
Oh, wherefore stand I dreaming here?

I'll hurry home, 'tis growing late,
I said I'd walk to the meadow gate ;
It was unkind to stay from Kate.

What strangers—they, that climb the hill ?
"Father" ! Oh God, my heart stands still ;
The head man walks like my son Will.

What burden do those others bear ?
Why, yes—it is wife's easy chair !
And she is waving, sitting there !

I've walked too far, my mind is dim,
In dreaming—all my senses swim ;
Could death come thus, not dark and grim ?

" Father " ! I hear the cry again ;
'Tis wife, tis Will, there's Tom and Ben
And all the boys, our stalwart men.

But who's that bright-eyed, sweet-faced child
With look like Helen's when she smiled ?
And am I dreaming ? Am I wild ? "

In the warm kisses that press his cheek
Far more is said than lips can speak ;
He starts and trembles, sadly weak.

'Tis only joy that fills his heart
And make quick tears 'neath eye-lids start ;
Tears, that well from out the heart.

"Ah, who is she?" His thin hand shook,
Her dimpled hand he gently took,
Hand of the child with Helen's look.

The fair young girl looked up and smiled
With great gray eyes like Helen's, mild,
And answered : "Grandpa's, grandchild's, child."

CO-EDUCATION OF THE SEXES—NATURAL
AND SUCCESSFUL.

BY MRS. JEAN FISH BERDAN.

Those who are opposed to co-education, say that a woman needs a different training from a man, and, therefore, that the sexes cannot be successfully taught together. If this were ever true, it is so no longer. Many women in every community are obliged to labor for their own maintenance and for the support of their families. They must labor in the same way, follow the same pursuits, and earn their living by the same methods as men. Then, why should they be differently educated? We are told that women have not man's capacity for study, and are not able to maintain an equal standing in their classes with young men. This assertion can but provoke a smile of contempt for those who make it. The register of every mixed school in the country proves the contrary. In all these schools young women are found to take the highest honors away from the young men. And so in the pursuits of life. The first English novelist of this day is a woman, George Eliot; and one of the most distinguished French painters is a woman, Rosa Bonheur.

It is sometimes said that young women should not attend mixed schools on account of the bad manners of the young men. We are charitable enough to believe that men are not naturally coarse and rude. But even granting that there is a natural tendency to rudeness in the masculine mind, then women should find it out for their own protection. Let women know the truth, see man as he is, and both she and he may be saved from the consequences of those serious and life-long mistakes, which are so commonly made through women's ignorance of masculine character.

But we are told that a general education in a mixed school makes women masculine Would you have them soft and pliant, —inert and helpless? Knowledge is power, and power is not found in weaklings. None but a weak man wants a weak woman for his companion. We believe that those who hold to this opinion are jealous of woman and afraid of competition with her.

There are those who claim that some of the studies taught in a mixed school, like Physiology, should not be taught to a mixed class. If this were true the defect could easily be remedied by forming separate classes for each in such studies. However, this is a an argument against co-education that can hardly have weight, since to-day all the professions are open to woman.

It is urged that so close an association of the sexes at so early an age leads to foolish love affairs—youthful and ill-assorted marriages. Upon so delicate a subject as this, I will merely venture to say, that it is best that young people should have their first attack of "love," as it is called, at the earliest age possible. It is like the other infantile maladies,—mumps, whooping cough and measles, contagious and indigenous to all states of society. The child seldom escapes it, and the longer the attack is kept off the more fatal it is when it comes. As this is so general an epidemic, why charge it upon mixed schools? You will find

young men afflicted nigh unto death with this melancholy
malady, in boys' academies and in their own homes, as well as in
mixed schools. Henry Ward Beecher said that if God had designed the sexes to be separately educated no man would have
been blessed with a family of both boys and girls. Every man's
children would have been either all boys or all girls.

Let us now look at some of the benefits of co-education.
It enables young men and young women to know each other's
character. It helps to dispel absurd and harmless delusions.
It shows men that women are not wingless angels, and it teaches
women to know that the embryo lords of creation are, indeed,
but sordid clay. Such a method of education cannot fail to have
a refining influence upon man. In the presence of women every
man is more gentle in manner, more careful in conduct and
more thoughtful in conversation. This refining and elevating
influence being reflex is therefore mutually beneficial. For by
the association with men women learn self-reliance and courage,
become more sober in mind and more fastidious as to dress and
deportment. They hear discussed the grave affairs of life and
business, and become more capable of taking care of themselves
in the rough struggles and sudden vicissitudes of life. Co-education induces a healthy competition in classes, and thus teaches
habits of industry. What young man, without contesting every
inch of ground, will allow a woman to stand higher in class than
he does? What woman will yield the first place to a man without a struggle?

Nor must the moral influence of co-education be overlooked.
Man and woman act as a counterpoise to each other, each giving
the other some valuable trait of character or some good lesson
in manner or conduct.

We may also refer to the economy of the system. Suppose
co-education be abolished. The expense of instruction would
be nearly doubled. Where you now have one schoolhouse you
would have two, and the force of instruction would need to be
greatly increased.

Therefore, upon all these grounds, social, intellectual, moral
and economical, I claim that the sexes should be trained to-

gether for the great work of life. Our creator has ordained the co-education of the sexes. He sends the boy and the girl into the same household, there to grow to maturity, and by the sports and studies of childhood, to assist in the development of each other's minds and formation of each other's characters. We ask only that this system ordained by God, shall be continued in the school ; that men and women shall be instructed by the same teacher and informed by the same great examples ; that they learn the same lessons of the past and shall have the same preparation for the trials of the future. In no other way can man be made worthy of the fidelity and affection of woman ; in no other way can woman be made a fit companion and helpmeet for man.

LIFE IS SO BEAUTIFUL.

BY MISS CARRIE A. BREESE.

Life is so beautiful,
   Often I say,
Would it were possible
   Always to stay.

Sorrow's dark shadows fall,
   Sitting, I grieve,
Life is so sorrowful
   Would I could leave.

Folding my hands I say,
   Merciful One !
Whether I go or stay,
   " Thy will be done."

THE DISOBEDIENT OWLS.

BY JOSEPHINE L. BALDWIN.

These four little owls
—Reprehensible fowls—
Have been out all day in the rain—
They sit on that post,
Forlorn as a ghost;
You would certainly think them insane ;

For they have a good home
And why should they roam,
Above all when the weather is bad ?
They had no wish to go
As the facts plainly show,
And the story is terribly sad.

'Twas the end of the night,
And just before light,
When, not heeding mamma who said "Boys !"
They quarreled and fought
For a rat one had caught,
And were making a terrible noise

When old Mr. Owl
—A very stern fowl—
Came home for the day to rest.
He wasted no words
On these quarrelsome birds
But turned them all out of the nest.

A cat ate the rat,
So they didn't get that,
And they shivered all day with the cold.
The morals you see,
Are as plain as can be—
" *Don't quarrel,*" and " *Do as you're told.*"

AN UNINTENTIONAL APRIL FOOL.

BY JOSEPHINE L. BALDWIN.

Samuel Walker was a boy of fourteen, considered bright at school, and ordinarily good as boys go. But he had one fault, which was a grievous one, and caused him much trouble at different times. The difficulty was that if he had some work which ought to be done, and some play that he wanted to do, it somehow happened that the play was attended to first; for Sam dearly loved play, and—I am sorry to write it, but the truth must be told—hated all kinds of work. Lazy, did you say? No, it couldn't be that exactly, because he worked a good deal harder in trying to avoid his tasks than any one else would in doing them. He had some pride about standing well at school, and yet when a difficult question was given him the first use he made of his mind was not to attempt to answer it, but to calculate whether any boy who knew enough to answer it was near enough to prompt him without being seen by the teacher.

Friday, March 29, 1889, had been rather a disagreeable day in Samuel's school. During the morning nothing went just right, and when the time for compositions came they were so poorly written and wretchedly read that the teacher's wrath rose with each floundering performance. Sam was the last on the list, and the alacrity with which he stepped to the platform was so unlike his usual motion that Mr. Kent regarded this, in itself, as suspicious. When he announced his subject, "Spring," and read of "budding flowerets" and "mists like fairy veils rising above crystal lakes and emerald valleys," the suspicion was confirmed, and the teacher knew as well as if he had seen him do it, that Sam had taken one of his sister's old essays instead of writing a composition for himself.

7

Then the indignation which had been smoldering blazed out; the scholars quailed beneath the talking to which they received, and were astonished as well as discouraged by the punishment.

"We will devote Monday morning to a composition exercise" was what they heard. Then a subject was given to each. When all but Sam had been inflicted Mr. Kent said, "Since Mr. Walker seems to know so much better than the rest of you how to write compositions, and has so fine a command of language, we will ask him to present a paper on 'How to Make a Composition,' which I am sure will be not only interesting but instructive. Any failure to have these essays prepared will be punished by the loss of recesses for the rest of the term."

Now, if there was one form of work that Sam disliked more than another, composition writing was that one; but, on the other hand, recesses were his great delight; so on the way home from school he determined to get his older brother, Ben, to help him with the essay the first thing Saturday morning. But when he came down to breakfast Benjamin had gone to the city on an errand for his father. Then Clarence Whitlock came over to get Sam to help rig up a windmill; so the morning slipped away. At dinner-time Mrs. Walker said: "Sam, your Uncle John has come in from the farm with a three-seated wagon, and wants to take you and Clarence and six other boys back with him to a candy-pull to-night. If your school work is done you may go, and they'll bring you back when they come to church tomorrow."

Sam was wild with delight at the thought of a candy-pull anywhere, and above all at Uncle John's. But the school work —that hateful essay! What should he do? Just then he heard Ben's voice in the hall, and, rushing out, told his troubles and begged his assistance.

"You just write it for me, won't you, Ben? You know how to make compositions and I don't, and if you won't do it I can't go to the candy-pull."

There were real tears in Sam's eyes, and Ben could not withstand the pleading, so he said: "Well, I'll do it this once be-

cause I hate to see you disappointed ; but it isn't fair or honest
for me to do your work, and I shall never do it again."

Sam scarcely waited to hear anything more than the first
words, but sped away to find Clarence. Ben, after eating his
dinner, applied himself to the task, thinking, as he did so, " What
a queer subject to give Sam ! He knows about as much about
making compositions as he does about the manufacture of Gat-
ling guns. It's a wonder Kent didn't tell him to describe the
process of bread-making and give object lessons. He couldn't
have intended this to be serious. Well, I'll see what I can do."

On his return Sunday Sam declared the candy was "awful
good " (as was proven by the generous samples he brought in
his pocket), and that he had "an awful jolly time ;" and this
was proven, if proof were needed, by the large amount of adhe-
sive sweetness which he had managed to get on his clothes and
even in his hair. Monday morning came and Sam started for
school without having once thought of the essay since Ben had
taken it off his mind Saturday. Near the gate he met a schoolmate who called out, "Got your composition?" "No," said
Sam, stopping short. Darting back he called to Ben to know
where the composition was. "On the desk in the sitting room,"
answered Ben from up stairs. Hastily turning over some papers
Sam saw at last the word he was in search of, and, snatching the
paper, ran hastily to school, reaching the building just as the
last bell rang. Mr. Kent was still stern and had a displeased
look, so that when he ordered, "Sit erect ; desks closed ; give
attention," no one dared disobey, and Sam could not read over
his composition, much to his dismay. When it came his turn he
opened his paper and began :

"How to Make Composition Tea."

"What!" thundered Mr. Kent. Poor Sam, with his face so
red it was almost purple, repeated the title he had read.

"Tea?" repeated the teacher ; "I fear that a decoction of all
the compositions read in this room would make very weak tea.
However, proceed ; but I would advise you not to attempt to be
funny."

Then, breaking a silence so profound that it seemed terrible to Sam, he read what he found on the paper before him :

"Take two ounces of boneset, two of slippery elm bark, and one ounce of horehound. Pour over the mixture three quarts of boiling water, and boil down to two quarts. Strain and add one pound of ginger, two ounces of cayenne pepper, and two ounces of cloves. Bottle, corking tightly. For colds and coughs, take two tablespoonsful in a cup of hot water before going to bed."

"Now." said Mr. Kent. "perhaps you will kindly explain what all this means. It cannot be intended for wit, for the only thing of that nature about it is its brevity. What did you write in that way for!"

"An April Fool," suggested a new scholar under his breath. but repented his rashness when he saw that he had been heard,

"No!" said Mr. Kent, glaring at the offender, "these boys agreed last year with each other and with me that they would not indulge in any such foolish tricks, and I know they will keep their word," he added in a kinder tone. "But, Samuel, please explain your conduct."

Then Sam, who had many manly qualities, as well as numerous weaknesses, bravely told the whole story ; the borrowed composition of Friday, the candy-pull, and Ben's assistance Saturday, and then, holding up the paper in his hand, he said : "This is some mistake, I am sure, Mr. Kent. I don't know how it happened, and I'm sorry."

The confession over, he hung his head to hide the tears that would come, and as Mr. Kent bade him take his seat he said, in a pleasanter voice than he had used that day, "I don't know that I am sorry. It has shown you perhaps, that your way is not the easiest. The old adage is true, 'Lazy people work the hardest.' You have been pretty severely punished, so all I shall ask of you now is to promise me that instead of using your time and talents trying to get out of doing your work you will devote them all to doing it as well and quickly as possible."

Sam, smarting under the sense of shame, readily made the promise.

About the time this was going on at school Mrs. Walker received a note which will explain itself :

" Dear Mrs. Walker : When I asked you yesterday as we came out of church for your mother's receipt for composition tea I had no time to explain why I wanted it. A few days ago my husband's throat began to trouble him very suddenly, and his cough since then has been most distressing. Saturday he said he believed if he could have some of the composition tea which your mother used to make it would help him ; so, more to please him than because I had any faith in the remedy, I agreed to ask you for it. When your coachman came away out here early this morning bringing the note from you I appreciated your thoughtfulness and kindness more than I can tell you. We drive into town often, and the most I expected you to do was to copy the receipt so that any one going from here could stop for it I went in the room where Mr. Dallett was, to tell him the receipt had been sent and to read it over before getting the ingredients together. The 'receipt' turned out so different from what I expected that I read it aloud, and now return it to you that you may read it, and perhaps better comprehend the effect that followed."

Mrs. Walker here opened the enclosure and read :

" How to Make a Composition.

' In order to do this it is necessary to have some paper, ink, a subject, a pen, and a few ideas. Take the subject and ideas, mix thoroughly, sprinkle in a tablespoon of commas, teaspoon of semicolons, and about a dozen periods. Stir well and then moisten with ink until the mixture is thin enough to spread easily on the paper with a pen. If, when all is used, it does not seem enough, more ideas may be added, but it must not be diluted with ink alone. Adjectives are good to give it a flavor if used sparingly.

" To show some mistakes of beginners in composition-making we will suppose our subject to be the cow. A favorite way for filling up the paper without using many ideas is to enumerate all the different kinds of cows, such as Alderney, Jersey, etc. This does not make an interesting composition. Neither is it wise to say : 'If it were not for the cow we could not have milk, cream, butter, or eheese.' The cow is here ; she has come to stay, and it isn't worth while to think what we would do if we didn't have her. The best way to make a composition is to tell all you know or can find out about the subject in the best way you can, and stop when you get through."

Mrs. Walker's face as she read this was a study, and her perplexity was by no means cleared away when she finished. "What can this mean ?" she thought. "This is Ben's writing, and I asked him to copy the receipt, and gave him the book, but—." Further thought did not throw any light on the subject ; so she turned again to Mrs. Dallet's note :

"When I read this to Mr. Dallett he began laughing at the idea of your dignified mother having such a recipe as this, and laughed so violently that he choked, and I became very much frightened, the paroxysm was so severe. I tried to do something for him, but the coughing continued with increased violence, until finally he coughed up a fish-bone which had lodged in his throat and causing all the trouble. So you see the recipe you didn't mean to send probably did more good than the composition tea would have done, and we are both a thousand times obliged.

"Truly your friend,

"CHARLOTTE A. DALLETT."

When Sam came home at noon he found out where the composition tea came from which had been so bitter a dose for him to take; Mrs. Walker discovered how it happened that the paper she took up hurriedly from the desk, though in Ben's writing, was not the one she wanted; and Ben was both amused and astonished to find what a disturbance he had innocently raised.

It was an April Fool certainly, but—perhaps because it was not intended for one—it turned out better than such things usually do. The fortunate result in Mr. Dallett's case we have already seen; and, last Tuesday, as Sam left the school-room, Mr. Kent stopped him and said:

"Sam, that composition tea of which you told us one year ago to-day is the most wonderful medicine I ever knew anything about. It has completely cured a boy with I am acquainted of a very bad habit. I just wanted to say this to you this afternoon, and (holding out his hand) to shake hands with Samuel Walker, who for the past year has been doing his own work and doing it well."

This was high praise for Mr. Kent to give, and Sam went home with a light heart and his face flushed with pleasure and honest pride. But he will always have a queer feeling when he hears any one speak of making or taking Composition Tea.

A WINTER SONG.

BY ANGELINA B. BOYLE.

At night the rugged hills look'd down
On barren fields, all drear and brown;
On trees, whose branches gaunt and bare,
Were trembling in the rimy air;
While mist was brooding o'er the earth,
To veil her darkness and her dearth,
As when, from void, she sprang to birth.

And truly on a world new-born,
In light and glory broke the morn;
Nor southern flow'r, nor orient gem,
E'er form'd so fair a diadem
As on the North's bleak landscape lay,
Where hung from ev'ry spear and spray
A jewel for the eye of Day.

The waste and grime of age were lost
Beneath the silver wand of Frost;
All rosy-hued in dawning light,
Grew spire, and tower, and portal white;
And wondrous fret-work overwrought
The fondest dream of sculptor's thought,
His fancies into substance brought.

The forest lifted lances keen,
Or droop'd in crystal fountains sheen;
Each sparkling rill a captive held
By fetters such as Fay's might weld;
We half forgot that Wintry morn,
The sunshine on the golden corn,
The scents and flow'rs of Summer born.

O snow and vapor, ice and cold,
We sing as sang the saints of old,
Summer and Winter, that fulfill
The wise monitions of His will;
Ye fair creations of His Word,
With all His works in grand accord,
Bless ye and magnify the Lord.

THE HEROES OF THE AMERICAN REVOLUTION—1775 TO 1781.

BY MRS. MAY WHITE BARKER.

Our heroes in the six years' struggle for liberty are like links in a chain,—beads in a rosary—and over each one, we, who are "heirs to the throne," should breathe a prayer of thankfulness, that they were made of such stern stuff! Our heroes: to do and to dare under oppression and tyranny!

In the long chain I can only glance at a few names and they

are samples of many others who gladly spilled their precious life blood in the cause of liberty and freedom. King George III did not reckon wisely with our bird o' freedom, in the years when she was young—the great American eagle had the instinct but her undeveloped resources for screaming when sat upon had yet to be tested and proved. We, English also,—for is not England our mother?—imbibed the taste of freedom from her.

The Anglo-Saxon blood directed our heart-beats, but it had the oxygen of a higher life and a bolder activity—it could brook no trammels which partook of oppression or injustice.

What made Great Britain great also made her first-born great! '

So the history of the Revolution is simply the fruit of English thought, relating back to "Magna Charta," the great charter obtained by the English barons from King John, A. D. 1215, "a fundamental Constitution which guarantees rights and privileges," the idea that the governed should have a voice in the shaping of the policy which exercised control.

Every domestic struggle which marked the centuries of British growth had this warp for every woof.

The interregnum of Cromwell was resplendant with national glory. Men became enthusiastic in the cause of liberty and they made the greatness of the people known in clear and significant tones. The drift of human thought was toward liberty and freedom, and the exodus of the colonists to America was the fruit of the misconception of the rights of the people and of the latent resistance which rules the life, whenever the soul makes duty its purpose and conscience its guide.

The Puritans of New England, the Huguenots of South Carolina, the emigrants of Maryland alike shared the impulse to escape from hierarchical control and work for freedom, self-government and the best interests of the governed. So were born under oppression the Revolution and its heroes—men of distinguished valor and intrepidity or enterprise in danger. In the skirmishes of Lexington and Concord our raw militia were set and determined to vindicate their rights as a free people by the test of liberty or life. So, fearless and brave, they faced the disciplined troops of Great Britain—they were inspired. Says a celebrated writer: "It was the method of an inspired madness." They swept back a solid column of trained soldiers, because the moral force of the energizing passion was imperative and supreme. No troops in the world could have resisted that movement. The men of that period possessed unusual intelligence and mental culture; this, united with the spirit of the struggle itself, made soldiers quickly. The leaders—those who controlled the public policy—were men whose capacity and moral worth were pre-eminent above all others—Washington, Greene, Lee, Maxwell, etc.

The success of the skirmishes at Lexington and Concord made the resistance of Brud's Hill possible. When the discipline of the English army was shattered; when their prestige and their glory went down before the rifles of the farmers, made these farmers confident of the physical strength of moral opinions. The farmers were plain men and handled plain firelocks; oxhorns held their powder and their pockets held the bullets. Coatless under the broiling sun, unadorned by plumage or service medals, looking like vagabonds after their night of labor and their day of hunger, they met the advance of the British army, which was like a solemn pageant in its steady headway, and like a parade for inspection, in its completeness of furnishment. It needs no painter to make the scene clearer than the records we possess. The British think it so easy to gain the victory, but not so; for right in the way were men with calm, intense and energizing love of liberty, awaiting the words of a single man—of Prescott. Warren, by his side, repeats it. The words run, like an electric current, along the impatient lines; the eager fingers give back from the waiting trigger; "steady, men;" "wait till you see the white of the eye—not a shot sooner;" "aim at the handsome coats;" "aim at the waistbands;" "pick off the commanders;" "wait for the word; every man steady!" It comes that word "Fire!" sharp, clear, and deadly in tone and essence; it rings forth, "Fire!" We all know the onset and repulse. Three hundred lifetimes in twenty minutes; another twenty minutes—five hundred went down. Thus the events of the day in which blood was first shed in the contest between Great Britain and her colonies, served to show that if the Americans were unacquainted with military discipline, they were not destitue of either courage or conduct. They knew how, and also dared to, avail themselves of such advantages as they possessed. A kind of "military fever" seized them, and they willingly risked their juvenile ardor in opposition to the matured strength of the parent state.

Thus "the expedition to Concord became the preface to the history of a Nation, the beginning of an Empire and a theme of astonishment to the civilized world," says Dr. Dwight.

Thus the "Minnte Men" were the first of the Revolutionary heroes. History relates: "Then the officers of these 'Minute Men' decided to march down to Concord Bridge and at least drive away the British soldiers stationed there." Captain Isaac Davis, of Acton, said proudly, "I haven't a man that is afraid to go"— and he and his company marched at the head. When they reached the Bridge the British soldiers fired and Davis fell dead. Then Major Butterick called, "Fire! for God's sake, Fire!" and the regulars retreated in great disorder, and Concord Bridge became a hallowed spot, where, in Emerson's grand lines, "the embattled farmers stood and fired the shot heard round the world." Paul Revere! we all know of his midnight ride, as sung by our poet Longfellow,—"Listen, my children, and you shall hear, etc." Also the battle of Lexington, sung by Oliver Wendell Holmes:

> "Slowly the mist o'er the meadows was creeping,
> Bright on the dewy buds glistened the sun—
> When from his couch while his children were sleeping,
> Rose the bold rebel and shouldered his gun, etc."

Another patriot, Joseph Warren, who stood out against the first British aggressions in 1774—he was President of the Massachusetts Provincial Congress, and the following year was made Major General. At the Battle of Bunker Hill, though offered the chief command, he refnsed, and served as a volunteer, musket in hand. He was killed in this action. Before the

battle, he said to a friend: "I know that I may fall, but where's
the man who does not think it glorious to die for his country."
Who has not read "Warren's Address," by John Pierpont:

> "Stand, the ground's your own, my braves;
> Will ye give it to slaves?
> Will ye look for greener graves?
> Hope ye mercy still,
> What's the mercy despots feel?
> Hear it in that battle peal,
> Read it on your bristling steel,
> Ask it, ye who will?"

and General Francis Marion, of South Carolina, he had his
camp in a swampy and wooded island, and from there he would
secretly sally forth and strike swift and telling blows at the
enemy.

Bryant has sung his paen, "The Song of Marion's Men:"

> "Our band is few, but true and tried,
> Our leader—frank and bold—
> The British soldier trembles, when
> Marion's name is told.
> Our fortress is the good green wood,
> Our tent the cypress tree," etc.

Nathan Hale, another hero. After Washington's retreat from
Long Island, September, 1776, he needed information as to the
British strength and fortifications. Captain Nathan Hale, a
fine young American officer, of twenty-one years, volunteered to
get the information. While inside the enemy's lines he was
taken prisoner and hanged as a spy. His last words were: "I
only regret that I have but one life to lose for my country."
Francis M. Finch sings of him thus:

> "To drum beat and heart-beat
> A soldier marches by,
> There is color in his cheek,
> There is courage in his eye,
> Yet to drum beat and heart-beat
> In a moment he must die."

The last verse is this—

> "From the fame-leaf and angel-leaf,
>   From monument and urn,
> The sad of earth, the glad of heaven,
>   His tragic fate shall learn;
> And on fame-leaf and on angel-leaf
>   The name of Hale shall burn."

and so they pass by like a moving panorama—one closely follow-ing another—hero after hero, until the closing scene at York-town, when the British commander, Lord Cornwallis, surren-dered his army of over seven thousand men to Washington, September, 1781. Whittier sings of the seige at Yorktown in his own inimitable verse :

> "From Yorktown's ruins ranked and still,
> Two lines stretch far o'er vale and hill,
> Who curbs his steed at head of one?
> Hark! the low murmur—Washington!
>
> "Who bends his keen approving glance,
> Where down the gorgeous line of France
> Shine knightly star and plume of snow?
> Thou, too, art victor—Rochambeau!
>
> "Shout from thy fired and wasted homes
> Thy scourge Virginia, captive comes—
> Nor thou alone with one glad voice
> Let all thy sister states rejoice!
>
> "Let Freedom, in whatever clime—
> She waits with sleepless eye her time—
> Shouting from cave and mountain wood,
> Make glad her desert solitude.
> While they, who hunt her, quail with fear,
> The new world's chain lies broken here."

So I close this article upon the Heroes of the Revolution in the language of the commander-in-chief in his last military order of the struggle itself : "Happy, thrice happy shall they be pro-nounced hereafter who have contributed anything ; who have performed the meanest office in erecting this stupendous fabric

of freedom and empire upon the broad basis of independency ;
who have assisted in protecting the rights of human nature and
establishing an asylum for the poor and oppressed of all nations
and religions."

A REMEMBRANCE.

BY EDITH B. BLACKWELL, M. D.

Down the long green slope of the hillside
  Where the cloud-shadows love to play,
They saw the snow of the daisies
  That was drifted away and away,
And the soft blue light that was sifted
  From the sky to the distant hills ;
They heard a thrush singing and singing
  His tender melodious trills,
And they felt how through all that is living
  The tide of rejoicing thrills.

'Twas a glimpse of the great wide summer
  That was blooming for thousands of miles
Into beauty and bountiful blessing,—
  One of Nature's infinite smiles.

Then they thought of the crowded city
  That had walled out the summer's grace,—
Of the ceaseless noise of traffic
  And hurry from place to place ;
And they sent where a child was pallid
  In a tenement's stifling heat,
Her playground the sordid gutter,
  The dusty, sweltering street ;

And she came to the flower-clad meadows
  She never before had seen—
Mysterious tents of the woodland
  With curtains of rustling green—
To the mosses and red-cap lichens,
  The lullaby croon of the brook,
To the largess of treasures unnumbered,
  Discovered in every nook.

The pink of the wild rose petals
  Had come to abide in her face,
And the gracious glint of the sunshine
  Relighted a childish grace,
When she came with a brown-gold daisy
  Dug up from the meadow loam,
Saying, "Oh, you beautiful country,
  I must carry a piece of you home!"

It may be on window-ledge lowly
  The flower-stars again may shine bright ;
I know that the thought of the summer
  Helps make childish burdens more light,
And surely its echoing visions
  Bring sweeter dreams into the night.

So when book, or a word that's inspiring,
  Brings us glimpses of grander fields,
That blossom with deeds more heroic
  Than our every-day toiling yields,
That blossom with thoughts that are higher,
  Akin to the thoughts we would pray,
We may gather some floweret of beauty
  In our souls to carry away.
And its grace will enoble and lighten
  The burden and heat of the day.

TANGLES.

MRS. A. SWAN BROWN.

"Come, daughter Nell," I said one day,
　　To my wee four-year-old;
"I want to wind the skein of silk,
　　And you may come and hold."

She took the shining, silken skein
　　Upon her chubby hands,
And I began to smooth the knots,
　　From out the tangled strands.

But little Nell became soon tired,
　　And said, "If I could wind
And you would hold, Mamma, 'twould be
　　Much nicer you would find.

For I could wind right fast, I know,
　　And get the knots out too,
I'd get it done in half the time,
　　Mamma, that it takes you!"

I smiled, but took the skein myself,
　　And let the wee one try
The puzzling task she fancied she
　　Could better do than I.

She sat to work in right good will
　　With tiny baby hands,
To bring out order from the mass
　　Of much disordered strands.

But soon her childish patience failed
　　For worse and worse it grew,
And looking in my face, she cried,
　　"I can't, mamma, won't you?"

And as she ran away to play,
　　Leaving the task to me,
I could but think how often I
　　Am just as weak as she.

When God asks me to hold the skein,
　　And wait for Him to wind,
Do I not often think that I
　　A quicker way could find?

But when I take the skein and strive
　　To smooth the tangles out,
And find it growing sadly worse,
　　Through twisting it about.

Seeing the task to be too great,
　　Beyond my power to do,
I lay the skein aside and say,
　　I *can't*, dear Lord, won't you?

And then my Heavenly Father takes
　　The knotted, tangled strands,
From out my weak and feeble hold
　　Into His mighty hands.

He gently smooths the twists and knots
　　That were too hard for me,
And then I see how weak I am
　　And how all-powerful *He*,

Oh, teach me, Father, when in doubt
　　Within Thy strength to rest,
Trusting Thy wisdom, love and power,
　　Assured Thy way is best.

Content to simply hold the skein,
　　Since Thou dost deem it wise,
Knowing that all will be made plain,
　　Up yonder, in the skies.

REMINISCENCES OF MRS. BRADFORD.

The Last of the Washington Circle.

J. J. BOUDINOT.

Perhaps the last of the old-fashioned homes of this country to retain its ancient customs and traditions, transporting one into the life of previous century, was that of Mrs. Bradford, of Burlington, N. J. Susan Vergerau Boudinot was born 1764, and married William Bradford, Attorney-General under Washington, in 1784. Her mother was Hannah, sister of Richard Stockton, the signer, and her father was Elias Boudinot, President of the Continental Congress, who as such signed the peace with Great Britain. Being a man of letters as well as a patriot and a philanthropist, he retired early from public life and spent his declining years with Mrs. Bradford, then a widow, in Burlington. Here he built himself a home, somewhat more elaborate than the one in Elizabeth, and much in the same style of his country seat near Philadelphia, in which city his town house was for some years in the near vicinity of that of President Washington. Many of the richest and most influential families in the country lived in Burlington, forming a charming society, among whom were tho Binneys, Whartons, Chaunceys, Shippens, McIlvans, etc., and here was the colonial home of Governor Franklin. It was a picturesque old town, with its many colonial houses, wide streets, and immense shade trees, and its green banks sloping down to the Delaware River.

Within the old mansion, all was profusion, comfort, and elegance, without waste or vain display, but accompanied with a certain old-fashioned formality and etiquette natural to the hostess and her surroundings, for she had come to us from another age, "the good old times," a perfect type of a lady of the old school. Her early associates had been the Washingtons, Lafayettes, Hamiltons, etc., whom in their generation she had long outlived. The writer remembers her as an aged woman, but with the erect carriage and bearing of one much younger. She was rather short than tall, but there was a decided presence about her. The expression of her face was placid and benevolent, denoting the serene calm of the evening of a well-spent life ; she had passed through the storms and anguish that must assail every true woman's heart, in the loss of all who are nearest and dearest, but she could, notwithstanding, clasp hands with the new generations in loving sympathy. Her soft gray eyes, however, had first seen the light in troubled times—"the times that tried men's souls." She seemed to breathe the very spirit of those patriotic days. She inherited from her ancestors courage, firmness and decision. Portia's speech has been aptly applied to Mrs. Bradford : " Think you I am no stronger than my sex, being so fathered and so husbanded ?" Her character was well exemplified in an amusing incident of her childhood. One evening, as an invited guest at Governor Franklin's, she was presented with a cup of tea. The stamp act had passed, and all good patriots were filled with resentment. Our little heroine politely declined the tea, and, being again and again pressed, she took the cup and with a grave courtesy raised it to her lips, but without touching a drop crossed and poured the contents from the window.

The family on one occasion during the war, having been levied upon by a party of British, an officer, reminded by her that her aunt had asked protection, remarked : " Not by your advice, I presume ?" "That it never was, I can tell you," she replied. Her self-possession was equally manifested when in extreme old age the house took fire in the middle of the night. To avoid opening the door by which the dense smoke would rush into her chamber, the attempt to rescue her was by reaching her room from the roof of the porch. The blinds being forced open, there she stood enveloped in a blanket, quietly awaiting, showing by look and mien as well as by word that she was not frightened, though her maid had disappeared in the darkness.

She would tell with a great deal of spirit and amusement a story against herself—how, when the family fled to Baskingridge during the war, she, being a little girl, was sent out with her maid for exercise ; firing being heard in the distance, she took to her heels, running as fast as her feet could carry her, rushed in at the street door and up the stairs, crying, "The British are coming ! The British are coming !" She was caught in Mrs. Washington's arms, soothed and caressed and told that her alarm was needless, as what she heard was only the practicing of our soldiers. She was present during an interesting interview between Washington and a party of Indians. A temporary stage had been erected, but no sooner had the forest braves been ceremoniously seated upon it, than the structure gave way and they were precipitated to the ground, and were with difficulty persuaded that it was not a preconceived plan for their destruction. Many families fled to Baskingridge during the march of the armies through the Jerseys, and were dependent upon each other for the interchange of various kindly offices. An amusing story was told of young Master Morton, who was sent with the only darning needle possessed by the community to a neighbor's house. He dropped it on the way, and to his infinite terror and disgrace was obliged to return home and confess the loss on which so much of the comfort of the community depended. A more touching reminiscence is that of a scene which occurred some years later, at the Washington mansion in Philadelphia, when Mr. Bradford was attorney-general. There being none but an intimate circle present, the conversation turned upon Lafayette, then a prisoner in Germany. Washington dwelt upon his sufferings, contrasting them with his former fortunes, and, speaking of his heroism in our cause, became greatly moved, tears coming to his eyes, and his whole being apparently shaken. On returning home, Mr. Bradford wrote some verses on this pathetic scene, entitled "The Lament of Washington." Private copies were circulated, and they were sung to a solemn

:air composed on the occasion of the execution of the queen of France.

Mrs. Bradford, as the mistress of her father's house during much of his public service, together with her family connections, was brought into close relation with the most eminent characters of the country; and now in her declining years she was a historic figure, the last relic of that famous coterie of revolutionary dames, of whom were Mrs. Rush, Mrs. Hamilton, Mrs. Madison, and Mrs. Carroll. Our minister to England, Mr. Richard Rush, was her kinsman. He writes to her: "I have always felt a just pride in the distinguished names of the maternal stock, from which I and mine spring; a feeling strengthened rather than diminished by my intercourse abroad.

"I think I wrote to my mother from London, that she might tell it to you, in what gratifying terms my estimable friend, Lord Teignmouth, of whom I see much, used to speak to me of your father, and that he and others spoke publicly in the same way. I venture to put under cover for you two humble little articles connected with some of the public questions of the day. Washington's name is about the main staple of both and the known respect and friendship he bore for your father must naturally superadd ties in your bosom, to the veneration and homage the whole world now cherishes towards his great name. I saw much of the Lafayettes at La Grange and elsewhere when lately in France; George, whom you probably knew when a youth in General Washington's family, and the head of his family during my mission to France, I am sorry to say, died soon after I got home."

Mrs. Bradford's hospitality was unceasing, and seldom indeed did boat or train arrive that did not bring some guest to her house, ofter the most distinguished men of the day in our own or from foreign countries. How beautiful was the welcome to her home! As warm as the great fires that blazed on her hearthstones. All felt the charm of her manner who came within its influence. As Mr. Rush again wrote: "From youth, from early boyhood, my recollections of her at her own house, at my uncle's, at my mother's, with whom she was reared in part as with a

sister, are all of the most grateful kind. Attaching in her manners to all, because they sprang from the many virtues and solid
excellence of her heart, their peculiar grace and kindness were
ever especially winning to the young, and now as I call up these
recollections, through back time associated with a thousand early
pleasures they come over me like delightful visions, no, not
visions, for at that time of life they are realities unmingled with
anything to take from the happiness and joy they give ; their
vivid impressions live forever and momentarily, at least, renew
in us the delight they once afforded." Only those who lived in
her house can know what a perfect gentlewoman she was ;
the dignified bearing was instinct, with self respect and the
refined thought that "thinketh no evil, the charity that suffereth
long and is kind, the love that beareth all things, hopeth all
things, believeth all things," were coupled with a humility
astounding in one upon whom fortune had always smiled. As
Bishop Doane said of her in his funeral sermon : " There lies all
that was mortal of the holiest woman that I ever knew and
therefore of the humblest. She was pre-eminent for her propriety and delicacy of thought and feeling. Who of the generation that has passed away in the light of her loveliness, who
that has lived to enjoy it in its lingering and declining radiance,
has ever met with a more perfect Christian lady?

She was instinctively refined and courteous. A courtier
would have called her elegant; to the last day of her long life she
never for a moment lost her native grace. Her charity was
great, no poor man was ever turned from her doors; she gave
away one-third of her income.

Among her many visitors were some very odd old people,
whose visits, I was about to say visitations, called for great cir-
cumspection on the part of the younger portion of the household, and were not a little tax on the good nature and self-control of the younger hostess, Mrs. Boudinot, into whose hands was
so gracefully resigned the control of this large establishment, as
the older lady felt herself growing somewhat infirm for so much
care. She insisted that there could not be two mistresses, and
with a delicacy and consideration all her own, she would ask per-

mission, as though herself a guest, did she wish for any change in the ménage. And how thoroughly her nature was appreciated and her wishes carried out by the one she had chosen as a daughter! Seldom have two such rare natures dwelt together under the same roof-tree. Mr. Boudinot, with his wife and children, had been persuaded to spend the winter with Mrs. Bradford before settling down at his estate near Philadelphia, they having left their home in Newark, New Jersey, for that purpose. But never for any length of time after would the elder lady part with the younger, and Burlington became their home. Mr. Boudinot was Mrs. Bradford's nearest living relative, and she, his senior by thirty years, bore towards him almost the relation of a mother. It was his pleasure as well as that of his wife to keep up all the associations of the house. Mrs. Bradford, for many years before her death, kept her room, where she received her friends. Some of the members of her household might be described as picturesque; certainly such was the little old French lady who had come there first, during the elder Mr. Boudinot's lifetime, as an amanuensis She was a refugee from St. Domingo, whose lover had been shot before her eyes, so went the romantic story, though the youngsters wondered that so old and grotesque a little body should ever have possessed a lover. She was, however, kind to the children, making them benicake, from seed which she received once a year from the south. They compounded her sins of eavesdropping, importance, and general fussiness, with various kindly deeds and gifts. Her broken English was only outdone by that of Ambrose, the old butler, whose African tongue could never accommodate itself to the English pronunciation. "He" with him was always "she," and " she " "he," as thus, in announcing the daily visits of Bishop Doane to his aged parishioner: "De bitchip man. Shall she walk up?"

Ambrose was a perfect servant, and, with the footman and coachman, wore still the mourning livery for the master, dead nearly half a century. The domestic grievance was not known in that household—its ten or twelve servants accomplishing their work with a magical quiet and precision. The housekeeper

made her daily round with the chambermaid, to assist in arranging the large, old-fashioned, high-post bedsteads, with their
gay and elaborate hangings in winter and white demity festoons
in summer. The hall was wide and contained some beautiful
statuary—four groups of seventeenth century work, the only
known specimens of the kind in this country. The stairs with
very low steps led to a landing on which stood the old clock, a
gift from Richard Stockton, the signer, which had measured out
the moments of those stormy times of the Revolution, and had
struck the knell of many a footsore, weary soldier on the frosty
banks of the Delaware. The house possessed also a well-stocked
library, with many editions of the Bible, from Mrs. Bradford's
father, the founder of the Bible society in this country and its
first president. Generations of children delighted in the "blue
lions," Chinese porcelain beasts, which stood upon the lawn, and
into whose grinning and capacious jaws they would stuff grass,
and sometimes to their terror drop a silver spoon. There were
two sets of servants, white and colored ; the former took their
meals in the housekeeper's room, the latter in the kitchen where
Crissy the cook presided. Ambrose had pet names for his favorites—as "Honey" for one of the best women that ever lived,
making sweetness wherever her influence came. She was a sort
of confidential servant and nursery governess to the children, a
most valuable and worthy young woman. She and her sister,
Mrs. Bradford's maid, lived in the family until the children were
grown up, saved their earnings with which they bought farms in
Canada, when they married, carrying with them the benedic-
tions of all the family.

Ambrose always called the two little girls "madam"; and
"misses"; that he had quite a vein in his nature, as when he was
heard to tell "madam" that he could make himself carpet for
her to walk on, and exclaim of the piece of statuary in the drawing room representing an African queen, "Ah, madam, dare's de
dignity." He said that he had been a prince, stolen from his
native wilds. He looked like a gnome, but was as good as gold.
He was religious, and would, on occasions, retire for prayer, to his
chapel, an old sedan chair, which was kept in a room in the cellar

after the family had ceased to use it. This mode of conveyance was sometimes resorted to, however, up to quite a late period, when Mrs. Bradford's visits to the parish church became more difficult; she was often conveyed thither by two stalwart negroes in the very chair of which I speak, from her own hall, the wide double front doors of which admitted of its egress with ease, and she would thus avoid any exposure to the weather. Greatly she loved to listen from the old square pew in the front of the chancel to her bishop's eloquent sermons, delivered in that terse and beautiful English of which he was so great a master.

Reference to the old sedan-chair reminds me of the antiquated coaches in the coach-house. The one most in use was a large double affair, lined with some rich stuff and set high upon springs, with steps which rather resembled a carpeted staircase, and which little buttons, the footman, springing from his perch behind the coach, where he stood up and held on by the straps, would let down and fold up. There was still older style of conveyance called the chariot. This somewhat resembles the other, but was lined with crimson satin and painted yellow, and had but two seats inside; the coachman's being very high with a hammer-cloth, the same behind for the footman. The livery, formerly blue and gold, changed at the time of which I write to mourning, was a dark-gray cloth with white bands, a cord of black velvet on each side, the hat with a wide silver band and buckle.

The hours for the meals were the old-fashioned ones. Breakfast at half past eight o'clock, preceeded by family prayers, consisted of something very light, as toast, Digby herring and rolls; meat was never seen, except, perhaps, as frizzled beef. Dinner at half-past two; beautiful damask, one large table-cloth and a small one which was laid on the top and removed before the dessert was served by a deft movement on the part of Ambros, catching the four corners with the help of another man, from the other side-cut glass decanters, and coasters. First came soup served from the head of the table, and then sometimes fish and sometimes not, meats and vegetables and salad, beef, turkey, game, ham or tongue, terrapin, all placed on the

groaning board at once. The dessert course was equally generous, consisting of pies, pudding, blanc-mange, jelly and custard,
served on a beautiful service of silver, after which the large cloth
was removed, and the polished mahogany appeared, on which
were placed the wine, fruit and nuts, with finger glasses. Grace
was said before the meal and thanks returned after. Mrs. Bradford was a beautiful and skillful carver. At half past six, tea
was handed in the drawing-room with the finest little scraps of
rolled-up bread and butter, finely chipped dried beef and cake.
At ten o'clock, supper—cold meats, nuts, apples, jellies, etc., with
wine; then prayers, at which all the family and servants were
present, after which the servants appeared with candles to light
the guests to their rooms.

The house contained several interesting portraits of Washington, for in that household, veneration for that exalted name
knew no bounds. There were also many interesting family portraits—two by Sir Godfrey Kneller. Mrs. Bradford had among
her keepsakes a pair of bracelets, containing the hair of General
Washington, the clasps of which were set with pearls, and also a
small cushion made from a piece of Mrs. Washington's wedding-
dress. A few of these she left by will to friends, some of the
large silver service to her favorite cousins, who were Miss Bay-
ards, and one of whom married the nephew of General Washington, another the gifted and greatly beloved Professor Dod, of
Princeton college, in whose families doubtless the silver still remains. With these few exceptions, the portraits, silver and statuary remains grouped together in Miss Boudinot's house in New
Jersey. One of Mrs. Bradford's relatives, when quite a lad,
witnessed a stirring scene, which picture, he said, could never be
effaced from his memory—Washington going to open the houses
of Congress in Philadelphia. This youth was one of a vast
crowd of spectators which filled the streets in all directions, in
front and around the State House. "The President's carriage,
white with ornamental panels, drawn by four beautiful bay
horses, drove slowly up through the densely packed multitude.
Alighting, the President slowly ascendeded the steps of the State
House, turned, and for a moment paused, waiting for his Secre-

tary, who followed him from a carriage behind, and who handed
him a paper, probably the speech he was to deliver. All eyes
were fixed upon that majestic form, as he stood before them clad
in a suit of black velvet, his hair powdered to snowy whiteness,
a dress sword at his side, and his hat held in his hand. Perfect
silence reigned, not a sound was heard, every heart was full, no
tongue could speak their unutterable admiration, and not until
the door had closed upon him did the crowd as with one voice
break forth into wild and prolonged huzzas. '

I close this sketch with a letter written by Judge Elisha
Boudinot, the brother of Hon. Elias Boudinot, to General Washington, the original draft of which is in my possession, together
with Washington's original letter in response. Judge Boudinot
writes :

"Amidst the general joy that is diffused thro. the states on the establishment of our Independence and a restoration of the blessings of peace,
will your Excel. permit an individual deeply interested in your happiness, to
give vent if possible to the feelings on this subject, and most sincerely to
congratulate you on the final accomplishment of our most sanguine hopes. The
thought that your Ex. has survived the contest adds a pleasure to the enjoyment, that no other event could possibly give. It has been my earnest
prayer that heaven would preserve your life to complete the liberation of
your country from tyranny and see her safely secured in peace, independence and happiness, and to receive the grateful acknowledgments of a whole
people. Nothing can afford a great mind more real pleasure than the idea
of being the happy instrument of giving birth to an empire, the future nursery of every principle that can enoble man, an asylum for the persecuted
of all nations, and in fact rendering happiness to one-quarter of the globe.
It is a satisfaction that an angel might aspire after, and which you Sir, are
justly entitled to enjoy. I am confident that the idea of this has supported
your Ex. in many distressing scenes you have passed through to the final
completion of our wishes. You have finished your part, it only remains that
your country should equal in gratitude the toils, the dangers and solicitude
you have endured for them. That they will do this collectively there is no
doubt, but something still remains to perfect the reward to convince you that
every individual feels that real affection and gratitude for you that they
ought to the Father and Deliverer of their country. This only can be done
by the representation of private persons, which will, I hope, apologise for
this intrusion. My public business calls me into every county of the state
and a very general acquaintance with the people, and I am positive I should

do the greatest injustice to them did I not assure your Excel. that there is scarcely a man or a woman among them, but what entertains these senti- ments, and but have a monument erected to you in their breasts, that can only be effaced with their lives. Were it possible for your Ex. to have a view of the whole country at once, and see the honest farmers around the fires blessing your name and teaching their children to lisp your praises, you would forget your toils and labors and thank heaven you were born to bless a grateful land.

When your Excellency is retiring from the field will you indulge the in- habitants of this state by spending a short time as you are passing thro., free from care, where you have spent so much in distress and anxiety of mind, that they may have an opportunity of personally convincing you of their attachment.

I take the liberty to enclose and beg your acceptance of a copy of an Ode written by my father-in-law Mr. Smith, on the occasion of our rejoicing.

Mrs. Boudinot joins me in entreating that you will be kind enough to make our sincere congratulations acceptable to Mrs. Washington, and to assure her that we participate in the joy that she, above all others must feel on this occasion, and that you may both long, long enjoy that cup of happi- ness which Providence has so completely filled. Is the fervent prayer of

Your obedient Servant

Elisha Boudinot."

Washington in his characteristic reply touches upon matters of public interest to all Americans. His letter is dated:

" Newburgh, May 10th., 1783.

Sir:—

Your letter of congratulation contains expressions of too friendly a nature not to affect me with the deepest sensibility. I beg therefore you will accept my acknowledgment for them, and that you will be persuaded I can never be insensible of the interest you are pleased to take in my per- sonal happiness, as well as in the general felicity of our country. While I candidly confess I cannot be indifferent to the favorable sentiment, which you mention my fellow citizens entertain of my exertions in their service, I wish to express through you the particular obligations I feel myself under to Mr. Smith for the pleasure I have received from the perusal of his elegant ode on the peace. The accomplishment of the great object we had in view, in so short a time, and under such propitious circumstances, must I am con- fident, fill every bosom with the purest joy; and for my own part I will not strive to conceal the pleasure I already anticipate from my approaching re- tirement to the placid walks of domestic life. Having no rewards to ask for myself, if I have been so happy as to obtain the approbation of my country- men, I shall be satisfied. But it still rests with them to complete my wishes, by adopting such a system of policy, as will ensure the future reputation, tranquility, happiness and glory of this extensive empire; to which I am much assured nothing can contribute so much as an *inviolable adherence to the principles of the union*, and a fixed resolution of building *the national faith on the basis of public justice*—without which all that has been done and suffered is in vain—to effect which therefore, the abilities of every true patriot, ought to be exerted with the greatest zeal and assiduity.

I am as yet uncertain, at what time I shall be at liberty to return to Virginia, and consequently cannot inform you when I may be able to gratify my inclination of spending a little time with my friends in Jersey, as I pass through that state. I can only say that the friendship I have for the people, from whom I have often derived such essential aid, will strongly dispose me to it.

Mrs. Washington begs Mrs. Boudinot and yourself to accept her best compts., and thanks for your good wishes, and I must request the same favor, being with sentiments of esteem and regard,

Sir, Your most Obed. & most Hble Servant,

To. Elisha Boudinot, Esq."   G. Washington.

This correspondence breathes that spirit which carried our patriot fathers through the struggle that bequeathed so much to posterity and to the world.

BEETHOVEN'S FIFTH SYMPHONY.

BY MRS. FREDERICK G. BURNHAM.

Long years ago, an eager child
I listened to the mighty master's voice.
I strove to understand his solemn joy,
To rise with him to heights of ecstacy.

But vague unrest possessed my lingering soul,
The wailing music filled my eyes with tears,
My heart with longing for a good unknown,
And tender strains that ever and anon
Come in to rest the heart from too much souring.
Seemed to me but the sad and dreary ending
Of a too mournful, tho' exalted dream.

But now with all my restless thoughts and longings
Interpreted by thee, oh Love !
I come again, in life's high noon
And joy to listen to the mighty music.
For now I know how Love and Faith lift up
And bear away the soul to heaven's gates
In a triumphant march of harmony.
No more my heart is beaten back in sadness
By undertones of solitary longing.

As the bird that's wandered out to sea,
And hearing the mysterious rush and roar
Of the great ocean throbbing underneath her,
Longs for the rest and peace of wildwood green
Where all the hum and crooning song of nature
Woos her to sit among the leafy boughs
And build her nest amid the sweet green forest,
So had I heard the monotone of ocean,
Of vague, sad, rushing strivings in the music.

But now the glad hymn bears me quite away,
I mount on harmonies of love and glory,
For life hath taught me of the glad sweet strain
Made up of sad and joyous intermixed,
Of broken bursts of song, of wailing grief,
Of discords even, till we know their meaning
And how they blend in truer harmony
In the Great Maker's plan of conqureing Love !
So soar we, resting on the Infinite ;
We mount on wings of mighty Love Divine,
That bears us up, and bears up all the world.

And ever, as the mighty strain rolls on,
Come in the closer, sweet and homelike notes
That tell of human love, of hearts that rest
On one another, while they look to heaven.

THE PATTERN SEEN IN THE MOUNT.

CATHARINE L. H. BURNHAM.

Go to the mount in the morning,
    Seeking thy pattern there.
Let the day at its dawning,
    Find thee engaged in prayer.

There, with the sky around thee,
    Removed from care and strife,
With the whole world lying beneath thee,
    There lay out thy life.

Dwarfed are the little troubles,
    Small do thy cares appear.
Naught can dim heaven's brightness,
    Naught can annoy thee here.

Mists that hung over the valley,
    Shrouding thy heart with care,
See how they melt in the sunshine,
    Light are they ; nothing but air.

Look o'er the wide horizon ;
    Dost thou not blush for shame,
That thou hast gazed so wholly
    On one little spot called by thy name ?

Earth, with its joys and sorrows,
    Sins, and pains, and cries !
Can'st thou not do thy portion
    To ease these agonies ?

Can'st thou not follow the Master,
　　Coming down from the height,
Moving with tender pity
　　Through these shades of night ?

Never forgetting the brightness
　　Up on the top of the hill,
Looking up for thy comfort,
　　When sorrows press thee still;

Knowing thou straight shall return there
　　When thou hast done thy best,
Knowing the sunshine is still there,
　　God and thy utter rest.

Clouds may enshroud the mountain,
　　But it will still be there;
Faith can pierce the darkness,
　　Soaring to clearer air.

Then, my soul, tarry never,
　　In the vale below;
Haste thee, morning by morning,
　　Up to the sunshine's glow.

And when thou comest down,
　　See that the world may count
Thee to have fashioned thy living,
　　By the pattern seen in the mount.

ESSEX COUNTY COUNTRY CLUB, (HUTTON PARK), ORANGE, N. J.

THE GOVERNMENT BUILDING OF THE
CENTENNIAL EXPOSITION OF 1876.

BY S. ELLEN BLACKWELL.

PHILADELPHIA, PA., October, 1876.

Standing today at the Centennial Exposition, in the centre of the United States Government building, surrounded by the beasts, the birds, the fishes, the insects, the vegetables, the fruits, the very fungi of this vast and varied country which we call our own—flanked in by its woods, its marbles, its iron, its coal, its mineral treasures, from the North, South, East and West, walled round by photographic representations of new and wonderful scenery ; our living interests represented on the one hand, and relics of singular and almost unknown predecessors on the other, with curious and unlooked-for information in every corner, I felt that I was where everyone might well wish to begin, who would look at this great exposition from an American standpoint.

I realized also that we ordinary people ought to go to school again in some such building as this, to begin to appreciate the treasures and interests here gathered together, concerning our own land. Then we might be prepared to pass out into other buildings and see the similar, yet different ; collections sent to us from other countries, bravely brought to us over land and sea —from our very antipodes.

After diving in and out among the beautiful and orderly cabinets of natural history, botany and mineralogy from the National Museum, I returned to the centre of the building feeling somewhat helpless and overwhelmed. I became hopeless of seeing the Exposition in a comparatively short time, and sure that I should fail for lack of knowledge in fully understanding what I did see. But plucking up my courage, I rose up again in

9

the face of an enormous grizzly bear who, rearing his huge bulk before me, held out a placard warning me not to touch him, because his "fur was poisoned." I turned my back upon the monstrous whales, the walrus and the sea lions, and gazed up at the roof to take in the general appearance of a building which, big as it might be, needed no very great stretch of intellect to comprehend. It is built in the form of a cross with a dome in the centre. It is painted in blue and oak ; it is draped from end to end with American flags. The dome is liberally surrounded by red and white banners. From the floor almost to the roof of this central dome rises a monstrous black column of anthracite coal in square blocks, supported by an iron framework, showing the thickness of one rich vein. This black column is surrounded at its base by masses of granite and marble, barrels of cider and wine, sacks of cotton, bundles of grain, etc., etc.—a little mountain of the human produce and the natural productions of the land.

The whole of one side and one end of the building are fully occupied by the exhibit of the Smithsonian Institute at Washington, and its ward—the National Museum. At the other end is the Army and Naval departments. Here, with much that is interesting, may be found also the most humdrum portion of the contents of the building. There are rows of hideous figures, life size, of painted plaster, arranged in American regimentals, ancient and modern. Wooden sailors, with stony eyes, keep watch over a very perfect model of the warship "Antietam," thirty feet long, imbedded in a sea of glass, in rugged little wavelets with soapsud crests. This model ship, with its polished decks, beautiful rigging, tiny guns, and little bags of shot, represents work to the value of thirty thousand dollars, for the most part freely given. Machinery is at work on one hand turning gun stocks and making other ugly instruments of inhuman destruction.

I passed rapidly through this portion unable to feel much pride or pleasure in such things, longing only for the time when we shall settle our disputes by brains instead of muskets. But one implement of war was certainly very curious. A torpedo or battering ram, looking like an enormous fish, to be propelled through the water by an electric battery on shore. This great soulless creature is expected to glide through the waves, and dash its sharp nose into the sides of ships, doing fearful damage among the hostile fleet.

We may well pause for awhile, with grateful and reverent interest before two cases containing the Washington relics, removed from Mount Vernon. There is his camp furniture, the battered iron plates, the two pronged forks, the rough knives worn thin by actual use, with rounded terminations for ladeling the food into the mouth, (suggesting an amusing picture of the father of his country and his beloved compeers, at their daily repast). His camp chest, his writing case, his treasure chest, the clothes worn by him on memorable occasions, the damaged china sets, the plate presented to him, and used by him at his table in his own residence. These cases deservedly hold their places near the centre of the Government building.

Near by are cases containing the models from the Patent Office at Washington. Tiny engines of every description, miniature stoves, tools, reaping machines, etc., just as perfect as their inventors could make them ; the successive products of the busy American brain in every inventive department. One case alone contains more machinery than the whole great busy building entitled "Machinery Hall."

Then we come to the Educational department, and have models from the early log school house, with its long wooden seats, consisting simply of planks laid upon cross legs, to the latest high schools, with all their modern appliances. We have the Art schools, the Universities, and now the Kindergarten, so rapidly taking root among us. We have specimens of the work done in all these institutions, among which the drawings from the Art school of the Cooper Institute hold a conspicuous place.

Near the eastern entrance gate, there is a model showing the late operations at Hellgate, near New York, to remove the obstructions which impeded the navigation of the East river. Here we may see the shafts that were sunk, and all the galleries bored beneath the surface of the rock, to be charged with dynamite. It is worth while to see this model to understand the mode of work which has proved so successful in this case, and to appreciate the long and laborous preliminary steps which had been taken before the explosion, which caused such apprehension in New York and its vicinity. Seven years of patient labor, and then—in one minute the work was accomplished!

Returning again to the Natural History department we take a more leisurely survey; first of the animals of America of every size and description, stuffed and arranged in due order. Then we have the fishes represented in as life-like a manner as possible. As fishes cannot be stuffed for exhibition, the method adopted is to make a plaster mold from a good specimen of each kind, then, carefully removing the fish, to color from it the cast obtained, so as to reproduce the original specimen as perfectly as possible. A coat of varnish suggests the natural glossy look of the living creature.

We have specimens of fruit obtained in the same manner made of wax, delicately colored, and we note especially a great variety of apples. No wonder Eve found them charming. I did   Then there are the insects carefully impaled, in rows innumerable. Then great Herbariums of plants and flowers. Finally a long and surprising row of edible fungi. As we regard these alarming-looking knobs, and discs, and ragged excrescences, we mentally exclaim, "Can it be possible that human beings have eaten all these dubious looking productions and survived the experiment?"

Since we hear every now and then of fatal poisoning from even a mistake in mushrooms, we reflect with apprehension upon the fearful results that would entail if the popular taste should, ever crave indulgence in such a realm as this. "For our part," we devoutly ejaculate, "Give us, oh give us potatoes and apples!" And so we pass on in admiration mingled with awe.

Along the walls stand cabinets of minerals, crystals and gems; specimens of marbles, and a great variety of native woods, in sections, with their leaves and flowers pressed and framed above.

But what justice can we do such collections as these by a pass-

ing glance? How many of us can even tell, as we ramble
through the woods and fields, the names and properties of the
weeds beneath our feet? of the forest trees above our heads, and
of the birds that flit through their boughs? The deficiency of
the popular level of education in this respect, is the great lesson
impressed upon us as we pass through this department, and we
resolve that our children shall know more of the natural objects
that surround them than we have known ourselves. Meanwhile
we rejoice that so comprehensive a collection should be gathered
together in the National Museum, at Washington, in the safe
keeping of the Smithsonian Institute.

At the northern end of the Government building we find
ourselves standing beneath a giant map of the United States : in
the headquarters of the most novel, perhaps the most interesting,
portion of the government exhibit.

Some time since, in view of the coming Exposition, $50,000
was appropriated by Congress for researches among the Indians
in the interior, and in the far Western and Northern territories.
The appropriation was energetically applied, and the consequence is, that more is now known of our distant territories and
ancient predecessors than ever before. Much information has
been obtained. Interesting photographs and sketches of scenery, Indian relics, pottery, costumes, etc., and portraits of the
Indians themselves have been collected.

But first let us consider the map before us. Nine men were
employed for nine weeks on its construction. It was built up
section by section, from separate ordinance maps, with the added
result of the latest explorations. It is the most comprehensible
map of the United States ever yet made ; and will remain as a
record of the exact extent of our geographical knowledge in this
Centennial year. After the exhibition is over, it is to be hoped
that our publishers will give us this map in sections in a popular
atlas, that we may have the opportunity of improving our acquaintance with our own land.

On going home, I tried in vain to find in the best atlas I
could obtain, some of the points I had noted down with interest
during the day. Beneath the map are models of the surface of

the country.   An attempt has been made to give some idea of
the magnitude of the Sierra Nevadas and of the Rocky mountains.

We hear much from our California travellers, of the magnificent valley of the Yosemite, and we are becoming somewhat
familiar with the general character of its bold and massive
scenery, but it is said to be far surpassed by others Canons of
the Sierra Nevadas, as yet unexplored.   The Canon of the Colorado River for instance, is two miles in depth and of great extent.   Beside it, this celebrated Yosemite valley sinks in point of
magnitude into comparative insignificance.

But we may look upon the the actual reflection of some of
this wonderful scenery.   At this end of the building there are
large windows, filled in with transparent photographs on glass.
They are very beautiful and effective, and we look upon scenes
of so striking a character that we say to ourselves that the most
celebrated scenery of Europe may find its parallel in our own
land, in regions not yet opened up to general travel.   How much
the impression produced upon us by grand and beautiful scenery,
depends upon association—How far for instance, the charm of
Swiss scenery depends upon the old names we have heard from
childhood, the little villages nestling among its wild grandeur
and filling it with human interest.   But as we look upon the
wonderful scenes before us, we say that the natural elements are
here, the snow capped mountains, the rocky passes, the lovely
lakes, the rushing waterfalls.

Who can say what romantic associations may gather around
these, as yet almost unknown scenes, to enliven the imagination, and to complete the charm to the future generations who
will look upon them with other eyes than ours.   As a a specimen
of the romantic and striking, we may instance the truly awful
mule road round the spur of King Solomon mountain, leading
to the mines of the "Mountaineer," and of the "North Star."
As illustrations of the beautiful, the lovely lakes of San Cristoval
and Santa Maria.   Some of the scenery of Colorado, such the
"Garden of the God's," and "Pleasant Park," near Colorado
Springs, is singular and striking in character.   Great sandstone

cliffs, corroded at the base and capped by masses of more enduring rock, have been worn by time into lofty columns with rude
and gigantic capitals.

In this Department of the Interior, we find among the records of a late geological survey, colored sketches of the region
about the Yellowstone River, in Montana, lately set apart as a
National Park. Here is one of the most singular regions upon
the face of the earth! Snow-capped mountains almost destitute
of vegetation, boiling geysers, depositing circular terraces of
flint volcanic rocks of strange forms and colors! We feel as if
we had arrived at some other planet, or had gone back to the
the primeval ages when the earth was unfitted for the habitation
of man or beast.

It is thought, however, that the atmosphere of this region
has some peculiar and beneficial qualities which may make of it
eventually a great national sanitarium. Here certainly is a region calculated to surprise and refresh the jaded business man,
to take him out of the ruts and effectually to change the currents of his thoughts. Here the monomaniac, dwelling forever
on his individual pains and sorrows, must be surprised for a time
into self forgetfulness, and he will enter into wider ranges of
thought as he gazes upon this new phase of creation. speaking
of things so far outside the realm of his troubles. We rejoice
that of such a region as this, there should be no possibility of individual ownership. It is right that it should be preserved forever as the heritage of the whole nation.

The researches among the Indian tribes, and the relics of
superior races now extinct, soon claim our attention. We are
surprised by the photographs of remarkable mountain dwelling's
in Northern Arizona, in the region of the Moquito Indians.

Here the mountain sides, steep and precipitous, expose to
view successive layers of different formations. Beneath a deposit
of rock there will be a deposit of clay or sandstone which has
crumbled away, leaving long, level galleries beneath the over-
hanging summit. The ancient race has availed itself of this
peculiar mountain feature, to secure fortress dwellings, imposing
in appearance, which still stand like ruined cities, from which

the builders have long since vanished. The overhanging rock has been supported by strong stone piers, built of the rocky fragments from the base of the mountain. The galleries have been closed in by stone walls with long rows of windows and doors opening on to a passage-way or external arcade. Then the steep declivity below has been smoothed and polished like glass, to prevent the approach of foes from beneath. Inside these dwellings we find pottery, showing considerable attainment in some of the arts of civilization. We wonder that a race that could advance so far should not have continued to advance. We can only suppose that it was swept away by internal dissension and the inroads of more barbarous tribes.

Another distinct race known as the Mound builders, has left also interesting relics. There is a fine collection of ancient pottery brought from these mounds. Some of it is original and peculiar in design ; some seem to suggest copies of vessels of European manufacture, so that the theory has been advanced that the Mound builders did not become extinct until after the advent of their European successors.

As a result of the effort now made to preserve a record of the still existing Indian races, we have cases of Indian costumes characteristic of the different tribes. These have been procured with great difficulty and expense. The Indians are now adopting so largely the European dress, with modifications, that it was found no easy matter to collect or reproduce the real Indian costumes. It was only among remote tribes that they could be made and were often only worn by the old men of the tribe. A valuable collection, however, has been obtained, and many of the costumes are very handsome and curious. The skins of which they are made are exquisitely dressed. There are blankets of down and of feathers which surpass in beauty and lightness our most civilized productions. No doubt they bear witness to the clever fingers of our Indian sisters from their earliest days ; and to the natural artificers sent by nature in all times. There is a great tent of leather dressed by the Indian process, which has this superiority over our mode of tanning: that it is waterproof, and does not harden or shrink in the rain.

There is an enormous canoe, sixty feet in length, brought from Vancouver's Island. It has been hollowed out from one great tree. It is symetrically formed, and painted in compartments with rude and probably symbolical devices. So large and so weighty is this great Indian achievement that it was found impossible to transport it without sawing it in two. Was it constructed for some great pageant or for the warlike descent of some redoubtable warrior, thirsting for the destruction of a rival tribe?

We have also very curious ancestral trees, purchased from the Hawaiah Indians of the Northwest. Each of the most distinguished families of the tribe owned one of these trees, carved in in successive stages with grotesque and hideous designs, painted in rude but durable colors. Each successive generation added a new compartment with new devices of idols or Indian warriors. These trees stood before the hereditary dwelling with an entrance door at the base, which opened only to admit the sworn friends of the family. Any one admitted through this portal was sacredly regarded as a friend thenceforth and forever. Among the Indians, as elsewhere, ancient families sometimes became impoverished, and hereditary dwellings fell into ruins. So it came to pass sometimes that the ancestral tree alone remained to bear witness to the haughty dignity of its possessor. But the ceremony of entrance at the front door was proudly retained, and was as binding as ever in its signification, though it should admit the guest only to a vacant space behind. Proud record of ancient lineage and invincible pride!

But the dark day has come when even the ancestral tree has been sold by degenerate descendants. It has come to grace the Centennial celebration of the new and aggressive race now stretching out its hand in every direction to take possession of a wide domain, and which has striven today to show to all the world the characteristic features of the land which it calls its own.

IN THE LONG AGO.

BY MRS. T. E. M. BEEKMAN.

On passing a very old, dilapidated and deserted stone building in the valley of the Ramapo.

Oh where are they who trod those halls,
And they, who gazed upon those walls !
    In the long ago, the long ago?

'Twas there, the bridegroom took his bride,
To love, and cherish by his side
    In the long ago, the long ago.

Perhaps the little children played
Under those old oaks, in the shade,
    In the long ago, the long ago.

In that old house, the feasts were spread ;
From that hall door, they carried the dead,
    In the long ago, the long ago.

But oh ! the thought will come to me,
If they lived for time or eternity,
    In the long ago, the long ago.

If they lived for God ! or lived for self,
And only to hoard up worldly pelf
    In the long ago, the long ago.

Or if they scattered far and wide
The gospel seed on every side
And told of Him ! who for them died ;
    In the long ago, the long ago.

TOLD BY A WATCH.

BY MRS. MARILLA CURTISS.

My earliest recollections may date some decades of years farther backward than one would suppose possible from the regularity of my movements,—I deem myself, however, quite in my prime—and I "take no note of time" only tick by tick. I first awoke to conscious life by the steady beating of my heart and the hearts of those around me, so seemingly in unison with my own pulsations of life. Was this then life? And were we brilliant ones; were we reallly living, thinking and reasonable beings, and would we in time learn to express to each other our own thoughts as they who went and came were accustomed to do? And would we as the years went by ever learn the power to love and hate? In fine what were we? And what the motive power controlling us? I confess to the convictions coming later in life, that all of our race are but fair creations for some minor purpose, and that we need not trouble ourselves about the weightier matters over which some puzzle themselves so much. Now whether we are a scale above or below these ever-reasoning and speculating ones remains to be seen in some after time. Be the case as it may we escape it altogether, and live only for the present moment. If there is a deeper emotional nature than we watches possess experience and close intimacy with those who are susceptible to fluctuations from outside influences are not to be envied by us. Brilliant, beautiful and unchanging we are through all times and changes. But what vacilliating weakness do we not see in our close intimacy with the many we have known! I, a staid and sober watch have realized the superiority of a firm metallic force over weak nerve power and learn to be satisfied to be just what I am, and the more an inanimate one like me *can* do this when it is seen in how many lives some can.

live, and how many (almost) deaths they die long before their
hearts really cease to beat. Now some one may remind me that
I am only an humble dependant upon the bounty and patronage
of some generous friend—in truth may say I am only a watch.
—Realizing this fact I recall with pleasure the confidence of
my several patronizing friends of the past. I think of the many
tete-a-tetes of love and betrothed to which I have listened, but
of which I must *"never tell."* Really, upon looking back over
my life and the lives of my distinguished friends, I must own to
great experience! But there comes a time in the life of a sober
watch when it is becoming to look a little to what is going on in
the world, lest in life's later decades there might come a time when
even a grand old watch might feel *loss of caste* which would be
worse than gout, any one may know. Nothing like keeping up
with the *time of day.* With these few suggestions will the LADY
ELGIN permit me to say to some other watch "what of the
night?" Or is it really the *dawn* of morning to thousands of
happy beings, whether mortal or immortal?

EXTRACT FROM "AUTHORS AND WRITERS"
ASSOCIATED WITH MORRISTOWN.

BY MRS. JULIA K. COLLES.

" The road taken by Washington and his army on coming to
Morristown, was, according to Dr. Suttle, through Pluckamin,
Baskingridge, New Vernon, thence by a grist mill near Green
Village, around the corner and thence along the road leading
from Green Village to Morristown, and over the ground which
had been selected for an encampment in the valley bearing the
beautiful Indian name Lowantica, now called Spring Valley."
It was, here, that the terrible scourge of small-pox broke out
among the soldiers. One cannot but wonder, continually, at

Washington's courage and serenity in the midst of such over-whelming difficulties. He had hardly entered his winter home, in the Arnold Tavern, when the loss was announced to him ot the brave and noble Colonel Jacob Ford, Jr., his right-hand man, upon whom he depended. He was buried by Washington's orders with the honors of war, and the description of that funeral cortege is one of the most picturesque pages out of traditional history. Then, came the alarm about small-pox, the first death occurring on the same day as Colonel Ford's funeral. Washington, himself, was taken ill, says tradition, with quinsy sore throat, and great fears were felt for his life.

It is interesting to know that, being asked who should suc-ceed him in command of the army, should he not recover, he, at once, pointed to General Nathaniel Greene. It was during this time of residence at the Arnold Tavern that Washington joined Pastor Johnes and his people in their semi-annual communion, after receiving the good pastor's assurance: "Ours is not the Presbyterian table, but the Lord's table, and we give the Lord's invitation to all His followers of whatever name." This is said to be the only occasion in his public career, when it is certainly known that Washington partook of the sacrament. The hollow is still shown behind the house of Pastor Johnes, on Morris street, (purchased February 3d, 1893, of Mrs. Eugene Ayres, for the Morristown Memorial Hospital) where a grove of trees then stood, when this historic event took place in the open air, while the church building was taken up with the soldiers sick of smallpox.

MIZPAH.

BY MRS. FREDERICK CRANE.

"The Lord watch between me and thee, when we are absent one from
another."

"Away from thee?"   Poor, silly heart,
  For this dost thou such burdens bear?
Since he and God are not apart,
  What matter though thou art not there?

Could thy soft walls a fortress make
  To gird him in from fear and foe?
Or could thy weakness undertake
  To be his staff the journey through?

Could thy fond foolishness devise
  The counsel which shall guide aright?
Foresee and quell, ere they arise,
  The dangers hidden from his sight?

But God his fortress is, and shield;
  Strong to sustain, all-wise to lead
In mart or waste, by flood or field,
  A very present help in need.

A steadfast rock when billows roll,
  A cheering sun when darkness blinds,
And for his tempest-driven soul,
  A covert from the rain and winds.

Or is he worn?—a place of rest.
  Or sad?—a comforter most sweet.
Lonely, perhaps?—a heavenly guest
  Knocks, enters, takes the vacant seat.

Ah, in such fellowship divine,
  With all high heaven pledged to his care,
What need hath he of thee or thine?
  What matter though thou art not there?

NORDENSKJOLD.

BY MRS. THOMAS J. CRAVEN.

The "Vega" was sent out by the Swedish Government, in the summer of 1877, to explore the North-west passage. They were within a few hours' sail of Behring's Sea, when the Arctic winter set in and entombed them in ice, almost within sight of a glad triumph; and it was not until July of the following year that they cleared the passage.

To the North east
Sailed, Nordenskjold, seeking
The way to the rising sun;
Through summer's seas he sailed,
Through nights that were days as well,
Either no man could tell.

And the hours sped
'Neath the keel of the Vega
Like running billows of the sea,
For the moments crowned with light,
Swift as drops of misty rain
Came, and were gone again.

Sweet the summer
Of the Arctics, sweet, yet fleeting;
And, soon, blocks of ice appeared,
Like ocean buoys set afloat.
"Winter is nearing," they said,
"There is danger ahead."

Still he sailed on
Till but a day, and scarce that,
Only a few hours more
Would accomplish his purpose,
And he rejoiced without fear
Since the end lay so near.

Then to him came
Faint, a breath from the Northland
From the ice-lands leading.
Only a sigh of the air,   .
But it said in accents low,
"Thou can'st no further go."

Soon before him
Cold and still lay earth and sea,
In winding sheets laying
Of snow and ice crystallant,
And packed ice still wider spread,
Like the ice 'round the dead.

Then at high noon
Of the year's darkest day,
Twilight of morn and eve met;
And the sun, by refraction,
Above the horizon reared,
Showed only hemisphered.

There was he stay'd;
While his frustrated purpose,
His baffled desire, peopled
The silence with strange shapes
That mocked him: eidolons grim,
That appeared unto him.

"We are the ghosts
Of those who wait," they cried,
Of unsatisfied longing.
"We beat upon the door
And no answer comes again;
So shall thou beat in vain.

"It is death's door;
Firm and close shut it stands;
No hand may loose its fastness,

No hand from hither-ward,
But only from the other side
May it be opened wide."

"High is the wall,
And impenetrable
As the walls of a tomb,
Overreached it thou canst not;"
Fiend-like they mocked him, and yelled
"Knock thou, then, Nordenskjold!"

Ninety-four days
And two hundred stared he this
Body of death in the face,
And it was as the face of one
With whom his desire must lie,
Yet who was still for aye.

Ninety-four nights
And two hundred the awful
Auroras blazed and burned,
With intermittent flashes,
Like corpse lights flying
O'er the face of the dying.

The flaming nights,
The lurid noons, were like
The days of the doomed
In the sin-lost nether world,
And life seemed a closed door
To him forever more.

But suddenly,
Like the hush of expectancy
That holds a waiting throng,
Brooded o'er ship and sea,
O'er land and all things near,
A warmer atmosphere.

And now was heard
A sound through the ice,
A rumble heavy and dull;
Far off it seemed to start,
And nearer and nearer come,
Like the boom of a gun.

Then with a crash,
Like the noise of joyous drums,
The ice beat and burst around,
And flung its glittering spears
High into air with a ring
As if it saluted a king.

And, lo! the way
Opened and rolled before them,
Like a scroll, on which was writ,
In golden letters, that they read:
"*Shield of the North*," thou hast won;
Pass on and greet the Sun!"

For the Sun had come
To meet him—had come
All down a royal road;
For, behold! all things were new;
The world had swung round once more—
Waiting and longing were o'er.

A LEAF FROM MY JOURNAL.

BY MRS. MARY GRANT CRAMER.

Though our recent voyage across the Atlantic was a pleasant one, I grew so accustomed to the motion of the Frisia that my head felt as if on a sea voyage for two or three days afterwards. The fine scenery from Cherburg (where my husband met us) to Paris seemed to possess a double charm, because we had not seen the green earth for eleven days. Paris looked so beautiful that it was hard to realize what effort had been made to destroy it, some years ago, by foes from without and within. We appreciated the change from our broken, untidy American streets, to the clean, smooth boulevards of the French capital, and think it would be well for our people to try the European plan of keeping the streets clean and in good repair; such a change would promote health, comfort, and economy.

As we crossed the Swiss frontier we observed at a great height a fort on a perpendicular mass of rocks, as if nature had placed them there for a boundary line. As we made our way deeper into the little inside pocket of Europe, the scenery became grander, and where the tunnels would let me, I stood gazing out of the car windows, lest I missed some magnificent views. The approach to Berne impresses the traveler favorably, for it has picturesque surroundings; there is such a tinge of country life in the charming walks around this quaint little city as I never observed elsewhere. Even from our windows opposite the Federal Palace we have a very romantic view of mountain and valley, with a graceful curve of the river Aare in the foreground. A little to our right is a pretty little park, from which one has a fine view of the Alps on a clear day, but such days are rare here this summer, and rain is abundant. I said summer out of respect to the almanac, for the temperature since our arrival here is too chilly for the season of sunshine and flowers. Yesterday we enjoyed an excursion on Lake Thun, though the clouds, like a torn garment, hid the mountains in places from our view; sometimes they came almost to the base of the mountains, resembling a smoky wreath. Our destination was an old castle, where we were invited to dine. The family, with a few invited guests, numbered twenty-one, as we partook of the sumptuous fare. My right-hand neighbor insisted on my drinking wine instead of water, and finally said I must do it, as he placed a glass of champagne beside my plate and desired to drink to my health, but our kind host at my left told me I need not to drink wine if I did not wish to, and it would be better if no one drank it. This is the first time I ever heard of this confession on such an occasion, for in Europe belief that wine is a necessity for those who can afford it seems universal, and water is considered a poor substitute. Yesterday a delicate looking lady told me she never drank water, and reminded me that the water of Berne is very unhealthy. I am not afraid, however, to risk its use.

After dinner we repaired to the picture gallery, where we saw ancient weapons and armor. In the knights' hall we seemed carried back to the Middle Ages; the furniture there has a very antique appearance, and the stained glass in the windows bears ancient dates. The prodigal son, in various stages of his sad history, is represented in some of the carved oaken panels on the walls; above these are white bas-reliefs.

In looking out of a window across the beautiful grounds I saw a rainbow resting upon the lake, with the mountain wrapped in mist for a background. After a visit to the library, our host took us up into a tower that is two thousand years old, and was built by the Romans. In the massive walls of this tower we saw small dungeons, where prisoners were confined in ancient times. In one of these a little light and air was admitted by a small aperature, or loophole; but in two others the victims could not stand, and no light ever entered their tiny prisons. In the center of the tower is a deep pit, in which persons were thrown to starve to death, and in a recess of the wall is a place where their inhuman judges sat to pronounce their doom. I thought that if those gloomy looking walls could speak, what a tale of woe they would tell! At one of the windows, or open doorways, are a quantity of huge bowlders that were placed there in ancient times to hurl down upon the heads of the assailants. The wheel for torturing victims, we saw stowed away in the attic, where the bats congregate in great numbers.

After the rain ceased we drove out along one of the most beautiful highways we ever traversed. The mountains rose to a majestic height, and sometimes their perpendicular rocky summits seemed as if they would fall on us. The grandeur of this wild scenery was enhanced by a serpentine stream rushing over a bed of rocks far below us, and which we crossed at intervals by bridges. Seeing a picturesque old castle perched like a bird's nest against a mountain, I asked how old the castle is, and the answer was, "Only eight hundred or one thousand years old!" After returning to Castle Spitz from our long drive, there was little time for us to look at the beautiful flower-beds that bordered the lawn, for the boat whistled its approach, and we hastened to the landing. As we sailed down Lake Thun amid the gathering darkness and the shower, we noticed little bonfires on the mountain sides, and were told it was in honor of a new constitution.

THANKSGIVING.

BY EMMA F. R. CAMPBELL.

Written after the assassination of President Garfield, when it was
thought he would recover.

Great God of nations, hear
A grateful people's prayer,
  Their hymn of praise,
As low on bended knee,
With trembling ecstasy
Of hope and joy, to thee
  Our hearts we raise.

When o'er our sunlit land
A mad assassin's hand
  Spread death's dark pall,
Above their prostrate chief
Millions are bowed in grief,
And for thy quick relief
  United call.

And not in vain they cry ;
Thou didst not let him die,
  But graciously
Withheld the fatal blow,
Stayed the red life-tide's flow,
Gave length of days below
  So wondrously.

Thanks, that thy watchful eye
And loving hand were nigh
  That fatal hour,

To guide the deadly dart,
Aimed at a noble heart,
So not one vital part
  Felt its full power.

Thanks for his courage true,
The dauntless soul that knew
  No craven fear ;
But calmly bore the ill
With iron nerve and will,
Sustained and cheerful still,
  And death so near.

Thanks for the nation's love,
All party feuds above,
  Now freshly shown ;
One heart from sea to sea,
One throb of sympathy,
One thrill of loyalty
  To him, their own !

God bless our fallen head,
Raise him as from the dead
  To life again ;
Long may his gentle sway
All fear of strife allay ;
United as today
  Our land remain.

Borne on the summer air
Let universal prayer
  With praises blend ;
Praise for the mercy sent,
Prayer with faith's deep intent,
"God save our President,
  The country's friend !"

THE ONWARD MARCH OF WOMAN.

BY N. L. CAMINADE.

Beloved comrades:—There is a part in a dish of salad, which if taken without its savory dressing, is not very toothsome.

You have, or will have, from others deliciousness, and "spices" in rich abundance, so by way of having a perfect dish, and also to give variety, I select the leaf itself, which is most necessary in making up a finished dish. "*The onward march of woman* and her relation to the great reform which brings us together."

In coming before you, in this new relation, and in this place, where as I look about, scarce anything but the old cupola on yonder college is familiar enough to remind me that it is at once my birthplace, and my "Alma Mater," you will pardon me, if with rapid glance, I, with you, look backward, less than half a century, and trace the then and now, and its relation to womanhood.

I see myself sitting in the old high-backed pews of this sanctuary, which is now so beautifully remodeled, and with childish awe listening to noted ones who were wont to occupy this place, but who long since have been admitted to a loftier pulpit ; never dreaming that one day I should stand within this altar, my face turned pew-ward, with a message to my comrades, yet so it is, and because it is, there is no wonderment.

History tells us that when a French girl attempted to found a girls' school in Dijon, in 1537, she was declared to be possessed of the devil, and her own father dared not openly countenance her, and yet her work, which began in a garret, with five girls, was twelve years later acknowledged, by carrying her in triumph through the streets of the same city, with the ringing of bells and flowers strewed all along her pathway. Coming down to our own century we find in 1840 only seven employments open to women, and one of these was household service, an employ- ment always relegated to women. Now, in one of the Eastern States, three hundred occupations are open to them, and nearly three hundred thousand women are earning their living in them, and this does not include those, who, either in home, or out at service, do household work. Boston, the centre of intellectual light, fifty years ago, would not allow girls to go farther in the public schools than the primary grade ; now the girl enters the highest, and in almost all her colleges, is given equal privilege with her brother. The West, the broad expansive West, in thought as well as domain, gives woman entrance to every intellectual door. In my childish days I well remember how far above me I thought my eldest brother, because he had been to a Medical College, and was conversant with bone, muscle and nerve, and how I wished I might know, too, but with no thought that it might be possible, yet to-day, our girls need only to desire and studiously persevere and success is sure.

It has been no easy task for womanhood to bring about this change in public sentiment; persecution, ridicule and much hard work have been her daily companions, yet we, of to-day and our foremothers, are solving a problem, which in the beginning was never intended, for " male and female created he them," but which through sin, selfishness and submissiveness, had come to be until the majority believed it was "so ordered by Providence" and we finite creatures, must not dare to change " His fixed unalterable laws." Yet a few courageous souls, of the minority, nothing daunted by defeat, for they knew no defeat, have left a legacy in thoughts and purposes, which have taken root on good soil, and grown to immense proportion, until now, in this closing of the nineteenth century, woman is by all progressive minds, given equal advantages with man, in intellectual progress ; while in the spiritual race she has long since outrun her brother.

It is true if a woman assumes a professional or public posi- tion, more is expected of her than of her brother, and conse- quently the strain is greater, yet we question if she is not equal to more, if she gives her possibilities full play, because she, as a class, is free from the tobacco habit, and the use of intoxicants..

And how does all this relate to temperance? Much every way, for the unions of our organizations, dotted here and there all over our broad domain, have been one of the most efficient agencies in the advancement of woman.

It has taken the ordinary woman in the little hamlet, and opened to her a vision of the past she has in the hastening of the time when humanity shall be so uplifted, that universal sisterhood and brotherhood is reality. It is shown the ordinary women, that lying dormant within her, are faculties and talents which, if used and improved, will help to perfect the plan of the eternal. It has taught the ordinary woman that duties are active as well as passive, aggressive as well as defensive, and that all things are possible, if with a strong faith, and earnest purpose, there be a determination not to cease until the victory be won ; not that all are called to the same positions, but each has her part to do in building this superstructure for humanity, then shall each share and share alike, for rewards are for faithfulness, not greatness ! So faint heart, look up ! not down, be all that God designed thou shouldst be, and then " 'tis well done ! "

So, looking backward nearly fifty years, we see how reform after reform have followed in quick succession, and that woman has ever kept step with this onward march of progress, intellectually and spiritually.

We think it no stretch of faith to believe, that, in the coming century, woman shall walk side by side with her brother in all the avenues of life, a real co-worker, and with her strong spirituality, lifting humanity up to the God-head of which we must be part to claim a rightful heirship.

" Ah ! but you forget the evil woman, your theory is right, if all women were good." Nay, I do not, I place them side by side with their evil brothers, setting for each the same standard ; but as Godhead if stronger than manhood, so I believe when woman uses her possibilities. by education and development, which now are dormant, and measures up to her God given opportunities, then will develop a race, so courageous yet so gentle, that God can rapidly carry out His Supreme will and the reign of righteousness shall be begun.

To you, who have heard the call (or if heard not heeded), to come out from your life of ease or pleasure, or who believe there is no part for you in this warfare, I say. look about you! Not far from the sound of my voice are children who work for twelve hours a day for one dollar per week, and women glad to make garments for seventy-five cents per dozen, and find their own thread, while others toil all the week amid surroundings that seem to be impossible, were it not a fact. Surroundings that would in you produce disease unto death, if only a day you were compelled to endure them ; yet these who toil are your sisters, and mine, and for whom Christ died. Alas! that human blood should be so cheap, and gold so scarce!

These toilers, with you, have no hand in regulating trade, nor in the legislation of laws relating thereto, yet they, and you, if violators of the law, are just as amenable to the penalty as if you helped make them.

Surely a change should be brought about, and can'st thou say, thou sleeper, that it is not high noon, and time for thee to awaken out of thy sleep, and "lend a hand," to establish a reform for blighted childhood, and wronged womanhood? When the open saloon, with its pitfalls, greets our loved ones as he leaves us to do battle in the world, at every corner, and yet we cannot save him, because we, forsooth! are women, and do not legislate, "for that would be unwomanly," (and I admit it would as men do, reform is needed in this department, if anywhere). Don't you think it is more than high noon? The time for the dawning of a new day, when not only manhood, but womanhood shall seek to make laws that will give equal protection to our boys with the fish in our streams, or the game in our forest? and that shall compel our government to cease to accept a revenue from a crime, which has for its capital, the very life of the Nation? To my comrades who are walking in the light as given them to see it, I say, step onward and upward in thought and action, listen to the Master's voice, that every step may tell. To the young, who will take up the work as we lay it down, ah!

what possibilities and opportunities await you. Enter every open door, yet ever watching for the Master's call, following only as He leads, that you may make no mistakes, then the very topmost height is yours because you have *earned* it ! In closing, I pray you, each and all to take as the keynote of your thought and action, in the coming years, and God's blessing will surely follow, these words of Dr. Locqueville.

> " Life is neither a pleasure or a pain
> It is a serious business ;
> To be entered on with courage,
> And in a spirit of self sacrifice."

JOHN DOUGLAS BEMO.

MRS. H. V. CONE.

In Mrs. A. E. W. Robertson's article on "Civilized Indian Tribes, " mention is made of the death of a Seminole bearing the name of John Bemo. His early history was well known to a former generation of Presbyterians.

Rev. John Douglas, pastor of Mariners' church, in Philadelphia, was accustomed to invite sailors, who, when in port, attended his prayer-meetings, to give statements of their religious experiences while on the great deep. One evening a young Indian arose and told a wondrous story of his conversion on the sea, through the teachings of a pious sailor, one of the crew.

Mr Douglas and the audience were thrilled by the simple, strange recital, and at once took him by the hand, inquiring into his history. The facts, as he gave them, being verified by the captain of his vessel, and also from the Christian sailor from whom he had gained his knowledge of the way of salvation, Mr. Douglas felt warranted in proposing that he should receive an education. This offer the young Indian accepted with grateful cordiality. He was shortly baptized with the Christian name of John Douglas Bemo.

The funds for his education and support were at first supplied by the Mariners' church and the pastor's friends. Afterwards he commenced a tour through the churches in Philadelphia and vicinity, addressing large audiences and enlisting much interest. He was a ready speaker, of good voice, expressing his thoughts in the manner of his race, by figures of speech, many of which were original and apt. At this period he was about nineteen years old, of tall, manly form, agreeable features, wearing his hair in one long braid, wound around his head.

He said his Indian name was Husti-Koluk-chee, and he was the youngest son of a Seminole chief. His older brothers being twins, were according to the customs of the tribe ineligible to the chieftaincy, and therefore he was to be the successor of his father, and as such was "the apple of his mother's eye." About the tenth or twelfth year of his age, his father took him to St. Augustine to see the white man's world. While there his father was killed in a drunken brawl. The poor boy, in his fright, ran away and was lost to his friends. He was found by some sailors wandering about the wharves of the city, and by them taken on board a vessel just ready to sail for foreign ports. On shipboard he learned to be useful, and gained some knowledge of the English language. The vessel was absent three years; returning, it entered one of the harbors of North Carolina. The captain, acquainted with his history, planned to send him to his friends. But, during the absence of the vessel, the Seminoles had been at war with the whites in Florida, and in the final settlement, had been removed to the Indian Territory. Thus the boy was unable to join his people. He had frequently mentioned the name of Osceola, claiming him as his uncle. This famous Seminole chief had been captured and imprisoned in one of the Southern cities, and died in prison. His portrait had been painted in life, and was at this time on exhibition. The captain, without explanation, took the young Indian to the gallery. He immediately halted before the picture, exclaiming.

"That is my uncle, Osceola!" Being friendless he sailed with the ship again to foreign shores, which caused another absence of three years. This time the ship entered the port of Philadelphia.

Through the good offices of the sailor friend, he was placed in a proper boarding house, and his acquaintance with Mr. Douglas began. In his public addresses he related many touching incidents of his childhood. Once in the forest he heard the Great Spirit calling him by name, three times, saying, "Go preach." He did not then understand the nature of the command, but evidently had had some strong impression of a Supreme Power made upon his childish intelligence. The ladies of Philadelphia supplied him with a suit indicative of his claim to the chieftaincy: a green blouse with red sash and appropriate moccasins, also a head-dress of feathers. His portrait was taken in this suit, and reproduced in colored lithographs, which were for sale, with his Indian and English autographs affixed. He remained at school for two or three years, but he never entered a Theological Seminary. When the time came for him to seek his people, he was commissioned by the Presbytery as teacher and preacher among the Seminoles. He hoped to establish his claim as chief, but it is not probable that he succeeded. From all that was ever heard from him, he became and continued a faithful and honored teacher and preacher of that gospel he had been so providentially taught.

MY DARLING.

BY NAOMI T. COMPTON.

Crimson the glow of the sunlight
As it fades in the far-off West,
The day has grown faint and weary
And longs for the night's sweet rest ;

A star comes out in the eastern sky
   And shines o'er the waters blue,
While I clasp the warm hand of my darling,
   My loved one fond and true.

The beach is all white and silent
   Save the breaking of the waves,
And we watch through the deepening shadows
   For the nymphs from the coral caves.
The amber tints grow deeper
   As the moon comes up from the sea
While the sweet voice of my darling
   Is breathed in love to me.

'Tis years since we sat together
   In the twilight soft and sweet,
And Time has kept up his marching
   With restless, tireless feet :
But the years have knit close and closer
   The silken threads of love,
And the meshes grow strong and stronger
   As down life's strand we move.

So we sit and talk in the twilight
   Of the times in years ago,
Of the hearts that sleep under the roses,
   But our own were covered with snow.
The moon climbs higher and higher,
   And its radiance soft and still,
Gleams over the sapphire billows
   And the lighthouse on the hill.

ROSE GROWING.

BY ANGELINE M. COLBURN.

When asked by amateurs, who confess their own failures, how I manage to grow roses in such profusion, I can but reply that I am not a learned botanist, nor have I been trained in the business. Somewhat late in life, after seeing what had been done by professional florists I became inspired with the ambition to see what could be done, in a small way, with the rose on a bit of adjoining land I had reclaimed from weeds. This occupation, I may say, has been my pastime, my study, my health invigorator, at odd hours, when other cares would allow. Of the several things requisite to success a fondness for the flower, for outdoor life, and an observing habit, so as to ward off its three especial foes: The elements, the parasites and drouth. The composition of the soil does not seem to be of so much consequence, as it is now shown that the earth is chiefly a holding ground or anchorage, and to some extent a saturated sponge, the bulk of the plant growth being derived from the air. Any soil which will hold the fertilizer will serve, and the added ingredients may better be in soluble or liquid form. I use decayed leaf mold, and rotted sod with the drainage from the stable, occasionally, applied in the dormant state not in the growing season. Winter covering or hilling with ashes serves a double use, nutriment for the plant, and protection from frost. Roses must have besides sunshine, plenty of water; they can hardly get too much or too often. Examine carefully, with a magnifier, the under side of the leaves for the eggs of parasitic insects, and spray at once a with a weak solution of tobacco stems, with hellebore. Note well that my flock of chickens assist in this duty, roaming at will among them, picking up the larger pests, and in this way doing far more good than harm. Cutting back, in spring, is also important. Failures, from over-caution or tender hearts, are often due to this error. For the more tender varieties I provide a thick screen of Scotch fir or other dense evergreen.

Sometimes I am asked, are you repaid for all your care and labor? I must reply: It repays me in several ways. Perhaps the thrill of pleasure I experience from brilliant hues may be due to some hypersensitiveness of the optic nerves. There is also the beauty of form from bud to full blown flower and fruit, to say nothing of the fragrance for which I care less. The expectant attention while watching the evolutions of plant life are also interesting, and make of these flowers agreeable companions, in spite of thorns. Moreover, I am convinced that their gaudy colors attract the merry song birds, nor am I insensible to the pleasure they give to my own specie, who admire them from across the fence, or gratefully receive them for the sick-room or hospital, not to mention festive occasions. Last but not least, they take me into the open air and sunshine, and these are soothing, tending toward optimism, conferring sleep, appetite, and rerfeshment. Whatever is lost to the complexion, is more than made good in general vigor otherways.

To sum up my twenty years' experience in growing roses out doors, in which I have had more than five hundred varieties, satisfies me that it is not so difficult or mysterous an art as many suppose. I retain nearly that number, including among them many classed as tender sorts, such as, in Teas, Catharine Mermett, Sunset, Pearl, etc. Dutchess Brabant, Cornelia Cook. Among my favorites in hybrid perpetuals are: La France, Louis Von Houte, Caroline Swails, Louis Odier, Mad Chas. Wood, Mad Gabrielle Lizet, Mad Trotter, Victor Verdier, Mad John Lang, Mabel Morrison, Baroness Rothchild, Marshall P. Wilder, Mellville D. Lyon, A Camille de Rohan, Rev. J. B. Canarn, Queens of Queens, Fisher Holmes, Chestnut Hybrid, Gloire de Dijon, Wm. Allen Richardson Gen. Jacqueminot, Hermosa, nearly all of which do well in this red clay soil of Central New Jersey. No collection however, is complete without the Mosses,

11

the Glory of Mosses, the climbing Jules, Margottin, Russell's Cottage, Cloth of Gold, Baltimore Belle, the apple bearing, Rosa Kugosa and the diminutive Polyanther. By judicious selections I am enabled to have roses in abundance from May until November.

For the benefit for those who are in doubt where to procure stock, true to name, and for satisfactory dealings, I ought to add that Messrs. Dingee & Conard of West Grove, Pa., leave little to be desired, their roses being grown on their own roots.

CAMDEN.

BY MRS. E. F. CHARLES.

I love, I love it, old Camden town,
With its homesteads, its streets and its old-time calm ;
It leaves the rush and bustle of commerce and gain,
To that vast city, founded by Penn,
Whose park, and whose tower,
Whose air of refinement, and brotherly love,
Are not to be found on this earth, anywhere,
Except on the shores of the broad Delaware,
The ships of all nations are welcomed by her,
The red cross of Great Britain,
The Mexican bars, the Austrian eagle,
The bear of the Czars, all spread to the breeze their
      proud ensigns of war,
As they rest on the bosom of that mighty stream
Whose waters are famous, in history and story,
For all those who delight in America's glory.

PURITY.

BY THEODOCIA E. CARPENTER.

In promoting the work of Social Purity, to advantage and with sure results, it is better to study the subject from a causative standpoint, to ask ourselves why it is, since children are born *pure* that we have such an appalling task of reformation to perform. How, when and where did so many lose that innate modesty, that natural diffidence belonging to innocence. Let us begin our research for causes among that great majority, the middling, well-to-do laboring class, the people who rent or own small houses and, in a small way, eke out a tolerably good living. By economy and frugality the daughters are kept at home till they are grown, when, if they do not soon marry, they in some way learn to support themselves. The boys generally begin young to look out for odd jobs, before and after school hours, and when a good permanent job is found the need and temptation is such that usually they quit school before graduating.

It is not small homes, plain living nor labor that demoralizes, but I will not say that small wages may not be a factor in the cause we seek, for, there is a relation between capital and amusement that it may be well to consider. Small wages obtain among men who begin to earn their own living before they have acquired scarcely a common school education. They toil all day and have to economize closely to make the same wages, that sufficed for two, do for a growing family; and which would be utterly impossible but for the untiring industry of the wife and mother who is nurse, cook, laundress and seamstress, in one. These men and women are too poor in pocket, too over-worked in body, and, necessarily, too dull in intellect to manifest a taste for reading. A paper containing only political news and the latest horrors may occasionally be taken by the father, but the mother does not have time to read. Subjects of work, dress and neighborhood gossip are the current interchange between parents and children. They try to appear as well as their means will possibly allow, and this is the height of their ambition. They can't afford pianos nor the cost of musical instruction and vocal music is confined to popular ballads which the younger members pick up here and there from their associates.

With uncultivated tastes for art, music or literature, will you ask yourself how, when they gather for a social time, they are to have the recreation they seek.

The majority of this class belong to or attend some church; the children generally go to Sabbath-school. Many of them would think it wrong to dance, and as music is a luxury and dancing without music altogether undesirable, this species of amusement is denied them. Still, some kind of fun they must have, and it is in the fun or amusements of all people that we must look for the undermining influences that lay waste so much purity.

The class in question, when brought together, have but one natural pastime which is that found in games since, as I have shown, want of means and close application to labor cheat them of more intellectual pleasures. What is left to the non-reading, non-musical portion of the community but games and games? Alas, nothing. unless it be eating to repletion.

Think of it, sisters, no amusements but games and such games allowed, beginning as children and keeping it up at almost every social gathering till they are grandmothers and grandfathers.

You who think this is not a true picture, let me ask you were you ever at an entertainment entirely outside your own social set? If not, then you do not know what is going on in any other circle. I recently attended a wedding anniversary, among the class I have described, where almost every person present was a church member or a Sabbath-school scholar. Here my eyes were opened to the facts I have but faintly given you, and I learned on inquiry that such order of entertainment is repeated at almost every social gathering of these people and those of like standing every where.

When I asked myself why this demoralizing state of things should exist, I reasoned it out and found that it would not be otherwise among those who have so few intellectual advantages.

The same amusements obtain among the servant class and among the poorest of our mixed population. I am told that often, very often, a few young men bring liquor and drink it on the sly with their companions, and the party, towards morning, is little less than a drunken rabble. Is it not plain to see how social impurity creeps into so many families and robs them of their brightest sons and daughters.

Once in the city of Poughkeepsie I went as a stranger to a church sociable held in a large hall, and as I entered you may judge of my amazement to see nearly the whole congregation there playing copenhagen. The minister was one of the most eloquent in the city and preached to so large an audience, Sabbath evenings, that many other churches complained of emptied seats. Yet, he was there, smiling and happy, but blind to the results that might follow a half-hour's promiscuous kissing between the men and women and the boys and girls of his large congregation, to say nothing of outsiders free to come in. Many were there who could not plead lack of resources for amusement. They had all the benefits of art, music and literature, but, as in almost every church, there were very many who had not these and who, knowing nothing but games, had led off in their own way.

It is as easy to put a stop to this and so nip a great evil in the bud as it is to pull up a tiny weed. You have but to denounce it and they see at once the impropriety of it, and by influencing only one, you can, generally, set right the whole circle of that one's friends. Once they have their eyes opened to the immoral tendency of such games they will ever after discriminate and play only those that afford innocent amusement.

All classes of society are more or less guilty, in their social diversions, of fostering that familiarity—which is to the weak but a stepping stone to ruin.

To the credit of the mothers and daughters, who play copen-hagen, let it be noted that they dress in high-necked, long-sleeved dresses, usually of some modest colored wool material, and never specially attractive in style. This is, in part, their moral salvation.

Many in the upper classes, who would be shocked at the idea of a kissing game, fit their daughters out in light gauzy material to look like angels, strip their arms and necks bare and let them go, without parent or other chaperon, to an evening entertainment accompanied by a young man whose private char-acter they know little or nothing.

The order of entertainment is dancing, and you all know what waltzing is like without my describing it, and there are few, if any figures so popular in the various dances now-a-days as the waltz. The painted, and powdered and perfumed beauty is whirled around the room by a host of young men, in fact she prides herself on the number. She is taught to permit an entire stranger, as soon as introduced, to take her hand and encircle her waist for the next waltz, and one stranger after another seeks an introduction and they go whirling around together until their heads swim.

Do you wonder that the native reserve of young woman-hood and young manhood wears off very fast? and you know when it is once worn off there is no putting it on again, except by affectation. I believe it wears off faster in the round dance and in the fancy undress of fashion than in the hilarious kissing games in which fathers and mothers join, and in clothes as mod-est as those of every-day wear.

Teach your children that God is Love, aad that aught said about Love without a sense of its sacredness is as if it were said about God and this wholesale profanity against Love and its Divine fruition, marriage, shall give place to moral reformation among old and young. All reference to Love should be in keep--ing with the subject, pure and holy, and there can be no real social purity until society is lifted to this standard.

ROSWELL'S WARD.

BY VIRGINIA JEROME COXE.

Roswell has returned from Spain and the strangest stories
are wafted back about him. He is accompanied by a little girl,
a brown Spanish child, ugly as Meg Merrilles, with not more
than ordinary intelligence to warrant anyone's interest in her.
She is not related to him—she is not the legacy of some in-
amorata; yet he has adopted her, is to educate her a la Anglaise,
and as the title and Roswell Hall revert to Carmean, she will be
endowed with his own private fortune. Fathom the mystery;
solve the problem. Roswell, the adamantine soul, the most
sceptical, unprincipled piece of humanity that ever breathed—
severe in his judgment of all women—pronouncing them all
treacherous and false, leaves Granada with a promise to pilot a
brown, elfish child "along this fleeting shore."

Perhaps he will educate, then marry her—no woman will
ever elicit his commendation unless moulded after the design
his conservative ideas prescribe.

"Thereby hangs a tale." Carmean Roswell is converted.
He left a sinner, returns a saint.

Worshiped at the shrine of a brown-eyed nun, I conjecture,
and she entrusted a protege to his care as a slight tribute of her
regard, etc., etc.—drink to my acute powers of divination. Am
I right, Duke?

No, order more cognac—ice the champagne, and I will give
you an authentic version. Roswell is my friend and he prefers
London's enlightenment to architectural designs upon so slight
a foundation as a child.

The bull ring at Madrid, the Plaza de Toros, is crowded
with its 12,000 spectators; crashing music, punctuated by tumults
from the crowd, roaring bulls, deafening cries of aquadores with

water jars, old women with pomegranates and oranges, now and then glimpses of fighters in tawdry glaring paraphernalia, relays of horses and a profusion of tinsel; all this permeated with excitement and expectation. The "Gaceta" has devoted columns to the praise of a young torera—a woman who rivals in skill, agility and artistic strokes the muscular men who have reigned here ; and there is something novel for the fiery Southern children in having a woman risk her life in so daring and blood-curdling occupation. The royal box is empty, but amid the forest of forms sit nobility and the hightest meteors of the land. In a prominent box, and with the party of a Spanish nobleman, enters an Englishman, and his inflexible, almost sneering countenance shares the gaze that is riveted on the beauty by his side—the cynosure of all eyes. What an antithesis! she young, brilliant, and possessing beauty in the superlative degree; he not more than a score and a half, but his stalwart form and Atlantean shoulders crowned by a gloomy, cynical face that trouble, not years, have aged. He leaves the box to speak to an English attache, who has entered an adjacent compartment. An elderly lady turns to the lovely Dona with this mandate:

"Inez, abandon the diplomacy you affect with that man. Why do you wish to flirt with him? I hear that something has darkened his life—a woman, I suppose, for his speeches about them are desecrating. I dislike to see you smile or talk with such a giaour. I am unacquainted with his past, but I know he seeks to submerge memories in dissipation of the wildest kind. He not only drinks and gambles, but his life is unhallowed in every way. He is a gentleman by birth and his status demands that your father should not ignore his presence in Madrid, but he expects you to keep him at antipodes."

"Money and birth covereth a multitude of sins, Duchessa," and a gay, light laugh complements the remark. "It is requisite that he should fall in love—it will prove an alkali to his acid temperament and divorce him from this irrational life."

Her vanity supercedes her wisdom and she imagines him already her vassal. "A rebellious spirit is worth conquering. I have flung away hearts as lightly as I would unripe olives, but

to own his would be holding the unattainable Sappho's apple.
No one can resist my charms—he will be plastic in my hands.   I
will reform, mould him to my mood."

The entrance of the Englishman terminates bravados, and
conversation gravitates to the girl who killed the bulls in a recent
corida, and who appears to-day.   Dona Inez is a feminine sword
of Damocles for a vulnerable hearted man—a beautiful, soulless
coquette, whose teleology is to ensnare and vanquish.   Her costume is studied; a lace mantilla—that most dangerous of weapons
—frames her face and is fastened in her hair and around her
perfect shoulders with costly jewels.   The fan assists challenges
from dark eyes, and prove that her monitor's injunctions have
fallen unheeded on barren soil.

Trumpets sound as the gate under the royal box opens, and
two marshals enter the list, mounted on richly caparisoned An-
dalusian steeds, whose heads are half hidden under their manes.
They clear the lists, report readiness, a flag is waved, and the
music sounds a march as the chulos enter escorting two
picadores.   The former, commonly termed "cheats," serve to
irritate the bull and divert his attention.   The animal rushes
out, the chulo flutters a bright cloak right and left, this unsteady
motion retarding the progress of the beast, and the former, on
reaching the barrier, leaps over.   A picadore is next attacked,
horses are killed, and two men maimed.   Until now toros has
been the aggressor, and the others on the defensive, but amusement has reached meridian—enough carnage for to-day, and his
time must come.   Fragosa comes forward, and, if any latent
interest is betrayed, it is dispelled with her appearance.   A typi-
cal Spanish girl on a large scale, strongly developed muscles,
symmetrical limbs, rather sinewy, and, consistent with this, keen,
sure, penetrating eyes.   Her costume borders on the Turkish
style, for convenience sake, and there seems to be perfect understanding between herself and the horse she rides.   A thunderous
salutation greets her, to which she appears oblivious.   She makes
the banderilla attack several times with swiftness and dexterity,
then arms herself for the final office of matadore.   A sword is handed her, which she conceals in the folds of a red banner.   Twice she

advances, evading her combator's aims and diagnosing her target
well.   The third, the sword disappears, is entered full length in
the shoulder of the victim and the cross at the hilt alone shows.
The creature rushes at the matadore, dying agony stimulating its
fury, but each time the blows are received on a deceptive buckler.
It is over and by a vociferous chorus of laudation, extolling her
name, tumultuous applause, the Spaniards manifest their appreciation of her art.

"What do you think of it, Lord Roswell?" queries Dona
Inez, as seated in the carriage they wait for the throng to part
ere they can be driven to the city.

"I have a keen relish for your hectic amusement—it intoxi-
cates ; resuscitates me.   Should I ever take up my abode in this
clime, Plaza de Foros will be the bait.   There was one detrac-
tion—one feature I must condemn ; Fragosa !   I cannot conceive
how a woman can put her life on a level with that of a beast—
there should be laws prohibiting it.   I would rather see a woman
at the helm of a guillotine sending souls to eternity, for then it
would be human versus human, but this ! my soul recoils in
horror ! I hardly feel that this coarse, brutal creature deserves
the name of woman !"

"Why witness what you do not approve?" says a clear voice,
and Fragosa, they perceive, stands near enough to have heard
all.   "Mi lord does not understand.   I am honest.   My soul is
as white as the fine mi lady beside him.   Not love of sport, but
bread for my afflicted parents brought me here.   There are many
people and little work in Madrid."

"Curse the plebeian for her impudence !   I hope she will
end her life some day in her beloved arena !   Take this gold to
heal your wounded pride?"

"I will not take your gold, but you have poured the first
hatred into my heart that it has ever held.   You have given the
first insult that has ever been offered me.   Were it in my power
to save your life ; were it left me to snatch you from the most
awful death, I would not do it.   I would laugh to see you tor-
tured into eternity."

The horses dashed away, leaving a girl's angry countenance

—a foreboding farewell. Roswell's thoughts were skillfully steered to the charms of Dona Inez, who proposed a visit to the royal picture gallery to feast on Velazquez and Tintoretto, and the disagreeable moments were forgotten.

The arena again; dazzling preparations to-day, for royalty will illuminate the gory empyrean. The usual clamor, flourish of trumpets, blasting music, mingled with enthusiasm is re-echoed. The Royal Guards enter, an imposing escort, and the cry "Los Reyes" passing from mouth to mouth as the subjects rise simultaneously, proclaims the crowned head to be with them. The Duchessa, Englishman and Dona Inez, accompanied by a brilliant party, occupy their box. The latter has a wager in rein —a wager prefaced by a boast of her conquest of the English-man. She has averred that in a perilous moment she will induce him to go into the arena.

"My lord," she murmurs, softly, "they tell me that you committed daring deeds in England ; your reputation for bravery preceded you here. I believe you to be a resurrected Knight of of the Round Table, for only weak men exist these days—a race of exhausted courage—whose deeds only disgrace the fair records their ancestors bequeathed them."

"I have never eclipsed my contemporaries. Good or bad acts always grow during a journey."

"I will test you now and see if rumor be true. I prize this fan; will you restore it to its owner?" As she speaks she drops it lightly into the enclosure below.

"My gallantry has never been doubted, Dona Inez, but to jump into the arena when the bull is about to be freed would be an act of madness. The days of chivalry—days of wild deeds for trivial motives is over. Make a reasonable petition. I will grant it. Ask me to risk my life, but in so doing permit me to reap a higher reward than a fan."

"It is immaterial; I merely wished to see if your laurels were merited. I see they are not."

"If it pleases you, Dona Inez, it is with pleasure I recover your treasure."

With this a long leap takes him into the ring below. There

is a wild shout from the spectators; a tardy warning from the alguazils who have just cleared the list; a cry of help from the women; an endeavor on the part of the men to assist a fellow-being, for at this moment the gates are opened and the bull rushes madly about, sniffing the air, pawing the ground and rushing toward the one person in his power. There is no escape—the walls are too high to scale; time too limited, for the attack is already made, and Roswell is unarmed. The din is deafening, the confusion depriving people of self-possession. Everyone is helpless, for it is hazardous to venture to his aid. But Fragosa has not battled with these animals in vain, and a sense of duty prompts her to try and save the martyr. She has been victorious all the time—why not once more, and another torera is not near, and no one else could strike the fatal blow. It is all done in a minute—the woman, then the sword, then Roswell appearing from time to time behind the huge animal. Then the latter falls, there is a mass of blood, the girl reels and is prostrate also. Roswell is wounded, but not disabled; Fragosa! the surgeon says she cannot live, and she is moved into an inner room, out of sight of the struggle.

"I want to see the Englishman," she says faintly. "I cannot live, and I wish to tell him something."

"Here I am," answers Roswell, "make any request you wish and I swear to spend my life in fulfilling it. Can—"

"Let me speak—my moments are short. I want to tell you that I did not know I was saving your life. I would have let you die had I known. I have not only saved your life, my lord, but your soul, for that is black and you were not ready to hand it to your God for inspection. I have a charge to leave you—my child—will you take her? She is fatherless. My afflicted parents and my child depended upon me for sustenance—will you provide for them?"

"Yes, yes, they will be cared for. I will make your parents independent; will take your child to my English home, educate her, raise her as I would my own. The reparation I owe you will be paid her; the debt will be canceled, and when I render my final account before the High Tribunal I will not fear to face you."

" My mind is steeped in peace for the first time; my life has been hard, but death has no terror, for I expected it daily in this deadly work. Do not forget your charge."

"And "in the gloaming" of that day Lord Roswell took charge of his new inheritance a changed man—changed for the better by two women—one, a pure pearl in rugged clay! the other, a fair flower with a deadly aspen hidden in its petals, but the poison flung at him by one was picked up by the other, who lost her life by the act.

THE OLD, OLD STORY.

BY SUSAN H. CARLSON.

I gathered my children around me
　One quiet Easter eve,
To tell them the story of Jesus,
　The story we all believe.

The day had been long and dreary,
　The burdens hard to bear,
My mind and body were weary,
　And I felt bowed down with care.

I had been tempted and tried that day,
　Beyond my power to bear ;
I had many times yielded to passion,
　And forgot to take refuge in prayer.

But now the tasks were all ended,
　The last pile of dishes was washed,
The numberless stockings all mended,
　And I could go to my darling's at last.

I found them quietly waiting.
　In mother's own room up stairs—
Waiting for their bedtime story,
　Ere they said their evening prayers.

I sat down there with my treasures,
　My baby girl in my arms.
The older one's close around me,
　Safe from all outside harms.

Then I told them again the old story,
　I had told them all their years,
How Christ came from his home in glory
　To dwell in this valley of tears.

How for us he was killed and buried
　Out of his mother's sight ;
How the other Mary had hurried
　To His tomb while yet it was night.

How she found not Him but an angel,
　And her tears began to flow,
But the angel had said "He is risen,"
　To His friends she could then gladly go.

How He dwells with the Father in Heaven,
　How He pleads for us day by day,
Asking God do deal mercifully with us.
　And to wash all our sins away.

I found as I told them this story.
　That I felt no more weary, but glad.
That, Christ had from His home in glory
　Sent comfort to my heart that was sad.

Then I asked the dear Father to help me,
　When tempted and tried again,
To let His dear love come around me,
　His love that can comfort all pain.

THE BRAVE MIDDY.

BY MARIA MCINTOSH COX.

This story is reprinted by courtesy of the editors of "The Youth's Companion," for whom it was written. It is absolutely true, and therefore historical. Commodore James McKay McIntosh, died September 1st, 1860, while in command of the Pensacola Navy Yard.

When I fir-t remember my father, his hair was already gray, and its white, close-curling rings lay upon the high collar of his blue navy coat. His bright blue eyes expressed sincerity and courage, and the smile upon his face emboldened his children to climb upon his knees, and make the most of his rare periods of leave from his ship.

We found in him our hero and our delight, and often begged him to tell us stories of what he had done and seen. I had a special liking for the adventure which I am going to relate, and I shall tell the story with as strict an adherence to the truth as I can attain to, with only the memory of years long past to rely upon. It was only briefly told me then, for if I asked my father for an enlargement of the story, with details which only he could give, he would put me down from his knee saying:

"Yes, yes, Puss, it is all true, but enough has been made of that. No decent lad could have done less."

The boyhood of my father had been a peculiar one. He inherited the qualities of brave Scotch ancestors, who had lost all in their adherence to "Bonnie Prince Charlie." At fifteen years of age he obtained a warrant as midshipman in the navy, and at once had opportunity, in the concluding events of the War of 1812, to show his boyish mettle.

After peace had been concluded with Great Britain, there came the expeditions against the pirates of the Gulf of Mexico, for which the famous mosquito fleet, under Commodore Patterson, was fitted out.

Chief and most troublesome of the pirate bands was that over which the Lafitte brothers ruled. Through the skill and audacity of Jean Lafitte most of the mischief was accomplished.

Almost all intercourse with the South and Gulf was then carried on by water. Beside passengers and merchandise, vessels carried gold and silver bullion and coin. Hundreds of thousands of dollars were transported in unarmed ships.

No entrance for large vessels then existed to New Orleans. The mouths of the Delta of the Mississippi were choked with mud, and were always of uncertain depth. The city was more easily reached by the clearer waters of the deep bayous, and by Lake Pontchartrain.

In the marshy grass—land that stretches out between the Lake and the Gulf, there were islands of firm soil. There were too, natural and artificially enlarged canals or ponds, and a great net-work of inter-communicating water passages.

Here Jean Lafitte and his band of buccaneers were at home, and here they had many places of refuge and of deposit for their plunder.

In swift, light-draught sloops, sufficiently armed for their purpose, these pirates appeared and disappeared like birds of prey. Large open boats, frequently twelve-oared and filled with armed men, also made great havoc, and the more cumbrous men-of-war vainly strove to track or conquer them. Hardly were they seen before they were gone, as mysteriously as if swallowed by the sea.

Lafitte appeared occasionally in New Orleans, and kept up the fiction of leading the life of a merchant while disposing of his plunder. He pretended that he was at peace with the United States and contenanced attacks, upon the Spaniards only.

The more the failure to check the career of the bold outlaw was recognized as a National disgrace, the more earnest became the men of the navy, in their purpose to find, follow, and capture him, but for a long time he baffled them as completely as if he had been a creature of their dreams. The ordinary course of his pursuers was from the Bay of Honduras, through the West Indies, and along the coast from Galveston to Mobile, where they knew the pirate crews might be lying, hidden safely and watching them.

As I remember my father's story, it was the brig "Enterprise" to which he was attached, and it was in the year 1815, when, after an unsuccessful cruise, the "Enterprise" was standing on her western course, that the incident took place which I am to relate. The brig had passed the mouth of the Mississippi, and was abreast of Grand Isle, the real shore of which could not be distinguished through a tall, coarse growth of rushes, and of the existence of which the officers were unawares.

It was here that the "Enterprise" came upon a merchant vessel, apparently at anchor. She lay within half a mile of the shore, about a mile due east of the point where the man-of-war lay to. She showed no flag; she did not answer any signal, nor could any token of life be seen upon her.

"There is something very singular about this vessel," said the captain of the "Enterprise." "She shows no sign of being a piratical craft. She is evidently a slow-sailing merchant ship. I cannot make her out. She must want to give Monsieur Lafitte an opportunity to board her, to lie at anchor in this neighborhood. I shall be obliged to investigate."

Lowering his two largest boats, and manning each with eight picked men, fully armed, the captain gave to his senior lieutenant command of one, and with reluctance entrusted the other to young McIntosh. The second lieutenant was ill, and the captain had no choice, though the boyish senior midshipman was nearly of suitable age for such a duty.

"Lieutenant," said the captain, anxiously, "use the greatest caution in approaching this vessel, and do not mistake recklessness for gallantry. You will be closely watched, and your signals instantly responded to. And you, Mr. McIntosh, let me caution you not to run useless risks. Take care of your men, and follow the orders of your senior officer. Remember that you are young for such responsibility."

12

The two boats pulled away in silence toward the motionless vessel. The mystery about her heightened the excitement and expectation of the reconnoitering party and the men watched eagerly the faces of their commanding officers.

They approached the ship's side without a challenge or the sight of a human face, though they could hear the sound of rapid movements. Rounding her stern, they saw that she was the " Mary Jane," of Boston.

This was not all they saw, for in a moment more they were in full view of two large cutters, filled with armed men, which, up to that time, had been effectually hidden by the hull of the ship they were robbing.

One boat was already laden, while into the other boxes and bales were being lowered. The ship's crew were evidently in confinement below.

A shout of defiance greeted the man-of-war's boats, and the cutter which was already loaded, made off with a rush in the direction of the shore.

" Follow her!" was the order of the lieutenant. "I will signal for help here."

Like an arrow from a bow McIntosh's boat gave chase.

"Give way, men ; we have caught them at last!" he shouted, and bent forward in his eagerness as if his wish could add to their speed.

The pirates were at a disadvantage on account of the weight of their booty, and the distance between the boats lessened fast.

"Pull away, men, we are gaining on them!" McIntosh urged.

The old boatswain touched his cap. "Excuse me, sir," he said, " but it's queer they don't fire. We are not much to run away from. It's my opinion they are leading us into a trap, amongst these rushes we're coming on."

"That may be Martins, but we are under orders to follow them, and are bound to while we can."

The separation grew less and less wide. They were nearly upon the pirate's boat, when suddenly it vanished among the rushes.

"Back! back!" shouted McIntosh, springing to his feet.

The long line of coarse rushes stretched before them, apparently unbroken; but there was a vibration at one point, as if surf had broken there, and in a direct line with this, within the marsh, rose a clump of cypress trees. The quick eye of the young officer fixed itself on the spot where the sedges swayed so roughly.

"Stand off," he said to the coxswain, "and head her for that spot!"

He pointed with a hand which trembled from eagerness. Backing, and standing off a couple of lengths to give the required impetus, the crew drove the boat into a scarcely perceptible opening, bending their heads and broad backs as they passed under the rushes which met above them.

The boat had not exhausted the momentum given by their vigorous spurt before they began to see daylight above, and to find that they were floating in a canal, wide enough to enable them to use their oars. In a quick whisper McIntosh said : "We have them! They are not a hundred yards ahead!"

The straight line of the canal made a sudden curve around the clump of trees which had helped McIntosh to discover the entrance. The pirates pulled hard, and were lost to sight again.

"We carry our lives in our hands, men," he said, "but our duty lies straight ahead. Give way, and we'll soon be alongside of the rascals."

"Aye, aye, sir," was the response.

A moment more and they, too, had rounded the bend, and were within a land-locked bay, partly natural and partly artificial. Upon the shore they saw a small, one-storied house, surrounded by huts. A crowd of thirty or forty men were gathered around the newly arrived boat. A cleverly mounted battery bristled from the hull of an old brigantine.

Scarcely three minutes had passed before the pursuing boat touched the muddy shore, within thirty feet of the cutter. A tall handsome man, dressed in green military clothes, and wearing an otter-skin cap, advanced rapidly. McIntosh had no difficulty in deciding who he was. Bidding his men keep their places, the young officer stepped ashore and awaited him.

The man's face wore a smile as he looked down on the slight figure of the beardless midshipman and noted his scanty escort.

"To what am I indebted," he said, "for the honor of this visit, sir? I suppose you know you are my prisoner."

"Am I addressing Captain Lafitte?" McIntosh asked in his turn.

The other bowed.

"I am an envoy, not a prisoner," said the midshipman. "I was not brought here by force, but came in pursuit of your boat yonder, which is filled with the property of citizens of the United States. I am attached to the brig "Enterprise," acting under the orders of Commodore Patterson. No doubt you are aware of the object for which he is cruising in these waters?"

"I am aware of the intentions of your commander and of the presence of your ship. I think small advantage has been taken of the opportunity this day afforded him." The accent on the adjective, and allusion to the youth of the midshipman, was satirical. "But I am not an enemy to the United States, and I am ready to respect your uniform; my men are even now demonstrating the restraint they exercise toward your flag and your service. Since you are here, come with me and tell me what your commander desires."

"First I must have assurance of safety for my men."

Lafitte frowned: "I will do all in my power," he said. "I have no desire that your men should be injured, but if trouble comes, you have brought it on yourself. This is a mad expedition."

In response to a shrill whistle, two men came out from the reckless group, who were talking and gesticulating violently beside the still laden cutter. Lafitte spoke to them rapidly in French, bidding them take charge of the boat and crew.

The men shrugged their shoulders. "We will do our best," "but it will be hard to restrain the men, who are much excited."

Lafitte declared that he should hold them responsible, and bade them summon him by a pistol shot if he were needed.

The angry crowd about the pirate boat looked on with astonishment as they saw their captain lead the way to his house. Arrived at the door of his low dwelling, he stood aside, with ceremonious courtesy, to allow the young officer to precede him into the bare little room, which showed no sign of the traditional luxury of buccaneers.

"Now, sir," he said, " pray be seated, and if possible explain your purpose in invading my private property and home."

I do not desire to sit, Captain Lafitte, I am not your guest. I represent my government, and I demand a return of the property of its citizens, and a guarantee that your men shall not attack our commerce.

Lafitte's face relaxed. He was noted for some grace of manner, and the brave bearing of the youth seemed to win his admiration.

"I beg you to be seated," he said. "If you are an envoy, let us negotiate articles of agreement amicably. As a preliminary, I give you my word of honor that I am a friend of the United States. But your flag protects the property of my enemies; your ships suffer for their own greediness in carrying Spanish money and merchandise."

"I could not restore what my men have taken today, if I wished to do so. The first hint of such a thing might cost me my life, as well as sacrifice yours. I will be frank; I have no intention of attempting it."

"But those goods are not the goods of your enemies," said McIntosh.

"The chances are ten to one that every article is Spanish property. The absence of my other boat, and the undoubtedly dangerous position my men were in when their comrades left them and you pursued, makes your presence very exasperating, and makes it tenfold more difficult for me to protect you. What else do you ask of me?"

"I desire," replied McIntosh, "a letter of apology to Commodore Patterson for the indignities shown the vessel your people have robbed, an admission that you cannot restore the stolen goods, and a pledge that our flag shall henceforward be re-spected."

" I will write a note to Commodore Patterson, and I promise you a safe return to your ship. Now, will you not sit down beneath my roof ? Do you distrust my word ?"

The clear, honest eyes of the young man looked steadfastly at his dangerous host, and their verdict was in his favor. He accepted the proffered chair. Lafitte bowed and then seated himself and wrote a few lines, which he handed to McIntosh to read. The blood rushed to the midshipman's face, and he instantly returned the paper.

" I will not take that letter. Captain Lafitte. It puts me in a false position, and insults my commander."

Lafitte sprang to his feet in anger.

" You will not take it ? How dare you refuse it ? What do you complain of ?"

" You say I know and acknowledge this booty to be Spanish property. I neither know nor believe this to be true. You accuse Commodore Patterson of interfering in matters not strictly in the line of his duty. This ship is from Boston, and I believe her cargo belongs there. Her officers were under such restraint that they could neither show themselves nor answer our signals."

Lafitte's eyes glared. Laying his hand with a strong grip upon his shoulder, he drew the young man toward the window of the room. From a gibbet the body of a man swung in the wind.

" There, sir," he said, " is where we place men who defy and annoy us. Are you ready to join that man's company ?"

" Sooner than subscribe to a lie, or be the bearer of an impertinence to my superior officer."

The boyish figure stood steady under the fierce grasp, and his eyes met Lafitte's with answering fire. The pirate's fingers relaxed.

" Sit down," he said, " recovering himself," your courage deserves respect, Besides, I seek no quarrel with your government. I will write again.

In less than five minutes he completed a second note. It expressed courteous regrets that his men had "mistaken the nationality" of the detained vessel, gave strong promises of friendship to the United States and closed with these words :

"I commend the young officer who bears this note to the highest rewards of his government. His intelligence and dauntless gallantry have saved his own life, protected his men and obtained assurance of good faith. His courage has compelled my respect and admiration."

A flush, this time of delighted surprise, covered McIntosh's face.

"I thank you," he said, putting the note within the breast of his coat.

Lafitte's face recovered its look of handsome indifference as he said :

"Now comes the difficult task of getting you and your men off in safety. For my men to obey me when conquest and profit are concerned is one thing ; to see an enemy depart in peace is a new experience. It is high time we showed ourselves at the landing, for your men must be anxious and mine growing ungovernable. I will get the report of my look-out before we go."

His whistle sounded again, this time with three distinct repetitions. A man appeared almost immediately, and did not wait to be questioned.

"Nothing new in sight, sir," he said ; "the vessel anchored this morning is under way, bound East. The United States vessel of war is standing off and on, making signals we do not understand."

"Probably trying to communicate with me," said McIntosh.

"No doubt. Anything more, Pedro ?"

The man hesitated.

"Speak out. Have you seen the missing boat ?"

"The boat is just inside the canal. She is either hiding or waiting for something."

"What else about her ?"

"She seems to have thrown over her cargo, and we think there are two wounded men lying in the stern."

"You can go," said Lafitte.

"Now, sir," he said anxiously, "I have allowed you to hear for yourself what cause you have to dread the anger of my people. I sincerely desire to have you return unharmed, but if fate orders differently, I trust you will not accuse me of treachery. I acknowledge to you that I fear much. But we have no time to lose."

As they approached McIntosh's boat, his crew stood up to salute him. Lafitte paused, spoke a few courteous words, and then, calling their guards to follow him, passed on to his own cutter.

In a short time the booty lay upon the shore, and a number of the pirates began to transfer it slowly, to the armed hull of the brigantine. Into the empty boat four men and one of the late guard sprang hastily and pulled toward the Gulf. Lafitte returned.

"So far, so good," he said to McIntosh, in a low voice. "Securing the goods will occupy them until that boat returns."

In half an hour oars were heard, and this time both boats came in sight. Lafitte's face showed intense excitement as he walked back to the landing. How he controlled them it is impossible to say, but after a brief and angry argument, in French, the men sullenly took up their wounded comrades and carried them toward the huts, though not without loud words and menacing gestures.

Lafitte beckoned McIntosh toward him.

"Leave at once," he said, "but do not show your haste. Here are the signal lights to guide the "Enterprise" in picking you up. It will be dark when you strike the Gulf. I bid you farewell."

The "Enterprise" was reached in safety. Promotion followed this exploit of the young officer ; and many years afterward, when he had performed a service, for which Congress thanked him, gray-haired men in the forecastle told the story of his visit to Lafitte.

JESUS OF NAZARETH PASSETH BY.

BY EMMA CAMPBELL.

What means this eager, anxious throng
  Which moves with busy haste along,
These wondrous gatherings day by day?
  What means this strange commotion, pray?
In accents hushed the throng reply;
  "Jesus of Nazareth passeth by."

Who is this Jesus? Why should He
  The city move so mightily?
A passing stranger, has He skill
  To move the multitude at will?
Again the stirring notes reply;
  "Jesus of Nazareth passeth by."

Jesus! 'tis He who once below
  Man's pathway trod, mid pain and woe;
And burdened ones, where 'er He came,
  Brought out their sick, and deaf and lame
The blind rejoiced to hear the cry:
  "Jesus of Nazareth passeth by."

Again He comes! From place to place
  His holy footsteps we can trace
He pauseth at one threshold—nay.
  He enters—condescends to stay.
Shall we not gladly raise the cry—
  "Jesus of Nazareth passeth by!"

Ho! all ye heavy-laden, come!
  Here's pardon, comfort, rest and home.
Ye wanderers from a father's face,

Return, accept His proffered grace.
Ye tempted ones, there's refuge nigh,
  "Jesus of Nazareth passeth by."

But if you still this call refuse,
  And all His wondrous love abuse,
Soon will He sadly from you turn,
  Your bitter prayer for pardon spurn.
"Too late ! too late !" will be the cry—
  "Jesus of Nazareth *has passed by !*"

MORN.

BY HARRIETTE SEYMOUR CAMPFIELD.

Awake little dreamer the bright sun has risen,
  And shines in full glory o'er mountain and vale ;
While forth from the meadow and woodland the sweet birds
  Are sending their carols of praise on the gale.

And all the fair flowers their heads are uplifting,
  To welcome with gladness the coming of day :
And brighter than gems on the brow of a monarch,
  The dewdrops are flashing beneath the sun's ray.

Far down in the hamlet the smoke wreaths are curling,
  And upward are floating away toward the sky ;
The harvesters long in the fields have been reaping,
  And gleaning and binding the wheat and the rye.

The milkmaid returning with pail richly laden
  And merrily singing, has passed from my view :
The shepherd his flock to green pastures has guided
  With trusty old Rover, so faithful and true.

Then wake little dreamer, no vision in dream-land
  Of jewels or palaces fairer can be ;
Then the fresh blooming flowers the dew-spangled leaflets,.
  And song of the sweet birds from woodland and lea.

THE FLOWERS' BALL.

BY MAIE PARKE COYNE.

"The Misses Calla Lily have issued over a hundred invitations to a ball which will take place Tuesday evening in the conservatory of Mr. Aster." Such was the announcement read from the "Morning Star" by Miss Rose to her mother, as they were eating their breakfast of morning dew and sunshine. "Oh, mamma, how delightful," said the younger Miss Rose, one of the season's buds "are we invited ?"

"Why, certainly, my child," her mother replied, "here is our invitation," and she handed to her daughter the invitation neatly written on an oak leaf. The Roses read it, and the eldest Miss Rose said: "Why, this is the new style of paper the Heliotrope girls are talking about—the ragged edge."

While the Calla Lilies were preparing for the ball, all flowerdom was discussing the great event to come off Tuesday evening.

The eventful day dawned. The Calla Lilies were all in a flutter, as also were their cousins, the Lilies-of-the-Valley and Miss Tiger Lily. "There never was such a day," remarked Miss Tiger Lily to her betrothed, Mr. Dandelion, a wild young man of country origin. The birds were carolling their merry lays. The blue sky was entirely free from clouds. The brooklets murmured gayly over the stones. The tinkle of the cow-bell could be heard in the distance—and the bees were humming drowsily and flitted from field to field culling the sweets to be stored in their hives. Alas! one of the cruel bees has killed Miss Honeysuckle, and she will be missed from the ball, for she was a favorite in society.

The day passed and as evening approached a golden haze covered the landscape. The soft summer air was balmy and all nature seemed joyous. Soon the moon came up and bathed the scene in its silvery light.

When the hour arrived all the Lily family were assembled in the conservatory awaiting their guests. How lovely they looked! The Calla Lilies were robed in white satin and the Lilies-of-the-Valley in white silk. The beauty of the gowns of the Tiger Lilies was enhanced by delicate dots of crimson and brown.

The guests began to arrive.

The butler, Mr. Ivy Leaf, very imposing in his green suit, ushered in the Roses, who looked regally beautiful in pale pink, red, white and yellow. Soon the Misses Camelia was announced, and as they entered a buzz of admiration went round. The Misses Heliotrope came dressed in gowns of delicate lavender. The Misses Hyacinth wore exquisitely shaded silks which had a delicate, clinging perfume. The Pansies looked their handsomest in robes of purple, yellow, white and brown.

The Golden-rods, Cowslips, and other country families were there, but in this group the modest Daisies in their simple costumes were admired the most.

The musicians, Mr. Whip-poor-Will, Mr. Owl and Mr. Cricket were now in their places, and soon the sweet strains of the fascinating valse, "Floral Days," stole out on the evening zephyr. The house was thronged with merry dancers, and Mr. Palm, Mr. Fern and other gentlemen of prominence declared that they had never seen such a galaxy of beauty before.

The hours passed rapidly until midnight, at which time the gay party dispersed. At one o'clock the scene changed, and only the croaking of the frogs in the distant mill-pond and the discordant quarrel between Mr. and Mrs. Katy, whether she did or didn't, disturbed the quietude of the hour.

"IF ANY MAN THIRST, LET HIM COME UNTO ME AND DRINK."—John 7: 37.

BY JULIA R. CUTLER.

We hear thy words, dear Saviour, still they sound
Down all the ages, with life-giving power.
As when, amid the throng at Temple gate,
Thou utteredest them, to those that heeded not.
As fevered patients rave of bubbling streams—
As travellers in the desert long for sight
Of fountains cool, that they may drink and live.
So do we, Saviour, long for promised draughts
Of thy pure spirit, full and fresh and free.
Our souls are weary, toil-worn, sad and lone,
This desert world can give us naught to quench,
The spirit's longings—naught to satisfy
Our cravings for the pure and good and true.
We plead thy promise, which can never fail,
To give, and freely give, to all who come.
So fill us with thy spirit, Lord, that we
May go rejoicing, strengthened, all our days.
As overflowing fountains, rippling streams
Bring beauty, verdure, joy to all around,
And men, and beasts, and birds their bounty share.
So may our hearts with love to Thee o'erflow
As through this world we onward take our way
That all among may the sweet influence share,
And hearts be gladdened, blest and purified—
Then leave behind, to mark our progress here,
A path of blessing, leading up to God.

LITTLE SUNBEAM.

A Story for Mothers.

MRS. I. W. COCHRAN.

Do we not sometimes miss a part of the blessing God means to bestow on us with a gift, from not receiving it in a proper spirit? Are there no homes where God sends little children, to whom but a grudging welcome is given?

Years ago a little daughter was sent to a household where there were already five little ones under ten years old. The mother's hands were very full of care, and at first, in the prospect of its coming, she felt as if it was almost a mistake, and that some other household, where there were not so many treasures already, might better have been enriched with this new one. But suddenly the words seemed flashed into her mind— was it not the whisper of the Spirit of God?—" Whoso receiveth one such little child in my name, receiveth me." She remembered how gladly she would welcome the Lord Jesus into her home, and the thought that this darling little girl was sent in His place, gave the mother a tenderness to her that was indescribable. None of the other children seemed quite the same, for was she not the Lord Jesus' little substitute? And there was something in the little one's lovely life that seemed to bear out her claim to wear so sacred a title. Her chosen text for the motto of the last year of her life was, "Even a child is known by its doing," and those who knew her well bore testimony that in her measure she was as "faithful in all her house" as Moses was.

Alas for the mother! It might have been said of her as it was of the Lord's own mother, "Yea, a sword shall pierce through thine own soul also." For only seven years was Kitty Sunbeam left to gladden her home, and then this little ray from the Sun of Righteousness went home to the city where she will shine forever.

How thankful was the mother that in all the blessed little life no thought but of love and tenderness and welcome had been given her. Perhaps the reason that Little Sunbeam was "such a little child" was because she was welcomed "In His Name."

NOON.

BY HARRIETTE SEYMOUR CAMPFIELD.

To the fair and verdant meadow where the flame-hued poppies
  glow,
And the daisies and the buttercups in rich profusion grow;
And the graceful, drooping willow leaning o'er the river's side,
Dips its long and swaying branches in the clear and foaming
  tide.

Come the mowers and the reapers from the noon-tide glare and
  heat,
Seeking 'neath the out-spreading elm tree, a cool and safe retreat.
Here they watch the clouds that gather, as they take their noon-
  day meal,
And the changing lights and shadows o'er the distant hills that
  steal.

Scarce a breath doth stir the leaflets and no other sounds are
  heard,
Save the chirping of a cricket or the note of some lone bird:
Or the murmur of the river, as it hurries through the lea,
Bending low the reeds and rushes on its journey to the sea.

At the crossing of the roadways, stands the little school-house
  red
O'er whose humble roof a giant oak, protecting arms doth
  spread.

And the sound of eager voices bursts upon the listening ear,
As the children rush from out the door and scatter far and near.

'Tis an hour free and restful from the cares and toils of life,
'Tis an hour free and restful from the noise and din of strife;
To the young and old it cometh, like a heavenly blessing down,
To the toiler in the hamlet and the toiler in the town.

But the hour is short and fleeting, and the harvesters must go
To gather in the golden grain, 'neath the summer's heat and
  glow;
And to school the children hasten, turn to tasks they'd laid
  aside,
And the busy world goes toiling on, until the even-tide.

IN MEMORIAM.

On the death of Miss Anna T. Pierson.

BY MRS. RUSSELL W. CHASE.

Gentle sister, thou hast left us,
 Waiting here, amid the gloom,
Left us for a brighter country,
 Left us standing at the tomb—
 Wondering, hoping at the tomb.

Oh ! how deeply sad our hearts are,
 When we feel thou art no more,
And we ne'er can hope to meet thee
 Till we reach the other shore—
 Reach the happy, golden shore.

Thou art decked with crown immortal,
  Which alone the Saviour gives,
Just within the heavenly Portal
  Where the angels cry, "She lives!"
  Shining angels cry, "She lives!"

So the golden Bowl is broken,
  So is loosed the silver cord,
So Thou'st gone from earth to heaven,
  To be forever with the Lord—
  Ever with the Risen Lord.

Here we leave the precious body,
  Resting in the earth's embrace ;
There we see the ransomed spirit,
  Gazing in the Saviour's face—
  In the Saviour's dear loved face.

We ere long do hope to meet thee,
  When life's work for us is done,
When we reach the deep, dark river,
  And pass over one by one—
  Leaning, trusting, one by one.

Farewell, darling, lovely sister,
  Sweetly sleep beneath the sod,
Till the archangel shall awake thee
  At the last great day of God—
  At the judgment day of God.

GRANDMOTHER CARTER.

BY MRS. I. W. COCHRAN.

One of the most vivid memories of my childhood is of an aged Scottish lady with a round, wholesome, sunny face, fresh complexion, and bands of shining white hair, stalwart form, robed always in deepest black, with a snowy kerchief crossed upon the broad bosom. The hands were large, white and beautifully shaped, the eyes with a gleam of quaint humor, the smile benevolent, the voice full and sweet, with strong Scotch accent. Her speech was " always with grace seasoned with salt," and her ready wit and repartee will not be forgotten by those who have heard it. Of this, one little specimen will suffice. When some-one was speaking to her of a person who had made a rapid rise from obscurity to eminence, and was somewhat carried away with the pleasure of his new position, "Ah," said she, "when soles get to be upper leathers they are awfu' stiff."

The writer well remembers hearing her tell an incident of her early life which may be an encouragement to some young mother, feeling the burden of a large family of little ones almost too much for heart and brain and muscle. She had always been accustomed from early childhood to attend the village church, morning and afternoon. When her first babe was born she was obliged to stay at home with it half of the day, and it was a sore trial to her to miss one service in the house of God. When the minister, good old Mr. Lauder, called upon her, she told him how greatly she felt the privation, and feared that she was losing many opportunities of growing in grace. Her wise old counsellor made answer: " I will give you a text to think of as you sit at home with the baby: "Take this child and nurse it for me and I will give thee thy wages." It was just what she needed, soothed and encouraged her, and afterwards sustained her in the bearing and rearing of her eleven children. And the promise was faithfully kept. She went down to the grave at the age of eighty-two, her children rising up to call her blessed.

> " The love of all her sons encompassed her,
> The love of all her daughters solaced her,"

Rich reward had she for all her faith and labor of love.

If the little ones are nursed for God, the wages will be paid. No work is surer of its reward. "He that goeth forth and weepeth, bearing precious seed, shall doubtless come again with rejoicing bringing his sheaves with him."

THE POCKET QUESTION.

BY ANTOINETTE CARROLL.

A woman who tries to be optimistic as to the progress of her sex was witness the other day of a scene with a moral. In a neat surrey drawn up to the sidewalk sat a trim and alert young matron ordering household supplies. As she was in the act of paying for them her horse started and in snatching the reins she dropped her portmonnaie. Of course it fell upside down and out poured silver and bills, a railroad ticket, several newspaper scraps, a formula for tooth powder, a piece of court plaster, two or three old coins, and some postage stamps.

The polite young man who rescued all these articles from the curbstone, the gutter and the immediate neighborhood of the horses' heels no doubt wondered, after the manner of his sex, why women would persist in carrying all their miscellaneous belongings in their pocketbooks.

The woman who looked on but who did not drop the portmonnaie is open to suggestions; indeed, she would like to ask any benevolent-minded masculine critic what he would consider a neat and handy receptacle for odd things. He wouldn't, one would suppose, look with favor upon a woman's putting them in her sleeves or the tops of her stockings or in her hatband, if she happened to have one, or thrusting them through with her hat pin.

There is one alternative—the crowning agony of finding the well-named "secret pocket" that the dressmaker has obligingly hidden somewhere among the fold of a woman's skirt—but consider that this would involve a rediscovery every time anything was wanted.

"Why don't you have your pocket where you can find it? Why don't you have more pockets?"

Just as if it were a matter of snipping holes wherever pockets are wanted, or tagging them all over one's gown on the outside.

The other day a man whose sympathies are catholic enough to include the pocket question was talking to a woman on the subject. "Just think! I have thirteen," he said, compassionately.

The woman couldn't think it. If he had said eight or ten, her imagination might have stood the strain; but thirteen (in pockets) was unthinkable. Then the man asked, "Where do you carry your pencil?"

"Anywhere and everywhere," was the gloomy reply, "and it never stays." The woman did not feel equal to explaining that a long pencil is an unyielding object that is particularly hard to stow away about the corsage of a fitted gown. There is one place, however, where it and a note book are perfectly at home—that is in the inside pocket of a loose jacket-front.

A woman possessing such a pocket is an altogether different creature from the woman who is obliged to raise her outer "drapery" to delve into the mysterious receptacle in her foundation skirt. This action is always more or less unseemly, and puts one in a timid apologetic frame of mind.

A long suffering ticket agent complains that after a woman has explored both sides of her skirt for the pocket, and has at last extricated her pocketbook, that she looks all through the latter for change, then remarks, "No, I shall want this," and concludes to break a ten-dollar bill. He does not know that there are profound psycho-physiological reasons for her unbusiness-like behavior. No woman with such a pocket can be prompt and decided in action any more than a woman in tight sleeves and collar can be perfectly in command of her nerves and temper.

Not that even one pocket is to be despised wholly. The capacious pocket of our grandmothers would probably hold all the articles that any reasonable woman could desire to stow away about her person, but the point is that they should not be huddled together in one place. What is wanted is a sub-divided and wisely distributed pocket. The higher the physical organism the greater is the complexity of structure and the more marked the adaptation of organs to special functions. The pocket of the future will contain articles of only one kind, whether documents or bonbonnieres.

In the meantime we can but note signs of progress, and look for consolation by the way. Most women have watch pockets. Many women have cash pockets : a few women rejoice in inside pockets in their coats.

And even the low estate of one pocket has its compensations. Women do not carry important letters around for a week before they remember to mail them. Women have not to undergo the going-through-himself contortions of a man who has left all his money in another suit of clothes.

" And then, too," remarks a sweet-faced young matron, " we get the men to carry our things for us."

THE DEER AND THE DOGS.

BY EMELIE S. COLES.

Last Sunday morning early our deer-keeper went to the park with food for the buck and the doe, and their beautiful fawn. As he reached the gate an ugly-looking dog, lying near, sprang up and leaped over the fence into the park. The poor frightened buck ran from the dog in great distress, but, instead of running to his kind keeper for protection, he thought he could save himself; so, giving a desperate leap through the wire fence, he escaped, all torn and bruised and bleeding, to the woods. Our gentle doe was unharmed, for her keeper was close by to "deliver her and her darling from the power of the dog," and she "trusted in him that he would deliver her."

Mr. Ritchie, that dear old gentleman who paints and engraves pictures so beautifully, sent my father the other day a very sweet picture, engraved by himself. A lovely young girl, whose name is Mercy, stands knocking at a high gate. Over the gate these words are printed in large letters: "Knock and it shall be opened unto you." Mercy is knocking very loudly, while the tears are rolling down her cheeks. No wonder! Outside the gate, where she is standing, she hears a great, cruel dog barking fiercely, and as he is close by, she fears he will tear her to pieces. Inside the gate she is sure she will be safe. So she keeps on knocking, knocking, knocking, until the gate is opened. When she tells the kind keeper why she is so frightened, he will lovingly say to her: "I will deliver my darling from the power of the dog."

That is just what our Lord Jesus Christ will say to each of you when you ask Him to save you from the power of Satan, who, like a furious and cruel dog, is going about, seeking whom he may destroy. Only our Lord Jesus can deliver you from his power, but you are safe when you can say : "The Lord is my keeper."

I have read that the Romans used to chain their dogs to their house-doors, over which they wrote : "Beware of dogs." The Apostle Paul in his letter to his Phillippian friends wrote these same words. I think the kind of dogs he meant were such cruel, wicked men as put our dear Saviour to death. "Dogs have compassed me ; the assembly of the wicked have enclosed me ; they pierced my hands and my feet." And such men as King Solomon warn us to shun ; "enter not into the path of the wicked, and go not in the way of evil men. Avoid it, pass not by it, turn from it and pass away." The prophet Isaiah also tells us of other wicked men, and perhaps the Apostle was speaking of these also. "They are all ignorant ; they are all dumb dogs ; they cannot bark ; sleeping, lying down, loving to slumber. Yea, they are greedy dogs which can never have enough." These were watchmen or shepherds which should have been like the faithful watch-dog, protecting the sheep and giving alarm when danger was near, but instead of this they were like worthless, lazy curs, only caring for their own comfort.

I am so glad that none of these dogs "can enter in through the gates into the city" of our great King, "for without are dogs ;" and here in this world they are all around us, and they trouble us if we are not under the constant protection of our keeper, the Lord Jesus Christ.

The deer-keeper has gone in search of his lost one. To day is Wednesday, and until this morning he had not found out where the deer had strayed. I am told that the poor creature has been hunted by the dogs the whole of last night, and would surely be killed tonight, for he has been seen, looking so forlorn, so worn out, so lame and bruised, that it would grieve you to to see the beautiful creature. While I write I hear the voice of the keeper ; he is returning home, and he is calling to me to come and rejoice with him, for he has found the deer. How bright and happy he seems, and how tenderly he looks upon the wounded animal. So our Good Shepherd goes in search of His

sheep, for He will not leave it to perish in the wilderness; and
when He finds it all "weary and worn and ready to die," He
brings it tenderly back to His green pastures, saying: "Rejoice
with me, for I have found my sheep which was lost."

LITTLE BARBARA'S HYMN.

BY CHARLOTTE E. CLARKE.

A mother stood by her spinning-wheel,
Winding the yarn on an ancient reel;
As she counted the threads in the twilight dim,
She murmured the words of a quaint old hymn:
   "Whether we sleep, or whether we wake,
    We are His who gave His life for our sake."

Little Barbara, watching the spinning-wheel,
And keeping time with her toe and heel,
To the hum of the thread and her mother's song,
Sang in her own sweet voice, ere long,
   "Whether we sleep, or whether we wake,
    We are His who gave His life for our sake."

That night in her dreams, as she sleeping lay,
Over and over the scenes of the day
Came back, till she seemed to hear again
The hum of the thread and the quaint old strain:
   "Whether we sleep, or whether we wake,
    We are His who gave His life for our sake."

Next morning with bounding heart and feet,
Little Barbara walked in the crowded street;
And up to her lips as she passed along,
Rose the tender words of her mother's song:
   "Whether we sleep, or whether we wake,
    We are His who gave His life for our sake.'"

A wanderer sat on a way-side stone,
Weary and sighing, sick and lone;
But he raised his head with a look of cheer,
As the gentle tones fell on his ear,
    " Whether we sleep, or whether we wake,
    We are His who gave His life for our sake."

Toiling all day in a crowded room,
A worker stood at her noisy loom;
A voice came up through the ceaseless din,
These words at the window floated in:
    "Whether we sleep, or whether we wake,
    We are His who gave His life for our sake."

A mourner wept by her loved one's bier,
The sun seemed darkened, the world was drear,
But her sobs were stilled and her cheek grew dry,
As she listened to Barbara, passing by:
    "Whether we sleep, or whether we wake,
    We are His who gave His life for our sake."

A sufferer lay on his bed of pain,
With burning brow and throbbing brain;
The notes of the child were heard once more,
As she chanted low at his open door,
    " Whether we sleep, or whether we wake,
    We are His who gave His life for our sake."

Once and again as the day passed by,
And the shades of the evening-time drew nigh,
Like the voice of a friend, or the carol of birds,
Came back to his thoughts the welcome words,
    "Whether we sleep, or whether we wake,
    We are His who gave His Life for our sake."

Alike in all hearts, as the years passed on,
The infant's voice rose up anon,

In the grateful words that cheered their way
Of the hymn little Barbara sang that day:
    " Whether we sleep, or whether we wake,
    We are His who gave His life for our sake."

Perhaps, when the labor of life is done,
And they lay down their burdens one by one,
Forgetting forever these days of pain
They will take up together the sweet refrain,
    " Whether we sleep, or whether we wake,
    We are His who gave His life for our sake."

HYMN.

BY EMELIE S. COLES.

Now lift we Hymns of heart-felt praise to Thee,
    Our King, Redeemer, Saviour. Brother, Friend !
And when Thy face we, in Thy likeness see,
    Our adoration-song shall never end :

Then shall we sing—when with our God we reign,
    Serving Thee, ever, in most holy ways—
" Worthy the Lamb who once for us was slain ! "
    That Song, forever new, of ceaseless praise.

While here we tarry in this world of need.
    Seeking the lost ones who in darkness roam,
Thy little flock, Good Shepherd, gently lead,
    And bear Thy lambs in safety to Thy Home.

MASSAGE AS USED IN INDIA.

BY A. B. CONDICT, M. D.

The use of the massage as a remedial agent is comparatively recent in this country, but if we turn our eyes to the changeless East we shall find that our *Huckeem* friends (Arabic for Doctor) have been using it for many centuries in India and Persia.

What we see done in those countries today is without doubt the customs that prevailed in the time of Christ. It was most interesting to me to visit Pompeii on my journey homeward. There I found the same style of kitchens that my food had been cooked in while in India. Those oil stoves I saw in Pompeii were identical with those just left in India. The houses even were the very same I so often visited in India up in the interior.

The daily life of the Pompeian no doubt was quite like that of the ordinary native of the East today.

Today like those days of Pompeii's glory, the new and old moons had their respective influences as they are now believed to have.

No one would dream of doing so rash a thing as to wean a baby in the old moon, or to perform ever so slight a surgical operation unless the benign influences of the new moon were in the sky. The actual cautery was then as now a favorite adjunct to the use of the drugs obtained from the dense jungles. Such inert substances as the ashes of pearls, or the ground dust of rubies is still in high favor, especially in the families of princes and rajahs. How amusing! to watch the cunning faces of those old Huckeems when the pearls and rubies were brought to be burnt or ground (?!) for the benefit of the patient just prescribed for. The question was did they ever get further than the grasp of the old Huckeem.

From these simple deductions shall we not conclude that the

rude "mallaise" (Hindustanee for Massage we now find in use
in India is the same as was used by remote generations of that
changeless people.

Our Huckeem friend succeeds admirably with his rude mallaise in the cure of a variety of diseases, where we often rush in
with more extreme measures.

Even fevers, rheumatism, malnutrition, the pains of child-
birth, sleeplessness, and many ailments akin to these mentioned,
are treated by the mallaise. The wealthy merchant, or native
prince has what he considers an indispensible adjunct to his
corps of household servants in the person of a middle-aged
woman who is skillful in applying this crude massage. She sits
cross-legged on the floor, by the side of the mat or soft Persian
rug, upon which her patient reclines. Beginning at the extrem-
ities she rolls, kneads, presses, beats softly with finger tips, or
applies continued deep pressure to every portion of the body.

To the fever patient this deep pressure is of the greatest
comfort, so that she often continues her almost superhuman
efforts for many hours at one time.   '

This "Ayah," (nurse) is also apt to be gifted in romancing
while she works, weaving fanciful tales of adventure or love, thus
diverting the patient's thoughts from themselves. In a monotonous tone of voice she spins these stories out, hour after hour,
till we are confident this was the origin of some of the stories of
the Arabian nights, evidently of Persian and Indian origin.
Their endless adventure, their fanciful endings. Today we find
this Ayah as of old reciting those wondrous tales, while the
cocoanut oil lamp burns dimly in the corridors and arches of those
Persian and Indian zananas. She gives the mallaise and weaves
those stories, robbing weary aching bodies of their pains by her
magic skill.

In the case of the lower classes who are unable to obtain so
skilful a manipulator, means of a still ruder type are resorted to
for relief. Where the dreaded malarious fever causes every bone
in the body to ache with the intensity of a toothache, the poor
patient so craves the rudest approach to the mallaise ! In his
dire need, perhaps a friendly neighbor may come to his relief.

While the poor patient lies on the ground with face downward, his friend walks with bare feet slowly up and down with measured tread the back and limbs of the naked patient till every blood vessel, however minute, has been emptied of its heated contents. Every nerve stretched to its utmost capacity. Every bone made to rub its fellow, and every limb move in its socket. The patient declares he is much relieved. In fact many poor creatures use only this treatment for the frequent attacks of fever they contract from the foul air of their dense jungles.

The beautiful and spirited Arab horse who is almost as one of his master's family is also accustomed to the mallaise. In some cases where it is an unusually elegant and highly strong animal, his devoted master regularly employs two strong men to apply the morning and evening mallaise. Even English gentlemen have been persuaded of the benefits of this, and use it for their finest horses. It is found that horses so treated require less food to keep them in good spirits and flesh, and do their work in the extreme heat with less evil results.

It is an open secret! Give the blood a more perfect circulation, stimulate the glands to do their duty. They can and will relieve the over-charged body many times of the poison accumulated. Inflamed organs will become healthful and disease less destructive. Even congested ovaries and uterus may be made to discharge their unduly engorged contents by removing the obstructions in every tiny capillary and vein. Giving nature a chance to right the wrong, and so cheat the skillful surgeon even of the chance to use his knife so often as he now does.

THE SHUT-IN SOCIETY.

BY JENNIE M. CONKLIN.

Its Origin.

Janet's weak fingers ran along the words. I was studying her face as she read, and I knew by the light that flashed into her eyes and by the tremor of her lips that she had found a new thought. I believe that Janet loves a new thought better than anything else on earth or in heaven, I was about to write, and I will write it, for what else can bring one so near to God as a new thought about him?

"What is it?" I asked.

So she read with a sympathetic thrill in her voice; "And the Lord shut him in."

"Well?"

"Don't you see if he shut him in—" hurrying along with little pauses, "it was right and best for him to stay shut in and to find out all that the shut in meant."

Poor Janet. She had been shut in for three years; three years of great pain and weariness, three years of inactive, restless life; but peace had been sent when she became willing to let God have his own way in her life, and to-day she was the happiest Christian that I knew.

"I have such good times with my books and flowers and letters, above all with my letters, you can't imagine how I look forward to mail time! Sometimes I awake in the morning wondering what the mail will bring me at night. When we can no longer look forward to our old pleasures, how God brings us new ones! Do you know what I have resolved to do?"

Janet had such a lively way of talking, not at all like an invalid.

"I am going to pray that I may find somebody shut in,

some one to write to, to do good to, and to receive good from!
It seems comical, but I only know one invalid beside myself.
Haven't I told you about Sue? We have been corresponding for
two years; she is a dear little maiden that is seldom taken out
into the sunshine, and never stands upon her feet. She suffers
very much from bronchitis and chills and fever and heart
disease. Enough, isn't it? Her quiet life is full of business;
besides teaching thirteen little children, she sews and mends,
reads aloud when she can, and gives her frail little fingers all the
work they are able to do. And she lives in the very presence of
God, she has not a thought that she does not tell Him. I'll find
somebody new to broaden her life as well as mine."

"How? Where?" I queried, "will you advertise?"

"I'll ask," she answered seriously.

That was nearly a year ago. I wish that you could hear
Janet talk about her invalids now. She calls them "Our Shut-in
Society." You shall hear about them all as Janet told it to me
last night as we sat alone in her chamber by her fire on the
hearth, for we live in the country where wood fires are still in
fashion. She was in her wooden rocker with its chintz cushions,
her feet upon a home-made foot-rest, and while her fingers were
busied with some light knitting, she told me about the answer
to her prayer, not as though it were anything new, but as another
proof of how our Father gives more than we know how to ask.
I was sitting on the rug, between her and the fire.

"It all chanced," she began, "for it was God's chance, about
a month after I began to ask for it. One day I had been suffering all day, and at twilight I sat here alone, feeling low-spirited
and miserable, so I cried a few tears, for I do cry sometimes
when nobody knows, and then I wiped my eyes and wondered if
God liked such tears. But he knew they came out of my nerves,
and not out of my heart, and so I know that he made excuse for
them. I had been reading the "Advocate and Guardian," what
a friendly, home-like little paper it is. But I had not found
much in it, and had dropped it on the carpet. Eliza intended to
send it away by mail that night, so I had had my last look at it.
Suddenly I felt as if I must look through it again, and the first

thing I saw was an article headed, 'My Invalid Friends.' I don't know why I had not noticed it before. I read it eagerly, although it was almost too dark to see the letters. It was written by a young lady confined to her room; for six years her feet had not touched the floor. She had cared so much for study, but had been shut in from every advantage. Since her first illness she had lost the sight of one eye, and at one time had feared that she must lose the sight of the other. The letter was so touching, so humble and grateful, that the tears began to come out of my heart instead of out of my nerves. And to think how near I came to losing it; for no one in the house had noticed the article. It must have been just God's minute for me to find it. Eliza came up with the lamp and I wrote a note to the editor of the paper, asking Elsie's name and address.

And I found that she had been praying for six months for a new friend, for some one to help her in a piece of work that she is doing; something that I understand better than any friend she has. I know that I can help her more than she dared to ask me, and we two are to pray about it as well as work for it. She says she gave thanks for her answered prayer before she had finished reading my second letter. Isn't it delicious to be an answer to somebody's prayer? And isn't it beautiful to think that all the world over, one prayer is the answer to another prayer? Her letters are full of cheeriness. She is always finding something to give thanks for. She makes the prettiest tatting, you saw it on Eliza's white apron. A friend came in one day, and when I told her that Elsie was glad to sell her tatting, gave me a dollar and said she would take four yards. Elsie's postal card in reply was a song. She said that a lady had engaged some tatting, and then had disappointed her about it, so she was praying that some one would buy it, for her postage stamps were all gone, and she had no stamp to answer the letter from a stranger that had come to her with the same mail as the dollar. The stranger was another invalid, and had written to her for comfort and encouragement. She wants a wheel crutch, thinks she could walk with it. In her last letter, she says, speaking of the crutch, 'If I could use it, and it is best for me, God will provide a way. How sure I am of that.' Perhaps he will surprise her with one; don't you think that he loves to make little surprises for us?"

"And then I found, through the 'Christian Union,' a poor, suffering lady who has no rest night or day. I can't tell you how she suffers, it would make you too sorry. At first I sent her leaflets, and postal cards, with the most comforting hymns I could find, copied in my plainest hand. Her letters, would you believe it, are just bubbling over with gratitude to God, and the friends He has given her? I never knew before where the happy people were. She sent me those autumn leaves on the mantel. She writes to Sue and Elsie, and Sue and Elsie write to each other. Elsie says in her last letter, 'What a happy little band we are.'

"Then, through Elsie, I found Mabel. She has lain nine years, just think, nine years in bed. She cannot even sit up in bed, and at night she take the change of rest by turning on her side. She sews and writes lying on her back. Her neat and pretty penmanship is a lesson to me. She says that when her sufferings are the hardest to bear, that Christ is always nearest. Her windows reach the floor, and, as she lives in a busy village, she has passers by enough to study. She has been taken out into the air seven times during the last eleven years. She writes as if her life were full of doings. Sick people have something to do, as well as to be and to suffer. I have no patience when people talk as if there were no work for invalids. Mabel teaches me that God will be just as good to me, if even a darker time come to me. It seems as if the shut-in people know best and most assuredly just the resource that God has.

"How did I find them all so soon? By keeping my eyes and ears open. Some one says the wise man does not find opportunities, but that he makes them. And praying for a thing is pretty sure to set one to work to get it.

"Several years ago, I met a lady who impressed me with her face, it was so homely, so plain, so ruggedly plain. I know that I am not a beauty, but her face haunted me, I was so sorry for her. She was spoken of as possessing a rare Christian experi-

14

ence. I remember I spoke of a book one day; she replied, 'I read nothing but the Bible.' Well, poor thing, now she is shut in, and it is the Lord who has shut her in. She has been sent to an insane asylum. The last I heard of her, they were teaching her to dance. I will send her our funny paper. It is said that the development of humor keeps the mind balanced.

"And there's another, I really don't know how to help her; it is her father who shuts her in. He will not let her come to the table with him and her brothers, or visit the neighbors, even. She has no mother. Isn't that a queer way to be shut in? I'm afraid that I shouldn't feel as submissive as I do now, but her father's heart is in God's hand, as truly as my neuralgia is. I hope that she thinks so.

"Only this afternoon I saw a letter from an invalid in the 'Advocate and Guardian.' I have written for her name and address and will trouble you to mail the letter on your way home. There are two postal cards also, and 'Heaven Anticipated,' and the last 'Christian Weekly' and 'Christian at Work.' They are great favorites with my invalids."

"Yes," said I, rising, "but I love to be out. How I shall enjoy my walk in this keen air! All the more for thinking of Sue and Elsie and Mabel."

"It is blessed to be out," returned Janet, brightly, "but I know that good is the will of the Lord concerning me."

THE STRANGE STORY OF A MANUSCRIPT.

BY ELLA B. CARTER

" None but an author knows an author's woes,
  Nor Fancy's fondness for the child she bears."

The light of a strong and new-formed purpose glowed on
Annie Morton's face.   In some way it seemed to expand the
whole personality of the little woman, and to make her look
larger.   Even unobservant Mommie saw Annie's silent look of
determination and thought that Annie was probably going to begin a big piece of fancy work, a silk patch-work quilt, or a tapes-
try covering for the large easy chair.

But Mommie was wrong.   Annie was going to write a story.
Pages might be written here, analyzing the subtle influences that
led to this project.   Suffice it to say that this Annie of ours, young
as she was, had felt " the sly dagger in life's hand."   She was lonely and unhappy, for she had had an unfortunate love affair with
a man who was not free to marry her.   After the quarrel he, in
in his chagrin, had given up his position on one of the evening
papers, and gone to Florida to live ; but Annie stayed in her
place and went on doing her work, for Annie belonged to the
great army of women who earn their own living.   She was a
clerk in an insurance office, and she and Mommie lived a Bohe-
mian sort of life ; It was sometimes light housekeeping and
sometimes boarding, as now at Mrs. Mulhye's.

She thought she would take Mommie into her secret at first.
With that end in view she veiled her intense anxiety for a favor-
able answer, and with careless air and a nonchalent voice asked
Mommie :

" Do you think I could write a story ? "

" No." answered Mommie ; " you couldn't write a story ; you
see you haven't traveled enough."

"But," demurred Annie, "people have written books who· have never traveled, and have laid their plots in places and described scenery they have never seen."

"Yes, but they had genius. You couldn't write a story, you dont know enough."

Mommie's words hurt a little, but discouraging as they were, they did not shake Annie's determination to write a story; but she resolved that it should be her own secret; she would write a story, and Mommie would be as proud as anybody if it made a a great hit, as it might some day. It would be impossible now to abandon the idea of writing out the story which her brain had been months in shaping; and then it seemed so capital a plan that the desire to see how it would look on paper was overmastering. Indeed, the whole thing was like a demoniac possession, a scribbling devil fully possessed her.

Of course Anna had a moral purpose in view. She believed that society would be vastly better if there were more good mothers. There had come under her observation a bit of tragedy directly traceable to a woman who had failed as a mother, and she intended to use this material in her story. Entertaining incident and bits of discription should cover a fearless reproof, and though she knew she could never turn this old gray world entirely from its sinnings, yet word of hers might give light to some other woman.

She had somewhere read that a celebrated woman writer always used yellow paper, and that Charles Reade wrote his novels on large cards. She stopped at a stationer's on her way home from the office, the next day after the talk with Mommie, and bought a pad of yellow paper and several yards of thin cardboard, which she cut into pieces seven inches by five inches in size. She placed paper and cards on her desk and was ready to begin work. She took up her pen; the very blood in her veins was tingling with eagerness and impatience to begin, but at that moment Doubt entered her room. The weary, subtle thing sat down upon her desk, spread his black wings above her, paralyzing her pen and whispering: "Don't you know that you are about to run the risk of failure, with its mortification, bitterness and hot tears,—you, who are unknown and unpracticed, will never catch the ear of the mad multitude—it were better, like Miss Primley, to make clothes for the missionary box." But she rallied her forces and routed him by her brave-heartedness.

Then she took one of the cards, the only one she ever used, and copied on it these words from her commonplace book: "All writing comes by grace of God, and all doing and having."

This she pinned over one of the pigeon holes of her desk, but she did not begin her story that day. Doubt had gained a partial success. She leaned back in her chair and fell into a listless mood.

Across the street, in her lace-curtained window bower, sat Mrs. Searles embroidering pink daisies on her baby's afghan. Mrs. Searles had a husband to take care of her, and she had two lovely babies. She spent her days embroidering daisies, and her most arduous mental work was to remember the cunning things the babies did each day that she might recount them to her husband when he came home at night.

Was it true, as somebody had said, "that no happy woman writes." How remote, how very remote, was the thought of writing a book from happy Mrs. Searles.

The next day Anna began her story in good earnest.

It was odd, but until she began she had hardly thought of a title. She invented, considered and rejected sixteen names for her story, and finally began without any. She knew the importance of a first sentence and the opening paragraphs; in them she made her bow, her first impression. Here must be the verbal felicity and the novel descriptions or psychic eccentricity that should catch the eye and rivet the attention of the reader.

She wrote at first painfully and slowly, then more rapidly. She wrote for three or four hours every evening, and read and revised what she had read in the early morning before she went to business. The task grew intensely absorbing and worked a change in her. She grew *distrait;* she was no longer a good listener ; she gave wide answers ; some way the real actors in the great drama around her interested her less than the men and women in her story. She could perfectly understand now why

Balzac should say to one who talked to him of some family affair: "All that is well, my friend, but let us come back to the reality and talk of Eugenie Grandet." She turned from Miss Primley's small talk with caustic remark. Why should she, "full of high thought unborn," listen to gossip about the neighbors?

The story, too, expanded itself; new characters were conceived in her brain, and severe mental throes were endured before they were born and lived on paper; the battle between idea and expression was incessant; she wrote and rewrote; amended, interlined and eliminated, and began to think that writing books should be done by people of large leisure, and she grew as niggardly of time as a miser of his gold, and was full of devices for economizing it.

She discarded earrings and bracelets and did not frizz her hair, for those things took time. She grudged the long bright hours of daylight that she must give to her business, for she disliked to work by gaslight; besides, she learned that the best literary work could be done in the morning, when brain and body were fresh.

Again and again she wished she could lock herself in her room for six or eight weeks, as Balzac did while he wrought like a giant. Those were the times when he would disappear, "fat, rosy, and come forth pale, flabby, with a black circle around his eyes and a *chef d'œuvre* in his hands." Annie was working with odds against her, but she bent again to her task. Ah, what matter the price, so it be a *chef d'œuvre* at last! The thought was intoxicating.

People began to observe Annie's abstraction and to comment upon it. She passed several acquaintances on the street without recognition. Apparently she looked often at people and things without seeing them, and folks wondered.

Mommie, too, began to complain in strain similar to that of Charles Lamb's father, when he said "If his son, when he came home, could not play backgammon with him, what need was there for him to come home?" Mommie said that if Annie were not selfish she would sit with her of evenings, and read stories to her, or rub her lame side with liniment.

So much are deep thought and great sorrow alike in outward expression, that Mrs. Mulhye, who loved her, gave as her theory of Annie's changed demeanor, that she was sorrowing over some private wrong; and Miss Primley, who was a gossip, coincided and whispered: "Yes, it is a disappointment in love —it may end in actual lunacy; seems like it now."

A whole year passed before Annie's story was written. She had given to the work as much as possible of her leisure, had sometimes burned midnight oil, and had spent nearly every minute of her Summer vacation in writing, and to expedite the work, had had the chapters as she finished them copied by a typewriter.

A feeling of relief came as she wrote the last word, and yet as she laid down her pen a sense of loss and loneliness crept over her, there had been so much companionship in the work. She had wrought long and with a "sad sincerity," and now it was done, and for all her effort, it was a poor production, an "unlicked incondite sort of thing," but it was the best of which she was capable. She had dug it from the mine of experience, she had heated it in the furnace of her burning woman's soul, she had tempered it in tears. and hammered it into shape on the anvil of thought.

Surely she had earned a rest, therefore she locked the manuscript in her desk and took a week's holiday.

At the end of the week, she took the manuscript from its hiding place to read it over with fresh eyes, as critically as she was able and if possible, as something quite impersonal. She began to read with a feeling of dread, she finished with feelings of delight and satisfaction, it was better than she thought. She wished, though, that she had the opinion of some experienced literary worker concerning it.

Oh, for a little human help! Her mind wandered to Colonel Elliott, who was away in Florida, working on his plantation and writing letters to northern journals. If he were near and they were on the old terms, how gladly he would help her, what a comradeship she had lost. She sighed a little, and tried to think of some one else who might assist her. There was Lizzie

Stevenson, who wrote clever poetry, which got printed and for which she received money, and whom everybody said had a literary career before her—she would ask Lizzie's opinion of her work.

She took the manuscript to Lizzie who gracefully consented to listen while Annie read it aloud. A sort of dumb wonder grew in Lizzie's eyes as Annie read, and when she was finished Lizzie said : "It is perfectly splendid."

"But, Lizzie, will you please criticize it freely. Tell me the faults and suggest how I can make it better?"

"Why," said Lizzie, still looking awed, "It is, as I said, perfectly splendid. I had no idea that you could write such a story. If I could write a story like that, I should think a good deal of myself. Who are you going to take it to?"

"Take it to?" Why I intend to send it to the—with a letter, of course. Take it, why Lizzie I never could get up courage to beard an editor in his den. I am afraid of editors, to tell the truth."

"Well," said Lizzie, "I think that a personal interview is better than fifty letters. Editors are very pleasant men, I think —that is, men editors. I confess some women editors have snubbed me, but men editors, never."

The interview with Lizzie was very unsatisfactory and made Annie doubt if much-praised Lizzie Stevenson possessed in smallest measure the literary instinct, and Annie concluded, after more thought, that an author must always be his own best critic, his inward approval the best test, and again she sat down to go over the manuscript again carefully and with a "critic's eye." It was too rapid, too laconic and too intense; why, one could almost hear the drip of the heart's blood in it.

She retouched and tried to remedy these faults. Still there remained crudities, but they must forgive her these; there is always something to forgive, much in some really great authors: but it had enough moral purpose to make it live, if that was what made Jeremy Taylor's "Holy Living," and some other books immortal. She decided not to adopt a pseudonym, but to sign

"A. L. Morton"; then, if it were accredited to a man, it might meet a better reception.   Last of all she added the title.

It was a singularly felicitous title, which had flashed suddenly upon her mind one day at the office.   Then she carefully wrapped, without folding, the manuscript, and one day when her office work was done, she went to the postoffice and dropped it into the receptacle for "Newspapers and Packages."   As she slowly went down the steps of the postoffice she felt a lightness of heart, such as she had not known in months.

The writing devil had ceased tormenting her; her task was done; she had sent her story to a periodical of high literary tone that would certainly appreciate her motive and her art; she had not rolled her manuscript, she had paid honest postage, and she had, in the whole action, been true to the impellings of her heart.

There had been a shower during the afternoon, and the sun was setting with the red light sometimes seen after summer rains. The hour and the association of the red sunlight Annie never forgot.   The tall buildings on the opposite side of the street were all aglow, and the hands of the clock in the market-tower pointed to a quarter of six.   As she walked across the little plaza in front of the postoffice, she seemed walking in a rosy mist.   A boy was selling flowers on the street; she bought a Jacqueminot rose and pinned it on her corsage; surely there was no incongruity in wearing a rose above her heart on this day when her hopes were like "the red, red rose."

In the days that followed Annie speculated much as to the result, if her story should be accepted.   Like a child, she began to "suppose."   Suppose it should be printed, why then the something within her—that longed-for expression—would be satisfied. Suppose it brought her a little money, she would buy a new rug and some lace curtains for her room, and a new tea-gown for Mommie.   But suppose it should be republished in book form, and should bring her a good deal of money—such things did happen to writers—why then she could adopt a child—she had always wanted something human to own and take care of.   She wondered if she would like a blue-eyed or a brown-eyed child

better   But suppose her story brought her fame—with the pub-
licity of which she had a horror—would the few people who
loved her love her still as now, or would they think she had risen
above and away from them, and perhaps look at her in the annoying awed way of Lizzie Stevenson and the typewriter woman
who did the copying.

Again she meditated that her story might bring her neither
money or fame, but it it might bring her, what was better, respect and the right to be heard.   Then there were the critics—she
had reckoned without the critics.   If she had stated her opinion
strongly, a host would arise and draw their swords and declare
that not better mothers but the ballot would save society—and
they would stab her to the heart.

While she was thinking about the dreadful critics, the post-
man handed her a bulky package.   She opened it with unsteady
hands for the name of the—was printed on the wrapper.   It was
her manuscript, and oh, horrors, they had rolled it.   A printed
slip fell out which contained about twenty lines.   Annie read
them slowly, but her dazed unreceptive mind absorbed only one
word, which seemed to stand out in letters of fire, the word was
"Overwhelmed."   She re-read the slip and gathered that because they were so overwhelmed with good stories, they were
obliged to reject many that possessed great merit.   She crumpled the slip in her hand   Once an irate, overtried editor had
suggested that slips be printed and addressed "To the idiots,"
who sent manuscript not worth the paper they were written on,
and this had led to the adoption of printed rejection slips ; they
were time saving, no doubt, but cold, unfeeling things.   She tore
the slip in small pieces, laid her head on her desk and wept bitterly.   That night she locked the manuscript in its old hiding
place, and her conscience troubled her sorely because of all the
hours she had wasted in the writing of the story, and as a sort
of pennance she went to Miss Primley the next day and offered
to make some garments for the missionary box.

But the writing devil returned.   It whispered : "There are
other journals and magazines innumerable ; of making them

there is really no end. Some of the world's greatest classics waited long for recognition, why not try again?"

She took heart of hope, but before she again hazarded a disappointment she would get the opinion and advice of some literary worker.

She ran over in her mind all the people she knew who would be likely to help her. The list was not long; it consisted of the minister, Tom Mackley, a reporter on the "Evening Greeting" and Dr. Adams Smith.

She selected Dr. Adams Smith, thought it would take a deal of courage to go to him of all others, for the doctor was learned and celebrated, and a very busy man. He edited a department in one of the great reviews; he was a noted archæologist, too, and he could write a score of letters after his name; his *ipse dixit* would be valuable.

It was presuming on a slight acquaintance, but to Dr. Adams Smith she took the manuscript. He received her in his library and laid down his pen to talk to her. She had met him and been introduced to him on three different occasions, still she was obliged to spend several minutes telling who she was, then she stated her business.

I hope you will pardon me for troubling you," she said. "I know you are a very busy man, and that it is great presumption in me to bother you; but I have written a story, and I am a good deal perplexed to know whether it has any merit or not. If you will allow me to leave it with you and will skim it over some time at your leisure, and then tell me your opinion of it, I shall be eternally grateful. If you find it unreadable, the merest drivel, pray tell me so frankly, and criticise it freely for my advancement in composition."

"Certainly you may leave it. I shall be very glad to help you. I cannot promise to look at it very soon. I am very busy rewriting my lecture on the 'Story of the Early Kings of Egypt,' as gleaned from the monuments, which I expect to deliver in Boston next month; but if you are willing to leave your manuscript for some weeks I will read it."

"Thank you very much," and then she added in a pathetic

voice: "It is such a poor immature thing to thrust upon *your* notice."

"I have no doubt it is a nice story," he replied, looking kindly at her.

Then Annie went away with a golden opinion of Dr. Adams Smith. How funny it was that so learned a man should use the adjective "nice" just as a girl would; and then he had been so hearty in his kindness and courtesy, surely Dr. Adams-Smith was one of the few men who

> " Bear without abuse
> The grand old name of gentleman."

She curbed her fiery impatience and gave him ample time to read the manuscript before she called again. As before, she found him in the library, and again he laid down his pen to talk with her. He took the manuscript from a shelf and turned its pages as he talked. He assured her that he had read it with no little interest, and that it was a good story. He spoke of the suspense in which she held her reader in one place, as good art, and the country scenes well done. Then he touched upon some faults; it was a pity she had not made the love affair turn out happily, it would please the young girls, who were the chief readers of romance, and it was better to bring about at the end what the reader wished for the heroine. The bit of tragedy he thought a trifle overdrawn. Then her ideal was too high; he wished the readers' taste did not make the standard, but unfortunately it was so. He saw no reason why the "Christian Chronicle should not take it, still she might find it difficult to find a publisher, so many people wrote now-a-days; so many thousands of manuscripts had to be returned every year. It did not pay pecuniarily to write; as a rule a candy shop, a laundry tub, or a sewing machine were more remunerative than the pen.

Annie asked : "Do you know Dr. Schenck, the editor of the *Christian Chronicle?*" "Yes," said Dr. Adams-Smith. "I know all the staff."

"Well, would it be asking too much to ask you to give me

just a word of introduction to him. A word from you might insure my story a reading."

"Oh, it don't come in Dr. Schenck's province ; the stories belong to Mrs. Joyce's department. Yes, I'll give you a line to her. She is a bright little woman, and her acquaintance will be worth much to you, even if she does not take the story."

He turned to his desk and wrote a note of introduction to Mrs. Joyce, in which he heartily commended the story. Annie took the note and manuscript and went home in high spirits. It was clear sailing now, for Dr. Adams-Smith had suggested a journal, had praised the story, had given her a letter of introduction to the editor. Again and again she blessed him for his kindness, and wondered whether in heaven where things must be rated differently from what they are in this world—if helping a living, lonely, struggling human being would not be counted greater than writing lectures on the dead Kings of old Egypt.

It was odd that Dr. Adams-Smith should call that overdrawn which was the only incident for which she was not indebted to her imagination.

Should she make changes and make her heroine marry her own true love and live happy ever after? But they did not in real life, as she herself knew, and she had determined to keep in touch with actuality. No ; what she had written she had written, and without changes she sent it with the note of commendation to the *Christian Chronicle.* Inside of two weeks it was returned. The editors thaked her in a printed blank for the opportunity of examining the manuscript, and regretted that they were unable to use it. This second disappointment was more bitter than the first. But she recalled that Dr. Adams-Smith had said "it was a good story," and she sent it to another periodical, which returned it as "not available." Then she sent it to a new magazine for women, which also returned it, but at the bottom of the printed slip the woman editor had written : "It is an excellent story, but too long for our magazine." She immediately sent it to a journal that printed long and short stories ; it was sent back after two weeks. Indeed, it was sent back so often that Annie began to be in such dread of a gray-coated mail carrier as to tremble when she saw one. These days were dark to Annie, but across the darkness their came a gleam of light.

There came home one day with the manuscript a kindly type-written letter, in which the editor said that "the rejection of a manuscript does not imply any lack of literary merit." The manuscript stayed away so long one time that Annie began to hope that it had finally been accepted, but she read in the newspaper that the editor had committed suicide. Then over-sensitive Annie began to think that perhaps it was because of reading her manuscript that the editor had gone mad. For a few hours she suffered the remorse of the murderer, till she read in another paper that it was the commercial editor and not the literary editor who had killed himself, and in a few days the manuscript came back as usual. She began to lose patience and temper, and to feel herself deeply wronged when she remembered some advice an editor had once given her in a note rejecting a competitive bit of writing done by her when she was a school-girl. She hunted up the note and read it slowly—the concluding words were : "Don't be vexed. Never be vexed at editors ; they are a merciless class. Try again. Yours honestly, etc." Try again ! She would try again and she did, to have it returned unread, "owing to the press of unpublished manuscripts on hand."

Thoroughly disheartened, Annie thrust the manuscript in the drawer of her desk, and locked the drawer and locked the desk. Never again would she hazard the torments of suspense and mortification and despair that resulted from offering a story for publication. But for all it was hidden away from sight and securely locked, she was conscious of the presence of the manuscript whenever she entered the room. This was so annoying that she surreptiously carried it up to the trunk room on the third story and placed it underneath her winter clothes. But still it haunted her. Like Frankenstein, she had created a cruel monster that murdered her peace ; ghost-like it walked the stair at night and attracted and drew her by its dread influence, till again she held it in her hands, again she sat retouching it, and again she sent it forth to seek an appreciative editor and a publication to which it was suited. This time the "crowded state of the columns of the weekly to which she sent it prevented its acceptance."

One morning about this time Annie met Tom Mackley as she was going down town to business.

" Heigho," said Tom in his bluff way. " Why, I haven't seen you in an age. You don't come to the meeting of the Socrates Club since Elliott left, I notice. Well, that's the way with girls. What have you been doing with yourself of late ? "

" You couldn't guess, Tom."

" I'll bet a picayune I can."

" Well, what do you conjecture ? "

" It's a crazy quilt, or a screen with red peonies painted on it."

" No, nothing of the sort. Tom, I've been writing a story."

" Well," said Tom, looking interested, " Did you make a strong indictment against Christianity ? "

" Why, Tom, I couldn't attack the Christian religion "

" Oh, I know it is the best thing in the world, but you must do something startling if you want your book read. What did you try to do in it ?"

" I tried to make it realistic, to make my men and women like living people, and then my main object was to point a moral, enforce a lesson."

" It is damned then if that is what you have tried to do. Why, didn't you know that sort of thing had gone out of fashion. The best that can be done has been done in that line, " the roll of great novelists is finished, the count is made," to paraphase Keats. Fantastic, grotesque, highly improbable wonder stories, not meat, nor milk, but condiments, are what take the public fancy now. However, there is one sure way to make your book a success, get the President of the United States or Chauncey M. Depew, or some other celebrated American to endorse it "

" But you know, Tom, there is no hope of my obtaining such sanction."

" If your sole object is to make money, why you might sell it to some of our great manufacturers for an advertisement.

Secure the interest of your readers by some tragical incident, and when you have gotten your heroine in a terrible dilemma, say she used somebody's soap or somebody's baking powder, and her broken heart was mended and all was well with her."

"How dreadful, Tom."

"Or, better still, when it comes out. I'll put in our paper that it is not a fit book for a woman to read—that would sell it."

"Oh, Tom," gasped Annie.

"Well, I am willing to do all I can to help you; here's my place to get out. Good-bye."

Annie's feelings had another rude shock before the day was over. She bought a copy of the "Evening Greeting" to beguile the ride home in the street cars. Looking over the column of book notices, her eye caught the name of a book, the joint work of a man and woman distinguished in the world of letters. Its title was the "The Responsibility of Parents." The hypothesis was that children failed because the parents failed in ethical training, and in a word it aimed to do exactly what Annie had tried to do in her unfortunate story. Annie grew sick and dizzy as she read the flattering words of criticism. Who would listen to her, after the king had spoken?

Upon reaching home she informed Mrs. Mulhye that she had a severe headache and did not want to be disturbed. Then she shut herself in her room. She would be alone in her misery. She paced up and down the room; it was a failure; all her faith in her work was forsaking her, and it died hard. Then sun set, the twilight faded and the gloom of night succeeded. Mommie came in at ten o'clock and suggested a Brown-Sequard pill. The pill was refused and Mommie was asked to please go away. She grew more weary and lay upon the bed and tried to sleep, but her brain seemed to be on fire, and the pitiless, crushing sense of misery and failure grew more intense. All her religion, her philosophy, her patience forsook her. Her soul asked bitter questions. Why, in her life, more than in any other woman's, must so many things fail? Why was it not given to her to work pink daisies on a baby's Afghan? Why was it given to her, with woman's heart, to live in isolation, and to do a man's work in the world. The clock struck three; again she essayed sleep; she said over all the dream charms of her childhood, but sleep would not come. She remembered in Mommie's room there was a box containing morphine; two of these pellets might bring her the blessed sleep she craved, and a larger dose would put her beyound the pain of life forever. But that was a wicked thought. She arose and sat beside the open window. A white mist was rolling up from the river; it entered the room and thoroughly chilled her, she was shivering with cold. Perhaps it was warmer in Mommie's room. She opened the door and stole softly into the room where Mommie, with her head wrapped in flannel to guard against draughts, was sleeping a deep quiet sleep. Annie laid down quietly upon a couch and counted the panes in the window. Suddenly the quietude of Mommie's body impressed her. She fell to meditating how much sleep is like death, then she began to imagine if Mommie were really dead how she would miss her and wish for her to be back, if only to be nagging her after the old way.

Again she noted the stillness on Mommie's body. Heavens, did she breathe? She sprang to her feet and bent over the bed. Her startled movement aroused Mommie from her slumber.

"Why, Annie, is that you?"

"Ye-es."

"What's the matter?"

"Oh, nothing. It was cold in my room, so cold I couldn't sleep, and the pain in my head, too."

"I told you to take a Brown-Sequard pill. Ah, Annie, if you would only sometimes do as I advise you. Well, get right in here by me, this minute; it's warm here."

Annie obeyed. Mommie put her fat arms around her and drew her close to her ample bosom; she grew warm and drowsy and was soon fast asleep.

"I can't help thinking," said Mommie, in her round-eyed way the next morning, "How cold you were last night."

"Yes, I was chilly. But what a foolish thing a nervous headache is."

15

"Yes; you see you ought to have taken the Brown-Sequard pills. I am glad today is Sunday and you won't have to go to the office."

And Annie sat in the steamer chair in Mommie's room and rested all that Sunday. On Monday, someone remarked her unusual pallor, and Mrs. Mulhye said it was the result of a nervous headache, and Annie overhearing it said within herself: "Oh, they little dream of the tempest that swept over me on Saturday night and of the grave in my heart."

Uneventful weeks and months followed. Evenings, after day's business duties, Annie read stories to Mommie and made garments for the missionary box, and she thought no more of her unfortunate literary venture. She believed her hopes in that direction were quite dead. However a slight incident worked a change. Walking up from the office one evening, a flaming red-lettered poster, in a book-seller's window, attracted her attention. The publisher of a magazine, which had printed a story that had obtained wonderful popularity, announced that, owing to the extraordinary demand that had exhausted the edition, they had printed a large number and were ready to "supply orders for this most popular work." Annie bought a copy of the magazine, and read it that night before she slept. It was a story of passion, written by a woman, who Annie thought would be sorely ashamed of her work when her hair began to whiten, or if she ever became a mother. It was unutterable trash, but it was "the sort of bait the public bit at." When Annie had finished reading the story she laid it upon her desk, and drew forth from its hiding place her own manuscript and compared the stories, with the result that her own story stood out in a sort of white light, and all her lost faith in it was suddenly restored. She understood now why one editor had written her: "I am obliged to decline many manuscripts that might otherwise have proved available, and to limit my selection to the class that have been found the most attractive to the general public."

During the weeks that followed the restoration of Annie's faith in her work, she renewed the old experience of frequently offering her work to some periodical, with this change, that when it was returned it no longer affected her as formerly; there were no tears now, no pangs of disappointment or despair. She received it calmly. She even welcomed it; it had become a sort of fetich; she tenderly smoothed out the crumpled leaves, mended the torn edges with court plaster, whispered to it "Remember there is always awaiting your return my patient love." Then she would bless it, and kiss it and send it away again.

But there came a time when she grew indifferent to the fate of the manuscript. This was owing to a physical weakness that began to creep over her. Mommie was sick a good deal that winter, and the hours out of the office were devoted to the exhausting work of nursing and she was no longer able to stand unusual demands on her strength. She began to realize that her literary work and worry in addition to her usual business had taken heavy toll of heart and hand and brain. The weariness increased daily ; it was a reluctant hand that took up the huge books at the office, it was a beclouded brain that did the work and made blunders. On one of these weary days the manuscript was returned to her. It would be curious to compute the hundreds of miles it had traveled and the number of cities and towns it had visited, meditated Annie as she received her manuscript for the last time. She had now exhausted a long list of possible publishers—there was only the "Coming Age" left now; a struggling paper of untimely birth ; which was so radical and so given to the championship of unpopular reforms that its circulation was not great—a paper which had this motto from an old Hebrew writer on the first page : "If thou dost not speak to warn the wicked from his way, that wicked man shall die in his iniquity; but his blood will I require at thy hand."

The old woman who lived in a shoe may have loved her children tenderly, but all the same she gave them bread without any jam, on one memorable night, and whipped each one and sent him or her early to bed. On this night Annie did an impatient deed; she put a new wrapper on her manuscript and directed it to the office of the "Coming Age."

She enclosed a note to the editor in which she said, "I have enclosed no stamps for the return of the manuscript. In case you do not want it, please throw it into your waste basket." "There," said Annfe alond as she finished, "I am rid at last of the bothering thing."

The lassitude continued and increased. Each day's work required harder effort ; bad weather depressed her, and she who once enjoyed battling with storms now dreaded the cold and cringed before the north wind, which in spite of her fur-lined over garment cut to the joints. She was shivering and benumbed on most days, and her thought wandered southward and brought back tantalizing visions of a more genial climate.

" Where the white magnolia's blossoms star the twilight of the pine."

One day her right arm refused to do its work and from inability to use it she was obliged to quit work in the middle of the day, and with the blackness of despair in her soul go home to Mommie. The physician called it nervous exhaustion and said that she must stop work for awhile, and that the arm would recover strength with the general system. Then there followed a resting time for Annie, when she sat at home day after day the centre of a circle who had grown strangely kind. Mommie was very tender. Mrs. Mulhye made special dishes. Mrs. Searles. sent over the baby for her to kiss. The clerks at the office sent flowers and Miss Primley read to her. She usually brought the newspaper every morning while Annie sat in the bay window to get the morning sunshine. At one of these morning readings Miss Primley exclaimed, as she opened the damp paper and glanced at the head lines :

"Oh ! there has been a terrible steamship accident—just outside of Sandy Hook, too—'Wrecked in Port,'—and several lives lost. Here is a list of the drowned. Wonder if there is anybody I know ?"

Miss Primley glanced down the column and breathlessly and with moving lips read the names. Annie watched her idly and thought how disappointed she will be if none of her acquaintances are in the list. Suddenly Miss Primley read a name aloud: "Lady Starkweather—Virginia Starkweather—the name is.

familiar ; oh, yes, now I recollect, she was Gordon Elliott's divorced wife ; she married an Englishman of rank and wealth, you know, and she is drowned. How dreadful ! Well, there is no one else that I know anything about. Shall I read the 'Marriages and Deaths' before I read the particulars of the steamship accident?"

Miss Primley read to one who heard not. Gordon Elliot's name had brought back a whole flood of recollections, of the casual acquaintance which had ripened into friendship, the depth and strength of which she had not dreamed till the day when he had told her that she had restored his lost faith in woman, that she alone could mend his broken life, and then the days of mental struggle and final determination to be true to her social standard, and then two people deeply in love with each other going a separate way, when life is so short and they might have been so happy together.

The advancing Spring found Annie still resting. The insurance people consented to a long furlough, and because her work possessed a certain quality, because it was done by a woman, and cost a little less than a man's, they promised to keep her place for her. The bright Spring days brought increased vitality to her. On fine days she rode out of the city into the blessed country and breathed the bracing mountain air and saw the budding trees make a golden-green mist on the meadow and hillside. And she dreamed at night of wooded sun-smitten slopes, of the pussy willow and violets by the brook, and of great drifts of dogwood blossoms in the hollow. While Annie was thus drifting with the tide. Colonel Elliot journeyed up from the South. He learned of the sickness of his old friend Annie Morton, and sought her to express his sympathy, and the old friendliness was renewed. One day they had an interview which began with these words :

. "Well, Annie, God has divorced me."

And then there followed a conversation with which you that read and we that write shall intermeddle not. But we have to do with results, one of which was that the Insurance Company were told to consider Miss Morton's position vacant, and Miss

Primley was busy for days telling far and wide that Colonel Elliott and Annie Morton were engaged to be married.

During the happy days that came to Annie now, when all thought of the old strenuous literary endeavor vanished from her mind, she saw in the "Coming Age" the opening chapters of her story. It looked a better piece of workmanship in print than she had thought it could, but someway it did not increase her happiness to know that it was published at last—some things come to late to give the joy they might have done, Gordon Elliott remarked, after reading the opening chapter :

"It opens well; this installment is certainly very clever, Annie."

He continued to praise as he read from week to week, and at the end he said in a low voice, looking at her with proud eyes:

"Annie, it is a work of genius; if I had known you had written this, I should never have dared to ask you to become my wife."

"Oh, did it nearly rob me of you, too?" she cried. "It cost me so much, so much; it was so long in finding an appreciative editor."

"I am not surprised, it is so purely ethical, so audacious.. Take this for instance, "Can there be any worse hell than a place where parents can be cognizant of what their children suffer in this world, as the inherited result of their vices."

"How pretty Annie Morton is growing." Miss Primley made no reply, she never praised another woman.

In the late October there was a quiet wedding at Mrs. Mulhye's, and after the wedding a party consisting of Gordon Elliott, his wife and Mommie started for Elliott's plantation in Florida, with everybody going to see them off, everybody wishing them every earthly blessing, and everybody invited to visit them during the coming winter. And so they went away, years ago, those lovers went away, to study out together the horticultural future of Florida, to collaborate in writing books and to a blessed companionship.

There is only left to record the last strange fact in this history of a manuscript. In time there came to Annie in her Southern home, from a Northern publisher, a copy of her story in book form, on the title page of which she read "Sixtieth Thousand," for Annie's story is a great success at last; already she is famous, perhaps some day she will be rich.

KALISTA.

A Portrait in the Frieze of the Parthenon.

BY JULIA E. DODGE.

You may see her on high Akropolis;
    She is noble and calm and fair and sweet
From the hand upbearing her sacred urn
    To the soles of her sandalled feet.

In marble! Aye, but she lived indeed
    More than a score of ages ago,
And I see her now through Phidias' eyes
    In her youth's unfading glow.

I fancy her roaming the Attic plain
    By the swift Ilissos she loved so well,
Fairest and first of a virgin train
    Binding chaplets of asphodel.

Or seated demure 'mid a half-hushed din
    Of girlish voices and distaff and loom,
With soft, skilled fingers waving in
    The web of the mystical pallium.

Meekly happy to bear her part
    In service to high Athene paid—
Athene, queen of her fresh young heart,
    Great maiden-honored maid!

What knew she better? The world's one Light,
  Not yet arisen, threw a twilight dim
Into such pure hearts through the darkness bearing
  Unconscious witness to Him.

I see her again as Phidias saw
  When the long procession onward rolled—
While the air was soft and the skies were blue,
  And the light was flecked with gold.

Soldier and gift bearer, minstrel and priest,
  Bellowing victim and rearing steed
And rumbling chariot, slow-paced age
  And youth with its ill-curbed speed—

Winding up the citadel's side,
  Past spear-sharp aloes, o'er soft young grass,
Through the stately gateway's marble pride
  And the glittering gates of brass,

Praying for blessings on people and town,
  Chanting praises for blessings rife :
"Paltos Athene! Spare thy frown,
  Thy smile to us is life."

A part of it all is my peerless maid,
  And the master's subtle, wondrous power,
Fixing for ages long delayed
  The glory of that hour,

Gives to my heart the joy to know
  How fair and fadeless a flower once bloomed
In that old, old world whose gods are dead
  And its glories deep entombed.

And I love to dream, as my fancies stray,
  How she lived here once in a life as sweet
As the farewell token I bring her to-day,
  The jonquils I drop at her feet.

OUR DECADE TABLES.

BY SUSAN GIBBONS DUVAL.

Under the loveliest of autumn skies, with the maples flaunting in our very faces their banners of scarlet and gold, with the sumac, too, hanging in long glowing sprays, we of Melas-sur-Melas have celebrated our bi-centennial.

Older than most of the settlements along the narrow strip of Atlantic seaboard, the quaint little town, proud of its antiquity, has always cherished among its rare old Lowestoft bits of spode that would tempt the last golden eagles from a collector—its ancient mahogany carved and fluted—an originality of ideas that when occasion demanded has always proved responsive, and that, too, in a very effective manner. With the first of the hyacinths, and again when the apple blossoms make every gnarled old tree a bower of beauty, this birthday of ours was spasmodically alluded to, but not until we had a *motif* did it assume fair and definite proportions.

The earliest suggestion of a Children's Home at the exposition, and needs for funds in its successful development, aroused our sympathies and supplied just what we had been waiting for—an object. To make it a *fête champêtre* there must be a touch of out-door life, and to guard against any designs the clerk of the weather might have upon us, we massed our forces in a new barn, cleanly and resinous in its floors and rafters, and being just on the edge of the town, entirely accessible. All the half-grown boys of our acquaintance we cajoled into bringing clover sods, a faint touch of brown showing among the green, to carpet the slope from the ground level to the wide open doors. You all know that "forewarned is forearmed," do you not? and as the day was exceptionally charming, the little tents outside, with rugs and skins disposed here and there, made attractive points for the afternoon tea we served at four o'clock.

But it was our "decade tables" I wanted to tell you about —the bright idea of a charmingly cultured woman, who arranged ten tables around the sides and inclosed end of the barn. On these were fancy articles for sale, and the costumes of the ladies presiding represented the changes in the fashions of the last century, taking them in lapses of ten years. The novelty drew the nicest people we knew from far and near, while the tickets of admission, fifty cents, kept out the rabble.

Yard upon yard of yellow and red—with holly, hemlock and cedar—we used in beautifying the interior. Golden pumpkins, with the lighter-hued feathery wheat, formed disklike ornamentations, from which were suspended the flags of different nations; for the Columbian celebrations were near enough at hand to impart some of the national enthusiasm.

One always feels sure of the success of such entertainments when the always available army of helpers can be provided for to their own satisfaction. Here we had ten tables, with the same number of young ladies at each, giving us from the very beginning one hundred enthusiastic workers, not only to swell the gate receipts themselves, but each by her own influence inducing those to come who might otherwise remain at home. Those who have safely piloted such affairs know there is nothing adds more to smooth working than well-disposed numbers. They give the appreciation. Two of our tables were set apart, one for archery, the other for tennis equipments, the latter coming to the dress of 1880, when it became so popular; and as both games were provided for out-of-doors, it made an additional attraction.

Commencing with our costumes at the beginning of the century, we made the periods between as near a decade as possible; sometimes a year or two less or more developed such startling transitions we could but glide over into it. We had at our command numerous old tomes that gave in the portraits of celebrities the costumes of the period.

The costumes of 1800 and its near-by years! One wonders

if they will ever have their place again in real life. The hats, some of them, have crowns very like the jam-pots of the present day, only very much higher, and some larger in width ; they set on an enormous flaring brim; we made them of pasteboard, and wired them to keep their place. One was covered with red satin, the lining of yellow; front and back, where the crown joined the brim, were loose, many-ended bows of red, while on the heavy ruche of tulle inside we perched another. In wearing it sets 'way back on the head, the ruche resting on the back part of the low-banged fluffy hair, which should fall in ringlets over the neck and shoulders. The gown with this was of yellow, thin and gauzelike, made full and short; a double band of Indian embroidery around the edge; its sleeves were just wide enough to form an easy loose puff reaching to the elbow, held in place by a band of embroidery, to have one large puff at top and a much smaller one below. The bodice, very short-waisted, was décolleté, and of red satin, as the hat; a tiny rose quilling of hunter's green silk concealed the joining at the waist-line, while one larger and fuller outlined the upper part. Round the neck was a very thick fluffy ruff of dark red; it was very like a boa, and tied under the chin with short ends of ribbon. For the feet were low slippers, crossed and recrossed over instep and up the ankles with narrow red ribbons.

It was only cheese-cloth, as it lay on the counter among the season's left-overs, but such a blue! and this is how we fashioned it: A long straight skirt, very skimp in width, with three rows of narrow black velvet set just above the edge and not far apart. Twelve inches up we put two more, and repeated the rows once again. This gave two enclosed spaces, which were filled with sharply defined vandyke points formed by two rows of the black. The bodice was *à la Josephine*, outlined at both neck and waist with this narrow velvet. Short full puffs formed the foundation for the sleeves, which were ornamented by a vandyked piece the same width, gathered in at the shoulder, the points caught at the sleeve band. A long gauzy scarf of yellow and white, its ends gathered into a point, hung carelessly down the shoulders and over the arms. The bonnet was of gray-

green tissue, cutting for its foundation a pasteboard the shape
of a poke bonnet, shorter at the ears, and running a trifle farther back. We took a double strip of the tissue over a foot in
width and three times the length of the inner edge of this poke.
On the raw edge we side-pleated it to the brim, which was covered by the fulled tissue; then by wires we shaped it into a full
high crown, standing up straight when on the head from the
brim. A band of ribbon drew it in somewhat about three
inches below the upper edge, and was tied in a bow at the back.
This formed a frill. Another band came a little below, while a
third passed around the crown piece, with a bow at the back for
a cape, then back again to the front. A bride reaching from
this, itself fastening on top, passed under the chin. A long
ostrich plume of light blue came from out this top frill and
curled over toward the front.

Ten years later, and we find the changes are very decided
from the waist line upward. An ordinarily pretty brunette
never looked half so charming as she did in her gown of thin
silky material, red stripes on a creamy white ground.

The hat should be of straw, very broad all-round brim, and
its trimming ribbon, ribbon, ribbon. One stiff bunch of bows
near the edge right inside the brim; again on each side where
the broad strings are set on; and on the outside wherever they
will appear the most assertive and defiant. Bunch four loops,
standing ones, put a strap across at the base and fasten on
the front of the crown near the top, then bring the ribbon down
wherever you wish another bunch, avoiding ends. Another
hat, also of straw, was suggestive of a sweet-pea blossom *en
profile*, and had these same stiff bunches of loops in pink ribbon;
at the back of the crown, where the scraping brim rounded up,
was a bunch, the strings coming out and passing under the
chin, where they tied. There was very little variation in either
hats or dresses at this period; for the former round flaring
brims sometimes weighed down with the immense bunches of
ribbon and gauze on the outside, but invariably the stiff clusters on the inner surface. Here commenced the era of the stiff

little curl directly in front of the ear, in vulgar parlance, the "spit-curl."

Ten years more and we find a gracefulness lacking in those which preceded. The skirts have grown fuller and are better hung, the leg-of-mutton sleeve is only one graceful swell (over an under-cushion of down) from shoulder to wrist. One such dress of the most exquisite yellow opened from waist to hem, displaying a yellow and white brocaded petticoat. Its waist was very low, both front and back having underneath a finely tucked chemisette with its high standing ruff up to the ears; on each shoulder two exquisitely thin ruffles lay well over the sleeves, a butterfly bow of ribbon serving as pretext for drawing them up slightly right on the top. The hair was either puffed in front, or in short curls standing out well from the head, and the huge bows on top had stiff ribbon loops to emphasize them.

Still wider skirts, destitute of trimming, made either of plain white or powdered with tiny clusters of flowers; still leg-of-mutton sleeves, but hanging limp over the narrow wristband. The pelerine has encroached, and, edged with lace, comes to the waist line; it has really developed into a cape; the fashions are not so pretty in 1840 as they were the decade before. The bonnet crowns are jam-pot shapes, but they carry a poke front and tie under the chin, the ribbons coming from round the crown; great bunches of flowers are massed on the outside. The hair is worn closely banded or drooping ringlets. But then we all of us know that youth, beauty and grace make any fashion attractive, and in the novelty of the effect produced by these costumes of the years that are gone every one receives more than a passing notice.

AN ORIGINAL POEM

Written by a great grand-daughter of Ann Halsted, a Revolutionary
heroine, and dedicated to the New Jersey Society, Sons of the American
Revolution, December 26, 1892.

BY SUSAN M. DAVEY.

A century or more sheds its dim and mellow rays
Over Revolution scenes and the deeds of other days :
 But let us part the drapery, enter into memory's halls ;
 And gaze with reverent spirit at the pictures on her walls.
There's the North Church steeple with the lantern swinging to
  and fro,
And the rider urging on his steed upon the road below;
 The hopes and fears that filled the soul of loyal Paul Revere
 As he sped upon his errand, were not voiced to mortal ear:
But as he passed the word to each terror-stricken band,
We can almost hear him saying : "God and my native land ! "
 There's the Hessian camp at Trenton, December 26th,
 The soldiers idling listlessly—their arms in stacks are fixed;
Still lingering o'e their Christmas feast, without a single fear,
They little dream of anything but comfort and good cheer.
 But the brave and gallant leader of the now disheartened
  band
 Is already on the Delaware and so the time has planned
That the mercenary Hessians are surprised and put to rout ;—
Then throughout the little army, courage 'takes the place of
  doubt ;
 One thousand of the enemy yield, with cannon and with shot,
 And the nation's fate is settled upon that very spot.
Another land and other scenes now come at Memory's call ;—
Nobles and lords—a regal court ; and grand among them all,

Plain Benjamin Franklin tells the heirs of luxury and ease
The story of his country's needs—the land across the seas.
They bend a listening ear to his projects and his plans
And the struggling little colony clasps the helping hand of
    France.
    The suffering at Valley Forge, of the Camp at Morristown ;
    The traitor's deed ; the dark, dark days before the victor's
    crown ;—
All come before our vision as we linger in the past,
And the names of martyred heroes crowd upon us thick and fast.

Not all the noble men went forth upon the battlefield ;
Some must remain the lands to till, the firesides to shield ;
    But when the Short Hills cannon resounds in thunderous
    tones,
    The fires are lit from hill to hill ; then from their various
    homes,
The " Minute Men " like swarms of bees assemble at their posts,
And in a trice the Morris hills are safe from hostile hosts.
    Another silent army gave their husbands, brothers, sons,
    To the service of their country, when they went to man the
    guns.
Were there no heroines in their ranks—no glorious martyrdom ?
Did they not suffer oftentimes a thousand deaths in one ?
    Brave Mollie Pitcher faltered not before the cannon's roar ;
    Ann Halsted donned coat, hat and gun and saved her father's
    stores ;
Gay Baltimore still celebrates brave Peggy Stewart's day;
The matron of Elizabethtown unbidden went her way
    To the Council Chamber where was broached the question of
    the hour—
    Submission to oppression and to a hostile power ;
Standing before her husband, with firm, unflinching heart,
She said : " If you submit, henceforth our ways do part."
    In Morristown, the women through the country far and wide,
    Ceased not to knit and spin from early morn till eventide,

And many a weary soldier, when he felt the hand of death,
Murmured blessings on their efforts with his last sad parting
    breath.
    The Revolutionary heroes have joined the shadowy throng,
    But their lineal descendants still live to right the wrong,
To resist the hostile inroads of a grasping, foreign foe,
To uplift the fallen statue of Libery laid low.

    The handful of brave spirits as the years have passed away,
Has become a mighty nation and beneath its scepter's sway,
    Dwell in one common brotherhood all kindreds, tribes and
        tongues—
    The hordes of pent up Europe—the Greeks, the Slavs, the Huns,
The Turk, the Celt, the Italian, the Spaniard, all have come,
By thousands and ten thousands to join the general sum ;
    The Dark Continent and India, and China, too, are here
    And each passes on his way, with none molesting, none to fear.
Sons of the Revolution ! What is your duty of the hour ?
Would you maintain undimmed the prestige and the power
    Of the heritage your fathers won in those dark and trying days?
    Then rouse up from your lethargy and fix your piercing gaze
On the mercenary troops upon on every side arrayed,
That would rob you of your birthright and in the dust degrade
    The principles for which they fought, for which they bled and
        died,
    And for which, in many a soldier's grave. they are lying side
        by side !
Let your Minute Men assemble ! relight your signal fires,
For the safety of your country and the honor of your sires !
Let the lantern be flung out from the North Church Tower
    again !
    Gird on your rusty armor and quit yourselves like men !
When the eagle leaves his eyrie, on your next assembly day,
Let him bear aloft this message to those long since passed away:
    That the dear old flag still floats and shall never cease to wave,
    O'er a land where all are free and o'er homes where all are
        brave.

THE GUARDIAN ANGEL.

BY LULU MAY FLEMING-DOWNS.

A group of angels gathered
  In the shining streets of gold,
And with eyes love-lit and beaming
  Their deeds of mercy told.
How they could best to mortals
  Show the glory of their King,
And how to cheer afflicted hearts
  And soothe the suffering.

One told of how another soul
  Had left the paths of sin,
And with eyes upturned for mercy
  Pleaded hard to enter in.
The angel group with one accord
  Struck up a hymn of praise,
And all the ransomed joined the song
  And sang their sweetest lays.

But one sweet angel stood apart
  With downcast, saddened eyes,
And joined not in the others' song,
  Nor let her praise arise.
And when they, wand'ring, asked her why,
  Down fell a pearly tear—
The angels wept in sympathy,
  For angels grief revere.

And then she told the pitying throng :
  " A few short days ago "
(For years are days in heaven,
  As all we mortals know),

I laid upon a mother's breast,
   A lovely, fragile child,
Whom God had lent her for a time,
   So pure and undefiled.

And I am the Guardian Angel
   Of that little one so sweet,
I've sheltered her from evil,
   And have kept her childish feet
From stumbling o'er the rocks and stones,
   Unsoiled by life's rough way,
For I know that He would call her
   To join us here some day.

And so I hovered o'er her
   With the watchful eye of love,
I've kept her soul as spotless
   As the plumage of a dove.
And if a childish fault was placed
   Upon the record white,
I dropped a tear upon it
   And blotted it from sight.

But the Savior loves the children,
   He has called her now to come;
And I'm on the way to bring her—
   You must sing glad welcome home.
It is not for her I'm weeping—
   She has found all pain's relief;
But I'm sighing for her loved ones,
   Bowed down with lonely grief.

But the kind and gracious comforter
   Will strengthen and uphold,
He will soothe their broken spirits,
   In his arms of love enfold.
She will be their angel guardian,
   Hovering o'er with heavenly peace,

Till they join their ransomed darling
  And their sorrowing shall cease.
*   *   *   *   *   *
Loud the songs of joy resounded,
  Robe and crown were quickly brought,
As the pearly gates swung open,
  Showing Heaven with glory fraught,
And the little one who entered,
  Borne by angels into rest,
Left behind all pain and sorrow,
  Folded to her Savior's breast.

Now she sings her glad hosannas
  With the angel choir above,
But she's watching o'er her dear ones
  With the tender eyes of love.
Think how sweet 'twill be when Jesus
  Tells you 'tis your time to come,
She will be the first to greet you,
  First to bid you " Welcome home?"

THE RIVER.

BY MISS ANNIE M. DOUGHERTY.

Slowly and gently flows the river
  Under the little bridge ;
It goes along with a little quiver
  Beside the high green ridge.

Over the fields and meadows it flows,
  Never stopping to think ;
And as it goes it sprinkles the rose,
  And waters the little pink.

In answer the flowers lift up their heads,
  And thank the river sweetly ;
Again they lie in their dewy beds
  That have been cleaned so neatly.

CLORINDY'S STORY.

BY KATE ERSKINE.

You'll see 'em up there on the ridge in about ten minutes,'' said Mrs. Hannah Stetson, rocking slowly back and forth in her little yellow rocker, as she laid down her knitting a moment to shade her eyes while looking in that direction. "I've got so in the habit o' watchin' for 'em that I find myself sort o' worryin' when they don't appear, an calc'latin' that Clorindy must be sick or somethin'. I don't worry much about Jabe, though ; trust him to be tough enough for a whole regiment. But, then, I don't s'pose they've missed meetin' up there in summer more'n a dozen times the past for years ; an' they keep it up pretty late in the fall, too. If you'll believe me, I've seen 'em up there in the winter with the snow on the ground, an' the wind blowin' Clorindy's clothes all round her while she stood there 's quiet an' meek as a lamb. You might liken Jabe to the shearer. There there be ! '' and Mrs. Stetson stepped to the end of the porch, followed by her friend and visitor, Miss Elvira Woodhouse, who, being of a romantic turn of mind, although somewhat seared and withered by time, took a lively interest in the matter.

"Poor dear !'' continued Mrs. Stetson, after gazing mournfully at the couple for a moment, and shaking her head slowly as she resumed her seat ; "an' that's all she's got, after waitin' more'n four years for that great fool of a Jabe Hutchins ; a piece o' bare rock to see him on, an' not the least chance o' his ever marryin' her—or rather her ever marryin' him.''

Miss Elvira coughed slightly, and gave a litte sigh.

"But there,'' said Mrs. Stetson, "I promised to tell you all about it, Elviry, from the very beginnin'; and here I'm commencin' at the very endin', as you might say. But it's all owin' to my not bein' able to bring my mind to bear on your bein' a stranger in these parts. It seems sort o' queer to think o' any-body's livin' an' not knowin' Clorindy's story. I'll just turn my chair round so's not to see Jabe Hutchins. He kind o' riles me up so "

Mrs. Stetson turned her rocker around, and then knit a few rows across her stocking in silence while she collected her thoughts before commencing the story. Miss Elvira leaned lazily back in her large chair, with the old buff cat curled comfortably in her lap, and her eyes fixed on the man and woman on the ridge. A couple of hens picked their way daintly about the porch ; and the buzzing of the bees in their hives, the tinkling of the cow-bells in the distance, and the general air of quiet and peace served as a fit setting to the story which Mrs. Stetson now commenced to relate in a gentle voice.

"Clorindy ain't much to look at now ; but if you could have seen her as I used to, with her cheeks as red as roses, an' her blue eyes bright an' shinin', you'd never forget it, but kind o' still put the red cheeks in the place of the pale ones, an' the shinin' eyes in the place of the sad ones, just as I do! Clorindy ain't but twenty-eight now, an' of course that ain't old. If she'd married she'd have been called a young woman now ; but as long as she didn't she seems like sort of old maid, an' yet not exactly like one, neither; as she says she still expects to marry Jabe.

"Clorindy used to have so many followers from the time she was seventeen or thereabouts, an' we used to calc'late among ourselves that she'd take first this one, an' then that one ; partic'larly Hiram Scott's son, who was the likliest young man around, an' just ready to eat Clorindy up whih his eyes when she sung in the choir. But she let 'em all go, one after another, 'an just when we was gettin' all pretty discouraged at the way she was goin' on, she appeared at meetin' on Sunday mornin' with Jabe Hutchins. Clorindy looked so happy, an' Jabe set so like a bump on a log at her side, that we all knew what it meant. My, wa'nt we surprised !" Mrs. Stetson dropped her work in her lap while she looked absently at the distant hills, and seemed to see the bright young face in the pew at church.

"But that was four years ago," she continued. "We all crowded round her after meetin' was over to try an' say somethin' pleasant on her account an' her mother's. But 'twas awful hard work. Not but what everybody liked Jabe ; I don't s'pose he had an enemy in the world, except himself ; an' that was just the trouble. You liked him because you couldn't help yourself, considerin' his sweetness o' disposition, an' also 'cause it wa'n't worth while doin' anything else. Although I was feelin' like death, I couldn't help smilin' to myself for the life o' me to hear all those people sayin' the same thing to Clorindy—'Jabe's awful good-natured, anyhow,' in the perlitest manner possible, an' yet sort o' helpless, too, as if they felt they wa'n't quite doin' their duty by her." Mrs. Stetson laughed gently, and then, after shooing the hens off the porch with her apron, and inquiring anxiously of her friend if she was "pufickly comfortable," resumed her discourse.

"Well, I guess we didn't any of us do very much talkin' the next few weeks except about Clorindy an' Jabe. We kep' at that stiddy."

"There, they're a-settin' down now," interrupted Miss Elvira, "an' he's takin' her hand."

"Yes, I daresay ; I know all their motions," said Mrs. Stetson, dryly, without turning around. "But I've got to hurry up with this story if I expect to finish it before candle-time." At this gentle reproof Miss Elvira relaxed into silence, although still keeping her eyes turned on the narrow ridge where the increasing dusk made the outlines of the couple more and more indistinct.

"Clorindy an' Jabe commenced right off to use that ridge as a meetin'-place. Most likely because it was just half-way between their two houses, an' then it always gave a good view of the settin' sun. Dear, dear ! how I used to set and watch for em' every night, just to see Clorindy in her clean, light calico, lookin', as I knew, so fresh an' pretty in the face (although I couldn't see that from this distance), an' Jabe aholdin' himself as straight as could be, an' prouder, too. They always kissed each other when they met, an' they'd chat for a while ; an' very often they'd hold each other's hand, just as you see 'em do now. Folks might think I'd been kind o' spyin' 'em all these years, but it ain't so ; only that I'm a lonely old woman, an' they made company for me—besides, Clorindy reminds me a little of my 'Lisbeth.

"Well, nobody s'posed they'd be married short of a year, say the next spring, but we did calc'late pretty freely on that, an' laid our plans accordin'. For instance, I turned the breadths of my black silk, so's to have it in readiness, an' Mis' Fisher did the same thing with her gray. Susan Pollard bought a new wreath for her bonnit, 'stead o' waitin' till the next spring, which would have been more thrifty. But the spring an' summer came an' went. Then we said we s'posed she preferred the cool o' the fall, but that came and went, too. People then commenced to talk, an' show more interest an' ask more p'inted questions than really they were called on to make. But Clorindy never answered 'em ; 'an, although she was always sweet an' gentle in her ways, there was a somethin' about her that kep' people off ; she's been that way ever since she was a little girl. For a wonder, Jabe held his tongue, too. But finally it leaked out. I've always suspicioned 'twas Clorindy's mother that told it, seein' she was the most likely to know, an' has always been such a perfect sieve she couldn't keep a secret over night to save herself."

The crucial point in her story had now arrived, and, fully appreciating it, Mrs. Stetion came to a full stop. Her needles clicked briskly as she cast covert glances at her friend's excited face.

"Well, now, Elviry, what do you s'pose 'twas ? What do you s'pose has kep' Clorindy and Jabe apart these four years, an' yet brought 'em nearer together all the time, as it were ?"

Miss Elvira searched her mind wildly for the most plausible reason, and then whispered hoarsely, "Jealousy."

"Nonsense!" said Mrs. Stetson; 'twa'n't nothin' but an old pig-sty an' a barn."

Miss Elvira flung herself back tragically in her chair.

"Yes," continued the narrator, satisfied with the effect she

had produced, "'twas just that an' nothin' more. It seems that
Clorindy asked Jabe, just after they was engaged, when he was
goin' to finish that pig sty, paint his barn, an' fix up the place
generally;· an' he answers in his easy way, 'Oh, before long;
there ain't no hurry.' But he never tetched them. Clorindy
didn't say nothin' more about it, but waited almost a year, an'
then told him she wa'n't willin' to be married till they was
attended to. You see, she knew Jabe just as well an' better'n
most folks by that time, an' mistrusted that if they wa'n't fixed
before she became his wife, they never would be. They say
Jabe's never thought she was onreasonable in the matter; leastways he's never said so. "Still, time went on, an' the pig-sty
wa'n't finished, an' the new barn, 'stead o' lookin' piney an'
fresh, commenced to look gray an' black. (You can see it over
there, Elviry, if you'll look sharp: behind that elum tree.) There
always seemed to be a somethin' 't kep' that fellow back from
finishin' 'em, an' doin' the other jobs around the farm—dear
knows, he's always been shiftless enough, though! Either he
couldn't get just the kind o' boards he wanted to finish the pig-
sty, or else he couldn't succeed in findin' the right shade o' red
to paint that barn with. But when I heerd tell how he'd sold all
o' his pigs, an' then told Clorindy, 'Of course, there wa'n't any
use in havin' a pig-sty when you hadn't any pigs to put in it,' I
thought I should die a-laughin', although I was just as mad as
could be all the time. There was a lot of other excuses that I
can't rec'lect just this minute; but Clorindy's never accepted
any of 'em, an' although she's been firm an' kep' to her word,
she's been just as kind an' gentle to Jabe, an' clung to him the
same as though he was a man to be leaned on. But it's wore on
her dreadful. Oh, Elviry! just think how she must love him!
She must find in him somethin' that none of us can see."

Both women wiped their eyes, and there was a silence while
the looked at the couple on the ridge.

"I wish I was near enough to see an' hear all that's been
goin' on up there," said Miss Elvira.

Two weeks had passed, and Mrs. Stetson stood on her front
porch looking anxiously up the road. "If Elviry don't come

pretty soon," she murmured to herself " I shall just bust. Cats are pretty good company," she continued, as the buff cat rubbed himself vigorously against her, " an' hens are awful knowin'; but there comes times when you feel as though you wanted a fellow-creature to talk to. Well, there! if that ain't Elviry now, walkin' as though nothin' hadn't happened!" and, hastily swooping hens and cat off the porch, Mrs. Stetson went forward to meet her friend. There was an air of suppressed excitement and determination about her, and an intensity of expression as she peered over her glasses, which made all superfluous conversation, such as a greeting, seem out of place.

Miss Woodhouse's tragic form sank on the first step as she whispered: "Hannah Maria Stetson, who's dead?"

" Now, Elviry Woodhouse, if you'll just get up, an' come an' set in this little rocker I've got out for you, I'll tell you about the goin's-on sence you left," was the firm reply. "Somethin's happened that's worth talkin' about.

" I don't wish to seem unkind, Elviry," she continued after they were seated; "for my not askin' you how you left the folks don't mean that I haven't got any interest in 'em. If you don't say nothin', I'll understand they're all alive, an' that Uncle Joe's rheumatiz is, as usual, 'middlin'.' But I've been holding myself in so, now for two days, waitin' for you, that I must talk about somethin' else. Dear! dear!—an' to think that we was settin' here only two weeks ago to-night, an' watchin' 'em on the ridge, an' talkin' about 'em just as though nothin' was goin' to happen."

" Then it's about Clorindy ?" suggested Miss Elvira.

" Of course it's about Clorindy an' Jabe, Elviry; did'nt I tell you before ?

"Yes, it's made a good deal o' talk," continued Mrs. Stetson, looking reflectively at the ridge. " I'm wonderin' whether they'll go up there tonight same's ever. But there! I want to tell you all about it.

" It was two mornin's ago that I was setin' out here shellin' peas for dinner (two quart pickin's from the back lot jinin'), and my brother Eli rode by on his mowin' machine, an' stopped to have a little chat about crops an' church matters. I s'pose w'd

been talkin' 's much as twenty minutes when Eli says, 'Too bad
'bout Clorindy.' (I forgot to tell you, Elviry, that I hadn't seen
her on the ridge the night before, although Jabe waited for her
some time; an' I'd been kind o' worryin' ever since). So when
he said that, of course I was all alive to know what was the matter. Well, men are cur'us bein's," and Mrs. Stetson laid down
her knitting while she looked absently at the old buff cat, who
had crept back on the porch, and was now playing with her ball
of yarn in the most bare-faced manner. "There's Eli; you
know he's Deacon, an' can pray in meetin' 'most as well as the
minister, an' knows the Bible an' the Farmers' Almanac through
an' through; then he's got a good head for business, too, an' can
drive as sharp a bargain down to the store as anybody; but he
couldn't give me the least idee of what was the matter with
Clorindy. Men don't seem to have any carryin' power in their
heads about sickness an' such things; although I knew Eli'd
heard all the partic'lars from his wife. First, he said she'd got
'chills all over, an' they couldn't get her warm nohow,' an' then,
the next minute, that she was burnin' up with fever;' an' he con-
tradicted himself twice. about sore throat. I tried to pin him
down to somethin', but 'twa'n't no use. Finally he got all mud-
dled, an' commenced scratchin' his head, an' tryin' to make out
he reckoned 'twas the 'measles.' When Eli commences scratchin' his head, you may know there isn't any use talkin' to him any
longer; so', 's soon's I'd done shellin' my peas, I put my hat on
an' went over to Clorindy's.

"Elviry Woodhouse, I'm never one to cry much, as you
know, but if you could have seen Clorindy, I believe you'd have
done just the same as I did—had a good cry." And Mrs. Stetson emphasized her remark by removing her glasses and weeping quietly, in which act she was followed by Miss Woodhouse,
whose emotions were easily swayed.

"There lay Clorindy on the bed, lookin' so pale an' sick,
just as if she was all tuckered out, an' wa'n't never goin' to get
up again. Her mother set at her side with a camphire bottle in
one hand an' a vinegar bottle in the other, which she was ap-
plyin' to Clorindy's nose promisc'ous. I declare, it just went to

my heart to see her a-doin' that, an' not a smell o' boneset tea in the house, when anybody whe knows the least about sickness knows boneset's the thing to give, no matter what's the trouble." Here Mrs. Stetson twitched the stocking, and then looked pity- ingly at it, as though she had Clorindy's mother before her. "I didn't say nothin', but I'd taken the precaution to bring a small basket of medicines with me, an' I can tell you, it didn't take me long to whip out that boneset an' go into the kitchen an' make a good, strong cup o' tea, wnich I give to Clorindy immediate. Then I set down an' inquired what was the matter."

"Well, it does take you to know how to do things," said Miss Elvira, admiringly.

"I do calc'late to know somethin' about sickness," answered Mrs. Stetson, placidly. "Clorindy's mother said the best she could express it was to say that Clorindy seemed to go all to pieces the mornin' before. Those were her very words, 'all to pieces.' So she just kep' her bed; but when it came time to go to meet Jabe, as usual, she tried to struggle up, an' seemed awful disappointed when she found she was so weak she couldn't stir. So she turned her face toward the west window, an' lay there with wistful expression on her face, she's had so much lately. She was lyin' there just the same when I first see her, but she turned her eyes on me once when I entered, with such a longin', questionin' look. I knew what it meant; so, 's soon's I had a chance, I drew her mother into the closet an' says, 'Hasn't he been here?' An' she only shook her head an' swallowed hard.

"Well, we did everythin' we could for Clorindy. I do' know as we left a single stone unturned; workin' over her all the time We tried a-sweatin' her an' soakin' her feet in mustard water, an' lots of other things; but nothin' seemed to do any good. I think she grew weaker, if anythin', an' finally begged to be just let alone. So we tidied her up an' fixed her just as comfortable as we could; propped her up on pillows, so's she could catch a glimpse o' the ridge when the wind blew the branches apart. Then her mother an' me set still, for there wa'n't nothin' more to do.

"So the time went by; but when it came towards sunset, we

both noticed how big her eyes were growin', an', now and then a tear 'd roll down her cheek.

I was watchin' her pretty close, thinkin' any moment she might faint away, when I see her lean forward a little an' the nex' thing I knew, Jabe had bust into the room a-wavin' a paint brush an' callin' out Oh, Clorindy! the pig sty's all finished, an' the barn's painted a beautiful red.' His clothes were all covered with paint, but he went right down side o' the bed, an' put his arms clean around Clorindy an' they both cried like children. Then he set an' told us how he'd been working more stiddy on 'em lately, an' that when he heard Clorindy was sick, he made up his mind he would not look her in the face, till they was both finished, an' the other jobs about the place. An' he had only finished the barn just that minute. Then he says, Clorindy when'll you marry me?" An' 'she says tomorrow Jabe.' Then he kissed her an' went away.

Her mother never suspicioned she'd be able to even get up short of a week, but her strength seemed to come back all of a suddent.

They was married this afternoon at the minister's house, an' Clorindy's mother said her cheeks looked pink as when she was a young girl."

There they be now? suddenly exclaimed Miss Elvira. I I can't seem to sense it said Mrs. Stetson softly, that Clorindy's story has come to an end an' that she's a goin' to be just like other folks now.

SUMMER SKETCHES.

BY CATHERINE THAYER.

A MAY SKETCH.

A sky of clearest blue, with fleecy clouds
Floating in dreamy softness o'er its face;
And outlined upon this, the distant hills
Are touched with gentle radiance by the sun.
Above the tangled alder thicket green,
The willows droop their golden-fringed boughs,
Until they touch the mirrored sky beneath
And idly kiss their image in the pool.

A JUNE SKETCH.

The rain has passed; the clouds which lately veiled
The highlands with a dim, enshrouding mist
Dispel with soft reluctance, as if loath
To vanish from a scene primeval fair;
Where the green woods are flecked with amber lights,
And all the meadow grass is daisy-starred,
And the wild rose, in sweet abandonment
Unfolds her perfumed petals to the breeze.

A JULY SKETCH.

Above the lake's expanse, where waters flash
Into faint ripples at the wind's caress,
Rise mountains purpling in the hazy glow,
On whose bold fronts the hand of Time has carved
With each succeeding year deep lines of age;
But Summer, with a verdant mantle hides
All scars, and clothes their slopes with forest dense
And undulating fields of golden grain.

AN AUGUST SKETCH.

Beyond a sand-dune's slope, where the pale grass
Clings with firm roots upon the shelving side,
A storm-ribbed beach extends its shining length,
A golden zone, confining the deep surge
Of the vast ocean's ceaseless energy;
The tide waves flash translucent in the sun,
Empearled with spray, then melt in snowy foam
With gentle, rhythmic murmur on its sands.

A SEPTEMBER SKETCH.

The grasses in the meadows by the bay
Blend in rich harmonies of autumn tints,
Faint russet, yellow, tinged with ruddy tones;
The glowing colors softened by the haze
Until harmonious with the water's hue
Of neutral gray—upon whose glassy calm
Are mirrored forth the outlines of the hills,
And the slow-gliding vessels' drooping sails.

A TWILIGHT SONG.

As the last glow is fading from the sky
    And twilight's dimness merges into night,
There floats above the reed's æolian sigh
    A whispered requiem for the vanished light.
A solemn silence stills with mystic spell
    The murmurs of the forest's myriad leaves ;
The fern-fronds droop dew-steeped within the dell,
    And drowsy poppies sleep among the sheaves.
Hark ! through the silence soar the rapturous notes
    Of a bird's song ; its cadence sweet and clear
Fills all the air with melody which floats
    Born by the breezes to the listening ear,
From where within the silent shadowy grove
    The nightingale sits singing of his love.

HER SPINNING.

BY AMANDA M. DOUGLAS.

Her summer spinning had this beginning—
   The day was June and gay with flowers,
   The birds sang through the golden hours,
   With sunshine sifted at our feet;
The meadow clover, was blown all over,
   With clouds of incense rare and sweet.

Her eyes beguiling I watched half smiling,
   Her hair astray from its dusty net,
   Tangling a thought like a snare all set;
   Her mouth of rose-red summer grace:
Her slim hand stirring, the wheel a-whirring,
   The half-turned, downcast, blushing face.

Said I—'Tell whether, you spin together
   The silver and gold of blended lives?
   The twisted thread where forever thrives;
   Love and faith and life in one,
Ah, no entreating, of my eyes meeting,
   I must be answered ere day is done.

I rambled the clover all over and over;
   I dreamed in the shade by a crystal spring,
   And painted a butterfly's turquoise wing,
   While a shadowy face stole unaware,
And still debating amid my waiting
   This spinning, I said, is part my share.

The dews were falling, the birds were calling,
    The wheel was quiet beside the door,
    The dusky sunshine drowsed on the floor,
    And her snowy thread was done;
My eyes were holden, nor gloom, nor golden
    Answered if I had lost or won.

From out the shadow like lark on meadow,
    Eyes entranced with their grace devine,
    Half hiding their tender light from mine
    Till my kisses set her free;
O, love this winning comes of thy spinning;
    Thou hast twisted the thread for thee and me.

RED-BEAKED BIRD AND PASSION FLOWER.

BY A. DURYEE.

In a legend, quaint and old,
    Runs this touching story,
When in hanging on the Cross,
    Bled our Lord of Glory.

Cruel the nails that pierced thro'
    Hands and feet so tender,
Cruel the heartless, gibing sneers
    Those in passing render.

Then a bird in pity flew
    To that body lowly,
Tried the nails with beak to take
    From the limbs so holy.

Thus a feeling artist wrought
    Bird with passion flowers,
Linking legend of the past
    To present world of ours.

MY TREASURE.

BY MRS. CHARLES EICHHORN.

'Tis only a little picture
  A girlish face and fair,
With dreamy eyes down drooping
  And wealth of golden hair.

Yet it has power to charm me
  And hold my senses fast,
Till I quite forget the present,
  In the magic spell of the past.

'Tis only a little picture
  That I see through blinding tears,
When I lift it from the casket
  That has guarded it for years.

But it tells a life's sad story
  Of love and promised bliss,
But life and love have faded
  And left me only this.

But this, a faded picture,
  And memories bitter sting,
Of all the wild hopes cherished
  When life was in its spring.

Ah ! the future cheats us ever
  And mocks at our despair,
When time has laid in ruins,
  Our castles in the air.

IN MEMORIAM.

BY ELMIRA J. FENNER.

Death comes to all ! To one with slow advances
   And to another with a swift embrace
   And this were, sure, by far, the friendlier grace,
To one who met the world with open glances.
Firm hand and valient heart ; no look askance
   Had pleased him like this greeting, face to face.
   If death must surely come. Nor need to trace
A fairer record ; years could not enhance
The simple grandeur, and the steady lights
   That shine to-day above his open grave.
   A conscience true as is the pole-star's ray,
A mind whose best endeavor aided right ;
   A heart as tender as it e'er was brave,
   A life kept useful to its latest day.

SONNET.

The day is passed when roses bloomed for me,
And lilies offered up their cups of gold
Filled with rich sweetness more than they could hold ;
And pansy's velvet leaves seemed made to fold
A thought intense and silent, that set free
Would fill the summer with its ecstasy ;
And yet 'twas sweeter that it lived untold
Looking from out the pansy's eyes at me :
But now the pansy and the thought are dead !
And my sweet summer, erst so warm and bright,
Died in the cold and darkness yester-night :
And winter's coming mocks my fear and dread,
Laying his icy touch on heart and head,
And leaving there his stillness, and his blight.

AS WE APPEAR TO OTHERS.

BY ISOBEL H. FLOYD.

In America we would call it a "boarding house," a place where the great army of the unhoused can have food and shelter, when, for reasons too numerous to mention, they do not care to put up at a hotel. In Dresden there are many of these places, and this one where our four Americans stayed is a fair sample of the class.

We secured in this "pension" three rooms, two bed-rooms, and a salon on the ground floor—parterre they call it—at the following rates: Two adults at 6 marks apiece per day, two children at 5 marks each per day. A mark is about 23 cents in American money. This included three meals as follows: Breakfast: coffee, bread and butter, and eggs; dinner: soup, two courses, fish and meat, vegetables and compot, desert and coffee; supper: either cold cuts of meat, tongue, ham and salad, or some warm side-dish, potatoes in some shape, bread and butter, and tea. Lamp in each room, 1 mark per week extra. Breakfast served in room for four persons per week, 1 mark extra. Good service included. Our rooms were well-furnished, good beds, every comfort, and a lengthy stay proved the meals to be most excellent. We give these figures to show the difference between the rates of any of our big American cities and those of Dresden. About a dollar and a half a day apiece, the best rooms in the house, in the heart of the city.

These transients were all of the well-to-do traveling tourist army, and we saw so many of our own countrymen and women that we began to understand at last why unfeeling foreigners do not admire us as a nation, why they object to our little peculiarities. What we formerly set down to prejudice, we now humbly acknowledge was only a simple statement of facts, and what we

took for narrow-minded criticism, we sadly concede was only too
true ! We have had rich Americans at the Pension Wahr from all
parts of the United States, and truth compels us to say that only
a very small per cent. of these behaved in a way to reflect credit
upon us as a nation of civilized and cultivated people! Americans
from New York, Boston, Philadelphia, St Louis, and ever alas !
from Chicago, were one and all, loud, boastful, rude, flippant, or
arrogant, according to their age and station. Our sparkling,
bright young girls,—and they did sparkle at times, both with
diamonds and with wit—were slangy and inconsiderate. Our
husbands and brothers were boastful and egotistical. Our wives
and mothers were pretentious, not dignified, and our children
were forward, and too self-assured. All nations have their weak
points, but our bad one is particularly bad, because it is so ob-
trusive.

We might sum it up in this and say we are "too loud." We
speak too loud, we dress too loud, we act too loud, we live too
loud. We want to be heard. Even if we have to yell to be
heard above our neighbors, we must be noticed. Well-bred
persons shudder at our war-whoop, and under their breath murmur unpleasant things about the American savage, but that
doesn't stop us, we go right on and do the same thing over
again.

Just then the old French woman who spoke good English
asked of the mother from Washington : "Is it true, madame,
that people in America of a certain station or class wear a dis-
tinctive robe, as do the German peasants?"

"Not that I ever heard of," replied Mrs. Brown. "What
makes you ask that?"

"Only zat I see on Prager-strasse so many American ladies
with blue cloth costume, and the sailor hat—old and young—all
alike—so many. I think, pairhaps, it is a national costume, n'est-
ce pas?"

"Certainly not !" answered Mrs. Brown, flushing angrily.
"I don't see how you could have thought such a thing. Some
of us do wear such a rig, perhaps, in traveling, but no one knows
better how to dress than we Americans."

Of our particular four Americans, Bub—was the only one whose irrepressible volubility we feared at the table—but, we had not done justice to his young level head. All through the meal he behaved with supernatural quietness, speaking only when spoken to, and generally covering himself with credit. Afterwards the colonel said to him : "What was the matter with you at dinner, Bub? Didn't you feel well?"

With his hands in his pockets, our boy replied : "Yes, well enough ! But those kind of Américans make me tired ! If I ever grow up to be like that, I wish you'd drown me, and don't go in mourning for me afterwards !"

MAMMA'S KISSES.

BY ALICE E. FABENS.

A kiss when I wake in the morning,
    A kiss when I go to bed,
A kiss when I burn my fingers,
    A kiss when I bump my head.

A kiss when my bath is over,
    A kiss when my bath begins ;
Mamma is as full of kisses,
    As nurse is full of pins.

A kiss when I play with my rattle,
    A kiss when I pull her hair :
She covered me over with kisses
    The day I fell from the stair.

A kiss when I give her trouble,
    A kiss when I give her joy:
There is nothing like mamma's kisses
    For her own little baby boy.

HEART BLOSSOMS.

BY ROSAMOND C. FOSTER CRANFORD.

"Oh, dear! It does seem as if everything went wrong to-day! And Elsie curled herself up on the sofa, and began to weep without restraint.

Quite natural and woman-like, you say. Quite human, I I think.

But it was a strange sight to see Gertrude Hamil standing by the side of her dearest companion, and not offering one word of consolation; yet there she stood quietly, a grand and grace-ful young woman, and it was so odd of her that another overflow came from the salt depths, as Elsie exclaimed:

"I really don't believe you care at all, Gert. Hamil, whether I break my heart or not, and I—I—," she faltered, and said no more, for her head was pillowed on Gertrude's shoulder, and Gertrude was telling her this:

"Yes, Elsie, I should care; and I know, too, why you are feeling so badly. Your mother said, as I came in, that she felt as if she needed you this summer, and could not afford to allow you to accompany us to Chicago. I am, indeed, very sorry; and I am sure you believe it. I did want you to go with the rest of us so much. But I've been thinking, Elsie, and I know what you can do."

Elsie half raised her head, questioningly, and then back it fell.

"Yes, I am quite sure you can do it," continued Gertrude. "You know you hope to go to college in the fall and have so coveted the necessary books. Now I, while I am away, will loan you my books and you shall study, which you love to do. And with other duties and plenty of rest you will be far better pre-pared, doubtless, than we shall be after our chase over the states. But I'll see you again to-morrow, Elsie."

So saying, Gertrude departed, leaving behind her a slightly comforted, but much injured young person; for vacation studies, even to a student, were hardly to be compared to a trip to the great exposition.

Elsie remained some time in her cozy room before she could face her nearest kin with a pleasant spirit. She had made up her mind to be contented—a great effort, was it not? And months after, when she had succeeded, she gave me permission to tell it. It is a pretty story, and I long to have you know it. But first, will you stir up the soil of your own hearts? For I want you to plant at least one good seed after you have finished reading this.

That night, really memorable to Elsie, she planted heart seeds; and in less than a week she blossomed. We all saw— actually saw the blossoms. She commenced in this way: she resolved to smile on all possible occasions, and it came about that she began at the tea-table. And could you believe it? in a few minutes, all were smiling, and all felt as though they were in an orange grove. Everything went so smoothly that week; and then, two little blossoms came out at each corner of her mouth. How pretty she was!

The next blossom came when she had forgotten herself in thinking of others. So Elsie kept on gaining and growing daily, and at the end of that year all could see or feel the outcome of those numberless grand seeds which she had planted and cultivated during the year. I need not tell you that Elsie's summer vacation was a glorious success. Of course she failed sometimes; we all do. But if good seed is once planted in our heart gardens; if it is carefully watched and tenderly cared for it can be trusted to bring forth good fruit. Some seeds, you know, fell by the wayside, but those that fell into good ground brought forth fruit, "Some an hundred fold, some sixty and some thirty fold."

THE SHIELD OF EXPECTATION.

BY JOSEPHINE FOLSOM.

In the legends of the Northland—
Of the land of Thor and Frigga,
Land of frost, and fire and tempest,
From whence sprung the mystic Eddas—
Many a gem of hidden meaning
Lurks amid the weird traditions
Of the strife 'twixt gods and giants
On the ancient hills of Asgard.

In a song of mighty Odin—
Odin, God of Winds and Tempests,
God of Mind and Inspiration—
There we read these words of wisdom:
"Man himself must yield to Nature,
Must lay down the sword of conquest,
But the fame of him who conquers
Never dies, but lives forever."

Hence, in wars of late ages,—
Ages when the Vikings flourished,
Ages dark with strife and bloodshed—
When a warrior won a victory
On his shield was graved his record—
Records of his deeds of valor;
Thus his fame if he but conquered,
Could not die but lived forever.

When a youth went forth to battle
All untried but strong and hopeful,
Full of bold anticipations
Of the foes whom he would vanquish,
From the old men, skilled in warfare,
He received a smooth, white buckler

Called the " Shield of Expectation."
His to bear through deadly combat,
His to grave with glowing record,
His to hang in Odin's temple,
That his fame, when he had conquered
Might not die but live forever.

Let us gird our armor closer,
Firmer grasp our burnished weapons,
Take our righteousness a breastplate;
Girt with truth, with gospel sandals,
With the helmet of salvation,
And the sword of Scripture teaching,
Keen, two-edged, and failing never;
Thus shall we go forth unflinching,
Victories win henceforth forever.

Still our armor is not perfect.
Still we lack a sure protection—
Lack a shield which, tried and proven,
Quencheth fiery darts of evil.
From our fathers, who have triumphed
Ages past as fire-winged martyrs,
We receive our shield and buckler,
Faith in Christ, our only Saviour,
Whom we know, once having suffered,
Rose again, and reigns in heaven.

Who is he that overcometh
But the soul that firm believeth
In the Son of God Immortal ?
In our Hope and Expectation ?
In the mansions of " our Father "
He is waiting to award us
Crowns of life and crowns of glory,
Crowns of righteousness eternal.
Saved from death, by faith victorious,
We shall reign with Him forever.

AN EDITORIAL EXCURSION.

JUNE, 1891.

BY MRS. CHARLES H. FOLWELL.

The annual trip of the New Jersey Editorial Association came off last week, and as children with new toys, the last always seem the best, so it is with those who participate in these very popular and enjoyable jaunts.

Monday, 10.15 A. M., June 22d, was the time, and Broad Street Station, Philadelphia, was the place for the rendezvous. Washington was reached at 2 o'clock, and the tourists promptly transferred to Willard's Hotel, where they were quartered for the night. Tuesday morning found the members ready and willing to turn their backs on the famous old hotel, with a lingering sense that its palmy days were over, and the most that remained to it was the reputation it had won in the times that are past.

From nine in the morning to six in the evening the excursionists sped down through "Old Virginny." On leaving Washington we crossed the historical Long Bridge over which our defeated and demoralized soldiers retreated after the disastrous encounter at Bull's Run, and found ourselves on the "Sacred Soil." The train halted a moment at Alexandria, and from the numbers of the unwashed that appeared there, and all along the route, we conclude that the negroes have not all emigrated North. We passed over the battle ground of Manassas, but scarcely a trace is left of the ravages of war; past Rappahannock and Culpepper, names familiar to the boys in blue; we reached Charlottesville and entered the beautiful Piedmont valley.

As an agricultaral country this portion of Virginia would hardly impress one fresh from Burlington County as being a success; there was very little corn, and that scarcely as advanced as with us; not much grain, and little hay, it was a question as to what supported the inhabitants, yet there were cabins and small towns all along the way; they could hardly live on the scenery, but that grew so grand and impressive as we approached the Allegheny mountains that we forgot about corn and potatoes and were content to enjoy the surrounding beauties.

It was all so peaceful and restful after the long day's ride, and the spacious rooms and wide piazzas and verandas were most inviting. The hotel with its rows of pillars, its worn floors and general air of old-time grandeur, together with the entire absence of an elevator of any kind impressed one with its primitiveness ; fortunately it was but three stories in height, so the guests were able to mount the stairs without much discomfort.' It was rather a surprise when we learned that the oldest portion of the building was only erected in 1857, and has since been added to until now it will accommodate 750 guests ; in addition there are about a hundred cottages on the grounds where families are lodged, taking their meals at the hotel. An effort is now being made to form a company and buy the whole property, selling 10,000 shares of stock at $100 each. The celebrated sulphur water was duly sampled by the New Jersey tourists with varied results, some being made quiet sick, while others pronounced it quite beneficial. The warm baths were tried by some of the party and voted a luxury ; others took in the drives, and as the delegates from Mt. Holly have a faculty for selecting something enjoyable, they did not make a mistake in choosing the drive.

Some of them got as far as Lewisburg, the county seat of Greenbriar Co., twelve miles distant ; it is a quaint old town that looks now just as it did before the war, with records that date back nearly a century, and was then written out by the oldest inhabitant in anticipation of his death, as he alone possessed all the facts of the early settlement of the county in his memory. This interesting data together with much other valuable information was ferreted out by our enterprising Prosecutor, who seems to have a natural drawing towards court houses and musty documents. The majority of the Mt. Hollyans contented themselves with going as far as Greenbriar River and fording in the carriages. It is about two hundred yaads wide with a stony bottom and the water reaches to the hub of the wagon wheels and is clear as crystal. On the bank stands a monster buttonwood, that two of the party succeeded in measuring, and the girth was fourteen feet. In the course of the nine miles over to the river a number of smaller streams were passed and all forded, a novel experience to our citizens ; and a prominent lawyer in the party remarked if Burlington County left the driving public to get through the creeks in that way our bridge bill would not be so heavy—a gratuitous suggestion to the Freeholders.

During the two days spent at the Springs, a small party visited the Natural Bridge, but as it was an all-day trip many who would gone feared the fatigue, and contented themselves with the quiet entertainments around the hotel. And just here can be added, the talent of our town was not slow in being recognized and was pressed into service, both for vocal and instrumental music.

Friday morning saw the delegates on their way to Luray, and many were the regrets among the younger part of the company at leaving White Sulphur.

It was a long but interesting ride through a portion of the Shenandoah valley, and that part of Virginia which is inviting capitalists to enter and possess the land. Basic City, at the junction of the Chesapeake and Ohio railroad with the Norfolk and Western, has made tremendous strides in the past year and a half; it now has a magnificent hotel, the Brandon, surrounded by beautiful grounds; more companies for developing the various resources of that section than we can name, extensive brick plants, car works, machine shops, etc., and it would seem as if Northern enterprise had taken possession of that locality in earnest. There are many other places being graded and laid out in town plots on the line of the railroad, and the old air of southern inactivity is relegated to the past.

The travelers were a pretty tired lot when Luray was reached at four o'clock, but the waiting dinner was quickly dispatched, and those who intended to visit the cave were promptly on hand. This feature of the trip simply surpasses our powers of description; those who have seen it are content to picture it for themselves, those who have not we advise to lose no opportunity of seeing it. It is a marvelous production of nature, and makes one believe this old earth is still a Wonderland. The Inn at Luray is very attractive and a most desirable place to spend a week or a month, and barring some dissatisfaction with the table service, the party were greatly pleased. The management certainly can improve on the way in which the guests are waited upon in the dining-room.

Saturday morning at seven o'clock the tourists were scheduled to leave on the homeward journey, and a special train of Pennsylvania railroad cars was sent to that point to convey them back to Philadelphia by the way of the Shenandoah and Cumberland valleys to Harrisburg. More historical ground was passed, of interest as connected with our Revolutionary War as well as with the War of the Rebellion. And from Harrisburg to Philadelphia the beautiful farming lands of Pennsylvania, with the magnificent fields of grain already in stacks or awaiting the reaper, and the great barns which completely overshadow the dwelling houses, were all noted as the train sped on. As we neared Philadelphia the good-byes began, many parting not to meet again for another twelve month. There is always a feeling of regret when these Editorial reunions come to a close, the regret that it is ending and not just beginning. From Broad street station, which was reached at four o'clock, each member directed his own way homeward, and the thirty-fifth Editorial Excursion was at an end.

LIFE AND POEMS OF MARY FENN.

Mary Fenn was born in the village of Clarendon, Orleans County, New York, on July 17th, 1824, and was therefore exactly sixty-two years and a few hours old when her death took place. Her parents were Chauncey Robinson and Damaris Fenn, plain but superior people, who followed farming, reared a large family of children and died at a good old age. Mr. Robinson was a man of rare intellectual endowment, however, and being a strong advocate of temperance reform, contributed vigorous articles to the local press on that and the leading political topics of the time. He died about twelve years ago. In her childhood Mrs. Fenn attended the village school at Holley, three miles distant, and at the age of sixteen entered the celebrated Ingham University at Leroy, New York, from which she was graduated with honors in 1846. In the same year she was married to Prof. Samuel G. Love, a teacher in Buffalo. Domestic infelicity lead to a separation after they had been eight years married. In 1855 she was married to Andrew Jackson Davis, with whom she lived happily for twenty-nine years. Again was she fated to become divorced, the second time through the act of her companion in taking advantage of a legal technicality by means of which the marriage was annulled. This blow was more than her gentle spirit could bear, and she died within a year afterward. She had assumed her mother's maiden-name (Fenn).

Mrs. Fenn's literary work began in 1859, when, in association with her husband, Davis, she conducted the *Herald of Progress*, then published in New York City, which was continued for about five years. Meantime she contributed poetical and prose articles to other current periodicals. Her residence, covering a period of nearly thirty years, was in Orange, New Jersey.

Mrs. Fenn is one of the few women who have won for themselves a national reputation, she being widely known for her literary work and her advocacy of woman's rights. In this latter work she was prominently identified with Susan B. Anthony, Elizabeth Cady Stanton and Lillie Devereaux Blake, who were among her dearest friends. She was for many years a member of Sorosis and a prominent member of the Woman's Club of Orange and regularly attended its meetings until her health failed. Mrs. Fenn was also a member of the American Akademe, and was recently elected Vice-President of the Alumni Association of Ingram University. Personally she was of an amiable, affectionate and sympathetic nature, ever forgetful of self. She at all times stood ready to champion the weak and down-trodden. Her poetical writings, though fragmentary, have been recognized and received as among the best contributions to the poetical literature of the day.

Her last published poem, which appeared in a local newspaper in June, 1886, just five weeks before her death, is here appended:

AFTER THE STORM.

At night, the sky was black with sullen clouds,
    In swaying torrents fell the hoarded rain;
The lightning's flash revealed the misty shrouds
    Of wind-swept trees writhing as if in pain.

At morn, the blackness vanished from the sky,
    O'er the glad meadows golden sunlight poured,
Leaves glanced, flowers bloomed, bright song-birds
        floated by,
    And far and fair the infinite heaven soared.

O heart on which the bitter blast has blown,
    On which at dead of night the lightning fell;
O human heart, appalled, bereft, and lorne,
    While waves of anguish darkly surge and swell.—

Let the storm rage, nor fear its turbulent roar,
    Though sorrow's whirlwind bow thee to the dust,
Round thee are sheltering arms unfelt before,
    And thou shalt rise into diviner trust.

Peace lies in wait for thee, grief-stricken one !
Morning shall dawn, and soft airs fan thy brow;
And rays will reach thee from the Eternal Sun,
Turning to good the ills that pain thee now.

Trust in the Love Divine that circles thee,
And on thy heart will drop its healing balm,
Till sweeter than thy dreams of Heaven shall be,
After the storm, the spirit's inner calm.

"SILENCE TO THE LORD." *

BY E. M. GIFFORD.

Art thou tired, oh, so tired,
Thou would's beneath the green turf lie?
Art thou so weary of this life
And all its cares, thou will not try
To let the heav'nly light shine through ?

Dost thou not know of that sweet rest,
That perfect " silence to the Lord,"
Which asks of thee, no strength of thine,
Not e'en to frame a single word,
Yet will thy fainting heart, renew?

'Tis not " the last ; " God ne'er forsakes
The soul which trembling rests on Him ;
He only asks for faith and love ;
Christ took the burden, care and sin,
And bought this " rest " for you.

* Marginal reading of Psalm xxxviii, 7.

FIRST PRESBYTERIAN CHURCH, MORRISTOWN, N. J.

THE FIRST EXPERIENCE OF A YOUNG TEACHER.

BY HANNAH E. FABENS.

The anniversary of my birthday had arrived. I was of age (in New Jersey) at eighteen, and had come into possession of my property—nothing; had also selected my "speah;" I was to become a school teacher. I had already accepted a position in a public school. How proud I had been to talk about it for months beforehand. But at last, when it came to leaving, and it proved to be a stormy day, I think the family found it as stormy inside the house as out. I can remember how, at last, my brother and I rushed boldly out into the storm—for he was to go with me, to remain until Monday, I being obliged to go on Saturday, in order to be in time to open school on Monday. I had on a hat trimmed with green—a most appropriate color—and by the time I reached my boarding place, my face was stained with green; and as it had been growing longer and for every mile that we had come, altogether I was disconsolate-looking, indeed.

We had not been able to reach there until about dinner-time. The dinner was a stiff affair until the dessert, when some dates were passed around. They seemed rather stale, and after eating a few, Mrs. Smith said: "I am sure I don't see what Mr. Jones made such a fuss about their being so che—nice for." At that my brother and I both laughed outright, and after that we were on a more easy footing. My face began to shorten materially, and spirits to rise proportionally, so that by the time my brother left on Monday, I was quite my usual self.

Monday morning came all too soon. I had made myself look as hideous as possible, by arranging my hair in a coil, although I had always before worn it in flowing ringlets. I also suspended round my neck a pair of eye-glasses, useless except for their

18

weight of added dignity, and started for the school-house. I found back of the church, as I had been directed—a little red wooden house with whitewashed walls and blue desks—patriotic, at least. The chair of state on the platform was mine. It was the happy possessor of three legs. Table there was none, but a stove which stood by the platform served me for that purpose. I placed my books upon it, at the same time noticing that there was a fire ready to light—prepared by some considerate boy, thought I—for the mornings were cool, it being only the first of October.

Before school closed I was made aware of the reason for the preparation of that fire, by the smell of burnt paper, and upon investigating, found only the covers of my books, and these in a smouldering condition. My boys had thought of that to escape the rest of the lessons; but, thanks to my normal training, I could get along about as well without a book; so the lessons for the day went on, and I determined to keep a close watch on the little fellows and be prepared for their tricks in the future.

We opened school by chanting the prayer and repeating in concert the Twenty-third Psalm, and singing, "I want to be an angel," to several original tunes. The one I started surprised me. At the best of times I cannot sing, and without anything to lead me, it was truly astonishing, the direction which the tune took.

I tried to write a sort of temporary roll, but as all the boys had agreed to have the same name—"Tom Smart"—I gave up the roll and concluded to call them all "Johnnie," or "That boy." Their ages were rather vague; some of them were "eleven, going on seven," they said. One very little boy said he was "months old."

We went immediately to work on the recitations of the day. My plans were good. For the very little ones I expected at first, to draw a picture to represent the words they were required to spell. The representations for boy, cat, dog, cow, house, and such common objects, were a success. One word in the book was "coat." Without any misgiving I drew the coat, and called

on John number one to spell. "C-o-a-t, shirt," he promptly responded.

Almost overcome with laughter, I turned to the blackboard
and put two pockets on this ambiguous object, and called on
John number two to spell. "C-o-a-t, coat" he responded, in
tones of thunder. "Correct," said I, "but could you not lower
your voice? we are none of us deaf." We were not deaf, but,
alas! he was. However, I finally succeeded in making him
understand my request, to which he readily acceded by spelling
in a voice which one would have thought came from his shoes,
it was so low. He was one of my well-dressed boys; most of
them wore no shoes. My most elaborately-dressed pupil wore a
pair of hose, with the worn-out feet cut off, so that they looked
like wristers on his limbs, and trousers that had originally belonged to his father, but had been cut off to make them a suitable length, and were now all seat, reaching to his ankles; and he
shared his hat with his brother, he taking the crown and his
brother the brim.

These peculiarities of dress were most of them pointed out
to me by my visitors. If they looked neat that was all I wanted.
Clean hands and faces were an exception, for the first few weeks,
at which I did not wonder, when I noticed in recess that quite a
number of the more fortunate ones had brought molasses candy.
One little boy, seized with an unaccountable fit of generosity,
offered his seat mate a bite, saying, "Taste it; only two cents
an ounce, and wo'th it, too."

As soon as recess was over, I found I was to be besieged
with questions, most of them taking the form of "Dares't I leave
the room teacher?" "Dares't I take a drink teacher?" etc. By
changing the order of lessons, and introducing some new exercises, such as rapid adding (the adjective inapplicable in this
case, however), I found they soon forgot their desire to leave the
room. This was proved by one little boy, who had seemed to
think his case so urgent that he had begun to cry when the lesson was finished, rubbing his eyes in order to squeeze forth some
more tears, saying, "O dear! what was I crying about?" Their
manner of addressing me as "teacher" became so monotonous,

after a few weeks, that I almost wished I could change my occupation to a boot-black, or anything, that they might vary my
professional title somewhat.

These little boys, with whom I have been associated about a
year, are some of them the brightest I ever met. One day, in
school, wishing them to pay close attention to their lessons, I
said: "Now, I want each one of you to put his eye on his book
and think of nothing but his lesson." I was not a little amused
to see one little boy put his book up against his eye. I found I
must be careful how I framed my sentences for him. When he
is naughty and has to be detained after school; at recess he
selects some good scholar and persuades him that teacher has
taken his name, and that he will have to stay after school. He
probably believes in the old axiom, "Misery loves company."

These little boys manifest their affection for me by constantly bringing gifts, such as they would appreciate themselves
—little china dolls, rubber balls, pop-guns and eatables—eggs
raw and cooked, tomatoes, fruit and quantities of flowers. I
never liked to accept these gifts, and always when I could pre-
vail upon the children to take them; would give them back at
the close of the school, partly because I had my doubts as to
their being honestly obtained (I have recently read in the paper
an account of baby thieves, in which is mentioned two children
between the ages of seven and nine who had been arrested for
theft, and it was said their first thievish acts were those of taking
slyly fruits and flowers for their teacher), and partly because I
thought they needed them more themselves, inasmuch as during
recess, one day, while I was eating an apple, one of the little
boys looked up and raising his hand, said : "Teacher, give me
that apple when you get done with it."

It seemed to be a sort of second nature with some of the
children to preface all remarks, even when not in school, by raising their hands, and this little boy was one of them. Always
when we met in the street, and he said "Good morning," his
little hand would go up first. I suspect he thought it was a
mark of respect, such as touching the hat by gentlemen, and I

doubt if he had any hat to touch. He probably thought raising the hand was used in the absence of a hat.

The ignorance of the parents of some of these boys was truly deplorable. For the first week or two we tried sending home notes to the parents, reporting on the conduct of their children at school. One little boy always took home a good note, and invariably brought a reply from his parents, signed in this way: "I beat him well, Peter Jones." Perhaps some one wrote it for him and signed it so, or told him that was the common way. Another one used to sign, " and oblige his parent, John Brown & Co." The writing and spelling were truly original. We thought our efforts in this direction were not appreciated, so the note-system was abolished, and the teachers were requested to call on their pupils.

I well remember my first call. It was on my largest girl. I knocked at the door of quite a neat-looking house for that section of the city, and on being requested to come in, I entered, and encountered Lena's mother, a large German woman, who, without any introduction whatever, placed me in the most awkward position by exclaiming : "You come to play with my Lena; she haf gone to work." I finally made her understand my position, when she was overwhelming in her attentions. There were three or four children in a clothes-basket in one corner of the room, probably put there to be out of the way ; and she called on Otto to get up and give to his teacher one chair. The next morning Otto and Lena came to school, each bearing a shoe. The pair, they said, was sent by their mother, because " They haf learn so much." Although I did not feel much encouraged about them then, I have since ; especially as they took the highest prizes in school at the close of the term, which showed that they must have had a desire to learn, as they had to compete with children who were much better acquainted with the English language.

Besides the prizes awarded at the close of the term, each pupil in the class was presented with a little gift. In my class they were favored with a package of torpedoes to celebrate the Fourth of July, which they did most effectually, I have

since learned.   One remarkable little boy, of an economical
frame of mind, has used one a day ; his will probably last until
we meet again.

— — — —

VISIONS.

BY LIZZIE E. FABENS.

There's a voice that's ever with me—
　　A voice so soft and mild :
'Tis the voice of my lost darling,
　　My angel, cherub child.

There's a little form that greets me
　　Ever at dawn of day:
'Tis the form of my lost idol,
　　Forever passed away.

There's a little grave where daisies
　　Look brightest in the spring ;
Where the robins come in summer,
　　And music round them fling.

And there my little darling sleeps
　　Low in a narrow bed ;
And I grieve and grieve forever
　　For my boy lying dead.

Ah, me ! there's a form celestial,
　　Wearing a crown of gold ;
It is calling me to heaven,
　　To join the happy fold.

O kind and merciful Father !
　　When will the moment come
When I can close my eyes in death,
　　And say, " Thy will be done ? "

WILD FLOWERS.

BY MRS. MARY FOREST—JENNIE NETTLES.

I l'oe the bonnie wild flowers,
   They've aye a wondrous spell,
That gars o'or thochts gae wanderin back
   Tae some auld mossy dell,
Some heich green knowe, or bonnie glen,
   An' aye my heart grows wae ;
Oh whaur are they that pu'd wi' me,
   Wild flowers the lee lang day.

Whiles daunderin' by some lane burnside,
   For hearts untouched by care,
We twined the wee forget-me-not,
   Wi' starry gowans fair,
An' speeled the auld hills rugged side,
   Mang wealth o' yellow broom,
O'er necks bedecked wi' sloes an' ha's,
   O'er heids wi' sweet briar bloom.

We skilipid barefit through the fields,
   Whaur scarlet poppies grew,
An' pu'd the cowslip frae its bed,
   Wi' petals drooked in dew.
Or searched the gloomy plantain's shade,
   Ilk howe an' flowry vale,
For Scotland's pride, the sweet blue bell,
   An' modest primrose pale.

Nae cultured flowers, hooever fair,
   Can touch the slumberin strings,
Nor life note o' the spirit wake,
   Whaur memory's minstrel clings.
Sae while the warm bluid rins I'll l'oe,
   Auld Nature's sweet wild flowers,
They speek o' forms wha shared wi' me,
   Blythe childhoods happy hours.

CARNIVAL WEEK IN SAMANA.

BY LOVE F. FABENS.

As Samana Bay and Santo Domingo are among the matters now "on the tapis" a little sketch of the manner in which Carnival was passed here might not come amiss. On the first day, which was Sunday, the bells rang gayly in the morning like marriage chimes. But church bells here are not like those in New York and Boston. They consist of three, suspended to a beam of wood, which at a distance resemble a gallows. Either a little boy, or in the absence of a little boy, the priest himself strikes on them with a hammer, slowly or quickly as the case may seem to require. Soon after the ringing of the bells, the people assembled in the church, and as we passed by it our way to the Protestant chapel, we could hear distinctly the priest intoming and the murmuring responses of the people. In the afternoon, at about four o'clock, a drum beat to call out all who chose to mask themselves, and they soon made their appearance on the plaza, where they danced until the drummers started for a march around the town. Then they and a horde of children as spectators, followed, stopping and dancing in whatever house they might be invited to enter. In the evening there were balls for the masqueraders, and the fandango was danced until late in night. On Monday the inagruation of the new Governor took place, but not being one of the privileged sex, I was not permitted to witness the ceremony.

Tuesday, "Madri Gras," was the last day of the Carnival. So the masqueraders appeared again in full force. At the close of the day the masks are all burned, with the exception of the wire ones, which are probably preserved for future use. On Wednesday, (Ash Wednesday) there were Lenten services. On Thursday, an exception was made to the usual rule of solemn service at the church in favor of the celebration of Domincian

Independence from the Haytian despotism. All officers of the Government attended the church en masse. As we were invited to be present we participated to the extent of listening. After the services the officers, accompanied by the Government guard, visited the heads of the several departments. When they reached the office of the Amercican Governor the populace were so anxious to see and salute him that the captain of the Guard, a burly colored man, lifted him bodily from the floor and held him aloft on his shoulder and that of his next neighbor, while a fife and drum played and the people shouted and cheered. The Governor's son, the Vice-commercial Agent. was then called for but he declined to be scrutinized in that manner and so noisily saluted. In the afternoon the masqueraders, improving the privilege of the day. again came out upon the plaza, running, dancing and cutting all sorts of capers, to the great alarm of some of the little colored children who stand in awe of the "Mardigras" as they call them. I had almost forgotten one little incident which occurred during the Carnival. As we were sitting at dinner one day I felt a trembling of the floor which I thought was caused by the trotting foot of my nearest neighbor, but when I discovered that his feet were perfectly still I supposed that the dog must be demonstratively showing his affection by furiously wagging his tail, finding however that there was no dog around, I could not imagine what was the matter concluding that it was a whitewash man in the near vicinity who in brushing shook our house for I certainly was being shaken, until a neighbor who called in the evening, inquired if we felt the earthquake and then I knew that we had lived through a real earthquake, but not so damaging in its effects as they sometimes are in tropical regions. Still it was sufficiently perceptible to one unaccustomed to such sensations.

ROMANCE OF A DROP OF WATER.

BY VICTORIA A. GONZALES.

My first recollection is that of being dashed violently into the Atlantic, and tossing madly about for hours in a darkness worse than Egyptian.

After what seemed to me an eternity, the waters that my lot had been cast with gradually subsided into a more peaceful state. During the elemental tumult, the only glimpse of light that I caught was from a foundering ship, as I dashed over its deck. Soon after this event, the pall of darkness that had enveloped us, changed to gray. I say us, because I learned in this, my first night with the sea, that it was made up of countless drops, like myself.

At first the knowledge bewildered me, and I feared that I should wholly lose my identity. But if I lost any of my component parts—they were so quickly replaced, that I did not miss them.

Ere long the brightness of the noon-day sun, so dazzled me, that I felt deeply thankful when some unknown power bore me steadily down among corals, shells, sea-anemones, and the slimy greenness of the lower deep. Rest soon restored my equilibrium, and I drifted slowly about, observing the weird wonders of the place; until (I rested at the base of a pink Sagartie), looking in amazement at a green Sea-Rease that held a lobster firmly clasped in its serpent-like tentacles.

I now congratulated myself upon being so small that nothing could harm me ; and for my power to glide about among sea-wonders, filling my head with knowledge, and not be caught like the unfortunate lobster. Just at this moment a school of herring dashed by me, pursued by a shark, which voraciously swallowed some dozens of them and myself as well, but after the manner of fish, it cast me forth again. So thankful was I for my escape that I made my way with what speed I could to the upper manes, resolved to bear patiently, any amount of jostling, but never of my free-will to again go down into the basement of the ocean. Above, all was placid, and I looked about for something to amuse me.

Close by, coming from the East, was a vessel of the White Star Line. My heart swelled with pride at the thought that my atom of strength would help to bear valuable merchandise, and more valuable living freight to their port. And when the "Adriatic" ploughed majestically by my companions and myself, dimpled and danced gleefully in its wake. I had become attached to my ocean life, yet one day the sun with a burning kiss drew me up into the air as a part of a white cloud.

I floated gaily about finding life more enjoyable than it was before my translation. With moon and stars above me by night, blue sky and glorious sun by day, and beneath me the ever varying landscape; oh! I was never weary of my aerial home—moreover my changing beauty was something to make me glad—for I was white by day, crimson and golden at sunset, purple black by night, edged with most brilliant silver.

One day when my spirits were hilarious, I discovered that the lower part of the cloud to which I belonged was no longer white, but a steely gray; and the shadow was gradually creeping upward.

I glared down into a lake over which I was passing and saw my face grow ashy-hued.

But I had no time to lament over my lost beauty, for a current of air drove us en-masse into a bank of clouds that had suddenly made their appearance above the western horizon.

I was wondering what new misfortunes were in store for me, when a fearful flash of lightning shot athwart the sky, followed by a deafening thunder-peal.

Blinded—I was driven headlong through space. I drifted down, down, for a time and then abruptly stopped in a state of agitation. I had fallen to the earth in one of Nature's hysterics.

—a summer-shower. A breeze that had kissed white poppies, passed over and soothed me.

My new home was the chalice of a lily. The storm passed quickly—winds sweeping the clouds into the eastern sky, while the sun gave prismatic colors to every rain-drop. For a moment I was envious, but consoled myself with the thought that even their gorgeous coloring could not prevent their falling; and being absorbed by the dark earth. Suddenly my fragrant habitation trembled. A brilliant humming bird was drawing sweets from its center. I feared that the feathered jewel would devour me; but it flashed away suddenly and I was unharmed. How long I lay in my scented chalice I know not; as I fell into a deep sleep—in my dreams I heard the rustle of fairies' wings, as the children of the night danced and sung upon the green. This was their song.

> " Our palace standeth in the air,
> By necromancy so placed there
> That it no tempest need to fear,
>   Which may around it blow.
> It standeth southward tow'rd the noon,
> Where lies a path up to the moon,
> And thence the fairy can as soon
>   Pass to the earth below.
>
> The walls of spiders' legs are made,
> Well mortised and finely laid ;
> He was the master of his trade
>   Who curiously it builded.
> The windows are the eyes of cats,
> And on the roof, instead of slats,
> Are deftly laid the skins of bats,
>   With moonshine that are gilded."

When I awoke I found myself on a velvety lawn ; from which the sun again drew me into the air. But I took no pleasure in this my second aerial flight, expecting soon to get another phaeton-like fall.

Instead of this, however, I came gently down in a soft rain ;

falling upon a slate-roof, whence I ran through the leads into a cistern.

How I detested the darkness that enveloped me ; longing for the power of the winged creatures that made their escape through an aperture, which gave the only glimpse of sunlight that we had.

Their song of freedom was such an aggravating buzz. One day I was rapidly drawn through a pipe with many of my companions in a miniature waterfall ; a boiler was our receptacle, so my joy was short-lived.

When the vessel was two-thirds full, a colored woman placed us over a furious fire.

For a few moments I was delighted with the warm glow that pervaded me, alas ! it soon ended in a raging heat, which was greatly *increased* when the aforesaid woman tossed a handful of soda into the seething water.

In the effervessence that followed, I hoped to escape.

Delusive hope ! with millions of my kith I was poured into a washing-machine.

Horrors ! was I to become a part of that detestable thing the first suds ?

Presently my wrath cooled somewhat, it was not so dreadful a matter after all to assist at the washing of a lady's dainty ruffles, and delicately perfumed handkerchiefs.

In due time escaped in a cloud of steam, through an open window, finding all nature sombre hued. Again I sought the clouds, and with them hung for days, threateningly over the earth. On a still night as a star-shaped snow-flake, I fluttered downward, lodging in the top of a kindly elm, that grew on the street of a large city.

My day in the elm seemed the shortest in my life, so many amusing things occurred around me.

Towards evening the sun dispelled the clouds and I nearly melted to tears, but when he disappeared behind a hill, I congealed almost immediately. I now felt the pride which it is often said precedes a fall.

Surely I was fit for a crown jewel. I clung to the limb to

which I was attached, congratulating myself that for me buffetings had finally ceased.

While complacently contemplating the glories of my elevated position, I fell to the ground with a crash.

Oh ! for annihilation.

THE ANGEL OF MERCY.

BY MARGUERITE L. GIBSON.

Upon the earth she came,
And round her holy head
There shone the light of heaven,
    The joy of day.
Bestowing grace was her delight,
And floating onward through the night
The crown of Mercy was the light
    That lit her way.

Sweet Charity, her floating shroud,
Enwrapped her like a fleecy cloud,
As onward through the starry night
    She seemed to sail;
And from her snowy hand there flowed
Rest to many a weary heart,
And in many a slavered land
    Peace prevailed.

Hearts whose hopes were crushed and broken
Seemed to flourish o'er again,
And the earth put on her loveliest,
    The darkest sky was cleared.
And when her mission here was done,
Behind the silver clouds that spun
The horizon, she floated o'er
    And disappeared.

THE DREAM OF A SUMMER.

BY CELIA E. GARDNER.

We have parted to-night, and forever!
  Oh my heart, is it true?
I shall look on his face again never;
  He has smiled his adieu,
His lips white with the bitter endeavor
  To be brave to the end,
And to hide that his warm heart had ever
  Loved me, save as a friend.

While the shadows grew fainter and slimmer,
  We two stood by the gate;
All around us the moonlight's soft glimmer,
  And the hour growing late;
But his face looked so sad in the shimmer
  Of the beautiful light,
That I felt, while my eyes grew dimmer,
  We were parting to-night.

We're parting to meet again never
  As to-night we had met;
And I knew, howe'er how strong the endeavor,
  I should fail to forget;
I knew, though no word now or ever
  Had shown me his heart,
To him, too, when the time came to sever,
  'Twould be bitter to part.

And I knew that the parting was nearer
  Than an hour since I deemed;
And I felt 'twould be sadder and drearer
  Than I ever had dreamed,

As the thought of "what might have been " clearer
   Was revealed to my heart,
And I saw how to each, each grew dearer,
   As the time came to part.

Yet we stood there in silence together,
   My hand on the gate,
In the beautiful September weather,
   While the hour grew late;
My eyes silently questioning whether
   My heart told me true,
That this was our last hour together,
   This our final adieu.

And he—'gainst the linden tree leaning
   Which o'er-shadowed us two,
Looked down with no effort at screening
   His pained face from my view ;
And his eyes took a new depth of meaning
   At the query in mine,
And I knew that I was not o'er-weening
   The sad truth to divine.

But I knew not the reason appearing
   'Neath the purpose I guessed—
Why the friendship like ours, so endearing,
   We no more might be blest.
I but knew that the parting was nearing,
   I knew nothing more ;
And my heart with its hoping and fearing
   Was heavy and sore.

The days had flown onward, swift speeding
   The sweet summer away ;
Days of beauty each other succeeding,
   Days too lovely to stay.
And the story we two had been reading
   We could never forget,
For our friendship to love had been leading
   Since the hour we first met.

But this low voice the silence was breaking,
  And I, listening, held still,
"My dear friend," there could be no mistaking
  The tremulous thrill
Which all through the words vibrated, 'waking
  In my heart deeper pain,
As I saw him the brave effort making
  Strength and calmness to gain.

But a moment he paused, then repeating
  The words he first spoke,
He continued, the sentence completing
  Ere his steady voice broke—
"My dear friend, do you know since our meeting
  Many weeks have gone by?
That the hours of a summer are fleeting
  As the breadth of a sigh?

"Do you know life has no rarer blessing
  Than a friend, tender, true?
Do you know that beyond all expressing
  I am thankful for you?"
Oh, how sweet was his voice, how caressing
  As it fell on my ear!
But it faltered—he paused in confessing
  That to him I was dear.

An instant, then slowly resuming
  He went steadily on;
His voice a new richness assuming,
  A new depth of tone;
"Will you think me unkind, or presuming,
  If I venture to say
These weeks have been glad ones, illuming
  My life day by day."

"If I ask you will sometimes remember
  In the days drawing on,

These beautiful nights in September,
  And the friend you have won?"
Did he need to ask me to remember?
  Did he think I'd forget?
While of joy naught was left but an ember,
  Naught of hope but regret?

Though each tone of his low, earnest pleading,
  I shivering heard,
My stiff lips, in the silence succeeding,
  Would utter no word.
Did he think me unkind or unheeding,
  That I failed to reply?
Or was he too truthfully reading
  My wide, anguished eye?

So I gazed in his face without breaking
  The silence that fell;
But the misery within my heart waking
  I never can tell;
While his eyes in the moonlight seemed taking
  A wonderful light,
And his firm lips, uncertainly shaking,
  Grew fearfully white.

Then he said: "Do you know time is flying.
  And I must away."
Do you know that 'farewell' I'm implying,
  When my 'good night' I say;
Have you guessed what I've vainly been trying
  All the evening to tell?
Will you bid me 'good-bye,' not denying,
  A 'God-speed thee' as well?

" But first I would ask—am I pressing
  Your kindness too hard,
When I ask for another the blessing
  Of your friendly regard?

For the bride, who, perhaps you are guessing
  Is waiting for me—
Who would love you beyond all confessing
  If your face she could see?"

Oh my God! could *this* then be the meaning
  Of this bitter farewell?
Had I heard him aright? was I dreaming?
  I in truth scarce could tell.
I but knew that my pain in brave seeming
  'Twas needful to hide;
And stepped back in the shadow, thus screening
  My face in my pride.

My cold lips, so slow in unsealing
  I forced to obey;
I crushed back the strong flood of feeling,
  Which I hardly could stay;
But the tide in my veins seemed congealing
  'Neath the terrible strain,
And my tired brain was dizzy and reeling
  With the might of my pain.

I scarcely knew how I succeeded
  In my pitiful task—
But I fear as I slowly proceeded,
  Very thin grew my mask.
I believe the good words he had pleaded,
  I faltering, said:
But I think the "good-bye" that was needed,
  From my craven lips fled.

But I know howe'er weak my endeavor
  It was graciously met;
That he tremblingly murmured,
  I never wilt your kindness forget,
God bless you and keep you wherever
  Your dear feet may stray—

Good night—fare-thee well—if forever—
  God be with you alway!

My hand was in his—with sweet daring
  He drew me again
Within the pale light, never sparing
  My too evident pain.
He gazed in my face, his lips wearing
  Their brave, tender smile;
I had thought him unheeding, uncaring,
  Were they not white the while.

One moment, and he had departed,
  And I was alone!
Stunned, and silent, and desolate-hearted,
  Too weary to moan,
To cry out at the sharp pain that darted
  Through my over-strained brain,
I leaned long 'gainst the gate where we parted,
  Then crept home again.

So the dream of a summer is ended,
  And what have I left,
But a love wildly, vainly expended,
  But a heart lone, bereft!
May God's infinite love be extended
  To His sorrowful one,
And peace with the anguish be blended
  In the sad days begun.

A SOLDIER OF FORTUNE.

BY HELEN MARGARET GRAHAM.

One raw autumn evening, in the year 17—, Cecil Stanley sat in his room at the top of a very high house, his eyes wandering listlessly to the roofs beyond, his thoughts moody and disconsolate.

All around him bespoke that he had come to his last pass; the bare, cold room, the empty grate and not a morsel of food.

It was the old story, Cecil was a gay, dashing young fellow, fond of pleasure and the gay world; too much so for his Puritan father, who, after one extravagance after another, had finally cast him off to shift for himself.

And now he was at his last pass, he had come the end of his tether, and the future rose blankly before him as a stone wall.

What can I do, he thought to himself, is there nothing that a strong, able-bodied man like me, can do? I might enter the army, I should not object to the fighting; there, at least, I could rise; yes, I will enter the army, or else—" Here his face, before radiantly kindled at the thought of a soldier's life, grew soft and and tender.

Yes, I will go home, throw myself at my father's feet, and ask his pardon and forgiveness. Ah, how I long to see it all again, the quiet country home, the rest, the tranquility will be most welcome after all the din and noise of the city."

He paused for a moment and laid his hand on his forehead, as if to stop its throbbing, then began to pace up and down the room.

"Yes, father, you were right when you said a time would come when I should want to return ; necessity and want have broken down all my pride, I will leave the old life now forever and start afresh in the right way this time." He threw himself down on the hard bed and soon was dreaming of the old home he had left for the gayeties and excitement of city life.

The next morning bright and early he was up and on his way to his father's house. The stage coach stopped at the inn of the little country village and Cecil was to finish his journey of two miles on foot. He plodded wearily along till with an exclamation of so much pleasure that it was almost pain, he beheld his father's acres stretching before him. No touch of the war that was raging so fiercely had marred the lovely scene that Cecil had impressed indelibly on his memory since childhood.

He is where he had lived as a little child, on that smooth lawn he had played with his brother Walter, now a cripple for life. There was the very brook he had dammed once for his own pleasure, the very trees he used to climb, some difficult, others easy. And his father and Walter, what were they doing? Would they know him? Would they be glad to see him back?

He sank down exhausted striving to somewhat regain his courage before entering the grounds, when a small company of five or six soldiers broke up his revery. "What have we here?" said one, "What a forlorn looking object."

At their first words Cecil started up, the men were rough and uncouth and very distasteful to him.

Finally one of them slapped him on the shoulder as he said:

"Well, Sirrah, how came you here? stand up and answer us. Who are you, and what are you?"

"Who I am is nobody's business," answered Cecil. "What I am I hardly know."

"I will soon tell you what you are, you are our prisoner."

The words struck Cecil like a thunderbolt. "Your prisoner; you are soldiers then, and, if I mistake not, British soldiers."

"True, we are all loyal subjects of King George, and you will have a chance to be one, too, soon. We were on our way to the Inn when we struck you and now you can go along with us and see our Captain." "You'd better enlist," said the first speaker, "its not such a hard life and if there's anything of the real man in you, which I think there is, you would enjoy our wandering, jolly sort of life."

"Come on boys," exclaimed one, "we are late already. Come along prisoner."

But Cecil, who up to this time had stood as one dazed, at the sound of the word "prisoner" sprang forward. "No," he cried, " I am a prisoner to no one, I am as I always shall be, free," and so saying he jumped one side and ran in hot haste, the soldiers after him into a labyrinth of evergreens. It was overgrown with weeds having been long neglected, but he was well accustomed to playing there as a boy and ran swiftly without difficulty through it till he came to the end and found himself in a remote part of the lawn shaded by large trees. They had darted into the labyrinth after him but soon lost sight of him and after going through it over and over again they finally gave it up and with much difficulty succeeded in getting themselves out. Cecil heard them and was watching them go off with a sigh of relief when a tall, stately looking man was seen walking slowly along under the trees. At the sight of him Cecil's face was transfixed and springing forward he exclaimed in a voice of agonized entreaty, " Father."

The man turned and for the first time in many years father and son stood face to face.

"Cecil, you here" began Mr. Stanley in a hard constrained voice " I thought I had forbidden you ever again to set foot here." " Father " he said again, "forget all that you said and let me come back to you again. Don't thrust me from you. I have nowhere to go now but to you, I know you have suffered much through me, let me now make reparation for it. Oh, don't turn from me I have come to you as a last resort."

"You have indeed fallen low" answered the father in the same severe tone. " To look at you I would hardly believe you were my son, but you have brought it all on yourself and must now suffer for it. You are an awful axample to others, so long as you have money to share with your ribald friends home and kindred are forgotten, then when they have squeezed you, you come crawling back to me. Go, I have done with you, I have suffered too much by you and through you ever to wish to see your face again. I have endured more than you can ever know, not only has my love and trust in you been betrayed but my grand ancestral name has been dragged in the dust in dishonor. Go, I have done with you."

"Father, won't you give me one more trial?"

"I tell you I have borne with you enough, such a life as you lead would not suit this Puritan household, here everything is strict and rigorous."

"It is by just such strictness and rigorousness that men drive their sons out into temptations. You say that I have fallen low, do you care so little for me that you can see me fall yet lower?"

"Be gone," exclaimed Mr. Stanley angrily, "you have forfeited all right to me, you are no longer anything to me."

"You forget that I am still your son."

"I remember it only too well, you bear my name but from now on we are strangers. You have brought me sorrow enough already, let my few remaining years be freed from the sight of you, you choose once to leave me and follow out your own destiny, you chose your own life, now follow it and leave me the little peace I have remaining."

So saying he turned and left the spot. Cecil stood for a moment spell-bound; all the fair beautiful scene before him suddenly grew dim and he walked slowly with bent head beneath the grand old trees, pausing when he gained the road, to look with a last sad fond glance at the home he was an outcast from.

No time must be lost, however, in brooding thought; something must be done, else he would starve. He would enter the army, British or Continental, it made no difference.

"I will entrust it to fate," he thought, as he took out his last shilling. Heads the British, tails Continental. The little coin spun and came down with the classic features of King George III, uppermost.

That same evening, as the soldiers were seated at the Inn, the young man who had been their prisoner suddenly appeared.

"I have come to you," he said, " to enlist on your side, I want to join the army." "Can you fight?" asked the captain. "I can try," he answered, "give me the lowest position, if you like, I don't care what, but I promise you won't be sorry that I joined."

"This sounds well," said the Captain, "we will enroll you at once. What is your name?"

Cecil started. It was not till he saw a man with a big book waiting, that he recovered himself and answered slowly, "Albert, Albert Page.

"Is that your true name, asked the Captain. suspiciously?"

"What do you care what my name is, so long as I fight for you. You must not ask me what I have been. what I am to be you will soon see. Come, fill me a bumper, and drink 'Success to King George the Third."

The toast was drunk with deafening cheers, and amid the general drinking and shouting Cecil Stanley ceased to be, and Albert Page, the British private, began his career as a soldier of fortune.

Two years had passed away, when one night there was a ball in progress in Boston in honor of General Carew, the Commander of the British forces. About the middle of the evening the General's nephew, young Algernon Forbes entered the room and proceeded at once to the General's daughter.

"I am so glad to see you, Algy," she said, but where is Captain Page, is he not coming?"

" Ah my fair cousin " laughed Algy " have you succumbed to to his charms like the rest? He has probably forgotten all about you by this time and will never give the ball another thought."

"For shame Algy, how can you talk so of an absent friend, I know Captain Page will come, for he promised me."

"I wish for him almost as much as you do Octavia, he is the best fellow I know of for a jolly good time, indeed, since he has been in the service we have done nothing but laugh at his jests, he is always so full of spirits."

"And yet," said Octavia, "there is to me in his very gaiety, a certain sadness as if it were a mask to hide some deeper emotion."

Captain Forbes laughed heartily at this, " you are growing too sentimental my cousin, of course there is nothing of the kind. Captain Page is my most intimate friend and there is nothing he does not confide in me."

" Has he confided to you then who he is and where he came from ? "

" You silly girl, certainly he is an Englishman like the rest of us, and a jolly good fellow in the bargain."

Here a commotion was heard and Captain Page and several other officers entered. He looked far different from when we saw him last. Now in the handsome red coat of a British officer he stepped up to Miss Carew.

" May I redeem my promise for the dance, or have I come too late ? " he said.

She looked at him ; a slight color rising to her face.

" And suppose you are to late ? I do not always wait on tardy guests."

" Will you make an exception when I tell you I have come many miles to dance this with you ? Remember I am the servant of the King and his caprice must ever be my law, but my desire and my pleasure are all centered here. May I have the honor ? " and he bowed low before her.

" I knew you would not break your word," she said, as she looked up at his handsome face, " but see, the sets are forming ; let us take our places."

Many eyes followed them as the gallant soldier and fair maid walked through the rooms.

At the conclusion of the dance they went some distance from the ball room and seated in an ante room:

" How soon must you return ? " asked Octavia.

" To-morrow morning will see me marching back towards New York again."

" What a good soldier you are ; King George should know how brave you have been. Algy has told us all about it, if the King knew of it he would reward you."

"I expected no reward and wish none."

"Perhaps there is some one over in England who would be glad."

"I have no one."

"The war will soon be over, it cannot last forever; what will you do then?"

"There will be other wars, I suppose," with a faint smile.

"Won't you tell me something of yourself? Tell me what you really are?"

"What you see me, a soldier of fortune."

"No, no, not that; what you have been, about your past."

"I have no past, I live in the present. Why do you ask me all these questions. I cannot answer them and they only pain me, why cannot you accept me as you see me without questioning me further?"

"Why" she answered confused, "is it so wrong to wish to know you better?"

"Ah if you only knew how I have longed to see you again, Miss Carew. Octavia, don't turn from me, I love you passionately, I came here tonight to hear my fate from your lips, I throw myself, my all at your feet, can you deign to look at me, to care for me, tell me do you love me?"

She raised her head and gave him such a look that he felt like clasping her to his heart but controlling himself he bent and kissed her hand. "I must go tomorrow, but I shall take your promise with me and keep it in my heart till I shall make a place worthy of you, then you will come, will you not?"

"I promise it."

"The next morning Captain Page was on the march, every mile of the journey bringing him nearer to his early home. The soldiers stealing and plundering by the wayside all they could lay their hands upon.

They entered the little village on the second day at sunset, the rays of the setting sun lending it a new glory, and as they stopped to reconnoiter a shout went up from some of the soldiers. "Here's richness, cows, pigs and all that the larder affords, come let us break in and make merry."

The fair, beautiful place of Mr. Stanley lay before them. The fine old house and grounds, unspoiled as yet by the war, and as Captain Page gazed on it, a thousand recollections of forgotten days swept over him. It seemed but yesterday that he was so happy there and his old father all alone, feeble, with no one to protect him from the pillage; there was no one but himself, and here he stood in the service of his country's enemy. Could he stand by and see all his tenderest memories swept away? No, not even if it cost him his life. He suddenly sprang forward among his men.

"Leave everything here untouched, the first man that steps forward will suffer for it."

A hoarse laugh went up from the soldiers.

"Do you hear that? Well, Captain Page, you can't stop us now. Our blood is up, we'll give the old Whig something to remember us by."

So saying they made a rush for the house, but Captain Page intercepted them. If their blood was up, his was too. "Back my men, back, every one of you; the first one that dares disobey me suffers for it."

"Let us pass," exclaimed one angrily.

"Never, except over my prostrate body; this place shall not be sacked as long as I can prevent it."

"Come on, boys, said one of the soldiers," one man can't stand long against us; merciful heavens, the house is on fire!"

Sure enough it was.

Captain Page grew as pale as death when he saw the smoke and flames, and hurried towards the house just as the old colored servant ran out of it.

"I've done it," he cried, "the tories can do their worst now, but they can't hurt the house."

Captain Page, little heeding him, ran on, and arriving at the house burst into a room filled with smoke.

"John, Adam, Joseph, where are you all?" he cried, and the trembling servants presented themselves.

"Quick! no time is to be lost; save what you can."

And saying this he lifted a heavy painting from the wall and carried it out on the lawn.

The servants, bewildered, followed his example, wondering where he came from. He worked prodigiously, fighting the flames, and a bad cut over his eyes he bound with a handkerchief to stop the bleeding and went to work again.

Suddenly he thought of his father. "My father! quick, where is he? tell me at once where I may find him."

"Up stairs, Mr. Cecil, but it is not safe for you to go."

Not heeding them he ran up the now scorching staircase. In a few moments that seemed like an eternity, he re-emerged, Mr. Stanley in his arms wrapped in a blanket.

He made his way down stairs and then out on the lawn, where he laid him tenderly on a hastily constructed couch and bent over him.

"Father, speak to me, tell me you are not hurt, father, it is I, do you not know me?"

The sick man turned uneasily, then turning slowly opening his eyes, fixed them on his son's face.

"Cecil, my boy, my boy," he sobbed out, "forgive me all."

And soon father and son were clasped in each other's arms.

That same evening a solitary horseman passed through the village and stopped at the inn, It was Algernon.

After greeting him, Cecil began hastily:

"I am going to leave the army. You can take my resignation to the General. I entered your service voluntarily; I leave it voluntarily; I have fought with you, I could never fight against you. You know now who I am and what I am. I leave you as I came to you of my own accord."

"You are a noble fellow," answered Algernon, but my time presses, Cornwallis has surrendered. I am on the my with the news now; the war is over; but I shall see you before we go back to England."

"Are you going back?"

"Certainly, there is nothing more to do here, I am going now directly to General Carew; have you any message for Octavia?"

"Yes," he said speaking with difficulty, "tell her the time has now come to redeem her promise. Good night."

Then Algernon rode out into the night, and Cecil entered the sick room.

It was many many days that Cecil tenderly nursed his father who daily grew in strength. After that first appeal to his son the night of the fire, all differences between them seemed at an end. Often when Cecil thought him sleeping he was watching him, and saw again in Cecil the face of his dead wife.

Once he said to him "you are nobler and better than I am Cecil, because you can forget an injury and I never could."

The house was found to be not much injured, only one wing really destroyed, and one warm April day Cecil was leading Mr. Stanley's faltering steps over the ground.

A lady and gentleman stood concealed in the shrubbery where they overheard Mr. Stanley's closing words.

"All this will soon be yours, Cecil. Walter grows weaker day by day in the warmer climate he has been sent to. You will inherit my all."

Then he entered the house and Cecil found himself face to face with Octavia. For a moment he was speechless but recovering himself he heard her say, "Why do you look so frightened? I received your message and I came as I promised, but I fear it it only to say good-bye."

"My dearest Octavia what would I not have given for the sight of your sweet face many many times since we parted. But what do you mean by good-bye?"

"My father and all the British sail next week for England and of course I go with them."

"Could you not care enough for me to be happy here? Could you give up all and become the wife of the man who loves you? I am no longer the nameless adventurer who first knew you. All I have I lay at your feet, can you care enough for me for this?"

"Her answer was so low he could scarcely hear it—a trembling "yes," and as Algernon made his appearance they all three started for the house.

Mr. Stanley, not finding his son, had come out on the piazza and stood awaiting them.

Cecil led Octavia up the steps and laid her hand in that of the old man's. "Father," he said, "Miss Carew is my affianced wife."

We will leave her standing thus on the threshold of the new life she was about to enter.

WHEN LOVE WAS YOUNG.

BY GRACE GOODWIN.

Love is bending above the stream,
  And his childish face is merry,
As with joy unbounded and hope supreme,
Among the ripples that dance and gleam
  He launches a roseleaf wherry.

Down by the willows the stream grows wide,
  On to the river sweeping;
And the roseleaf boat, in its dainty pride,
Is torn and muddy and tossed aside
  While Love on the bank is weeping.

Tho' Love grows older, tho' now the lips
  Are grave that once were merry,
Tho' across the sea sail his great white ships,
Yet I know that still, as each strong bow dips,
  He sighs for the roseleaf wherry.

THE PLAQUE DE LIMOGES.

BY MARGARET GARRARD.

You hang upon her boudoir wall,
    Plaque de Limoges !
She prizes you above them all,
    Plaque de Limoges !
Yet do your blossoms never move,
Although she looks on them with love,
And treasures your hard buds above
The gathered bloom of field and grove,
    Insensate, cold Limoges !

Brilliant in hue your every flower,
    Plaque de Limoges !
Copied from some French maiden's bower,
    Plaque de Limoges !
But still you let my Lady stand --
The fairest lady in the land—
Caressing you with her soft hand,
Nor breathe, nor stir at her command,
    Cold-hearted clay—Limoges !

Would that I in your place might be,
    Plaque de Limoges !
That she might stand and gaze on me,
    Plaque de Limoges !
I'd live in love a little space,
Then—fling my flowers from their place
As her dear feet to sue for grace,
Until she'd raise to her face.
    Happy, but crushed Limoges !

"HECTOR."

BY CELIE GAINES.

Not that son of Priam, the beloved of Andromache, but still a real prince of his race, and greatly beloved by one small woman. A magnificent mastiff is Hector, as brave and bold, not to say as gallant and noble, as many a hero with two legs less. As for dogs not being able to think, anyone who can entertain such an idea deserves to live in "a chill condition of doglessness" to the end of his days. I will tell you about Hector, and you may judge for yourself.

Having been suddenly thrown upon my own resources, as so often befalls a girl brought up in luxury in this swiftly whirling maelstrom of our American life, I determined to cultivate the only decided talent I possessed, that of painting. Dresden was recommended to me as a place both cheap to live in and offering unusual facilities for art study. I accordingly went there. Without a chaperone? Certainly. I was to be a person of affairs, and what was a business woman to do with so costly, not to say inconvenient, an appendage as a chaperone? All winter I studied and copied in the gallery, and when summer came, I took the little steamboat which runs up and down the Elbe, bowing its smoke-stack so deferentially to all the bridges, and hunted up picturesque castles to sketch.

"Lieben-felsen" was the beautiful old schloss I fell specially in love with; so I finally persuaded an old couple who lived near it to take me to board for a few weeks. They had rather a nice little house, and a garden that sloped down to the water's edge. There, under the over-hanging trees, I used to sit for hours gazing up at the massive towers just on the other side of the castle wall. Now and then a feeling of loneliness swept over me, and my heart yearned for some of the pleasures of my joyous past.

20

One morning I asked my landlady if any of the numerous German laws would be infringed if I should go in swimming. At first she declared I would drown immediately, but when I assured her that I had known how to swim since a child, she finally consented, with a protest as to the general unusualness of American behavior.

How refreshing it was! What happiness to plunge fearlessly into the cool, clear water. Not a living soul was to be seen; not a sound to be heard. Suddenly a great splash startled me. I felt my bathing dress seized between my shoulders and myself dragged vigorously out of the water upon the bank. I was thoroughly terrified, but fortunately made no resistance. As I looked up, an enormous head appeared, and a large pair of eyes gazed inquiringly into mine. I had always loved dogs, but this monstrous disturber of my peace was so formidable that I dared not move. He, too, was motionless; and I read on his collar the name " Hector." At last I raised my hand very gently and patted him on the neck, and to my infinite relief, I perceived a slight vibration in the tip end of his tail. Just as I was wondering how far I dare presume upon that friendly symptom, he lapped his rough tongue all over my face. Then I sat up and laughed, and he jumped and frolicked, as large as a young lion, as gentle as a kitten.

Presently I tried to go back into the water, but to this he forcibly objected, and I was obliged to submit. When I returned to the house, he accompanied me, to the terror of my hostess. " He belongs up at the schloss,,' she exclaimed; " the young graf is away traveling, and almost all the servants are afraid of him."

Poor fellow, I thought; he has been lonely too; that is what we read in each other's eyes. After that Hector and I were inseparable. He came every day, and we explored all the surrounding country together. I am sure he thought—yes, thought, just as much as you or I can think—that he saved my life and consequently ought to appoint himself my guardian. To me he seemed like a living link to the beautiful old castle, a protector and faithful friend.

One morning as we were returning from a long walk, I saw advancing that always novel sight to American eyes, a woman and a dog harnessed together, dragging a cart. In this instance the cart was full of vegetables. It was evidently a market frau taking produce to town. Now Hector was a true knight, valiant, loyal and gentle, but he possessed also that other characteristic of knighthood, he brooked no intruders ; and no sooner did one of his kind appear than he challenged him to combat. I knew this and trembled, but hoped for the best. Unluckily, however, that plebeian dog, as he approached, presumed to give a defiant bark, which settled his fate. Instantly, Hector gave one spring, and seizing his boastful adversary, shook him out of his harness, in less time than it takes to tell of it, overturning the cart and scattering the vegetables in every direction. I was distressed beyond measure and I called Hector in the most commanding tones I could assume. Then I coaxed him, all of which he entirely ignored. Meanwhile, the other one of the span was by no means quiet. She was indeed perfectly furious—she abused Hector ; she abused me ; she abused the aristocracy, to which she seemed to think we both belonged, as highway robbers and assassins ! In my desperation I picked up a stick to compel Hector to obedience, but she mistook my motive and advanced upon me in a rage. "Silence !" We turned quickly. Just out of the wood came a young man in uniform, evidently an officer. The dogs stood still an instant, and I rushed forward and grasped Hector's collar.

He did not consent kindly to being led off, but the other dog had been pretty well chastised by this time. Hector felt his knightly powers had been duly established, and he quieted down in a deferential sort of way, as if he were only consenting to it on my account. Then the market-woman began to wail that her wares were spoiled and she might as well go home; but when I gave her some money, and the gentleman kindly added some, too, she harnessed herself and her dog again and resumed her journey. Then I turned to thank my preserver. Hector, whose collar I still held, was restlessly dragging me forward, so we walked on together.

"I'm so sorry," I began, "that my dog should have made such trouble."

He smiled. "Happily," he said, "the damage was not irreparable."

"I am very much obliged to you for interfering just now," I went on, rather excitedly; "it gave me a chance to bring Hector away."

"It was courageous of you to do it," he replied. "He is a huge beast for you to defy."

"Well!" I protested, "he would not hurt me. He is such a noble fellow, and we are very fond of each other, Hector and I. Indeed, he has been my best friend all summer."

He looked down on me and smiled again. "I am glad of that," he said, "for Hector is my favorite dog."

This, then, was the Count, and I had been claiming his property. No wonder Hector had quieted down at his voice!

He must have read the disappointment and mortification in my face, for we had just arrived at the castle gates, and Hector had bounded away into the grounds, when he raised his military cap with a graceful courtesy and said : "Fräulein, we shall let Hector choose between us. If he prefers you, I shall never claim him, and shall moreover admire his taste."

He walked toward the gate while I went on; but Hector rushed out past him to me and whined pathetically, then he ran back to the Count and stood defiantly in his path. To humor him his master came out again, and I turned and faced him. Hector's joy was unbounded. He jumped around us both wildly, and showed by every sign in his power that he had no intention of "cleaving to the one and forsaking the other." It was so evident and so amusing that we both laughed heartily, which seemed to establish a friendliness at once.

"He is determined we shall not part, fräulein; will you permit us both to accompany you home?" They did so, and on the way I assured the Count of my intention to return shortly to the city, when he would probably have his favorite's undivided affection again.

The next morning, when I took my accustomed place out

under the trees, Hector soon came trotting gayly along the bank, holding in his mouth a small object of dark blue and red cloth, which he deposited at my feet. I picked it up. It was a military cap! You may call it accident if you like, and say any dog will pick up a hat and carry it off, but you will see how mistaken you are. After a while Hector's tail, as he lay at my side, began to hammer the ground with gratified thumps, and I looked up questioningly. The Count came towards us laughing—to get his cap, he said, but he must have forgotten his purpose, for he stayed to watch me sketch, and the next day he came again, and the next.

I did not return to Dresden as soon as I had intended. Indeed, I finally decided not to return at all, but to make my home in the beautiful old castle. I had always been opposed to American girls marrying foreign noblemen, and the Count had had, he told me, a most disapproving opinion of American girls in general; but, you see, Hector had made up his mind—yes, his mind, not to spare either of us, and he is such a fine fellow, we could but acquiesce in the matter.

TO THE POSTMAN.

BY JULIA IRVING GRAHAM.

What news does't thou bring
   My friend dressed in gray?
Is there sorrow or joy
   In the mail bag to-day?

Have hearts e'er been broken
   By tidings of thine?
O, wilt thou not promise,
   Thou'lt never break mine?

Sometimes thou bearest
  From dear friends apart
Sweet messages, bringing
  Great joy to each heart.

And sometimes a letter
  Is written so fast
In the first heat of passion
  Remorse come at last.

One tells of a death-bed,
  Our brother at rest,
His last words, his weakness,
  His dying request.

Oftentimes letters
  Tell of a love
That was only half guessed
  By the soft turtle dove.

Another penned badly
  In dire distress,
Begs humbly for charity,
  Money or dress.

This little one here
  Has a delicate scent,
'Tis the work of a bride
  In her new-found content.

Some good and some bad,
  You bring them together
As you go on your way
  In all sorts of weather.

BESSIE'S MOUSE.

BY SARA L. GUERIN.

Bessie felt cross; Bessie had been *so* naughty, and Grandma had said, "You cannot go out of the garden to-day," which was a very great disappointment, for the little girl loved to roam through the fields and woods.

She stood leaning against the pear tree now, and I wish I need not tell it, but she was pouting, an ugly frown disfigured the usually pleasant face. Suddenly a shout and merry laughter from the other end of the garden drew her attention to the fact that Phil and Bert were having a good time over something, and she walked slowly over to the old pump where they were. All at once the fretful look left her face, for what they were pumping water on was alive, yes, really alive! Bessie could see it move, and it was a dear little mouse.

"Oh, Phil, Bertie," said the tender-hearted little girl, "don't be so cruel; don't hurt it any more, it's most dead now," but the boys were having fun, they said, and would not stop for her.

Bessie thought if Grandpa were only there he would make them, and punish them, too, for their cruelty, but alas! he had driven away to town an hour ago. At last a bright thought occurred to her, and she said quickly, "I'll give you my silver half dollar, boys, if you will let me have it."

The boys were delighted to make the exchange, and the half-drowned little mouse was transferred to Bessie's gentle care. She rolled it up in her apron and ran to the kitchen door with it.

Grandma was making cookies, and laughed when Bessie unrolled her treasure. "Why, bless me, childie, she said, "puss will surely catch it."

"But, Grandma," answered Bessie, "may I keep it? I will

not let puss know I have it at all, and oh, darlingest Grandma, what can I do for it; it seems so weak it can't stand up."

"Well, dear, if it was you I would give you a warm bath, rub you with alcohol, roll you up in a blanket and put you to bed," was the laughing reply, all of which Bessie did, and in a little while the mouse was as lively as ever, and then the strangest thing happened; it became quite tame, and was very cunning; it ate out of her hands, ran up and down her arms, frolicked among her curls, and when tired would nestle on her shoulder and take a nap. "Grey" became very dear to the little girl's heart. Indeed, every one in the house was fond of it. Her brothers wanted to buy it back again, but Grandpa said, "You need not think the mouse would be as tame with you; you were too cruel to it. If Bessie gave "Grey" to you, he would soon run away."

It *was* strange, but the little mouse never tried to get away from Bessie, and it seemed to return her affections as well as it could. It grew even more tame as the summer drew to its close.

When Bessie's mamma said it was time to go back to the city, papa prought out a little cage, and "Grey" traveled with them very comfortably.

Bessie and her pet were the admiration of all the little friends in town, and "Grey" lived a long time; indeed, he died of old age. Best of all, this is a true story, for I saw "Grey" myself, and I know Bessie very well.

A STUDY OF INDIVIDUAL INFLUENCES RELATING TO OUR NATION.

BY MARY MARGARET GILE.

Knowledge, it has been stated by some philosopher, is made up of facts. These facts are constantly increasing in number, as the ages roll on, and we must content ourselves if we are not acquainted with anything more than a limited number of the great sum of these happenings.

As regards our nation, it will be far better for us to be able to trace some of the influences brought to bear upon the vital interests of our civil history than to accumulate a knowledge of isolated facts without studying their relations.

It is my purpose, then, in this paper to trace some of the individual influences that have helped and do help to mold affairs in our beloved land.

We are passing an important point in the history of events. We are coming to the close of the nineteenth century. Can we do better than to try, with the aid of our individual experiences, to look through the last four hundred years, to the end of that wonderful epoch in the history of the nations, the last of the fifteenth century?

The light, and gladness, and beauty of this festal season in our nation, shine far along the path through the centuries, and throw a halo of interest upon some of the notable scenes of four hundred years ago. And what are the notable ones for us? Let us see. In one, there is a lad earnestly studying the science of navigation. His intentions and convictions are altogether honest, manly and worthy. His patience and industry arouse our admiration. His zeal knows no bounds, and his fellow students feel something of the inspiration of this untiring worker. But what is the motive of this earnest young man? Does he wish to make himself famous? Why does he toil so unceasingly? Let us study his motive for a moment.

In a sermon preached not long since in this vicinity, the preacher likened human effort to the tin composing a part of the delicate machinery of a watch. Of itself, this common metal could do nothing effectual, but when charged with diamond dust, which the preacher likened to the Holy Spirit of God, it performed its duty quickly and easily, according to the text, "Not by might, nor by power, but by my spirit, saith the Lord of Hosts."

The efforts of our hero, now praised by all, were human, and of themselves they would have accomplished very little, but he had a divine purpose in his soul, and it is this divine purpose that should interest us today.

Hear what a writer of literary fame has said of Columbus: "His piety was earnest and unwavering, it entered into, and colored alike his actions and his speech. He was pre-eminently fitted for the task he created for himself. Through deceit, and approbrium, and disdain, he pushed on toward the consummation of his desire, and when the hour for action came, the man was not found wanting."

The Spanish love of gold and gain, the cruelty to the Indians in North and South America, can have no place in the contemplation of the motives that actuated the discoverer of this continent, as he worked "on, and on, and on." He did not live to know what he had accomplished, but we have lived to understand that our nation, with its civil and religious liberty, its wise government and its free institutions of learning, and its happy homes, can never separate itself from the influences that speak to us this day of the high aims of the great Columbus.

In this connection, let us draw our attention to another individual whose generosity we can but admire. That court scene at Cordova, so intimately connected with our nation's history, has two central figures—the great navigator, who supplicates for patronage, and Queen Isabella of Castile. Who can measure the importance of her decision? What is the impulse that will cause her to consider or reject the favor that is asked of her? There-are other interests than those seen in the mind's eye of our adventurer, as he stands and waits. Interests nearer home, for the Moors are even now clamoring at the very doors of the palace of the fair lady. O gentle queen! Is there a ray of light that comes from afar—from the glittering summit of snowy Shasta of the western Sierras—that falls on the jewels in your hand, and whispers to your soul of "Columbia, the gem of the ocean"? Does some spirit of prophecy show you the beautiful "Golden Gate," or the "Falls of Minnehaha," or the "Bridal Veil," or the "Wisconsin Dells"? Does it spread before you the sweet serenity of "Seneca Lake," to which our own Longfellow has sung:

> "On thy fair bosom, silver lake,
>   The wild swan spreads his snowy sail,
> And round his breast the ripples break,
>   As down he bears before the gale.
>
> "On thy fair bosom, waveless stream,
>   The dipping paddle echoes far,
> And flashes in the moonlight gleam,
>   And bright reflects the polar star."

The written record of the thoughts in Isabella's mind, as she listens to Columbus, we may never see, but the record of her generous action we can claim as our heritage, and we can but assume that she was actuated by no "sordid hope or vain desire." We can point to her self-sacrifice as among the powerful influences that helped to develop America. If posterity fails to honor her, by not erecting some appropriate monument to her memory, her history will be none the less significant to those who seek for the foundation stones, in the structure of our nation. Coming down through the centuries from the dawn of America's life, we could often pause to note acts of unselfish devotion to lofty principles that have helped to mold the affairs of our country.

What devotion to such principles filled the breast of young La Fayette, as he heard read at an English banquet, the Declaration of American Independence? The historian tells us that "he was won by its arguments, and from that time joined his hopes and his sympathies to the American cause." He had much to gain by remaining in his own country. His domestic ties, his social and political duties demanded his presence, but the struggle for liberty which breathed in every line of that wonderful Declaration called to him from over the seas, and he heeded the call—a call to assist the patriot in a foreign land! Was his effort to carry out his noble desire free from discouragement? Alas, no. His family had no sympathy with his plan for aiding America. The British Minister, very naturally, would gladly prevent the young nobleman from hazarding his life and his prospects in such an apparently hopeless enterprise. Last of all the French King said "No," but still he did not abandon his project.

Time will not allow us to note all the difficulties that follow the track of that friendly band of gallant men from sunny France, nor to trace all the results of that kindly aid so finely appreciated by our beloved Washington. It is fitting, however, to state that side by side in the same park, with the statue of the Father of his Country, stands that of the noble La Fayette, and the influences of those statues speak for themselves.

And just here let us glance at a quiet home, as it appears after the war of the American Revolution. In this unpretentious home in old Virginia, in the village of Fredericksburg, with her garden hat, among her garden flowers, is Mary, the mother of Washington. She sees a visitor approaching her humble abode. One of her grandsons conducts him to her presence, and as the boy spies her, he exclaims—"There, sir, is my grandmother!" Our friend, for it is La Fayette, has come to offer his tribute of praise to the mother of the Commander-in-Chief of the armies of the young republic. After listening to the tribute, she replies in those memorable words, " I am not supprised at what George has done, because he always was a very good boy." Her simple attire and graceful bearing make a profound impression on the mind of her visitor, and he may be thinking of the English banquet of four years ago, and comparing the simplicity of this scene with the grandeur of that. Mary Washington is in the habit of attending to the affairs of her home, and so we see her busy with her garden tools. Not at all disturbed by her plain attire, she says, further, "Ah, Marquis, you see an old woman, but I can make you welcome without a parade of changing my dress." Here are simplicity, goodness, modesty, hospitality; and their possessor has had an influence upon our country's progress, for was she not the mother of Washington, and was he not our nation's pride, our worthy leader in the stern necessities of war?

Following our train of thought toward the present time, we pass along the lines of great historical events, and as we move on, this inscription claims our attention. We pause with reverent tread to read the solemn words: "Our Martyred President." Volumes would not suffice to record all the important issues that this inscription calls to mind. They are of such recent occurrence that detailed accounts of them have been penned by many writers of the age, even by actors in the very scenes representing these great issues. It is important for our purpose, as we go on our way, to notice that all these writers are of one accord in their estimate of Abraham Lincoln. One says of him, "His wan, fatigued face and his bent form told of the cares he bore, and the grief he felt; kind, earnest, sympathetic, faithful, democratic, he was anxious only to *serve his country*." Hence all the nation responds to the beautiful sentiment: "With malice toward none, with charity for all," so appropriately inscribed at the foot of the statue of this truly great man.

It is commendable in us to feel proud of the fact that he was a representative of America's citizens, and influence such as his who of us can measure it?

The memory of his sudden and tragic end reminds us that "Death loves a shining mark," and, as in 1865 a procession of mourning friends reached all the way from Washington to Springfield, Illinois, so, in 1881, from Elberon through Washington to the Lake Shore Cemetery in Cleveland, Ohio, where the lamented Garfield was laid to rest, the people of the United States joined their voices to pay tribute to one whose noble sentiments and Christian character throw lustre on every page of history which records his name.

And now, while we have been looking at some of the shining threads in the fabric of American history, it is fitting that we should join in the universal expression of sorrow that reaches all over the length and breadth of this land, because of the death of Mrs. Harrison. The many interesting accounts of her rare qualities give us another evidence of the value of character. We do not have to look far to determine how people of the North esteem the eminent graces of the President's wife,—but what do the Confederate veterans, lately convened at Dallas, Texas, think of them ? In a recorded copy of their resolutions they say : "We regarded Mrs. Harrison as not only an exemplary and warm-hearted Christian woman, but as also representing the *highest order* of *American motherhood.*

Some of the noble qualities that enter into the minds and hearts of individuals for good place them high above the " petty strifes and follies " of politics and society. Above their "petty strifes and follies," but not above politics and society, nor above the consideration of political and social science.

The study of the lives whose influences I have tried to trace may serve to show us that we have a noble heritage to leave to the rising generation. A heritage of civil institutions founded upon principles of justice, morality and Christianity. A heritage of free education, open churches and open Bibles. And it becomes us, as friends, sisters, teachers and mothers, "Daughters of the Revolution;" to do what we can to inculcate the spirit of true patriotism in the hearts of this rising generation, that it may not sell its "birthright for a mess of pottage."

La Fayette, in that English banquet to which your attention has been called, heard the Declaration of Independance read, and believed in the " spirit of its argument." All honor to the writer and signers of that noble document ! But let *us* appreciate it, my dear hearers, and study the "spirit of its argument," and not have to confess that we do not know the difference between the "Articles of Confederation," the " Declaration of Independence " and the " Constitution of the United States."

Why do we hear young people say among themselves, " Memorial Day has no interest for me further than that it is a

holiday?"   Or why do some of our young men spend more time
in matching the color of their necktie with their boutonnière
than in studying the principles of the political organizations of
this great republic?

It is a duty for each and all to have an intelligent outlook
upon the great political and social questions of the hour, and the
merry music of the marching thousands upon thousands of children, citizens, soldiers and veterans, and they pass along through
memorial arches and under fluttering banners, to celebrate the
anniversary of the " Landing of Columbus," will lend us an inspiration as we study.

Then unroll the records of American Independence, unfurl
the stars and stripes, and while we give thank for what Columbus, Isabella, Franklin, La Fayette, Bartholdi, and many, many
more have contributed toward our costly heritage, let us sing,
in the language of America's national hymn :—

> " My country ! 'tis of thee,
> Sweet land of liberty,
>   Of thee I sing ;
> Land where our fathers died,
> Land of the pilgrim's pride,
> From every mountain-side,
>   Let freedom ring.
>
> Our fathers' God to thee,
> Author of liberty,
>   To Thee we sing ;
> Long may our land be bright
> With Freedom's holy light ;
> Protect us by Thy might,
>   Great God, our King ! "

THE QUEEN'S REPARTEE.

BY MRS. MARY A. GILLETTE.

He was a king, yet well he knew
    The worth of gold for payment;
She was a queen—a woman, too,
    And fond of costly raiment.

" This is a dainty cap," he said,
    " Fine as a cobweb, truly.
What was the price ? She shook her head:
    " You'll think it cost unduly.

" Men should not ask what women pay
    For ribbons, caps, and collars.
But this was a bargain as you will say,
    'T was only just ten thalers."

" *Only* ten thalers ! You cannot mean
    You paid such a sum of money
For that small thing, my darling queen ! "
    He looked o'er the landscape sunny,

And beckoned a guardsman, poor and old.
    "Here ! you are no imposter:
Tell this lady the worth of gold;
    What should that lace thing cost her ? "

On his clumsy hand he turned the cap.
    " I've but a feeeble notion
Of the cost of women's gear   Mayhap,
    It cost her many groschen."

" Groschen, man ! Such a bit of lace
    As that costs ten whole thalers.

This pretty lady with smiling face
   Pays dear for caps and collars.

" Ask her to give as much to you—
   She can afford it surely."
He held his hand with small ado,
   She gave the sum demurely.

Then said with a gesture arch and sly:
   " This gentleman so stately
Standing here, is richer than I—
   His wealth is increasing greatly;

" All that I have he gives to me—
   Thankfully I receive it.
Ask *twice* ten thalers, and you'll see
   He can afford to give it."

Laughing, the king bestowed the gold—
   Such grace his rank befitted,
And merrily oft the story told
   How he had been outwitted.

INDIVIDUALITY IN DRESS.

BY ELSIE A. GARRETSON.

We may be the very perfection of physical beauty without possessing that charm of all charms—individuality. Ethnology, psychology and biology show that specialization is a higher grade of evolution. All individual traits are developed equally as we proceed higher in the general physical and intellectual scale.

The form of Venus is exquisite, the face perfect; but it lacks expression; there is nothing in the face to love—it possesses no human softness.

21

We can take our analogy through all the highest forms of past civilization down to the present day, and we find that it has been left to our own age to recognize and develop variations and expressions, and create new and individual types, both of men and women.

Individuality, both in dress and sentiment, is of the greatest importance to personal success, and he or she who lack it, shows truly an evidence of inferiority. This craving to be and dress like some one else, is nonsensical, not to say the least absurd.

"You walk this peopled earth alone."

*　　*　　*　　*　　*

"None like thee ever yet was known."

It is a mark of weakness to be eccentric in dress and to devote all one's time to it. But it is a greater weakness to care nothing whatever for our personal appearance.

We have all, no doubt, said, and also heard others say, "that a person's hat looks just like them," and thus it should be. That indefinable something that is all our own should ever linger about us as a halo. We are all more or less original, but alas! few ever seem to know their own selves.

An ill-dressed woman is a discordant note and jars on refined taste. A well-dressed woman is a recognized power. We cannot help but associate fine detail with refined personal feelings. The human form is the most wonderful of Divine creations, and is a type of order demanding orderly attention.

What exquisite satisfaction there is in feeling one is well and suitably clothed! Such a person is never awkward in manner, being at peace with herself she is at peace with all the world.

WASHINGTON FORTY YEARS AGO.

BY MRS. LUCY WILLIAM HAWES.

Compared to the Washington of to-day, the city was very shabby. I use the word unreservedly as I recall particular instances of shabbiness. Pennsylvania avenue was poorly paved, poorly lighted and covered with mud. The old canal was a receptacle for the filth of the city. Jabbering negroes filled the market place with miserable carts tied up with ropes and drawn by poor, jaded animals. Their market truck was anything but inviting. A gentleman who became tired of waiting for the family coach that was to take him into the country for dinner, strolled from his hotel to the market place and found the vehicle, in which he seated himself to await the coming of the black Jehu. He felt something moving under his feet, and lo! it was a little pig which was to be sold and the proceeds taken to buy fruit and nuts for the entertainment! In the guest-chamber of a prominent Western member was a wooden mantel with coarse red brick hearth and tiles, and iron dogs supporting a smoky fire. When we went to this room for our wraps, after an entertainment, we found two small children nestled in the bed. The climax of shabbiness was perhaps the hall in which Thackeray delivered his lectures on "The Four Georges." Like a country schoolhouse of those days, it had bare seats and no carpet. On the platform was a table without a cloth, and behind the distinguished lecturer was a great window with a broken pane and a gaudy curtain flapping in the wind. But a finer audience was seldom seen—the President and his Cabinet, foreign ministers, officers of the army and navy, General Scott, Washington Irving and many distinguished men and fair women.

The most elegant home in Washington in those days was that of Mr. Corcoran, the banker. When we felicitated him on

being the possessor of Powers's Greek Slave, he said very pleas-
antly, "and that is the only slave I own, for you know I am an
Irishman." The yellow guest-room of his house was greatly
admired. He had rendered some service to Messrs. Baring &
Company of London which could not well be repaid in money,
and they sent him a gorgeous covering for his bed. It was of
superb yellow satin with Chinese embroidery of flowers and
birds in fine showy colors. Three sides were heavy with a
many-colored fringe and the lining was of rich white silk. He
told us he had a bedstead made to accommodate this gift. It
was of rosewood with headboard of lattice work through which
yellow satin was pricked. The pillows were covered with blue
silk and the cases were of finest linen cambric trimmed with
costly lace.

At a reception at Mr. Corcoran's, Madame Bodisco was the
belle of the evening. She wore a dress of corn-colored brocade
with low neck and bare arms; the black bugles of her bertha
were so fine that they appeared like lace. A wreath of wild
roses surmounted her brow and fell over her fair neck. The
old Count was very proud of her. She never accepted an invitation to waltz without his consent. While she was dancing
he turned to a friend and said, "My God! is not Madame
Bodisco very beautiful?"

Among the noted beauties were Mrs. Riggs, with her coro-
net of auburn hair; Miss Cutts, who married Stephen A. Doug-
lass, and the handsome widow, Mrs. General Ashley, betrothed
to Senator Crittenden, of Kentucky. A young daughter of
Mrs. Ashley, when dressed for a ball, said, "Oh, mother! don't
you wish you were as young as I am?" To which the mother
responded, "My dear, don't you wish you were as handsome as
I *was?*" The fashions in those days were not elegant. Middle-
aged ladies wore caps of blonde with flowers or marabout
plumes, high waists with vests, and flowing undersleeves of rich
embroidery and lace. The dresses were of moire antique or
brocade, but seldom of velvet. Mrs. Fillmore wore a red velvet, though she was a blonde; her daughter Abigail looked best
in blue silk and white laces with a wreath of water lilies.

The Fillmores found the White House in a miserable condition, dirty and bare, with no corner that seemed like a home. The great room over the Blue Room was covered with a straw carpet made filthy by tobacco-chewers. Underneath this was found a good Brussels carpet of the old pattern, a basket of roses upset. Mrs. Fillmore had this cleaned, she sent to Buffalo for her piano and Abigail's harp, shut off much of the space with screens, and with a wood fire and comfortable surroundings made the place very pleasant.

The old black cook, who had served many years at the White House, was greatly upset when a range of small hotel size was brought to his quarters. He had managed to prepare a fine state dinner for thirty-six people every Thursday in a huge fireplace with cranes, hooks, pots, pans, kettles and skillets, but he could not manage the drafts of the range, and it ended in a journey of the President to the Patent Office to inspect the model and restore peace to the kitchen.

At that time there seemed to be a dearth of great men. Clay, Webster and Calhoun were gone. When Mr. Sumner took his seat in the Senate, Mr. Benton said to him in a patronizing way: "Sir, you have come upon the stage too late. Not only have our great men passed away, but the great issues have been settled. The last of these was the National Bank—that has been thrown over forever. Nothing is left you, sir, but sectional questions and petty strife about slavery and fugitive-slave laws, involving no national interest." How little did Mr. Benton and Mr. Sumner foresee the things they lived to see!

We went to Mount Vernon, escorted by Mr. Powers Fillmore, who took a note to Mr. John Washington from his mother, asking admittance for Mr. Washington Irving to the room in which General Washington died, as Mr. Irving was finishing the last chapter of his great work, " The Life of Washington." But Mr. John Washington was very surly, to say the least, and did not consent that the room should be opened. Of course, Mr. Irving was hurt and chagrined and our party disappointed.

At a state dinner we met Mrs. Alexander Hamilton, whom Mr. Fillmore escorted to the table—a plain little old lady and

very plainly dressed.   The dinner consisted of nine courses, and
we sat from seven to nine.   Through the entire length of the
table was a mirror about a foot in width with a sort of bird-cage
arrangement at the edges, on which at intervals were placed
vases of artificial flowers.   We saw very few natural flowers,
and there was no conservatory at the White House.   It was just
forty years ago that everything was made ready for President
Pierce, as it is now made ready for President Cleveland.   Mr.
Fillmore was very popular in the entire South after signing the
Fugitive-Slave bill, and his family were making preparations
for a trip southward immediately after the inauguration.   Mr.
Fillmore rode with President Pierce on that day, while his wife
went in her own carriage and secured the best possible place,
but being deaf she could not hear the inaugural and stepped
out on the cold, wet ground.   A neglected sprain and a severe
cold caused her death in a few weeks.   She died at Willard's
Hotel and was taken to her home in Buffalo by her sorrowful
family.   She was a most excellent woman and bore her exalted
position with great propriety and dignity.   Though often the
subject of severe criticism, she never lost self-respect, and
among her friends and associates her name will be forever
cherished.

POLLIE'S SACRIFICE.

BY M. O. HALSEY.

"Mother," said Polly, "what is a sacrifice?"

"What put that into your head, little girl?" asked her
mother, smiling at the serious little face upturned to hers.

"Well," said Pollie, drawing a long breath, "last night I
heard grandma telling Joe about her grandma; she said when
the colonists made up their minds to fight the red-coated English soldiers, so we could be free and have 'Fourth of July,' the
colonists had to melt up lead things and make their bullets out

of them. They didn't have nearly enough, so the other colonists gave them all they had. Grandpa—Joe's and my great-great-grandpa—mamma, said, 'I haven't got any,' and was very sorry about it, and the men were going away very sorrowfully, when his wife, whose name was Comfort Prudence Alden, said: 'Oh, yes, we have, here is some,' and she ran to the old moon-faced clock, unfastened the heavy weights and gave them to the soldiers. Grandma says the colonists' soldiers were called 'Minute Men' because they had to be ready to fight at a minute's note. Our grandma says it was a great sacrifice for her grandmother to give up the old clock weights, 'cause her own mother and father had brought the old clock from England in a ship, called the 'Pilgrim,' ten years after the 'Mayflower' had landed, and now, mamma, please tell me what a sacrifice is, right away," concluded the little girl, taking a much-needed breath.

"Giving up something you prize for the good of others," explained Mrs. Patterson.

"Can little girls make sacrifices?" asked the child, eagerly.

"Oh, yes, indeed, and I know of one who is making one now, this very minute," replied Mrs. Patterson, looking up from one of the new shirt waists she was making for Joe, Pollie's older brother.

"Do you mean me? what's the sacrifice? and how am I doing it?" demanded Pollie, excitedly.

"Yes, this little girl's name is Pollie, and her sacrifice is just this—instead of being at play with the other little girls, although it is Saturday afternoon, this special girl is helping me by darning a big pile of stockings, so I can finish Joe's new shirts by Thanksgiving."

"But that is such a tiny little sacrifice, all the other girls I know do that, too. I wish I could make a great big sacrifice, like my great-great-grandma did. I can't give away lead to make bullets now, 'cause there aren't any 'minute men' to want it now, anh I haven't got anything to give away 'cept the big white turkey. Father gave me Whitey 'cause I helped him shoo all the others home lots of times, when it was going to rain.

Aunt Jane thought father ought to sell Whitey with all the rest to Mr. Rolks, but father said : ' No, Jane, Whitey belongs to Pollie, and no one has any right to sell him but her.' I was real glad to hear him say that, for I love Whitey, he's so splendid and big and never nips me, and I don't want him to be hung up on a big hook with all his feathers off, and some horrid little girl or boy to eat up his precious drumsticks," and Pollie shook her head over the dismal prospects of turkeys who were not Whiteys.

The next two weeks passed rapidly, the sky was a clear, cold blue, and the wind put splendid winter roses in Pollie's plump cheeks, and danced gayly among the gables of the little farm-house that had been her only home. Spicy odors stole from the big kitchen in which mother and Aunt Jane made all sorts of good things ; for it was the week before Thanksgiving, and everybody was busy. All the other turkeys had been sold to Mr. Rolks, and Whitey, the only survivor, strutted prouder than ever in solitary state in farmer Patterson's big turkey yard.

That same day, Pollie running in from school, found her mother reading a long letter with a very sober face. "Why mamma, what's the matter?" asked Pollie, struck by the expression of sadness on the usually serene face.

" I've just received a letter, dear ; it's from a poor woman out West whom I was able to help a good many years ago. She asks me to send her a little Thanksgiving dinner for her three hungry little children—their father died very suddenly last summer. She tells me she has managed to get along fairly well by doing sewing and odd jobs which came to her hand, until she slipped on an icy pavement and broke her arm. All the little money she had managed to lay by has had to go for medicine and doctor's bills ; and worst of all, her daughter, who had been ill with a low fever, has been taken sick again—she has some trouble with her back—and her mother is not able to buy any strengthening food, or even a warm comfortable for her delicate little girl who feels the cold very keenly just now."

" You'll send them a real nice dinner for Thanksgiving, won't you mother?" pleaded Pollie, interested directly in this every day, although none the less pathetic story of suffering and want.

"Well, dear, your father and I will send a nice Thanksgiving dinner of turkey and cranberry sauce and vegetables. Aunt Jane is going to send a bottle of wine, and grandma a new book for the sick girl. I am afraid that is all we can do, although I would like very much to send a comfortable, a warm wrapper, easy slippers, and a few other comforts, to this poor child, as well as something to help with the rent; although Mrs. Meyers only asks for something for a little dinner," and Mrs. Patterson gave silent thanks, as she glanced at her own small daughter, happy, rosy and warm, safely sheltered from cold and hunger, and rich in the possession of a father's loving care and affection. "But," she added, a little sadly, "I can't, for father has had heavy expenses, too," and Mrs. Patterson sighed as she thought how sadly the comforts were needed in this particular instance.

"I declare I was sorry I didn't have another turkey to sell Rolks," remarked Pollie's father, as he sat by the fire that evening with Pollie on his lap. "It seems the demand for my turkeys this year is greater than ever. At the very last minute Rolks says a crusty old gentleman stalked into the store and gave him an order for 'three of Patterson's turkeys for Thanksgiving.' He pounded on the floor with his gold-headed cane, and declared that my turkeys were the finest he had ever eaten. Rolks said that two were all he could let him have, as all the rest were spoken for; Rolks says the old gentleman got in an awful rage, told Rolks he wasn't fit to keep shop, would not hear of letting him send to the city for the other one, and departed in a furious heat, blowing up everybody in the store. Rolks says the old gentleman, whose name is Staunton, said he'd give twenty-five dollars for another Patterson turkey. He says his six grandchildren are coming to spend Thanksgiving with them and the old gentleman promised a drumstick to each one on his word of honor. He is as rich as he is queer, and would doubtless give twenty-five dollars for one of my turkeys, simply because he fancies them."

All the rest of the evening Pollie was very quiet, looking thoughtfully into the heart of the open grate fire, which threatened to roast her rosy cheeks. But she did not mind that, for her thoughts were a jumble of something like this : " Whitey, the little sick girl, an old gentleman, ' Patterson's turkeys,' and ' twenty-five dollars.' " All night long she tossed restlessly in her little white bed, but when morning came Polly had made up her mind.

" It's a sacrifice, only it's Whitey instead of the old clock's weights. Twenty-five dollars will buy the nice warm comfortable, and a red wrapper and slippers, and lots of other things, and if there's anything left over I'll send it to her mother to help pay the rent with," cried Polly, clapping her hands joyfully, with the pleasure of the thought of making sad and sick hearts glad, and a little ten-year-old girl making a " real live sacrifice," just like her "great-great-grandmother."

There being no school, after breakfast Pollie put on her little gray ulster and red hat and, tucking her warmly mittened hands into her two little pockets, trudged out to find the old gentleman, sell Whitey, and make her sacrifice.

After quite a long walk, Pollie found the house, and her brave little heart sank for just a minute. It was such a big place, and the stone griffins above the iron gate were really very alarming and seemed to frown upon the little stranger.

The smart, white-capped maid seemed very much surprised to find only a rosy-faced little girl standing in the tiled vestibule when she opened the door. " If you please," said Polly, politely, " I would like to see Mr. Staunton. It's—it's something about a turkey."

"What's that about a turkey?" called an authoritative voice from one of the side rooms, "show the person in immediately."

Obeying a sign from the maid, Polly walked across the big hall with its polished slippery floor into a handsome room whose walls were lined with immense cases full of big books. Before the open fire sat a rather fierce-looking old gentleman. For just a minute the little girl was almost frightened, for his eyebrows were thick and bushy, his gray eyes were very sharp and keen-looking and his voice sounded like a giant's to this timid little maiden.

"Well, child, what do you want?" asked the ogre of this castle, in a somewhat milder tone.

Seeing something in the stern old face which gave her courage, Pollie came shyly forward. "If you please," she said gently, "I'm Pollie Patterson, the turkey man's little girl. I live in the little brown house by the brook, Joe's my big brother; my great-great-grandmother gave the weights out of the old clock for a sacrifice, and do you think you could buy my Whitey? He's my turkey. He is splendid and big, and his drumsticks are nice and fat. I don't want your grandchildren to be disappointed. Mr. Rolks told father all about it. Aunt Jane wanted father to sell Whitey to Mr. Rolks with the others, but father wouldn't, 'cause he said Whitey was mine, all my own. It's all right, you see. Did you know," added Pollie, feeling perfectly at her ease now, "that if turkeys get left out in the rain they will catch the croup and die?"

"No, madam, I did not," replied the old gentleman, who was really very much entertained by all this; "but what about the sacrifice?"

"I'll have to 'splain that," replied Pollie, laying one red mittened hand on the arm of the old gentleman's chair.

Then she related in her childish way the story of her great-great-grandmother's sacrifice, told of the letter which had come to her mother, and of the little sick girl, and of the many little comforts which the twenty-five dollars were to buy for the sick child. "I'm so glad," she said, cheerfully, "for I've made lots of tiny little sacrifices like darning stockings and amusing baby when her teeth hurt, but I didn't ever thing I could make a big sacrifice like my great-great-grandmother, and send help to a little sick girl, and make her get well—and sell Whitey and not even feel sorry about it," concluded the truthful child, lifting her pretty blue eyes to the keen gray ones.

Now Mr. Staunton had no intention of giving twenty-five dollars for a turkey when he had spoken to his butcher that morning, but this pretty little girl's simple trust in his word of honor (which, by the way, was a thing upon which the old gentleman prided himself) pleased and flattered him. "Well, my little girl," he said, "a bargain is a bargain," and taking a capacious wallet from the side drawer of his writing table, Mr. Staunton placed five crisp green bills in the little red mittens' eager clasp.

"I'm ever so much obliged to you, and so will the little sick girl be, 'cause I'm going to write a piece at the bottom of mother's letter and tell how you helped me make a sacrifice; 'cause," added Pollie, seriously, "if it hadn't been for you, and dear old Whitey I couldn't have made any sacrifice at all."

After a few minutes more conversation, Pollie bade the old gentleman good-morning and started on a run for the "little brown house by the brook," holding the precious new bills tightly in her two small hands.

"Why, Pollie, what ails you? I believe the child's lost her wits," declared aunt Jane, as the delighted child danced around the big kitchen.

"I haven't lost my wits, it's the sacrifice. Look, mother!" and Pollie counted the five bills in a perfect ecstasy of delight.

"Well, I declare, that beats all!" answered aunt Jane, as Pollie finished her story.

"It's a lovely sacrifice, and I am as proud of my unselfish little daughter as I was of her great-great-grandmother when I first heard the story," declared Mrs. Patterson, kissing the fair childish face, which dimpled with pleasure at the honest praise so heartily given.

"It's going to make a real Thanksgiving Day for us all, and best of all, dear, it will please One who said : 'Forasmuch as ye have done it unto the least of these my brethren ye have done it unto me,'" remarked grandma, in her soft old voice.

That afternoon Pollie and her mother made a special excursion into town, and it was wonderful what the twenty-five dollars bought. A pretty warm red wrapper, a pair of soft slumber slippers to ease the weary feet, a down cushion to comfort the sick back, a gay red quilt, soft and warm, and light as thistle down and still there were five whole dollars left to help with the rent.

Two days before Thanksgiving the expressman left two great boxes at Mrs. Meyer's door, and later on came a letter to Pollie and Mrs. Patterson, overflowing with gratitude and thanksgiving from a truly grateful heart.

But Mrs. Meyers was not the only surprised person that Thanksgiving morning : for while Pollie was eating her oatmeal a mysterious rap sounded on the front door. Joe opened it, and Polly fairly gasped, for straight over the doorsill, right through the entry and out into the kitchen, strutted a white turkey, larger and even prouder than the late lamented Whitey ! On its neck was tied a card on which was written in a decidedly masculine hand, "Polly Patterson, from her friend and admirer, Frederick Stauhton."

" It's my ' turkey gentleman.' How lovely ! " cried Polly.

Yes, Polly was right, and her friendship grew and flourished long after the new Whitey was stuffed and eaten. And, thanks to the "turkey gentleman," Polly had pleasant surprises from the same quarter, even after she wore long dresses and called herself Miss Patterson.

OLD VIRGINIA CORN-PONES.

GRACE VIRGINIA HALSEY.

Sho, yeh needn't tell me nuffin bout yeh cakes, and yeh pies,
    Kase I'se made 'em fo' de light you eber see;
De omlecks, and de salads, and de creams am mighty fine,
    But dere's nuffin like de cawn-pones for me.

'Pears like de sun's a-shinin' on meh old Virginia home.
    An' de peart birds a-chirpin' in de trees,
An' de yello' roses climbin' roun' de pillars ob de po'ch,
    An' de red popies burnin' in de breeze.

I kin see meh deah young mistiss come runnin' down de paf,
  Wid her pooty cheeks a-glowin' rosy red,
An' de sunshine a-kissin' ob her leetle sof ' white han's,
  An' dancin' on de brown curls ob her head.

I kin heah her sweet voice callin', yes, as if it was to day,
  To dat lazy nigger Gawge, "whar I be;"
'Kase she say de " Brompton people" am a-comin' up de road.
  An' dey'll wan't A'nt Liza's cawn-pones for tea.

'Clar' to goodness, dey'd come troopin' to yo' very cabin do'!
  Wid a " Howdy, Mammy Liza, how ye be ?"
An' dey'd split dier sides a laffin', as they frowed de copper cents
  To de picaninnies hangin' aroun' to see.

Oh, de singin' and de dancin' when de yello' moon was full,
  An' de cawnfiel's jes like a silber sea;
Wid ole Mose a-scrapin' ob his fiddle to de bones,
  While Cæsar tummed de banjo on his knee.

Lor'! I done forgot meh ole sef in tinkin' ob dose times,
  An' de folks at Mas'r Alec's dat I see;
But de mos' hab cross' de ribber to de shinin' golden sho',
  An' de horn'll soon be tootin' up for me.

Den, when meh white soul's carried to dat bressed, shinin' sho',
  An' meh own deah Miss Lucy's face I see,
I reckon dat de heab'nly food dey eats aroun' de throne's
  Gwine ter tas' like angel cawn-pones ter me.

NOTES TO TEST QUESTIONS ON CIVIL GOVERNMENT, FOR THE USE OF TEACHERS.

BY JENNIE V. HORSLEY.

The Vice-President is first sworn into office before the Senate. The oath is then administered to the President by the Chief Justice.

44.—The presidential mansion, called the White House, is provided and maintained by the government for the use of the President.

45.—These officers, appointed by the President with the consent of the Senate, form what is called the President's Cabinet. It is their duty to aid the President in matters pertaining to their several departments.

The Secretary of State holds the highest and most dignified office in the Cabinet. He attends to all matters relating to foreign affairs; the Secretary of the Treasury is head of the treasury department and minister of finance; the Secretary of War presides over the war department, supervises the United States Military Academy at West Point, and has charge of all military matters; the Attorney General is the legal adviser of the President and of the executive departments; The Postmaster General is the head of the post-office department and attends to matters relating to post-offices and the carrying of mails; the Secretary of the Navy has control of matters pertaining to war vessels, naval forces, etc , and has charge of the Naval Observatory at Washington, and the United States Naval Academy, at Annapolis; the Secretary of the Interior has the management of public lands, Indian affairs, patents, pensions, etc., and the Secretary of Agriculture has control of matters relating to agriculture and agricultural products. It is his duty to publish, in the interest of commerce and agriculture, all reports of signal service concerning condition of the weather, etc.

Each Cabinet officer has an annual salary of $8,000.

57.—Territories are admitted as states under special acts of Congress. As a general thing, when a Territory has a sufficient population, the people send a petition to Congress asking permission to be taken into the Union. Congress then passes what is called "an enabling act," by which the inhabitants are authorized to form a State constitution. When they have framed a constitution which is free from objections and in conformity with the Constitution of the United States, Congress passes another act admitting it into the Union as a new State.

91.—Nineteen amendments have been proposed by Congress, but only fifteen have been ratified by the requisite number of States.

No amendment can be made which will deprive a State without its consent of its equal suffrage in the Senate.

Every amendment, when once ratified, is equally binding on all the States.

THE DAY AFTER CHRISTMAS.

BY ROSALIE M. HILL.

Tis the day after Christmas, and everywhere
Not a thing is in order, book, table or chair,
While small fragments of candy and nuts strew the floor
From the library table clear out to the door.
Poor nurse says, "It's just dreadful the way things is thrown!"
And the cook goes about like a Western cyclone!

Brother Fred got up late and with terrible frown,
Dragged his coat on and cap, and then started down town.
While papa said, "You're joking; it can't be so late!
Well, we never count Christmas; the office can wait!

So I'll just take things easy for once in a while,
And I don't mean to hurry," he said with a smile.

Aunt Kate's "quite prostrated," and has gone back to bed,
With a bandage of vinegar tied round her head.
Mamma fusses around from one thing to another—
Won't notice the baby, but just says, "O, bother! —
Such a terrible racket I never can stand ;
How I wish all those trumpets were out of the land !

" Mary, look at your bonnet, thrown down on the floor,
Right under the lounge, child, and see there by the door
Is Katie's new dollie. I declare it's shame
To give children such things. I said that when it came
But grandma would do it. O dear ; what's the matter ?
Jack, get off that hobby-horse! Do stop your clatter!

" Nurse, please rock the baby, or he'll just drive me wild !
My, I never did hear such a troublesome child.
It all comes from that candy and pudding and cake.
He has eaten too much. There? I said that would break !
Now go up stairs directly, you mischievous boys ;
It's mere wasting of money to buy any toys !

" I'm fairly worn out, and just ready to die !
I can't get things tidy; it's no use to try.
Why, I've cleared up this room fully six times, I vow,
And I'm sure no one would think it to look at it now!
Well, I'd better give up, and just take a good rest ;
There is one consolation, we've all done our best

" To get everything right ! and yet why should we care ?
Jackey dear, let mamma have that nice easy chair !
Here, nurse, I'll take the baby, and rock him awhile,
The poor little darling. O! now just see him smile !
Well, there, I feel better ; it's of no use to frown.
I believe it's far wiser for us to sit down
In the midst of the litter with hearts full of cheer,
And give thanks for the Christmas that comes once a year."

22

MAGNETIC PHENOMENA OF THE DEAD.

BY ROSALIE M. HILL.

"Hi! Ted; there's a funer-rell!"

"Is they! Say, lessusgo!"

And the two boys, who had been absorbed in a game of "hop Scotch" a minute before, started along the street as quickly as their bare feet could carry them." The younger of the two, "Ted," paused as he came to a vacant lot, inclosed by a broken-down fence, just long enough to shout, hand to his mouth, "funnel fashion"—"Sa-ay, Mickey, few-ne-rel!" then on again like the wind. Next minute half a dozen boys, ragged and barefoot, climbed over the broken-down fence and raced after the other two. All breathless and eager, animated alike by one end, one aim—"few-nee-rel!"

Looking along the road in the direction they were running, I could see some distance off, the white fence, group of weeping willows and high iron gate, which mark the entrance to so many "cities of the dead." And winding in slowly under the archway, a long train of carriages bearing one quiet sleeper to his or her last resting place. "Now," I said to myself, "what is there about a funeral to so attract all these urchins, that they leave everything else to run and look at it?"

A few minutes before this, the two boys had been so intent on their game that although I had stood watching them for some moments, they apparently had not even seen me. Yet long before I myself was aware of the fact one of them had spied the approaching funeral and, "Presto change!" had vanished.

While I was still wondering over this I gradually became aware that I was no longer alone, nearly every window of the adjacent house, the doorsteps and small yards were filled with women and children. They none of them gave me more than a passing glance; but riveted their attention on the black line of coaches in the distance, which they watched until the last one entirely disappeared, when they, too, one by one, slowly returned to their occupation.

"Now," I thought to myself, "what is there about a funeral to attract all these women, so that they leave their domestic duties to come and gaze after it?"

Standing in the open doorway of a house nearest to me was a stout, pleasant-faced woman. She was quite out of breath from the haste she had made to get there, and she had come too late to see even the wheels of the last coach. She gave me a smile and cheerful nod as she came out, and altogether looked so inviting that I drew nearer and accosted her.

"Good morning!"

"Good morin', madam! An' it is a foine day to be walkin'."

"It is, indeed," I replied, "so fine that I have walked further than I intended. Were those two boys yours who were playing here just now?"

"Wan of thim is, madam. The other lives on beyant."

"They're a couple of nice lads. I wanted to have a talk with them, but they ran off so fast. It's odd a funeral should have so much attraction for boys."

"They do always run loike that, ma'am, when they sees one;" then she added, half apologetically: "You see it do be littie pleasure they has in their lives anny way."

I shuddered involuntarily, then with a strange feeling of pity in my heart for the boys whose lives were so barren of joy, that they found pleasure in funerals, I raised the flat stone in the "hop Scotch" square and placed two nickels under it. Then asking the woman to see that they got the money when they came back I turned away.

As I walked I pondered rather sadly over this new phase of life which I had suddenly discovered, and wondered wherein lay the remedy. Education? Possibly; certainly these boys were uneducated, and that might account for the singularity of their taste. And also in some degree account for it as depicted by their mothers, aunts, sisters, and the rest of the women, who had really seemed as much interested in the funeral as the boys themselves. Even so, granting that education, or rather the want of it, were the foundation ; it still left a good deal to speculate over.

So musing I walked along till I reached a wide business street, thronged with people. Two richly dressed ladies came out of one of the large dry goods stores just as I came up to it, and paused a few moments talking. They were saying goodbye, when one of them exclaimed, "Oh ! Mary ; see, there's a funeral going into St. ——— Church. Let us go over, may be we can get in and find out who it is." And at once off they started.

" Now, who would have thought," I said to myself. "These two cultivated and refined looking ladies are possessed with the same mania."

Looking after them I saw a funeral cortege passing slowly along the next avenue and halting front of a little stone church.

At the windows of the handsome residences near by I noticed many faces, all intently watching a—funeral. This gave me more food for reflection, evidently " education " had nothing to do with it then.

Now for my own part I always rather shun a funeral, not from any feeling of horror, or superstitious dread; but because I love life, and although for me life has not been all kind, or too happy ; still I love to live, and to see living, breathing objects.

My meditations were interrupted at this point by observing two thin, sharp-featured little girls standing in front of an undertaker's window admiring the "lovely coffins !" And I hurried away in a somewhat cynical frame of mind, and started to cross the long bridge over the river which divides two large cities. Near the centre of the the bridge I met a funeral procession, and and noticed that all the foot-passengers, with scarcely an excepion, were standing to look at it. Some even came back to walk after it, while dozens of small boys were running along trying to see into the coaches. 　　*　　　*　　　*　　　*　　　*

I had nearly reached my home, when I came upon a group

of little girls playing "house" on one of the door steps, with dolls, and dishes ranged in order, and all laughing and talking at once. One sunny-faced little one was sitting in a small rocking-chair, with a doll wrapped in a blanket in her arms. She looked so sweet and earnest that I couldn't help looking at her and admiring. Imagine my feelings when she suddenly cried out to her playmates :

"Oh, say, girls ! I.e's make b'lieve she's died, and have a funeral !" And from the exclamafion of delight which followed, I judged the suggestion was one universally approved. * * *

What a very odd world it is, to be sure ! And one of the oddest phases of humanity to be met with can be summed up in : "Hi ! Ted ! There's a funer-rell !"

REQUIEM.

BY MARGARET CARPENTER HODENPYL.

Sleep beloved! Night before
   Never brought thee rest like this.
No to-morrow for thee more,
   Waking thee from endless bliss!

Not again shall anxious eye,
   Through the long and dreary night,
Watch, with strained intensity,
   For the prayed-for morning light.

Weary feet! Their race is won.
   Tired hands! Their task is o'er.
Troubled heart! The day is done,
   Rest is thine forever more!

Lay thy work now finished down,
   Listen to the welcome sweet;
"Faithful one receive thy crown,"
   And thy Lord with rapture greet!

CLEVER OCTAVE THANET.

BY ELIZABETH DOCK HASTINGS.

It was my great good luck this summer to spend a day and night in the same large country house out of Boston with the authoress of "Expiation" and "Knitters in the Sun"—the former book her first novel, the latter a collection of her magazine stories.

My first thought upon meeting her at the dinner table was,. What a bewitching voice! It was a combination, low and soft,. and the western drawl, which, in the mouth of a cultivated man or woman, is quite a different thing from the same voice in a rough diamond state.

Then my first question was, "How did you choose your nom de plume?"

"Well, I scarcely know; it came to me. Octave with a long 'a' was the name of a favorite schoolmate, and Thanet I picked up while on a coaching tour in Scotland years ago."

So, instead of what many have always imagined was a purely French name, it is English and Scotch, the first letter in Thanet being sounded. There was no absurdly mysterious reticence about her with regard to her work; she was always pleased to gratify the interest or curiosity of a friend or acquaintance when asked about it, and I enjoyed again hearing, this time from her own lips, the story of how one of her Western dialect stories provoked a rude attack upon her writings from an irate native. She valued his criticism enough to reply and explain that the idioms she used were in vogue during and directly after the war, and were not manufactured, and that she had at one time lived among many of the people of whom she wrote, and, therefore, knew whereof she wrote. Her letter was so satisfactory and courteous that she received a speedy apology, and a cordial invitation to Mr. Thanet to "come right down and he would have some of the best hunting the country afforded."

Then again, the soft answer that turneth away not only wrath but the double-edged pen of one skillful critic, made a firm friend and admirer of Howell's.

Her gestures, like her speech, are well chosen and deliberate, indolent, one might easily say, until they found each movement was made for a purpose, and that purpose was generally accomplished. The evening was very warm, and in the absence of the ideal east wind of Boston myriads of mosquitoes were doing their deadly work. We hit and missed, and finally contented ourselves—bon gre, mal gre—with flourishing our fans and handkerchiefs, but Octave Thanet would quietly put one soft, white hand upon the other, and on as quietly removing it she would say, "I have killed him," and she succeeded each time. Thus in her quiet, gentle way she accomplishes all she intends doing.

One of her family told me that her first story she sent to Harper's Monthly Magaze, and after a long and weary waiting it was published in the Bazaar, as being not up to the mark of the Monthly Magazine.

By this time every one who reads knows that Octave Thanet's real name is Alice French, which she writes in a small, round and beautifully legible hand. She makes her home in Davenport, Ia., notwithstanding the earnest entreaties of friends and fellow-writers to live among them in New York or Boston. Her summers are generally spent with her family, mother, sister and brothers, at Pocasset, in the Cape Cod region, where she can enjoy the yachting and bathing and pursue her chief recreation of photography in the fresh unspoiled bit of coast. It is nearly opposite Marion, and the sail across is a favorite one with her. She tells with great pride how she rents an entire old deserted mill from its owner for the modest sum of $3 a summer, and develops her pictures in a dark room fitted up for the purpose. Her friends are anxious to have her write a novel upon the scenes and people she encounters during her vacation. Her working hours are from twelve to fourteen each day, and yet she cannot begin to supply the demands that her interesting work has brought her.

A younger brother, Robert, a sophomore at Harvard, has lately written a story for the Harvard Advocate, and his style bears a genuine family likeness to that of his gifted sister.

Besides writing because she loves it and cannot help writing, Octave Thanet tries to bring wrongs to light and to right the many grievances that oppress humanity whenever she can do so, in such a manner as only a woman of her strong moral perceptions, her keen wit and her warm heart can successfully undertake.

As a raconteuse she is charming, and from describing vividly the horrors of an accident which she once witnessed in a quicksand, to making young girls go to bed shivering from the effects of a ghost story they insisted upon hearing, was an easy transition for her imagination. The ghost story was too ghostly and bloodcurdling to be other than fiction.

Her hold upon the public is now so great that five of the largest and best publishing houses in New York have each begged for a novel from her pen to be brought out by them; one of the number, and a successful one, is the source of my information, and I think each one of us reads eagerly in magazine or paper everything that is signed with the quaint name, Octave Thanet.

CHILD OF SILENCE.

BY SARAH E. HEALD.

Sad Child of Silence!
In vain for thee the earth resounds
On every side with sweetest sounds
In vain for thee the wild bird's song,
Or hum of insect, borne along
By whispering wing, till all the air
Is filled with melody so rare.

All, all " Earth's voices " do but seem
To thee a past, a pleasant dream.

Lone Child of Silence!
And in thy silence all alone
Thou ne'er canst hear the sweetest tone,
The ringing laugh of happy child,
Rustle of leaves, or temptest wild.
Silent to thee the voice of mirth,
Whispers of love, and songs of earth.
Thy words of prayer and hymns of praise
Only in silence canst thou raise.

Meek Child of Silence!
Bend meekly to the Father's will,
And since He bade the world be still,
And hushed for thee each pleasant sound,
That swells the earth and sky around,
Humbly believe His will is best
And still content in silence rest.
No storm can break the willow bent,
And grace to humble souls is sent.

Glad Child of Silence!
And be thou glad, O silent heart,
Sweet sounds of earth are only part
The moan of pain; the wail of woe
May still be heard where'er we go.
Thou canst not know the unkind word;
The rough, harsh tone is all unheard.
Be glad—so live, when death shall come,
Thou'lt hear the angels call thee home.

STORY OF A DUCK'S BREAST

BY SUSAN JACKSON HANNAHS.

I re-read, the other evening, " The Colonel's Opera Cloak,"
following with the greatest interest the career of the innocent
garment which was the cause of so much sorrow, as well as happiness. , As I closed the book and laid it down, I thought of a
duck's breast which had played its part most effectively in a
family of girls whose wants and needs were many, but the par-
ental purse, alas! far from plethoric.

How well I remember the commotion in church the first
Sunday that duck's breast made its appearance there! Louise
Wilton was tall and stylish, and gave an air of elegance to the
plainest costume; but the new turban, with the silvery duck's
breast made a princess of her. There was positively an added
air of deference in the manner of Ned Hart as he stepped to her
side after church to walk home with her. Good clothes bring
self-respect in their train, and "fine feathers" do make fine
birds. Louise was conscious of this feeling and yet not vain
with it all. It gave her courage to invite Ned home to dinner,
even while she knew the repast would be a plain one, and, worse
than the dinner, there were two very badly worn places in the
parlor carpet.

On the way home, Bess and Lillian, two younger sisters,
and bright girls, joined her; and while Ned chatted with Lillian,
Lou told Bess in an undertone that Lillian and she must stay in
the parlor during Ned's stay, and occupy chairs placed over the
bad places in the carpet. This pleased the girls; they were quite
willing to sit in and enjoy Ned. The dinner went smoothly and
tasted well flavored, as it was with spicy conversation, for wit
and good humor were always to be found at the Wilton's table.
True to Lou, the girls were back at their posts before Ned could

discover their scheme, while he, poor fellow, waited, hoping they would retire, and leave him alone with Lou. From the room overhead were heard peals of laughter. Papa, mamma and Nan, for Lillian had managed, while at table, to explain the situation to her mother. Ned grew restless. He had been in love with Louise for six months. Ever since the surprise party, when Lou looked so fresh and sweet in a plain pink cambric amid the silks and laces of the other girls When she chose Ned for her partner in the Virginia reel his heart did palpitate, and what contempt he felt for Alice Geer, whose lip curled at the pink gown, Sateen was at a discount, and there was for Ned "a corner" on cotton goods at once. The Committee on Chairs grew weary and felt sadly in the way. Ned wondered—will they never go? I really believe, if I could see Louise alone I would try my fate. Then suddenly he said, "Miss Lou, suppose we take a walk. Will you go?" And Lou, grateful for a break in the awkward state of affairs, ran up stairs for her hat.

The turban, unadorned, was the property of Nan, who had entered into a partnership with Lou ; each was to have the use of the turban and duck's breast when the other was at home. Nan, supposing of course that Lou was located permanently for the afternoon, had donned the hat and gone down to her Aunt Anna's, anxious to be the first to display the new acquisition. Here was a dilemma; and how to get out of it. Lillian and Bess were so much younger that their hats were too juvenile ; mamma dressed in mourning, so her bonnet could not be borrowed ; and as for wearing her own shabby everyday straw hat, with the blue veil pinned around it, that could not be thought of.

There was only one way out of it ; to go down and decline to walk. And then came the thought, "Why Ned will think I'm fickle, and perhaps he'll never come again."

Tears filled Lou's eyes, and her temples throbbed so that when she did go down and say she had a headache, even Ned was impressed with her change of manner, as well as the girls, who jumped off their chairs when the front door had closed on Ned and exclaimed :

"Why Lou! What is the matter? You look as though you could cry!"

"Well, I can," said Lou; and then the flood-gates were opened, while amid tears and sobs she told her grievance.

"What a goose you are! Why didn't you tell Mr. Hart that Nan had gone out and worn your hat?" said Bess, who was frank to the extent of saying everything—but her prayers.

"Then he would have said, 'Wear some other hat;' and what then?" sobbed Lou.

"Well, my dear thing!" answered Bess, giving her a hug and a kiss, "dry your tears and 'brace up,' for it will all come right in the spring;" and the trio went up to mamma's room, where more sympathy was given, and a pleasant feeling restored. * * *

Meanwhile Nan had been enjoying herself thoroughly. Uncle John and Aunt Anna had filled her cup of pleasure to the brim by their admiration of her as she appeared in the new hat; the duck's breast had been complimented to the fullest extent, and "the crowning joy" laid carefully on the bed in auntie's room.

It was almost dark when Nan rose from her comfortable chair before the open fire, to prepare for home. Chatting briskly she buttoned her Newmarket and tied her lace scarf about her pretty throat, then went into the next room for her hat, and then a scream—such a scream!—brought her uncle and aunt to the spot. From end to end of the bed feathers were scattered in every direction, and the duck's breast, which but an hour ago was "a thing of beauty," was now a hollow mockery, only a mass of white cotton remaining intact to show where it had rested in its beauty.

"That horrid cat!" cried Nan. "I told you, auntie, you would rue it some day, keeping the nasty beast. And to think that I should be the victim—and not I alone, but poor dear Lou. What will she say? How can I go home and tell her?"

Poor Nan! The complication of disasters was too much for her, and she threw herself down amid the ruins of her finery, and gave way to her grief. Auntie meanwhile gathered the shining feathers one by one, till she had them all, and taking the turban in her hand, seated herself to see what could be done.

"Jet," the family cat—the destroyer of the peace—had vanished. Having searched in vain for her, Uncle John kicked a hassock clear across the room as an outlet for his wrath, looking all the while from under his bushy eyebrows at Nan, who, by this time, had become "a dissolving view."

"Nan, I believe I can press the cotton back into shape and then put these feathers on again with mucilage," said Aunt Anna.

"Nonsense!" said Uncle John. "How long do you suppose mucilage will hold those feathers on? The first shower will send them flying, and make the poor child look as if she had her halo on ahead of time! If you had not been so fierce to join that Audubon Society, and destroyed that box of wings and breasts you had, we could have fixed the hat up for her."

"We might go around to old Ferguson, the taxidermist on High Street, and see what we can do," suggested Aunt Anna. "He's a queer old fellow, but I think he would serve us in an emergency like this."

"Oh? do!" acquiesed Nan, who had quieted and was ready for action.

"Have some supper first, dear," said Aunt Anna.

"No supper for *me*, auntie. 'am full to choking now; and I know Lou will expect to go to church tonight. Every minute counts;" and Nan took the turban, now robbed of even the cotton of the pretty duck's breast, and putting it on her head, turned to Uncle John and continued, "Come uncle, supper an hour latter means nothing to you," and dear old sympathetic uncle John took his hat and followed Nan as she hurried down stairs and out the front door.   *   *   *   *   *

Petted and pacified by Bess and Lillian, Lou got through the afternoon very comfortably. Tears soon ceased, and laughter flourished in the sunshine which the girls made for her. Presently there came a ring at the door-bell.

"It's Nan," said Bess, as she ran to the top of the stairs.

"Deal gently with her, Lou, for life is short, and joys are fleeting."

"And to be the first to exhibit the duck's breast to Aunt Anna is a boon very sweet to dear old Nan," said Lillian.

"'She cometh not!' It's a messenger boy with a note for 'Miss Wilton.'" This from Bess, who had reached the foot of the stairs. "I'll sign the paper;" and giving Lou the note, Bess bowed out the Mercury in livery.

SUNDAY, 4 P. M.

"DEAR MISS LOU:

I find it a rather difficult to reconcile your kindness to me today with your coolness as I left your house this afternoon. I am at a loss to account for your change of manner, as you declined to take a walk after having accepted the invitation,—as I fancied, with some degree of pleasure. I hope you will be at church this evening; and may I infer, from your presence there, that I am privileged to accompany you home?

"Very sincerely yours,

"EDWARD HART."

Then she handed it to Bess.

"Hurrah for Ned! He's a man after my own heart!—excuse the pun, dear sister," shouted Bess as she finished reading. "*He's* not going to let a trifle 'down' him. Didn't I tell you it would all 'come right in the Spring'? And—— My! but you look happy!" and putting her hand under Lou's chin, she laughed to see the color in her cheeks, and the light in her beautiful brown eyes,—so sad but a moment ago. "If Ned could see you now, he'd say, 'Heaven bless thee! Thou hast the sweetest face I ever looked on' and his tone would be as tender as dear old Rignold's, and that, you know, dear, is saying a great deal."

"You are a saucy flatterer," said Lou, as she slipped away from her sisters and went to her room.

This little rift had made strange music in her soul, and showed Lou how deep her feelings were for Ned. Yes, she would go to church to-night, and then—well, she dared not think.   *   *   *

Of course the shop of the taxidermist was closed ; but a dim light could be seen, and upon knocking hard, a door at the remote end of the establishment opened, and an old man, bearing aloft a kerosene lamp, came slowly forward, and unbarring the front door put out his head and asked what was wanted. In a few words Nan's uncle stated the dilemma they were in, and the old man opened the door wide enough to admit them.

Upon looking around they found themselves in the presence of a motley crowd of beasts and birds of all colors and climes. The ubiquitous owl looked down from his perch, and when Nan, with trembling fingers, laid before the old man the wreck of the duck's breast, he actually blinked, did this old owl; while the squirrel, on the shelf, indulged in a dry chuckle as the old taxidermist said :

"Well, the cat did knock the stuffin' out of it, and no mistake ; but cheer up, miss, I've mended worse jobs than this."

"How long will it take?" asked Nan.

"If you'll call around in the mornin', I'll try to hev it ready for you. You see I'll hev to heat my glue, and fix a good foundation for the feathers, and then dry it out well. If you want a good job, you must give me the time."

Saying she would call for it early next morning, Nan and her uncle left the shop, and Nan started for home alone, preferring to tell the sad story of her mishap without even Uncle John as a spectator.

The church bells had ceased ringing, and services had begun.

"I do hope Lou was not intending to go to church tonight," Nan said to herself as she hurried home. "I hope to goodness Bess and Lillian have gone, for I can stand Lou's frown better than their fun. My! but I'm hungry!"

She rang the bell. The door opened, and she was dragged into the hall by Bess, who shouted:

"Kill the prodigal! The calf's returned! Better late than never, but better never late. Gracious! What's the matter? You've been crying! You poor thing! Who's dared to hurt your feelings? Why! what *have* you done to your hat? Where's the duck's breast?"

By this time Nan was surrounded by the family, and had succumbed again to tears. In detached sentences, she gave a hysterical sketch—in water colors—of the catastrophe. Lou mingled her tears with Nan's, in a truly sisterly manner, and mamma did her best to comfort them both. Lillian brought Nan some supper, whileBess, who had been too full for utterance —walked up and down the parlor, "sniffing" suspiciously. Finally she sputtered out:

"If I live till tomorrow I'll join the Audubon Society. No more birds for *me!* No poultry on *my* hats, after this. That horrid duck's breast has brought us nothing but trouble!"

Poor Nan! When she heard of Lou's misunderstanding with Ned Hart, it was the last straw. Feverish and sobbing they put her to bed, and all thoughts of the duck's breast were forgotten in their solicitude for Nan.   *   *   *

It seemed strange to see the Wilton's pew in church vacant, as two or more of the family were usually in in it, both morning and evening. Ned Hart sat where, should Lou come in, he could watch every turn of her pretty head. Every rustle of garments in the vestibule and quick step up the aisle gave him a queer feeling in the region of his heart; but when the hymn and prayer following were over, and the minister began his sermon, Ned knew it was all up with him, and that Lou would not be at church *that* evening. The service ended, he went directly home and to his room.

"I have taken too much for granted, and she has served me right," he soliloquised. "So much for being in a hurry. If I had not written that note, and she had come to church,—why, I might take my chances on seeing her home. Well, it looks very much as though I had got my *congé.* By Jove! It's hit me harder than I dreamed of." Then, as he turned out the light and retired: "I wonder if there's anybody else she likes? But, pshaw!" And giving his pillow a couple of thumps, as though it was the imaginary rival, Ned lay and brooded over his disappointment till past midnight.

Sleep and rest had given back to Nan her color and courage. She met the family at breakfast, with a smile for each. As she entered the breakfast-room, Bess sang in a mockingly plaintive tone:

"Nor storms shall beat, nor billows roll
Across my peaceful breast."

Nan joined in the refrain, and Bess saw that she was impervious to all teazing; so the meal was eaten without further allusion to Sunday's mishap.

After breakfast Nan hurried to the taxidermist's, where, on the branch of a most impossible tree of domestic manufacture, hung, high and dry, the duck's breast. It was "a good job"; each silvery feather lay slick and smooth, as though it grew there and feared no foe.

While adjusting it on the turben, Nan was profuse in her praise of the old man's skill, and paid him his price—half a dollar—ungrudgingly. Her bright face, as she left the shop and turned toward home, was a happy contrast to the sad countenance of the day before.

"Why, there comes Ned Hart!" said Nan. "I've a good mind to tell him what happened yesterday, and then he'll understand why Lou stayed from church last night."

Quick as a flash she ran across the street and waited until Ned came up with her. The color left his face as he exclaimed, "Why, Miss Nan! Is anything the matter?"—lover like, thinking only of Lou, and fearing she might be ill.

"No, Mr. Hart. There's nothing the matter, only—I am so full of calamity (Nan wondered afterwards how she chose that word) that befell me yesterday, that I want to tell you about it;' and she did, in a very cute way, never intimating that Ned had any personal interest in the melodrama which had been played.

As Nan finished, Ned grasped her little hand and said, "I can't begin to tell you, Miss Nan, how grateful I am to you for telling me this;" and then, with a slight hesitation, he continued, "Do you think Miss Lou would object to a morning call?"

Nan laughed, and Ned blushed as she said, "You might try. Just say you saw me, and that I will be at home in a little while;" and Nan turned the corner and hurried to Uncle John's to show

23

Aunt Anna and him how successfully Mr. Ferguson had repaired the duck's breast. But not a word said the dear girl of the repairing she had been engaged in !

One hour later Lou met her at the door, all smiles and blushes, and whispered:

"It is all right, you darling ! Your 'calamity' has proved to be a joy; and I, yes, and dear Ned, too, will always cherish and think tenderly of 'the duck's breast.'"

THE DEATH OF TENNYSON.

BY AUGUSTA W. HILLIARD.

Truly the night knew a poet was dying,
   And whispering to nature, vesper bells rang,
To tell all her subjects where he was lying ;
   And the sad Autumn wind his requiem sang.

Calmly he lay there, nature's fond lover ;
   Bard, whose gray head the laurel had crowned,
Waiting for death with never a shudder,
   He who in life so much sweetness had found.

Surely he saw that the shadows were falling ;
   Felt that the angel of death hovered near ;
Knew that beyond Heaven's chorus was calling—
   Sunset was fading, but the pathway was clear.

Glorious moon-beams, but no earthly taper,
   Guided him gently death's journey through,
Far o'er the Border where all are safer,
   In the limitless realms beyond the blue.

HEREDITY.

BY MRS. J. W. HUMPREYS.

The word heredity is of recent origin, but the subject is older than the human race.

By the roadside we see a cedar and a buttonwood growing side by side, drawing nourishment from the same elements in soil and atmosphere, and yet how different in foliage and fruit—one deciduous, the other evergreen. By culture or lack of it, they may be enlarged or dwarfed, but the characteristics of each remain the same. We turn to the first chapter of Genesis and read: "God said let the earth bring forth grass, the herb yielding seed and the fruit tree yielding fruit after his kind, and it was so;" and echoing down the dim aisles of the past we may hear the refrain: "As it was in the beginning, is now, and ever shall be."

The study of plant life is full of beauty, from the sprouting of the seed to the full-grown tree blooming and bearing seed. In some kinds, notably the oaks, the variation of species is very great, yet there is no mistake; an oak is always an oak, bearing acorns and not chestnuts, though the chestnut oak is very similar in leafage to its namesake. Our beautiful pansies have all been produced fromt he common field and meadow violets, through the culture of two hundred years. Our lovely roses have been gathered from all parts of the temperate zone, and through careful culture and crossing of different varieties, have attained to such distinction that when some new seeding beauty appears, the names of its parents are recorded. Our large and luscious strawberries originated from the little wild ones.

The farmer is a believer in heredity. He knows full well he cannot "gather grapes of thorns or figs of thistles." When he sows wheat he expects to harvest wheat. If he is a stockman he pays great attention to the pedigree of his animals, and can tell the qualities and worth of an animal by the herd-book and the care it has received. The most careful attention is paid to blood in breeding stock, in consequence of which rapid improvement is being made, and the trotting, pacing and draft horses are fast approaching perfection. Salem County is well up in this knowledge. Where can you find finer stock farms or more beautiful herds of cattle than within our own borders? The farmer's wife, too, can tell you the relative merits of the fowls in the poultry yard. One breed makes better mothers, another better layers, while a third is best for the table.

When the world comes to study and understand these things ; when as much loving care and forethought is given to the human species as to the flowers; fruits and animals, then shall we have a higher, nobler race of men and women. Miss Willard's mother has often said to her : " Frank, above all things else thank heaven you were a welcome child." She was born one year after the death of a baby sister, and no doubt owes much of gentleness and spiritual character to the influences surrounding her mother before her birth. It is because so many children are denied their birthright and are not welcome, not born into the kingdom of love and truth and purity, as every child should be ; because parents have failed in their high calling ; because fathers and mothers alike do not feel the importance and sacredness of their work, that so much evil is abroad in our land. For every other work in life we fit ourselves by study and careful preparation, but for this holy of holies, where the crown of motherhood is given us, we rush in haphazard. Is it any wonder that children are born maimed and weakened in body and mind, and that society must be hedged about by all the safeguards of the law to give us even the appearance of a peaceful, God-loving people ?

Dr. Stackhouse in her lectures used to say so forcibly, holding up two fingers : " There are just two reasons for marriage— first, affection, and affection that overrules all others ; second, desire of offspring." Would that men who are to wed or who are fathers would pause and reflect that their acts, be they good or evil, will live after them ; and that every maiden, wife and mother would understand who she is, and thus be more careful to whom she commits her love and keeping and more vigilant in preserving her natural rights.

We prefer to study heredity from the sunny side, for we know that good traits, more than evil, are handed down to the third and fourth generation, because good is in itself persistent and a principle of life and health, while there is no law of evil.

> " For evil is good that has gone astray
> And sorrow is only blindness,
> And the world is always under the sway
> Of a changeless law of kindness."

The law of the universe is order and fitness, and this law is superior in the matter parentage. Children often seem to carry out and develop the slighted talents which the parents have been unable to perfect in themselves. A talent for drawing which went no further than scribbling on the slate, in the second generation develops the artist. An ear for music, never satisfied in the parent, is inherited by son or daughter who comes to be the composer or professor. Miss Willard, in the closing chapter of " Glimpses of Fifty Years," says : "A great new world looms into sight like some splendid ship long waited for. The world of heredity, of pre-natal influence, of infantile environment, the greatest right of which we can conceive, the right of the child to be well born, is being slowly, surely recognized."

It is no narrow sphere we are filling. It is deep and broad as the need of the soul, wide and large as heaven. The fields are ready for the sowing. Our children and our children's children for untold generations will carry on the work we begin. The little seed we scatter by the wayside today shall be a mighty fruitful tree in the future.

This afternoon you will hear something from the Department of Health. These two (Health and Heredity), both being preventive, have been placed under one head. I hope something will be said in one or both papers that will touch some heart in every Union represented here, and the response will be, " Here

am I, that is the department I should like." To all who earnestly pursue the work a blessing will come.

> " Think truly, and thy thought
> Shall the world's famine feed :
> Speak truly, and thy word
> Shall be a fruitful seed ;
> Live truly, and thy life shall be
> A great and noble creed."

KEEPS DICKENS'S MEMORY GREEN.

One of the happiest and brightest women in Jersey City is
Miss Alice A. Holmes, the oldest and most noted blind resident
of the city. A classmate of Fanny Crosby, a musician and a
writer of poems, Miss Holmes has led a very active life, with
too little time to grow old or become despondent. She has
lived in Jersey City since 1830, and now, at the age of sixty-
seven, is spending the close of her life in writing an account of
her life and reminiscences of those she has met.

Of herself she says: "I have always been compelled to
work for my own support, and it was a puzzling question at
first what to do. I began to write verses, and in 1849 published
a book of verses entitled 'Poems by Alice Holmes.' In 1860 I
published 'Arcadian Leaves,' and in 1868 I had my last book,
entitled 'Stray Leaves,' issued."

An interesting incident in the visit of the younger Dickens
to Jersey City was an interview Miss Holmes had with him
after one of his readings. When the elder Dickens was in this
country he gave $1,700 to Dr. Howe, of Boston, to have "Old
Curiosity Shop" printed in raised letters for the blind. Miss
Holmes sought an interview with the novelist's son to express
to him her gratitude for his father's generosity.

CHRISTMASTIDE.

BY MISS ALICE A. HOLMES.

Again the joyous Christmas
  Is drawing very near;
And tokens of its coming
  In varied forms appear.

The fleecy snow is robing
  The ground in spotless white,
And through the holly branches
  Gleam berries, red and white.

The churches, halls and mansions
  Are hung with evergreen;
In cot and lowly dwelling
  Its festive wreaths are seen.

The mail is large and heavy
  With missives from afar,
Where friends with joy are hailing
  The bright and morning star.

And greetings warm they waft us,
  That through the festive tide
Goodwill, with all its halos,
  May in our midst preside.

The stores, with wares the choicest,
  Are crowded to the door,
And thronged with eager people,
  Who purchase, less or more.

The markets glow with plenty
  The fairest in the land;

And signs of merry Christmas
Appear on every hand.

And Santa Claus as usual,
For little girls and boys,
His sleigh is kindly filling,
With candies, books and toys.

And with his airy coursers
He'll waft them o'er the snow,
And softly down each chimney
Saint Nick himself will go.

And from his pack of treasures
The children's stockings fill,
And greet the elder people
With kindness and goodwill.

Oh; hark! the chimes are ringing;
The Christmas tide is here;
What gladness dawns upon us,
What festive joys are near.

Behold the Prince of Glory
Descends from heaven to earth;
With sweet hosannas hail him,
And celebrate his birth.

And may this welcome season,
Upon its joyous wing,
To every clime and people
A happy Christmas bring.

THE HUSKING NIGHT.

BY ETTIE HENDERSON.

The Autumn night was sinking fast,
  Tingling with gold the West,
As Mollie, with her brand new gown
  And bonnet, smartly dressed,
Ran to the neighbors, right and left,
  To tell them one and all
We're going to have a husking night.
  The first there's been this fall.

There's pumpkin pies, and doughnuts too,
  And cookies that I've made,
And John will have the cider brewed,
  Least so my father said,
And the barn is swept all nice and clean
  And the floor all sanded over,
The beams are wound with Autumn leaves
  And blossoms of sweet clover.

"I hope I'll get the first red ear
  When Frank is standing by,
Come early girls; 'tis scarcely eight
  When the moon is up full high.
The fiddlers ordered for the dance,"
  Moll merrily laughed outright;
She knew the partners she would have
  This moonlit husking night.

Fair Luna from her realms of space
  Cast long, low shadows round
As the boys and girls unbound the sheaves,
  And tossed them on the ground.

The golden corn rose heaping up
    Midst laughter far and near,
When Mollie screamed, "It's mine, I vow,
    I've got the first red ear."

She looked around, Frank was not there
    The man to kiss was Jim,
"I hate a moonlit husking night ;
    Well, I won't be kissed by him,
I feel I'm turning white and red,
    I'm tingling just all over,
And Nance is laughing silly, 'cause
    She knows that Frank's my lover.

There's Jack and Bob, and Dick and Ned,
    All waiting for a chance,
Oh, I can't stay here all night to kiss,
    Come on, let's go and dance."
Into the barn she ran to seek
    The face she sadly missed,
And plump into his arms she dropped
    It was Frank she really kissed.

     *   *   *   *   *

And Mollie trembling, blushing came
    To father next day morn,
And told what Frank had said to her,
    After they'd husked the corn.
"I've got my cottage, cattle too,
    And all yon land in sight
Is mine and yours, sweet Moll, my wife
    Before next husking night.

AN EASTER EMBLEM.

BY STELLA LOUISE HOOK.

One cool August afternoon, when the air was tingling with a suggestion of the frost that would come in a month or two, a large caterpillar looked down from the branches of a hickory tree growing by the road. He had passed a very pleasant summer in that tree, nibbling its green leaves and enjoying the warm sunshine ; but this exhilirating weather, that gave everyone else such appetites, took his away completely, He did not like to feel that the summer was at an end, and came crawling down the trunk of the tree in a melancholy frame of mind, thinking he would find some quiet place in which he could go to sleep until the cool weather was over.

"Look at that great green worm !" exclaimed one of a group of children passing by. This epithet might have hurt the caterpillar's feelings, for he was not at all like the blind, red-brown worms that crawled in the earth without legs. They had no expectation of ever changing their ugly bodies for anything better, but he had great hopes for the future. However, perhaps he did not heed the remark, for he continued on his way down the tree. "And how ugly he is," said one little girl, cautiously poking him with a stick. This was true. However, he expected to be very handsome by and by, so he paid no attention to this criticism ; but he did not like to be turned over so roughly, and clung to the stick with all his sixteen legs. What his fate would be when the children lifted him on the stick and carried him away, he had no idea, but he felt too drowsy and dull to care much about it.

At last the boys and girls arrived at the house in which they were spending the summer, and the caterpillar soon found himself in a comfortable airy box, with some of his favorite hickory leaves by his side ; he walked slowly up and down his prison, carefully examining it at every part. At last he selected a place that seemed convenient, in the angle formed by the top of the box and its side, and there settled himself.

It seemed rather hard that the poor sleepy caterpillar should have to weave his own blankets before he could take his rest, but he went to work contentedly. He began operations by securing a little gum to one side of the box. This gum, which in the air soon hardened to silk, came from two little tubes opening into his mouth, and thus when he drew back his head he left a long sticky thread. Fastening it to the other side, he stretched another fine strand across his body, and though he did not work very fast, his head moved back and forth with such regularity that he was soon covered by a mesh of silken cords, and was only to be seen dimly through them. However, as the fabric grew thicker and thicker, it was plain that the caterpillar was still working within, and after his outline could no longer be perceived through its close covering, many were the conjectures as to what he might be doing.

The caterpillar himself, snug in his warm silken bed, paid no attention to outsiders, nor thought whether they had any designs against his peace or not; so he calmly took off his bluish-green skin, rolling it into a careless little ball, and became a mummy-like black object, with neither eyes nor legs. Of what use are eyes and legs when one is lying still, sound asleep? By the time he was ready to get up he would doubtless have new ones, for he had never yet lacked anything he really needed, and had no reason to suppose he ever should. So, perhaps wondering a little what his mysterious future would be like, the caterpillar, who had now changed his name as well as appearance, and was called a chrysalis, composed himself to slumber within his quiet cocoon.

It was so deep a slumber that nothing could rouse him. It might have disturbed some dreamers to be shaken about in their beds just to hear them rattle, which I regret to say happened to the unfortunate chrysalis occasionally when inquisitive small fingers pried into the box; and certainly few people would have slept so peacefully when jolted about on a railroad train for several hours; but this, too, befell the chrysalis, and he never knew anything about it.

The winter passed, and no note of time was taken by the sleeper in the silken cocoon.

But great changes were going on there, without sound or motion, and the warmth of the house hastened this marvelous work. Had the chrysalis spent the winter in the outer air, he would have felt no inclination to leave his snug retreat before the summer sun shone warmly upon him, but indoors, April was as balmy as June, and the chrysalis stirred restlessly. He felt mysterious new powers, and wanted to try them ; and at last struggled out of the black mummy-wrappings, wide awake. Now his only thought was to get out of his silken prison, and, with much difficulty, he began to force his way through the fibres that he had spun so carefully the year before. Occasionally he paused to rest, for it was hard work, and when at last he drew his long, pale body through the opening he had made, he had scarcely strength to move.

How great a change had passed over him ! He had only six legs now, but they were long and slender and elegantly formed, his eyes were round and bright, and composed of many tiny eyes put together, so that he could see in every direction ; and he had two long things on each side of his body that puzzled him very much. They were damp and crumpled, and impeded his movements ; but in the sunshine which came through the window they began to dry and expand. As his strength returned, he waved them to and fro, and felt them grow larger and firmer, and then he knew that they were wings, and that he need no longer crawl slowly over the ground.

The moth—for he was a full grown moth now—felt unspeakably happy. His powers of enjoyment were so much greater than he had ever known before. In the sunny window some tall white lilies were blooming, and shed their fragrance abroad on the air. The moth rose on his pale-green wings, and fluttered toward them, rejoicing in his freedom and in the beauty of the spring day.

It was Easter Sunday; but the moth knew nothing about that, and could not understand why the passers-by looked up at the window with such interest. "What a beautiful Luna moth!" said one ; and the moth remembered how he had been called an ugly worm but a few months before. But when they said, " It is a lovely emblem of the resurrection," he could not understand it at all. He knew nothing of the truth that we remember especially at Easter—that we shall wake from death's sleep to a higher life, which, unlike the moth's, will never end ; he only knew that he was surrounded with brightness and beauty, and asked for nothing more than God had given him.

ALUMNI.

BY JENNIE THOMPSON HILES.

A woman sits in a far-off land—
  A woman with grave brown eyes—
And she holds two babies close in her arms
  At the hour when daylight dies.

She's thinking, and over the quiet mouth
  Falls the tremulous hint of a smile;
The sunset has carried her far to the East,
  And she's tarrying there for a while.

She spins a tale through the growing gloom
  For the listeners twain on her knee,
Of the pleasant and quaint old Jerseytown
  Where their mother used to be.

She tells of the flowers that used to make
  The place like a bower in June;
She tells of the whistles that used to blow
  And the bells that rang at noon.

She tells of the old Academy, too,
   With its stately avenue trees,—
The edifice crouching far behind
   Like a giant down on his knees.

Of the happy days she has lived just here;
   Of the eyes that have met her own;
Of the lessons she's taught the boys and girls—
   The men and the women grown.

She tells of the gay, good times they had—
   The boys and the girls and she;
Of the wise young principal over all—
   O, jolly and kind was he !

Her voice grows tender, and through the dusk
   There's the flash of a tear on her cheek
As she thinks of the earnest and helpful words
   It has been her lot to speak;

For those have passed through the high school's door
   Who have chosen their paths in life
Through the gentle words and the sound advise
   Of the Oregon lawyer's wife;

And she, in her far-away home, has thought
   Of the four years back today
When she looked her last on six of her boys
   And girls as they went away.

PERDITA.

BY GEORGIANA K. HOLMES.

Perdita stole my heart, she did! she did!
And whirled and twirled me as she bid,
She did; and stamped her silken clogs at me just when she
    would,
And shook her saucy head—you know she could,
            And can,
        Compel the heart of any man.

Perdita vowed she loved me; mortal man
May doubt Perdita if he can,
He can; I could not, would not if I could, and humbly
    vowed
To love her in my sleety shroud,
            And do,
        And so, you know, would you.

Perdita's fancies have half driven me mad;
She really, truly is too bad,
Too bad, but so enchantingly, bewitchingly divine,
And quite entirely mine
            You see—
        I know you envy me.

Perdita's maid must twirl and quirl her hair
Like any pyramid in air;
Take care to twist it out again and have it spread to bleach
On pasteboard circle where the sun may reach
            And bake—
        Gold locks of black locks make.

Perdita's clogs must be the richest kind
  Of satin ones, before, behind,
Soft lined and covered well with twills of filagree;
Her petticoats of satin must agree
    With them
    From waist to hem.

Perdita's fluffy skirts embroidered round:
  Sleeves, big enough for any gown,
I found must from Damascus come, or some far, heathen
    place,
Alack! and then there was her corsage lace—
    And is;
    Truly a shame it is!

If all San Marco's riches were but mine;
  If I with ducats did but shine
And twine my fingers into gold at every lapping fold
Where doublets could a single ducat hold
    I yet
    Perdita's needs had never met.

Perdita scores my heart, she does, she does;
  My ears are deaf with such a buzz,
A buzz, and when I would be sleeping sweetly in my bed,
I must be twirling in a dance instead,
    And smile
    As if I liked the style.

Perdita will yet have me dead, she will;
  My limbs are lank; I stoop until,
Until, my breath it goes so weasened when I try to sing,
She tosses back her head and laughs—the wicked thing!—
    My hair?
    A dozen spears stand in the air.

Perdita vows if I should dare to die
She would detain me from the sky,
And fly beside me, but I know for all she would not go,
She likes it mighty well below,
And soon
Would chant a different tune.

———————

A STRAY LEAF FROM THE DIARY OF A MEDICAL STUDENT.

BY FRANCIS HENDERSON.

It was in the year 18— that I went to Paris as a medical student. I was just eighteen. I rented a room in the Pays Latin or Latin quarter. This section of the metropolis is inhabited entirely by students. I had been living here about two years, when some one suggested that it would never do to leave Paris without attending a masked ball at the Opera Francais. I gave directions to the old woman who cared for my rooms to have a good fire at seven in the evening, and sallied forth in search of a costume. As I went out I could not but notice my charwoman. Although her face gave full evidence of her being fifty, her figure was one which many a young girl might have envied, and her light, springy step seemed to promise many years of future usefulness and activity in her humble calling. The eventful evening came at last. I was not in a festive mood, but I had not been long in the room, however, before there was a complete revulsion in my feelings. A female domino had followed my steps with a pertinacity which attracted my attention. There was no mistaking the figure—that sylph-like form, that light and graceful step, those piercing black eyes could belong only to a girl of sixteen. I did not stop to inquire how a girl of sixteen could have got into that pandemonium. It was quite enough for me that she had sense enough to discover my superior merits. I entered into conversation with her. It is true, her voice was scarcely as melodious as that of most young girls. Her hand, too, looked rather large. The conversation was most animated. What was my surprise to find that the fair unknown was acquainted with all my habits. Here was a regular love affair. For the last two years this lovely girl had been watching my steps. In church or in the Tuilleries, on the Champs Elysees, or on the Boulevards, with the tenacity of disinterested affection she followed all my movements. Yet the iron laws of society had prevented her from ever giving me a hint of this romantic devotion. She had never said she loved. I trusted that "concealment had *not*, like a worm in the bud, preyed upon her damask cheek." My heart was full. I made her the most passionate vows of undying love, and slipped a costly ring from my little finger on to her gloved hand. I begged for an interview, and assuring me that we should meet again, she slipped away, and was lost in the crowd. In what a delightful dream I remained!

My companions rallied me on the conquest I had made; they were as sure as I was, that my fair one was, at least, some duchess in disguise. The ball had taken place on Wednesday; all day Thursday and Friday I waited for some message from my innamorata. I glanced into every crested carriage with servants in livery, hoping to see a tiny note fall out at my feet. But no! a cruel father, doubtless, held strict watch over that loving heart. On Saturday there was to be another masked ball. I determined to go, and gave the old charwoman one of my door keys, with orders to have a good fire ready for me at midnight. I started alone for the ball, but on turning the corner of the street received from some one accidentally turning the corner at the same time a blow on the nose, which almost stunned me. Feeling that that valuable organ was rapidly swelling out of all proportion, I concluded to go home. In a fit of vexation I threw myself on the bed, and was fast losing my senses in sleep, when I was startled by the creaking of the door. Judge my surprise and delight when I saw by the door, with a lantern in her hand, the beautiful domino of the ball of Wednesday. Was it then possible? Had she heard of my accident and come to seek me? I was spellbound by joy, and could neither speak nor move. I silently watched the fluttering of the pink silk robe as she advanced towards the bureau. She opened a drawer and took out a pair of my white kid gloves. As she stood before the mirror, she noticed something wrong about her domino. She took it off. Great heavens! *It was my charwoman!*

SPEAKING EVIL.

BY MRS. PAULINE W. HOLME.

Speak we evil of our sister,
   Evil of our erring brother?
In us do we hide no error
   That we would not in another?

When we hear our neighbor slandered,
   Do we join the band accusing?
When no voice in kindness echoes,
   Do we sit in silence musing?

Aye, 'twere better we were silent
   Than our neighbor's faults be showing,
Speaking lightly of their errors,
   Sets the sparks of hatred glowing.

True we make no false assertion;
   Only bring the sins to view
That were lurking in their bosom,
   And they hoped unseen by you.

Do we thus the precept follow,
   That our Saviour oft did teach!

"As you would be kindly dealt with
  Thus in mercy deal with each."

Let our search be for the beauty
  That in other souls may lie :
And if naught we can discover
  Then in silence pass them by.

Let God judge them ; He is holy,
  We are poor and weak at best ;
He has told us all to love them,
  Do we heed his wise behest ?

We will learn to love each other
  If the love of God we seek ;
We will count their honor precious,
  Of their failings will not speak.

Only when our Lord obeying
  Wrapt in sympathy we go.
Face to face, ourselves forgetting,
  Him alone his faults to show.

Then we do a Christ-like service,
  Prove our friendship true and strong
All unlike the flatterer's praises
  Whose sweet poison does thee wrong.

Then speak not evil of thy brother,
  Nor fear his faults to him to show,
Thus shalt thou bless him and in blessing
  Peace within thy heart shall glow.

JOHN BROWN.

BY RACHEL N. HANCOCK.

Lines written while he was imprisoned under sentence of death for endeavoring to liberate slaves in 1859.

Those in bonds he did remember,
　And with them he now is bound,
Yet from out this gloomy prison
　Light shall spread its radiance round.

Light to show this guilty nation
　To be safe it must be just,
And that all its false enactments
　Soon must crumble into dust.

For the seeds of dissolution
　Ever grow on Error's tree;
And though Truth may seem to tarry,
　Yet her advent is to be.

Faith in this sustains the martyr
　When he bleeding lies and bound,
Faith in this makes tyrants tremble,
　Though with earthly honor crowned.

Speed! oh speed then, Holy Father,
　Speed the coming of the day
When by Light and Truth uprising
　Error shall flee away.

When no more thy helpless children
　By their brothers are oppressed,
But with loving and believing
　Every nation shall be blessed.

PROFESSIONAL READING A FACTOR IN THE TEACHER'S WORK

BY MISS PHEBE HANCOCK.

In the far-away ages, from the shades of classic lands, comes to us echoes, prophetic of the advanced ideas of today, and promises that in the far-future, they should be part of the web and woof of our educational life.

Surely those old schoolmasters builded better than they knew; or did they with prophetic eye and unwonted prescience see that in these later centuries, the thoughts they breathed would take living form, the ideas they originated would be developed, and become the keystone of the teaching of the present?

The creator of any system intended to lift the world to a higher plane or make it better is worthy of all reverence; of being placed on canvas or chiseled in the enduring marble. Such were Socrates and Plato and those old philosophers. We are the wiser for their having lived—yes—and better. For he who shows us how to reach young minds and awaken the intellect, so that it may make the best use of its grand faculties has lived to purpose. All honor to these sages of the past and to their teachings!

Good reading is education, and the well educated man has simply read more and retained what he has read better than others. It may not have been done in school or amid favorable surroundings, yet he is more highly educated who reads and retains most of what is worth reading. Theodore Parker, Robert Collyer, Caleb Cushing, and many more, found in their love of reading the open "sesame" of all future knowledge, and when one sees the power of books, he feels like repeating with Charles Lamb—"Grace before reading" not "Grace before eating."

The advancement of Professional Education suffers from want of preparation by those who would be teachers, and the whole body suffers from the contempt this brings. Those can only drill—not do efficient work—who are so indifferently prepared. They have but little influence in the school room and scarcely any in the community. What kind of barrister would he be who had never looked inside of Blackstone, or done any reading pertaining to his profession? We certainly should not consult such a one in a situation needing knowledge of law. And what think we of the minister, even if he have been dubbed D. D., whose book shelves are destitute of works on theology, and whose mind is a blank as to the knowledge contained in such books? The physician, too, with whom we trust our lives. Would we be so confiding did we think him behind the age in his knowledge of diseases and their remedy? That he was unacquainted with modern thought and the wonderful discoveries in medicine and surgery? A thousand times no! Is not the same true of members of our own profession? Shall we depend on the little obtained from the schools? At these, we receive only the start, and were the knowledge thus gained all we have for the race in life, we should dwindle to merest intellectual dwarfs. It is the reader who is ahead, and he who reads and applies, what the men of widest views have written on the subjects related to our various professions, will, himself, expand in views.

Professional reading will do more than any one thing to advance the profession. Let us not be indifferent to the spread of educational literature, and let us search constantly for the light coming therefrom. Plutarch says, " Books have brought some men to knowledge and some to madness." The reading of good books has brought them to knowledge. Let us be scholars if we can, but let us above all things possess educated minds. The memory may let the fact slip, but the impression of the thought upon the man lasts forever. Let us be economical of time, for in the minutes we may gather the thoughts that will prove a circlet of pearls.

FIFTEEN SUMMERS AGO.

A Romance of the Nineteenth Century.

BY EMILY HOFFMAN—(HELEN THORNE.)

My pretty Annette, you haunt me yet
With your beautiful eyes of liquid jet;
And try as I may, I cannot forget
Those halcyon days when first we met
    Fifteen summers ago.

Not as you are tonight my queen,
With your regal air and your diamonds' sheen.
But when you were blushing " sweet sixteen,"
And I was twenty, tall and lean,
    Fifteen summers ago.

I was a college youth from town,
You were a country girl (don't frown)
Sweet simplicity—pure white gown,
Tangled curls of darkest brown,
    Fifteen summers ago.

I swore that I loved you—I thought I did,
(I was always a very susceptible kid)
And when my boldness you softly chid,
Your dimpled hand in my brown one hid—
    Fifteen summers ago.

The first time I kissed you—remember the night?
We stood on the porch in the pale moon-light;
Like a startled fawn you looked up in affright,
And murmured, I don't think that can be right;
    Fifteen summers ago.

I called you " my darling, my angel, my dove ! "
And swore by the tranquil stars above
That you were "my first—my only love ! "
And, like the late Romeo, talked of your " glove,"
    Fifteen summers ago.

Like the fickle knight in the ancient lay,
I falsely "loved and I rode away,—"
Left you with vows to return " some day "
And—forgot you so soon in the city gay,—
    Fifteen summers ago.

But you did not worry, my lady fair,
For instead of pining in proud despair,
Or romantic'ly climbing the golden stair,—
You married a gouty old millionaire—
    Fifteen summers ago.

FORKED ROADS.

BY KATE LIVINGSTON HAMILTON.

It was an unattractive little settlement, with no more of beauty in itself or its surroundings, than of euphoniousness in its name. The earliest inhabitants had been strict utilitarians. Whatever served an immediate definite purpose was accepted with slight questioning as to possible improvement.

For years a grist mill had stood just at the point where the road to the county town of Grafton branched from the main turnpike that led to the great city of L——. When a few houses began to cluster around the mill and then a store, and at last a church, was there any reason why the spot should not be called Forked Roads still?

Each of its fifteen or twenty dwellings bore a close resemblance to every other. They were four-square as to shape, dingy white as to color, and, externally at least, absolutely without ornamentation. This dismal bareness was not due to poverty, for it grew in time to be quite a prosperous neighborhood. But this prosperity had been reached by means of labor so constant and severe that it had well-nigh overcome and banished all interest in aught except work.

The largest farm in Forked Roads belonged to Robert Green, and his house stood in the choicest situation, just where it commanded a view of all that passed from either direction.

At an upper window, one afternoon in late November, sat his oldest daughter. There was nothing in her appearance, her surroundings, or her life, if you had known it, that would have led you to select her as the heroine of any story. She was not even the heroine of her own day dreams, as with hands idly folded, she gazed intently out over the monotonous landscape. Indeed, her reverie could hardly have been called day-dreaming. She was asking over and over the question that seems born on the lips of every American—" Will it pay?" To judge from the weary, discontented, half cynical expression of her face, life with her, thus far, had not paid for the trouble of living. At twenty-three that seemed a strange verdict, but for years she had been looking forward vaguely to something different. She could scarcely have told what. She had no dreams of fame, no desire for "a sphere," no pet hobbies to ride. Only it seemed as if somewhere there must be a more interesting, more palpably valuable state of existence than any of which she was cognizant. Just where, or when, or how, the meaningless round of necessary work in which she found herself was to be merged into this larger life she had no idea. Yet of late the abstract question had begun to take on concrete form, or rather circumstances were gradually forcing her to choose between this misty ideal and a very practical reality.

She was almost tempted to give up the vision. Perhaps, after all, she had been mistaken. Perhaps these things that did not quite satisfy her were worth living for, and the lack was rather in herself than in them.

To be the most notable housekeeper within their circle of

acquaintances was her mother's ambition; and a more cheerful contented woman would be hard to find. Every foot of her father's land had been bought with his own earnings, and his pride in the fact was none the less because it seldom found voice. The friends of her own age seemed tending in the same direction. With all due regard for sentiment an improvement of wordly condition was an ideal requisite of a happy marriage.

From one point of view there was a certain completeness about this scheme of life. To do one's work well, to possess a comfortable amount of property for week days, and a becoming amount of religion for Sundays, to live and die respected of one's neighbors, made a very fair sum total. All this lay just within her reach. Toward it for months she had been drifting, almost without volition, yet now that a decisive moment had come she was still loth to resign herself to its limitations. There were few girls in Forked Roads who would not have been glad to exchange places with Rachel Green, few who did not think her fortunate in having attracted the attentions and regard of Ralph Weston, the most prosperous young merchant in Grafton. For a year he had been her escort at all merry-makings and social gatherings. By every one, except the two immediately concerned, the marriage was considered a foregone conclusion. To "live in town," to keep a servant, to dress handsomely, was a mode of life several degrees more desirable and more "genteel" than to marry a farmer and settle down at Forked Roads; hence the general verdict that it was "a good match." Rachel herself had nothing to urge against it. She liked Ralph. She had never seen any one whom, on the whole, she liked better or admired more. It was not by force of contrast that she intuitively felt a want of harmony somewhere in their natures. True he was not an ardent lover, but he prided himself upon his practical sagacity and his strength of will. The former had shown him that Rachel Green, aside from any consideration of her father's broad acres, would be to some one a good wife. The whole force of the latter was bent on making that some one himself. He was neither domineering nor selfish. He honestly believed he could make her happy. He would have honestly tried to do all that in him lay toward that end while they both lived, and she would need stronger support than the misty outlines of a dream, if she successfully opposed his suit.

As she rose to put away the sewing that had lain untouched in her lap a little folded paper fell to the floor. It was a printed circular that had been handed to her in Grafton the day before. With a sigh of relief that something had interrupted her perplexing thoughts she opened the paper.

The enigmatical letters, C. L. S. C., which headed it, fraught with meaning as they are to thousands of people, told her nothing of its contents. Indeed the keys of our destiny rarely come plainly marked into our hands. As she read of the various schemes of study which Chautauqua typifies and embraces, she caught only a glimpse of what it might become to her. Perhaps the dim ideal she sought might be in this world of books. At least the plan had the charm of novelty, and the experiment was worth trying. A decision, with Rachel, was equivalent to an immediate beginning of the work in hand, and the unavoidable delay before the volumes could be ordered and received only increased her interest. The more she thought of her new undertaking the greater inspiration she drew from it. There was companionship in the idea of belonging to a class of several thousand, even though one never saw one's fellow-students. When the books came she looked eagerly through them—science, art, history and literature, names only, or wearisome tasks when she studied in the district school—delightful possibilities now, since she sought them voluntarily.

In the family the experiment was called "one of Rachel's freaks," and her enthusiasm did not prove contagious. She cared little for that. Like mountains through a vanishing mist the answers to many a question were slowly dawning on her vision. Nothing around her had changed—except her point of view. Yet the earth itself seemed new, its history clothed with a wondrous fascination that not even the technicalities of geology could entirely disguise.

History was no longer a dry fragmentary record of names and events—interesting doubtless to the actors therein, but of little importance to succeeding generations. It was a living, breathing thing, a complete logical story of which her own times formed a chapter. Its endless continuity of cause and effect she perceived but dimly, yet that faint perception aroused a thirst for knowledge, not easily to be quenched.

Out in the world, the great busy world beyond Forked Roads and Grafton, men and women were living the lives of which she had dreamed, lives potent for good to themselves and their fellows, yet made up of the very things she had despised. Could it be that these dull, colorless fragments at her feet could throw such a radiance over the earth when illuminated by the light of noble motives? Not work for work's sake, not even work for work's tangible results, was worth living for, but work for its influence on characters that were to develop throughout all eternity—ah! that was another matter. That was the key missing which made discord out of life's grandest harmonies. * * * A year passed, and it was rumored that Rachel Green had refused Ralph Weston. No one could guess why—Ralph, perhaps, least of any. He had pleaded long and earnestly. "If it's this new notion you've taken to books," he said, "you can have all money will buy—and all the time you want to read them. I never calculated to make a slave of my wife as some men do" "It isn't that, exactly—" "Then what is it?" he interrupted, half angrily. "Do you know so much that you are ashamed to marry a man who has only been to a country school?"

"Oh, no, no! I don't know anything but"—— "I want to know and you don't," was on her lips. She checked it there. She had, in her blindness, so nearly made shipwreck of her own life that she was tenderly pitiful of his. With all the power of a somewhat narrow nature this man loved her. It was neither his fault nor hers, that her larger gifts, her wider out-look, forced their future paths far apart.

If she had only discovered it soon enough to have saved him this pain! Yet she, too, had suffered in her groping after light, more than he would ever believe. Her questioning was at an end now. It was best for both as it was. Perhaps he, too, would see it so some day. Meanwhile her self-condemnation was greater because, deep in her consciousness, resolutely crowded out of sight, lay the knowledge that another might be to her that which Ralph Weston never could. Little by little had been revealed the harmony of hopes, intents and aspirations that had been so painfully wanting before. Shut her eyes to it as she might, she knew that she would find supreme content in giving her life into his keeping, in pursuing with him labors that should reach their fullest consummation only in "the life which is to come."

In view of all that had so recently passed could it be right to accept this crown of joy? And clear-sighted Love answered "Yes."

LET HIM, THAT HEARETH, SAY COME, THIS IS THE WAY, WALK YE IN IT.

BY MARIA HARRISON.

O come with me, the evening shadows fall—
   Time hastens on, and soon we shall be gone—
Life's little hour is hurrying to its close—
   O tarry not, but listen to my call.

The way's not dark if faith points out the road ;
   Even as we go it opens on our sight ;
Press on and soon we will gain the blest abode,
   Where reigns our *Saviour* in eternal light.

Once there, all sorrows shall forever cease,
   And joy ineffable possess the soul—
There shall our songs of rapture swell in peace,
   "While onward countless ages yet shall roll."

O Jesus, Friend and Brother, Saviour, God—
   Send down thy Holy Spirit from above—
To guide our weak and wandering footseps right
   So we may be forever with *Thee*, Lord—
      Or we will linger in eternal night!

LANTERNS AND UMBRELLAS.

A Stormy Drama of the Road.

BY FLORENCE HOWE HALL.

SCENE I.

A Sitting room in the Tear-all mansion. Mrs. Tear-all is seated beside a center table, darning stockings. A large basket-full of sewing stands beside her. On the opposite side of the table sits Master Tom Tear-all, with an enormous pile of school books at his elbow, and a Greek volume open before him. The hall and front door are plainly seen through the doorway. As the scene opens, the door-bell rings, and Mr. Tear-all enters, clad in yellow oilskin, and dripping streams of water on the floor.

MRS. TEAR-ALL.—Oh, John ! I'm so glad you've got safely home, this wet and dismal night—though you do look like a young waterspout. But where's Keate Tupperling ?

MR. TEAR-ALL.—Why, isn't he here ? He started to come out on the four o'clock train.

MRS. T.—No, I've seen nothing of him—but he'll come on the next train, I'm sure he will,—lets have our supper, and not wait any longer for him

MR. T.—Come on the next train, woman; you don't know what you're talking about ! I tell you he started two hours be·fore I did, and what's happened to him, Heaven only knows !

MRS. T.—Pooh ! nonsense ! what should happen to him ? Probably he stopped for a political meeting, or jubilee, or whatever you call these endless outings; you know as well as I do, John, that no man can be depended upon to come home in this dreadful campaign, which seems to go on just the same now that election is over !

MR. T.—Do you suppose, Martha, that people are waylaid

on trains, and entrapped by highwaymen, into political meetings? No, I know he's been robbed, or drowned, or garroted,
or something in the streets of New York. It's perfectly ridicul-
ous for these poets to attempt to go about alone—can't be done.
They go moving around, and the first thing anyone knows they
turn up in Australia,—I believe he's on his way there now; dear
me, sas. And what will his father say to us? Why didn't you
telegraph me that he hadn't come?

MRS. T.—Now, John, you're very unjust. I thought he was
coming with you; and you know you always say that's no use to
telegraph! And, besides, I never knew that he was a poet. Oh,
dear! what *shall* we do? Why didn't his father keep him at
home?

MR. T.—There's no use in going back to the Deluge, Martha,
with your foolish questions—this present deluge is enough for
us. Yes, I must start right out again, with all my rheumatism,
and my wet clothes and NO supper, because it's never ready, (he
becomes more and more excited in mannerr) and all in the dark,
because you would let the baby play with my lantern and smash
it. No, it's no use ringing the bell for tea—I must go now to
my DEATH. Tom, can't you lend me your rubber boots? (exit
Tom) mine leak—I shall fall into the canal on my way to the
station, all because you *would* ask a young man to stay with us
without first inquiring whether he was a poet! *Never* ask a
young man to come into your house again, Martha, without first
finding out whether he is a poet. (re-enter Tom, with an enormous pair of rubber boots, which Mr. Tear-all proceeds to put
on.) It's fatal—this careless, slipshod way of doing business,
but you've seen the last of me, Martha; good-by, forever!

MRS. T.—Oh, John! what ARE you going to do? Oh, I'm
worried to death! Oh, DON'T go out in this storm!

MR. T.—Do? I'm going to see whether he's stopped at
Weehawken, at his uncle's—and if he isn't there I'm going to
New York to ALARM THE POLICE! We shall search the
slums, Quarantine, all the haunts of wickedness, where no man's
life is safe one minute (Mrs. T. shrieks)—and where he's been

25

lured by some designing villain, who asked him to play backgammon—and who is now no doubt stabbing him in the back
(Mrs. T. wrings her hands and dances about in mute anxiety)
with a red-hot poker—unless he's been carried off to the cholera
hospital, where I shall CERTAINLY follow him.

Mrs. T.—Oh, John, John! You shan't go—the father of
seven children—to go and have hot pokers in his spine! you
can't—you *shan't*—or be drowned in a canal; oh! oh! and your
life isn't insured, and we've been married sixteen years on next
Friday week—and so happy! (sobs) and you MUST buy a lantern,
if you will go—but don't, don't (she seizes the lapel of his yellow
coat).

(Mr. T. tears himself away with a dramatic gesture, and
rushes out of the door, brandishing a huge, faded cotton
umbrella. Mrs. Tear-all drops into a chair, shuts her eyes and
moans bitterly.)

Tom Tear-all (studying aloud).—O TEKNA KADMOU.
(suddenly looking up from his book) Hulloa! What's all this
row! the governor going! (He starts to run after his father.)

Mrs. T. (throwing both arms around Tom's neck.)—No, no,
Tom; you're all that's left me now. No, you shan't stir ONE
inch!

(Curtain.)

SCENE II.

(This scene passes in dumb show. A wide and very muddy road, on a pitch
black, rainy night. Occasional flashes of lightning illuminate all objects, and reveal a canal, running along beside the road, and a little
way from it. Enter Mr. Tear-all from the left, wearing his hat very
much on one side; he holds a lantern aloft in his right hand and an
umbrella in his left. His whole bearing is that of a determined, Guy
Fawkes order of conspirator, and he walks along with great strides,
waving the lantern—which, however, only illuminates a small portion of the road,—and keenly scrutinizing the muddy path.)

(Enter, on the right, a curious crawling object, which a flash of lightning
shows to be the poet Keats Tupperling, proceeding upon all fours,
with an umbrella held over his back. He feels of the road carefully as

he creeps along, and is evidently much afraid of falling into the canal. His eye-glasses are wet with the rain, and his gaze is fixed upon the the ground. He passes Mr. Tear-all, on the opposite side of the road, and they leave the scene, at opposite ends.)

SCENE III.

(The same room as in *Scene I.* Mrs. Tear-all is vigorously darning white stockings with red thread, and Tom is still at his Greek, with his elbows on the table and his hands buried in his hair. The door-bell rings half dozen times.)

Mrs. T. (jumping up quickly).—There, Tom, there's your father! Oh, what a relief! Do hurry and let him in! (They both hasten to the front door, and Tom works at the key, which refuses to turn.)

Mrs. T.—Oh! that key never *will* turn! Your father's the only person who can manage it, and we may NEVER see him alive again. What *shall* we do?

Tom.—I can fix it; just wait a minute. (Tom leaves the scene, and reappears in a moment bearing a monkey wrench.)

Mrs. T.—How quiet your father is, Tom! He doesn't usually like to wait. (Tom applies the monkey wrench to the key, which finally yields and the door flies open, disclosing Keats Tupperling; his tall, lank form is dripping with rain, but he beams through his wet eye-glasses with a perfectly serene, unruffled air.)

Mrs. T.—(In a high excited voice).—Where's Mr. Tear-all? Where's my husband?

Keats T.—Oh! Isn't he here? Didn't you get my telegram?

Mrs. T.—No, no; oh! why did John go? I knew it would all come out right—and now he's alarmed the police—what shall we do? Where have you been?

Keats T. (with great sweetness).—I've been to Philadelphia —I forgot all about looking out for Orange, you see—and then they called so many different Oranges that I got a little confused, and as I was composing a new sonnet on the Chicago car strikes—a fine, thrilling subject—somehow I never noticed where

we were till too late. I'm rather hungry, but then, I've had a
hundred miles free ride ; that was very interesting !

Tom T.—Mother, I'd better go right after father, and stop
him at Weehawken, or telegraph to the police at New York that
Mr. Tupperling isn't dead—only writing a sonnet—

Mrs. T.—I'm nearly frantic ! First John, and then my precious Tom ! O Mr. Tupperling ! how could you do so ? It's absurd
to compose on the way to Orange ! Dear, dear ! None of the
commuters ever do it ! Why, John says he has hardly time to
compose himself before the train stops. Oh ! I can't let Tom
go alone ! (Tom goes out to get his coat and hat. A frightful
clap of thunder is heard). You must go with him !

Keats T.—Why, yes, I will, of course. I'm so glad, now, that
I borrowed this lantern of the man across the river.

Mrs. T. (in horror and surprise)—Across the river ?

Keats T.—Why, yes ; you see, I crossed the river and went
up the mountain by mistake, but a kind man lent me this lantern ; indeed, he offered to bring home here. He seemed to think
I might not be able to find the way by myself.

Mrs. T.—Oh ! you only went about three miles out of your
way. Where's Tom ? (Re-enter Tom). Oh, your father has got
your boots ! Dear, dear ! Oh, I can't bear to have you go.

Tom.—Good-by, mother ; we'll be all right. Come along,.
Mr. Tupperling. (Exeunt Tom and Mr. Tupperling).

(Mrs. Tear-all seats herself in a rocking chair and rocks
back and forth in gloomy silence for some minutes. Her eyes
are fixed upon the front door, and she wears an expression of
calm despair).

Mrs. T.—Yes, they'll find him in the morgue. I'm sure of
it, and he had on all his old clothes, too ! Or else in the foundling asylum, of course, John is rather old for a foundling, but I
suppose the police will take him there—if they find him alive !
(A terrific clap of thunder is heard, accompanied by a blinding
flash of lightning. Mrs. Tear-all claps her hands in her ears,.
springs to her feet, and walks up and down the room, dragging
after her several stockings and a ball of worsted).

MRS. T. (wringing her hands)—It's of no use. I can't be calm! O John! why did I let you go—and my blessed Tom?

(The door bell rings violently and continuously. Mrs. Tear-all hastens to the door, which she opens with some difficulty, revealing Mr. Tear-all, holding Keats Tupperling by the arm, and Tom Tear-all. They are very wet and splashed with mud. Mrs. T. utters a scream and throws herself into the arms of Mr. T., knocking him against the poet, who staggers and tumbles against the hat rack.)

MRS. T.—Oh! say you're not dead, John! I know you've been struck by lightning and paralyzed, you move so queerly—

MR. T.—Good heavens! Move queerly. I guess you'd move queerly if you'd been hunting for moon-struck poets in the ditches all night, with rheumatism in both shoulders, and no supper, and then had a 250 pound woman strike you with the force of a cannon ball—queerly; oh, yes! I'm not the queer one, but I know who is, and I've been telling Mr. Tupperling here that if there were a whipping post in this town, I'd take him to it p. d. q., too.

MR. K. T. (with great sweetness).—Yes, you're quite right! To think that we passed each other on the road! I can't account for it! It must have been when I was feeling of the ground, to keep out of the ditches—or else when the drunken man walked me into the big tree—

MRS. T.—What drunken man?

MR. K. T.—Why, you see, I didn't know my way up from the depot, so I asked a very pleasant man, who was going to the village, whether he'd show me the way—and so he did very kindly, but after we ran into a great tree, I thought perhaps I'd be safer without him, especially as he smelled very strongly of whisky, and I had to hold him up to keep him from stumbling!

MRS. T.—But where did they find you, John—not—not in the morgue?

TOM.—Why, mar, you must be crazy? We found the governor at the depot,—I only wish you could have seen him! There he sat on the bench outside the station, leaning on that horrid old gray umbrella, watching the track like a—a ferret or a detective.　He looked sterner than any old Roman—actually I wonder the trains dared to pass by. he eyed the track with such a tremendous and eagle eye !

Mr. T.—Why, of course, I did ! I got Mr. Tupperling's telegram at the station—and I said 'to myself that fo—, ahem, that goose of a poet will go shuttlecocking up and down this railroad all night and never remember to get out at his own station ; so I shall just sit here and watch, and pull him right through the car window by the head and ears if necessary!

Mr. K. T.—It's all very funny; even the storm can't damp our spirits, eh? Don't you want to hear my adventures, Mrs Tear-all ?

Mrs. T.—Oh, not tonight, Mr. Tupperling—I can't hear any more adventures tonight ! Besides, the servants have all gone to bed and I must get you something to eat. And you must all change your wet clothes—

Mr. T.—Yes, that is, if Mr. Tupperling can be trusted to go up stairs alone ! It would be a pity to have him walk into the cistern, or the coal bin,—no more sonnets now, Mr. Tupperling ! All the boots and trousers in the house are wet, so we can't go after you again tonight, no matter WHAT happens !

Mrs. T.—Never mind, John ! All's well that ends well,—do come now and have some supper !

(Curtain.)

THE GRAY NUN.

BY MRS. VIRGINIA B. HARRISON.

There comes each dying day to bless
　A little while before the night ;
A gentle nun in convent dress,
　Of clinging robes all gray and white.

She lays her cool hand on my face
　And smoothes the lines o fcare away ;

Her tender touch with magic grace
  Dispels the worries of the day.

She folds the mystic curtain by,
  That hides from view the shadowy throng
And gives me those for whom I sigh,
  The vanished friends for whom I long.

Sometimes she brings a perfumed spray
  Of flowers that bloomed long years ago,
The breath of summers laid away
  'Neath many a winter's drifted snow.

No other guest gives such delight,
  Nor can of peace bestow the same
As she who comes 'twixt day and night,
  And Twilight is the gray nun's name.

PRESENCE OF MIND.

"Honi Soit Qui Mal Y Pence."

A silken string which though snow white
  With Phoebe's brow could not compare ;
It's golden clasp not half so bright
  As Phoebe's wealth of shining hair.

Upon the floor it lay, half curled
  Around her little satin shoe ;
I wonder still what in the world
  Turned Phoebe's face to such a hue.

As, picking up the dainty thing
  With sauciest smile she said. " Please note
The latest style " and clasped the string
  Of ribbon round her slender throat.

FALLEN LEAVES.

AMELIA C. HOOPER.

Our Autumn days are here again ;
    To me they bring unrest,
And as the deepening twilight falls,
    My soul is sore depressed.

Past sorrows rise with every sound
    That falls upon mine ear :
That which I loved in other days
    I now feel sad to hear.

'Twas music once, the echo of
    The whip-poor-will's lone song,
And all the little voices that
    The evening brought along.

Now all is changed and ne'er can be
    The same as in the past,
Ere death had o'er our joyous home
    His growing shadows cast.

'Tis hard indeed to chase away
    The heart aches and the gloom,
Or cease to mourn for each dear one
    Now resting in the tomb.

Alas for me ! Our little cot
    Seems desolate and bare.
Go where I may, no sunny spot,
    No sweet young voice is there.

There's left for me one sacred place
    In solitude to tread ;
And there I hold communion with
    The silence and the dead.

A CAMP IN THE ADIRONDACKS.

BY JESSAMY HARTE.

When an enthusiastic Adirondack lover has finished reading Murray's "Adventures in the Wilderness," he is apt to be very discontented, and longs to have been among those mountains twenty-five or thirty years ago, when the great North Woods were indeed a vast wilderness; when no axe had sounded along its mountain sides, or echoed across its peaceful waters. But in spite of the amount of desecration this exquisite forest has suffered at the hand of civilization, it still contains in its depths, far from the madding crowd of hotels and boarding houses, the same majesty that awed the first band of discoverers who trespassed upon its solitude. The great trees of the "forest primeval" are there with their towering branches like huge arms stretched out in loving protection above the heads of their little ones.

And yet, notwithstanding the thousands of people who annually visit these mountains and flock about the hotel verandas, comparatively few have ever known the joy of standing beneath one of these monarchs of the forest, and of having camped under its deep shade. Many fashionable young women with Saratoga trunks journey to these mountains, only to sink exhausted upon the hotel piazzas, where they remain for the most part, going hardly beyond the hotel limits during the rest of their stay. Of course, those who are great invalids must of necessity be content with the superb views which are so graciously spread before them; but for those more favored mortals who are capable of appreciating the physical as well as mental enjoyments of the wilderness, camp life is the Elysium for which they are looking, and the Adirondacks their "Happy Hunting Ground." Camping, until of late years, has been the most exclusive enjoyment of men,

women having been considered rather useless and burdensome
under the circumstances; as incongruous, in fact, as a Dresden
vase would be. But now that women have proved that they are
not so frail and helpless, and that total exhaustion does not necessarily follow the ascent of a hill, and that they are quite as
capable of enjoying the rough life and thriving on it as their
masculine friends, camp life has taken on a new charm, and the
men are glad to have the companionship of the fair sex upon
these expeditions.

There is such a novel charm about the old forest, and such a
fascination in being removed from ordinary daily life and of living a sort of romantic holiday. Many stand a trifle in awe of
the vast woods, and the proposal "to camp" is often met by the
following despairing objections: "Won't we catch cold? Aren't
you afraid? What shall we wear? Won't we look like guys?"
It is a mystery to me why people think that the moment they
give up the restrictions of conventional social life, they must necessarily make themselves look as ugly and unattractive as possible. Some of the costumes which I have seen must verily have
offended its critical eye.

Crimson is a picturesque color for the feminine camping
dress. A very striking costume for a young lady is a short kilt
skirt, a little above the ankles, of some blue material; a short,
blue corduroy velvet jacket, blue and white striped tennis shirt,
russet leather leggings, and big, red felt sombrero. The men's
get-up varies little from the ordinary mountain garb—short corduroy velvet trousers and jacket, woolen tennis shirt, and leather
leggings. The latter are essential both for girls and men on account of the enormous amount of underbrush one encounters.
You cannot imagine how picturesque these costumes look
around the roaring camp-fire in the evening, or in groups on the
shores of some beautiful lake. A gentleman once said to me,
while admiring some pictures I had of "camp": "Why, how well
you all look! Do you know, I thought that in camp the women
wore healthful but hideous garments, and the men went unshaven
and looked slouchy." So you see no young lady need ever be

afraid of appearing at a disadvantage in camp, nor is her sweetness wasted on the desert air.

It is rather an arduous task though, to get up a congenial party, one that will hang together "in clear and stormy weather," as the saying is. In selecting your party you must not forget your funny man ; he is as essential to its success as a clown is to a circus. He is the life of the camp always ; the one who is always getting you into scrapes, and the only one who comes out of them unharmed. You must also have a recognized head, or leader, with an aptitude for managing, two or three trusty guides, and among the rest of the dramatis personæ, good singers, story tellers, etc. Then too, that "necessary evil," the chaperon, should be of semi-angelic character, else she will never successfully accomplish the care of such a party. With such a chaperon and party success is sure.

The three-sided log camp or "lean-to" has become a substitute almost entirely in the Adirondacks for the ordinary canvas tent, and as the floor is also made of planed boards, there is no danger of the dampness which was an evil of the floorless tent. The "lean-to" has a slanting roof at the back, two perpendicular sides, and is open in front. There is a bed at the back resembling a stateroom berth, which is made of boards thickly carpeted with balsam boughs and covered with blankets. There is no more comfortable bed in the world ; the odor of the balsam is most conducive to sleep, and insomnia is unknown in camp. At the front of the "lean-to" are usually hung curtains, generally of Turkey red, and when these are draped back during the day the effect of these little houses, with the never-dying camp-fire burning before them, is picturesque in the extreme. This fire is kept burning as religiously as were the old Vestal fires of Athens, and the guides, though rather rugged priests, are as faithful as the Vestal virgins.

We camped once on Long Lake, Hamilton County, one of the most beautiful of all the Adirondack lakes. Near its head stood one of the mountain hotels, and close by were several rude farm-houses and a country store, but the rest of the shore was delightfully wild and picturesque. Here and there at considerable distances one could discover camps peeping out from beneath the pine trees. We started from the hotel for our destination, which was at the extreme end of the lake, at about three o'clock on one of those clear, refreshing afternoons so common among the mountains. Three of our boats were rowed by the guides, who took care of our " duffle," meaning luggage in camping parlance. We rowed under the floating bridge near the country store in single file, and past the last farm-house (our Sandy Hook) about a half mile above. We reached our camp at sunset; the guides having already arrived were unloading the boats and pulling them up along the shore.

The camp stood on a high bluff which projected into the lake, steep and precipitous on one side, but gently sloping down to a smooth, shiny beach on the other. There were nine or ten "lean-tos" scattered along the cliff, while on the beach near the lake was a rough bark building, with a long table in the centre, which we were informed was our dining hall. The owners of the camp who had built it the year before had arranged pieces of sail cloth like curtains on each side, in case of stormy weather. We scrambled up the rocks to our new abodes in a state of great excitement. We were all novices at camping, except our chaperone and her husband, who knew as much about the woods as the guides themselves. The huge camp-fire was already built and crackled away in the most friendly and cheerful manner. Suddenly the clear notes of a cornet were heard from the beach below, and then a shout: "Come boys, grub's ready!" which was meant to convey to our scandalized ears that supper would be served in the log house below. Alas! the demon of slang had already taken possession of the dude of the camp and transformed him into a backwoodsman. We were all very hungry, the breath of the pines having exaggerated our already healthy appetites. Our first meal was a novel as well as merry one to us all. The long bark table was set in a most unconventional manner, tin plates, brown china cups (no saucers) and old knives and forks, the table being decorated with leaves put under the plates and around the dishes. In the centre was a long, green olive bottle filled with wild flowers and decorated with ferns, making a charming jardinière. The view from our dining hall was superb; the lake stretched before us in all its wild romantic beauty. Far off in the distance the peaks of Santanoni and Mt. Seward, with their rugged outlines, stood out against the rose-colored sky. There was that peculiar hush that comes at sunset; only the sound of the water lazily lapping the shore, and now and then the baying of a hound far away on some distant lake broke the silence. Oh, how we did enjoy our unconventional supper; but I am afraid our table manners suffered greatly from its very unconventionality.

After supper we proposed rowing across the lake to see "Mother Nichols," as she was called, an eccentric old woman, the widow of an old woodsman who had died several months before. No one could persuade her to move from their little log cabin where her husband had brought her a bride, some sixty years before. Her house stood about a mile from the shore, half way up the mountain side. Our guide told us that "folks said the view from there was extry fine," and as the moon would soon be out there was no danger of being lost. So we started, leaving two guides behind us to take care of the camp. When we reached the opposite shore we sounded the camp call; it was immediately answered by the report of a gun fired from camp. The path leading to the cabin was very rocky and hard to climb; and when we arrived at the hut we were surprised to see no signs of life anywhere. "Why, it's deserted!" "Where's the old woman?" we cried. "Hush," said our guide, "she's there all right taking her evening smoke." "Good evening, Mother Nichols," said our chaperone, addressing space; "we have come to pay you a little visit, and to take a look at your beautiful view." "I am proud to see you, ma'am." said a cracked voice from the shadow, and an old woman stepped out into the moon-light. In one hand she held her clay pipe, the other she extended to each of us as we were presented to her by turn. This ceremony seemed to please her greatly, and she insisted upon getting us some cider and apples. She said that "since the old man died" she was in the habit of sitting there in the darkness and enjoying the view herself; but if she had known she was going to have "kempany" she'd have "lighted up a spell." She pointed out to us the innumerable lakes we saw in the distance, calling them by name, and relating some little story or legend about nearly every one of them.

When we left her she insisted on coming half way down the rocks with us; it was wonderful to see how agile she was, refusing all assistance that was offered her. As we rowed away she seemed to us like some wizard who owned the great view she loved so well.

As we neared the camp, the friendly light of the camp-fire glowing through the trees seemed to welcome us back. The great forest had fallen asleep, so still it seemed. Our guides had some sandwiches made for us, thinking we might be hungry, and we sat around the fire, listening to marvelous stories from the guides, singing and playing on our banjos, until it was time to retire. If the rest of our stay was to be as jolly as the evening we had just spent we would indeed be willing to camp for the rest of our lives, so deeply in love with it we had already become. We climbed all the mountains about us, and explored every lake or pond for miles around. Our friends visited us from neighboring camps, when we entertained them with some impromptu charades given in the open air. The stage setting was a trifle Wagnerian, I will admit, a most fitting background for a Seigfried or Brunhilde, but we trusted to the imagination and indulgence of our audience to make our performance successful as social dramas. Every manner of game from whist to leap-frog was indulged in at camp. On rainy days we would all assemble on one of the largest "lean-tos" or in the dining-room, where we played games and sang, and in fact amused ourselves in a hundred different ways.

Our dances, too, under the pines, were a never-to-be-forgotten enjoyment of the camp. As we were all fond of dancing, these rural hops were indulged in, so that it was necessary to have a platform built for that special purpose. Numberless Chinese lanterns were hung on the branches above, and the huge trees encircled our ball-room with a weird charm. Our invitations were written on pieces of birch bark and delivered by the guides when one of these fêtes was about to occur. At eight o'clock the guests would arrive, the men arrayed in picturesque tennis suits, and the girls in all their finery ; muslin dresses that had lain asleep all summer were permitted to grace the vanities of the world once more. Our orchestra consisted of two fiddles and a cornet, which were played by the guides with exhilarating effect. Waltzes and polkas followed in rapid succession, but we usually ended our dances with a good old-fashioned Virginia reel.

When the hunting began, those who could shoulder a rifle wandered off with the hunters far into the forest, leaving the others to keep house at camp. Many a time I have waited on a rock at the end of a "run-way," with bated breath for the appearance of the game ; but alas, no deer ever came near me. I am afraid the men thought the girls talked too much to be successful hunters ; perhaps that was as true as it was uncomplimentary. However, we had some fine rifle matches, when we distinguished ourselves with our high scores, and we quite outstripped the men in catching fish. We went on many exploring expeditions, rowing up some lovely little river, suddenly finding ourselves on some unnamed wild lake or pond, white with lillies. What exquisite views we saw about us daily, for we never looked out from our "lean-tos" but to feast our eyes on some charming picture. The wild, romantic lake always before us, the stately mountains ever in view. We grew to love every tree that shaded us, and I am sure this great intimacy with nature and mother earth could have had nothing but a helpful and inspiring influence upon us. The material for the artist to immortalize is always there, the silent thoughts for the poet to utter are there too, in the deep shadows. The rest for the weary ordinary human being there awaits him.

> "And so in mountain solitudes—o'ertaken
> As by some spell divine
> Their cares drop from them like the needles shaken
> From out the gusty pine."

THE OLD MEADOW.

BY AMELIA N. HENSHAW.

I often on a summer's day,
To the old meadow wend my way,
When shadows lengthen hour by hour,
Soft in the sun's declining power ;
And resting on a mossy stone,
With vines and clustering ferns o'ergrown,
Watch the gray shadows, deepening still,
From rock and tree and grassy hill.

The tiller of the soil likes not
The uncurbed growth of this lone spot ;
For viewed through keen, long-practiced eyes,
Tis but a space to utilize ;
For axe to cut, and fire to burn,
And with the plow the sod upturn,
Quell the rank weeds, enrich the field,
Till it a full, ripe harvest yield.

All kinds of trailing foliage run
Luxuriant in the quickening sun ;
Broad spreading vines, in weavings thick,
Entangle every bush and stick,
And make the winding, old rail fence
One long continuous arbor dense,
Of wild grapes purpling full and free,
Inwoven with red mercury.

The toadstool brown, and crimson, too,
Spring quickly up, in midnight dew;
And overhead are hanging bowers,
And underneath bloom low, wild flowers.

And round about, soft to the feet,
Thick moss and grass embedded meet ;
While wafted from the rich buckwheat,
The passing breeze bears odors sweet.

Just in the slope from the upland,
Two gnarled old apple trees close stand ;
The robin with the yellow breast,
In secret here has built her nest ;
And undisturbed, she lightly flits,
Collecting all the dainty bits,
For th' unfledged, tender, little brood,
She rears in peaceful solitude.

Low in the bushes' deepest shade,
There lies a well, by nature made,
Of rough-hewn rocks, which, ever fed
From springs within its stony bed,
Is hidden in reflections green ;
Nor to the passer-by is seen,
Save for one glimpse of bright, blue sky
Thrown in it from the zenith high.

And countless birds their thirst here slake,
Whose joyous songs the stillness break ;
And mingling, too, to take his fill,
Comes the sad note of whip-poor-will :
And when the sun sinks very low,
A heifer, white as falling snow,
Lights up the pool, as from the brink,
Reflected clear, she stoops to drink.

The cricket in the grass close hid,
And the repeating katydid,
Add low-voiced harmonies, scarce heard,
Amid the chirp, and song of bird.

26

And skimming just above the ground
A grasshopper gives forth a sound,
Recalling, as it near me gets,
Faint, lightly stricken castanets.

With heedful caution peering round.
Half startled at the slightest sound,
Sometimes a rabbit softly hops
From his dark covert, sudden stops,
One moment looks, erects his ears,
Then hastening onward, disappears ;
His gray form lost in grayer shade,
By duskiness of evening made.

And myriad charms remain untold,
By nature held in this sweet fold ;
Yet everywhere, if rightly sought,
Lies unknown wealth for finer thought ;
And oft, when intellect and art,
Glow full and warm in cultured mart,
I sigh for sunny, pleasant hours,
'Mid birds and vines and low, wild flowers.

— . ----------

VENTNOR, QUEEN OF THE ISLE OF WIGHT

BY MISS MARY HITCHCOCK.

If there is any spot in this world which can furnish food for
the pen of a ready writer, it is the charming and romantic Isle
of Wight. My pen is poor and unpretending, but perhaps
some of my gentle readers may like to learn something of
the little town of Ventnor. The town lies on what may be
termed the outside of the Isle of Wight, where the deep blue
waters of the English Channel dash against the white chalk
cliffs and rocky shores of the Island. Nature has bestowed upon

Ventnor a full share of its blessings and such a complete harmony of sea, mountains, and-inland beauty is not often seen. It
is a spot which to see is to love, and the very air seems to
breathe peace and happiness. It is a modest little town, yet
glorious in its way, and may be called Queen of the Island, and
its very charm lies in its unconventionality.

Wandering on the cliffs and downs, and climbing the steep
foot paths over the hills or through the woods are all alike
attractive, and the air is full of music of the birds and babbling
brooks. The lark which to us Americans would seem a fabulous
bird, has its home here, and from its nest in the grass it
springs ; then with a sweet, wild note, it soars into the heavens
and is lost in the blue space.

The fields are full of poppies and daisies and the hedges are
masses of ivy and wild roses. This is truly an island of flowers.
If we follow the rocky path over what is known here as the land-
slip, we see the little village of Bon Church, nestling against the
hillside high above the sea. There is the site of the oldest church
in England, said to have been built in the seventh century. In
the quaint old church-yard can be seen the grave of the Rev. W.
Adams, author of the "Shadow of the Cross." There is an iron
cross suspended over the white stone, which covers the grave,
causing the real shadow of the cross to rest upon it.

One of the most charming ways of exploring the Island is
upon the top of of a four-in-hand coach, and as the Isle of Wight
is only twenty-two miles by fifteen, it is but a short lived pleasure. Less exciting vehicles may be had in the shape of pony
and donkey wagons, which jog up and down over the hills at
very modest rates, both as to speed and price. The climate of
Ventnor is said to be almost Italian in winter and ice and snow
are seldom seen here. August is the beginning of the season,
when people come rushing down from London in hot haste for
Ventnor's life-giving breezes, and things are changed in this
quiet little town, but it is lovely in all its phases and once having
seen it, no one can forget it. It makes an impression on the
mind as strong as the eternal rocks and white cliffs which guard
one of the most heavenly spots on God's earth.

THE KING'S DAUGHTER.

BY MARY LOWTHORP HENDERSON.

When you was out a lady called
  A lady foine and fair,
Wid swate blue eyes, and purty mouth
  And lovely banged up hair.

And when she asked ef you was in
  Says I " No mum, she's not,
But ef you'll lave yer card with me
  I'll see it's not forgot."

" O niver moind," says she,
  " I came a little news to bring,
About some poor we're doing for,
  I'm dau'ther av the King."

Then " houly saints," I lost me wits,
  And curtsied down so low,
That whin the Princess left the door,
  I niver saw her go.

But gittin' quick me sinses back,
  I hurried down the strait,
And bowin' low, says I to her
  " Pray won't yer hoighness wait ? "

She looked at me and smoiled most swate,
  With all her white teeth showin'
" No, not today, I'll come again,
  Tis time I must be goin'."

Now though I am a Dimmycrat,
  All Kings and Queenses hatin',
And bein' a American,
  All white folks aqual ratin'.

I'd loike to know the Princess' name,
  And who moight be her father,
And what she's doin' over here
  So far across the wather.

And ef her royal hoighness wants
  A maid to wait upon her,
I'll do it on these blissed knaes
  Shure's my name's O'Connor.

THANKSGIVING.

BY CLEMENTINE HOWARTH.

For today a nation raises,
  From its fruitful sod,
Offerings and Thanksgiving praises
  Unto Thee, O God !

From the temple of the Holy
  Flows the lofty strain ;
And the cottage of the lowly
  Echoes back again.

Upward floats the clear Hosannas
  From the freeman's mouth,
O'er the fields and broad savannahs
  Of the balmy south.

And Columbia's sons and daughters,
  Though afar they rove,

Send fond wishes o'er the waters
  To the land they love.

We who have the well filled larder,
  And the store of grain,
Unto those whose lots are harder,
  Let us give again.

Let the happy wife and mother,
  To the lowly home
Where the soldier son and brother
  Never more may come.

Bear her gifts, the wolf is pressing
  Heavy at the door,
To the rescue! win a blessing
  Helpers of the poor.

And where sons and sires are lying
  On the prison bed,
Send the cheering voice, replying
  To their cry for bread.

" Brothers! there are bosoms glowing
  In the northern home,
And with hearts and hands o'erflowing
  To your aid we come!"

For today Columbia raises
  From her fruitful sod,
Offerings and Thanksgiving praises
  To a gracious God.

OUR NATIONAL FLOWER.

BY HELEN M. T. HEADLEY.

The great centennials of '76, '87 and '89 have passed. The echoes of the cannon of our nation's birthday, have died upon our ears. This historic year and century with all its hallowed memories and associations is drawing to its close, to be numbered with those before the flood. Is not this an appropriate time for us to choose a national flower, that it may take root in the " new century." grow with our growth and strengthen with our strength? I think so. And would urge the merits of the Kalmia, the American laurel," as such a flower.

It is a genus of evergreen shrubs, peculiar to North America, belonging to the "Natural Order of Ericaceæ It is dignified, graceful and beautiful, and in great request in European gardens for its foliage as well as flowers. It blossoms in the early Summer, speaking of youth, prosperity and victory. It was discovered in America, in the middle of last century by Peter Kalm, a pupil in Linnæus, and named by that prince of naturalists—"Kalmia," in his honor. He remained here three years studying our flora, and on his return found his teacher, Linnæus, ill with the gout, and unable to move, but the sight of the specimen brought by Kalm, so exhilarated and enlivened his spirits that he forgot his bodily anguish and recovered. It is said that the flowers went to him to be named as the animals went to Adam.

The sight of the "stars and the stripes" has brought new life and a quicker pulse to many a weary exile, away from home and friends. I would that we could re-christen the American laurel, plant it anew in this centennial year as our national flower, beneath the shadow of the "star-spangled banner," that one may ever recall the other, that we may point to it, with as pardonable pride as England to her rose, France to her lily, Ireland to her shamrock, or Scotland to her thistle.

Since the lay of the first minstrel was heard in the land, history and poetry have crowned the brows of her heroes with laurel, but not our American laurel. Theirs was the Lauras nobilis (sweet bay) of the old Linnæan class of Enneandria, and grew in the southern part of Europe and northern part of Africa. Their leaves were very similar to ours, lanceolate, leathery and perennial, but their flower was small and inconspicuous, four-cleft, of yellow-white, and grew in recimes, three or four together upon a common peduncle in the axilis of the leaves. Our flower appears in corymbs, profuse, large, and very showy. in brilliant hues from deep rose to nearly white, has ten stamens confined by their anthers in ten cavities of a star pointed monopetalis corolla. One blossom is suitable for a "boutonniere." Many, beautiful for a vase. The American laurel is found in all sections of the United States, from ocean to ocean, from lake to gulf ; it belongs to us ; is ours. Sentiment or art has not yet discovered its beauties. It is unknown in story or in song.

The Epigæa, the ground laurel or trailing arbutus is of the same family, the Ericaceæ. But let the Pilgrims have it exclusively. It was the first welcome received by them on the shores of their "ice-rimmed bay."

> " God be praised " the Pilgrims said,
> Who saw the blossoms peer
> Above the brown leaves dry and dead
> " Behold our Mayflower here."

Then let it be their flower, theirs alone, while we adopt the Kalmia, the American laurel, our native mountain laurel, as the national flower of free America. Its evergreen leaves, its monopetalous corolla, seemingly many but only one, one and undivided, speak for the American Union.

E pluribus unum.

THE PRACTICAL DREAMER.

BY MISS E. M. HEADLEY.

DREAMS.

Laboring among the shepherds,
  In the olden, golden time,
When the Lord, his will revealing,
  Spake to men in words sublime.
Was a youth, who had been favored
  Somewhat more than all the rest,
Who with coat of many colors,
  And the father's love was blest ;
And thus spake he to the others ;
  Brethren hear this dream, I pray
Which I dreamed—so strange, unnatural,
  Yet seems in my mind to stay,
Lo ; as we the grain were binding,
  It seemed as if the sheaves
Had both life and motion given
  To their stalks and grassy leaves.

And the sheaf I bound stood upright,
  Lifting up each withered leaf ;
And your sheaves, all gathered round it,
  Made obeisance to my sheaf,
Then the brothers filled with anger,
  For the vision touched their pride,
With their minds made keen by envy,
  To their brother, thus replied
Shalt thou indeed reign over us ?
  Thou, the youngest of our band ?
Art thou in thy dreams aspiring
  To be ruler of the land ?

From that hour their hate and envy
  Deeper grew within their breast,
Daily sinking, deeper. deeper,
  Giving to their minds no rest.

Yet another day the dreamer
  Of his visions spake once more
To his father and his brethren :
  Hear this dream I now implore.
Behold ! in my night-time vision.
  I beheld the light of day;
And I thought the sun in setting
  Beamed on me a kindly ray,
Even seemed to do me reveience
  Just before it left the sky;
And the silver moon towards me
  Bowed its pale face from on high ;
And I saw as evening deepened,
  One by one the stars appear,
And my heart was drawn toward them
  As to something near and dear ;
And of all that host, eleven
  Seemed the brightest and the best,
Seemed the clearest, nearest, dearest,
  Dearer far than all the rest ;
And as I admired their brightness
  So strangly fair to see,
They assuming forms and faces,
  Made obeisance unto me.

Then the father speaking sternly
  As a wise reprover seemed ;
My son, what is this thy folly?
  What is this that thou hast dreamed ?
Shalt thy father and thy mother
  Come and bow before thy face ?

And shall these thy elder brethren
  Yield to thee, the highest place?

In these later days of privilege,
  Scattered over all the land,
Many an earnest soul is dreaming
  More than it can understand.
Though when seeking fame and glory,
  Providence our pathway bars,
Yet the soul, set free by slumber,
  Dreams of sheaves of grain and stars;
Dreams of toil, success rewarded,
  Burdens borne, and then laid down,
Of the "Well done faithful servant,"
  And of an immortal crown;
And the various plans of labor,
  For the general good may seem
Even brighter, wilder, weaker
  Than an oriental dream.

Should we tell our earnest purpose,
  Who of all around would hear?
Who would heed us? who would help us?
  Who would give us words of cheer?
Surely would the brethren scorn us,
  Surely would the fathers chide.
Can we bear the father's sternness?
  Can we bear the brother's pride?
Ah! my proud heart, weak and cowardly,
  Dumb-struck by the scornful gleams,
Doubting, fearing, trembling, fainting,
  Cannot dare to tell its dreams,
Such the power of human friendship,
  Worse than worthless must it seem,
When the soul stands mocked and silenced
  For the dreaming of a dream.

TRIALS.

Behold! this dreamer cometh
    In his beautiful array!
His bright robe of many colors
    We descry though far away.
Idle dreamer! Busy schemer!
    One or both of these is he.
Shall his dreaming or his scheming
    Ever prove reality ?
Even now he wears the token
    That he rules our father's heart.
Shall he rule his elder brethren ?
    Shall we yield unto his art ?
Here while we the flocks are tending,
    Night by night and day by day,
Our father sending him to us,
    Learneth all we do and say.

Shall we bear with this informer ?
    Brethren, let us now be free.
Let us slay this scheming dreamer,
    And his dream's fulfillment see.
Thus the brethren madly reasoned,
    Knowing not their secret heart;
Knowing not the power above them,
    That would take the dreamer's part,
Soon their minds were changed in purpose
    By that mighty power above,
And they strip him of his raiment,
    Given by a father's love;
And with cowardly hearts they sell him
    To a rude nomadic band;
Vainly thinking thus to thwart him
    Without bloodstain on the hand.

In the service of his master,
    Sadly in a foreign land,

Behold ! the dreamer toiling
  With an earnest steady hand.
Though a stranger, and in bondage,
  Truly he performs his part :
Nobly he resists temptation
  With a firm undaunted heart ;
With a heart unmoved by slander,
  Fearing not the tyrant's rod,
Trusting for a sure protection,
  In the faithfulness of God.

Time has passed.   Behold ! the dreamer
  In a gloomy prison cast !
What can now avail to cheer him ?
  Surely now all dreams are past !
Even here the Lord was with him,
  Helping him perform his part.
Even here some work was found him
  To employ his hand and heart.
When dark sorrows throng us, fill us,
  We are oft morose, unkind.
God be praised that he has given
  Unto some a nobler mind.
Like our dreamer, who, by kindness,
  Gives his fellow prisoners cheer,
Sympathy and gentle accents,
  As he seeks their woes to hear,

FULFILLMENT.

Who is this in princely raiment ?
  Whose may this chariot be ?
Behold this dreamer cometh !
  Unto Joseph bow the knee !
Thus the honor of a ruler
  He receives from every class.

All his days of grief are ended,
　All his dreams are come to pass,
All his friends are gathered round him
　And his brethren too have come
To bow themselves before him,
　And accept from him a home.
Not by aught of fraud or violence,
　Rather by the mighty hand
Of God blessing all his labors
　Which he wrought in Egypt's land.
To that land he proved a blessing,
　By his hand the poor were fed,
And from many distant nations
　They came to him for bread.

Let us not forget the story,
　Or the great example spurn ;
Let us from this noble dreamer
　This noble lesson learn—
Should God, in his boundless mercy
　Send us light before untold,
Let us never fear to show it,
　Let us not the dream withhold.
If we labor on through trials,
　Brave keep the end in view ;
If we trust our God for guidance
　We shall find the vision true.
Men may strip us, sell us, bind us—
　God shall still work out his plan
For the nation's full salvation,
　And the help of fallen man.

LATITUDE AND LONGITUDE.

BY HENRIETTA A. HOLDRICH.

I was going from Boston to Philadelphia to see my Aunt Rose. I was only a little shaver, so they sent me by steamer, under the captain's care—Captain Floy. Just the nicest man! Gray eyes, with the look in them that real sailors' eyes always have, and such a kind, fresh look about his whole face. I wasn't going to talk about him, though—not yet—but about her.

She came down awhile before we sailed. I liked her at the first, for all she looked so tired and sorry. The captain and I were on the dock when she came down. He looked at her for a minute. Then he went up and touched his cap and said, " Are you going aboard, Miss ———"

He stopped there, as if he'd been going to say her name, or wanted to know what it was. She didn't take any notice, though; just said she was. Then he asked would I show her the way. So that was how I first came to speak to her.

There weren't many passengers that trip, for it was along in the fall, pretty late.

I wanted to know her name, so I had to look in the book she had been reading for it. I was so surprised that, before ever I thought, I had blurted out, "Agnes May Wyvern! Are you Agnes Wyvern? Why, I've heard my mother talk about you so often."

She looked at me sort of queer, and said, " What is your mother's name, Gus?"

I knew I'd made a big blunder, but it was too late to back out, so I said: " She's Mrs. Lawrence. No, she don't know you " (for she looked sort of surprised); " but she wanted to, the worst way. Say, Miss Wyvern, you're an awful swell, ain't you?"

The captain just laughed out. Then he made out he was very busy looking at a ship in the offing.

She laughed too at first. Then she stopped and turned red. "No Gus," she said, "I'm not a 'swell,' as you call it."

"Then why did mamma want to know you?" I asked.

She hesitated a moment. Then she said, quite gravely, "It was very kind of your mother to wish to know me, Gus, but probably she is very glad now that she did not."

"Why," I said, "ain't you awful rich?"

"Not now," she said.

"But your uncle is?" I asked.

"My uncle—my uncle is dead," she said, and her face got white again, and the tears came into her eyes, till I was so sorry I didn't know what to do.

Then the captain began to talk to her, and I was glad enough to get out of the way.

We were up bright and early the next day, Agnes and I. Agnes had taken off her hat, and her head was wrapped up in some sort of fleecy white thing. By-and-by the wind began to blow the pink into her cheeks, and the light into her eyes. It caught her hair too, and twisted it into little rings and curls around her forehead, and she looked just awful pretty. The captain came along, and he looked at her in such a pleasant sort of way, and then he leaned over the bulwarks beside her and began to talk. Agnes and I had both been to Florida, and we didn't think much of it. So had the captain, and he didn't think much of it too.

"The Windward Islands are better, Miss Wyvern," he said, and Agnes looked at him, sort of surprised.

"I was there once," she said, "in my uncle's yacht. We cruised about among them all winter."

"The Agnes," said the captain. "Yes, I remember her well."

"Remember?" said Agnes, looking puzzled. "But you—"

"Oh, you would'nt recollect," said the captain. "I was only skipper of the Agnes."

"What! Captain Ben?" cried Agnes. "Why, how could

I ever forget you? You were always so good to me, and I must have been a perfect plague. I was only fourteen, you know."

"Never a plague to me," said the captain, in a queer sort of half-voice, looking away to the horizon—"never a plague to me, and all the sailors worshipped you. It was a bright day to all when you came on board."

He stopped all of a sudden. Then Agnes said just, "You know?"

And the captain said, "Yes, Miss Agnes, I know."

And then they both looked at me, and then they went on talking about those wonderful islands.

Why do I call her Agnes? Because she told me to, of course. I called her Miss Wyvern till she gave me a kind of shudder, and said, Don't call me that, Gus. Call me Agnes, or, call me Miss May. I hate the name of Wyvern.

"Oh," I said, "I'd just as lief call you Agnes. But, I say, why don't you like Wyvern? It's no end of a jolly name, I think."

"People don't always like their own names," said Agnes. "Besides, May is my name."

"Yes, I know," I said, and I picked up the book where I had read it; but it wasn't there any longer. Fly-leaf and all were gone.

Along toward afternoon the captain brought up his quadrant, and began to teach Agnes how to hold it—in her left hand, you know, with the right on the screw.

"Now turn the screw gently," he said, "until you bring the sun down to the horizon, with just room to heave a sea-biscuit between. Then look where two lines exactly meet, and ——"

It was all Greek to me, so I went off, while Agnes and the captain did sums. After the lesson was over, Agnes began telling the captain about some shipwreck. As I came up I heard him say:

"So everything went down?"

There were tears in Agnes' eyes, but she only said: "Everything. No hope, and, worst of all, no pity."

27

" Was it a shipwreck, Agnes ? " I said. " Who was wrecked? You ? "

Agnes sort of jumped when I spoke, but she only said, "Yes," and I went on.

" Was the captain lost, too ? And only you saved ? How funny ! Who saved you ? "

I'm not sure that I was saved," said Agnes, with a sort of deep, dry sob.

I stared. " Not saved ? " I said. " Why could you be here, else ? Tell a fellow about it. What was the captain's name ? "

" Wyvern," said Agnes.

I was going to ask a lot more questions, but the captain caught me by the arm.

" See here, Gus," he said, when we were the other side of the deck, '' Don't you know that sometimes when people have been through great danger, they can't talk about it ? Queer ? Well, I don't know, but it is so. No, I'm not scolding you ; only don't ask any more questions, and don't talk about this shipwreck to anybody—to anybody, mind."

I promised, and then I got to thinking.

" Captain," I said, '' Your'e not a bit like any of the captains I ever knew. Why is it ? "

" I don't know, Gus," he said. " How am I different ? "

That puzzled me. " You're all different ! " I said. " You look different, and you talk different—softer, somehow, and—and and— Oh ! I can't tell ; but what makes you ? "

The captain gave a sort of smile. " Gus," he said, just as I thought he wasn't going to say any more, "suppose that once, for a little while, a bit of heaven had come into your life—"

"An angel, do you mean ?" I said ; but he just smiled, and said :

" Call it an angel, if you like. You didn't come into the angel's life, you know ; only touched for a moment its outermost circle ; but the angel came into yours for all that. Even though it spread its wings and flew away, and you knew that most likely you would never, never, see it again, don't you think that the memory would stay by you, and that you would try to make yourself and your life worthier of it ? "

" Where did you see the angel, captain ? " I asked. Was it in the Windward Islands ? "

For there seemed to be such queer things there that I thought maybe there was something the captain took for an angel. The captain didn't seem to understand, though, for he looked hard at me for a moment, and then he began to laugh.

" It doesn't do to talk in parables to you, youngster, I see," he said, and then he got up and went away.

Just then Agnes came up. " Come here, Gus," she said. " I want to give you a lesson. Some day, you know, you may be cast away at sea, and want to know where you are. How would you find out ? "

" Guess, I s'pose," I said ; but Agnes put on a shocked face.

" Oh dear ; that will never do," she said. " If you couldn't find your latitude and longitude, where would you be ? "

" Just where I should if I could," I said.

" Yes, but presently you'd find yourself just where you shouldn't," she said, laughing. " I want to teach you what the captain has taught me."

It was very good fun to peep through the little spy-hole, and turn the screw until the sun hung, a great red ball, just over the water, but when she began with the addings and that, I stopped her.

" Now, Agnes, it's no good," I said ; " I never could do sums, and I'm not going to be a sailor, so where's the odds ? "

" But let me teach you—pray let me teach you," she begged, and I gave in.

" Teach away " I said ; " but you won't make anything of it ; " and she didn't.

When she'd gone on for half an hour about circles and degrees and chronometers and Greenwich time and that, I didn't know quite as much as I did when she began, and I told her so. She just stopped short, and when I looked at her she was looking down at the quadrant, with the tears running down her cheeks.

"Why Agnes," I said, "What's the matter? If you want to
know the latitude and longitude so bad, I'll go ask the captain.
He'll know."

"It isn't that," she said, laughing through her tears. "The
trouble is I am to be a governess, and I wanted to see whether I
knew how. I worked out the latitude and longitude this morning, but if I can't teach you how to do it, how can I teach my
pupils anything? That's what worries me.

Agnes Wyvern a governess! That stumped me.

"Who are you going to governess?" I said. "Or don't
you know yet?"

"Of course I know. Do you think I am starting out to seek
my fortune, like a princess in a fairy tale? I'm going to 'governess' the children of a Mrs. Robert Caryl, in Philadelphia."

"Mrs. Robert Caryl! My eye! Cricky!" was all I could
say.

"Why do you know her?" said Agnes. "What's the
matter?"

"Matter enough," says I. "Mrs. Robert Caryl's my aunt
Rose, and her young ones are my cousins—worse luck. Of all
the brats! You'll find out fast enough."

"Are they so bad?" says Agnes, 'most crying. "Oh Gus,
what shall I do?"

"Do?" said I. "Why, don't go. Or, if you must go, just
you give 'em a good thrashing first off. That'll teach 'em what
to look for if they're up to any of their shines.

"Oh, do stop Gus," said Agnes, laughing. "What a young
barbarian you are!"

It had been getting rougher while we talked, and all of a
sudden the ship gave such a lurch that the chairs we were sitting
on went over like a shot, and landed us all in a heap in the middle of the hurricane deck.

"Hope you're not afraid of a little knocking about," said
the captain coming up to us. "It's coming on to blow. You
two had better go below."

So he helped us down, while the ship began to wabble and
dance and bump about at a great rate, and—well, that was the

end of me for one while, you bet! Agnes stayed with me most all day, and was in and out of my state-room a dozen times in the night, for I was just the sickest little shaver you ever did see.

The captain came into my stateroom and just picked me up, bed-clothes and all.

"You'll never get well here, my little man," he said. "Just you come along with me and Miss Agnes too, if she will."

Well, where do you think he took me? Why, into his own stateroom, with its big bedstead and its lace curtains and its sofa and almost as fine as the spare chamber at home.

"This is yours for the rest of the voyage," he said, as he dumped me down in the middle of the big bed. "It's no use to me, for I've got to spend my nights in the pilot-house till the gale blows itself out. There's a sofa for Miss Agnes, if she'll have it. You'll find it pleasanter taking care of the youngster up here."

Then he was off, before we could thank him.

"Say, Agnes," I said, "the captain thinks a lot of you, don't he?"

"Of you, you mean, Master Gus," she said. "It wasn't to me he gave this room."

"Of—I'm not a bat," I said. "You knew him before, didn't you?"

"A long time ago," said Agnes. "He was skipper of my uncle's yacht on one cruise. Then my uncle took an interest in him and helped him up in the world, and I suppose he is grateful."

That reminded me. "I say Agnes," I said, "did you ever see anything like an angel in the Windward Islands?"

"What do you mean, Gus?" said Agnes, looking as if she thought I was off my head.

So then I told her what the captain had said about it. Agnes was still a minute and then she began to laugh in an unsteady kind of way, and said:

"No; I think—I am sure there were no angels there. It was only the captain's fancy."

Then the ship began to wabble and dance and bump and roll

worse than ever. All I knew was that there was a very sick little boy somewhere, and that Agnes May was taking care of him. I wasn't quite sure who the little boy was then, but, come to think of it now, I guess it must have been me. It was a long, long while before I began to wake up, or it seemed like that to me and I found the ship was getting steadier. Then the captain came in.

"It's all over at last," he said, "but I'm blessed if I know where we are. It's the first time I've ever had to take the latitude and longitude since I've been captain of this steamer, but I've got to do it now. Would you like to help me, Miss Agnes?"

So Agnes said yes, if I didn't mind, and I didn't; so she went. When she came back the captain came with her as far as the door. I heard what he said to her:

"It is no new thing, and it will be the same forever. I never hoped, and under other circumstances I should never have dared to speak. Even now ——"

"Oh, brave heart! true heart!" said Agnes, with a sort of sob; and when she came in her eyes were all soft and teary, and her lips quivering.　　*　　*　　*

Lily and Angelo! I just wish you could have seen 'em. Lil was a skinny sort of a young one, with sharp, snappy, black eyes and straight black hair. In old times they'd have put her on a bed of hot coals and let her fly straight up the chimney, and serve her right! Angelo was fat and flabby, with big staring blue eyes and hair like tow. He was as stupid as a log, but Lily had brains enough for six—such as they were. Aunt Rose wasn't a bad sort of a fellow, if she hadn't been so wrapped up in those brats. There wasn't any uncle Rose. I wish there had been. He wouldn't have let her make such a fool of herself, I'll bet.

"Come here, darlings, and see their nice new governess that Mrs. Lovell sent them." "She will make their lessons so easy that it will only be fun to learn them; won't she, my lammies? Miss May, I must warn you about these dear children. While I wish you to bring them on rapidly in their studies, I cannot have them irritated or thwarted in any way. Above all, they must never be punished. If they require correction, I am the proper person to administer it, and I must request that such cases be always referred to me."

Angelo stood with his thumb in his mouth, staring at Agnes, and Lily grinned from ear to ear, like an imp, as she was. I was mad enough to whop 'em both, but that wouldn't have done any good, so I went off with Agnes.

"Oh, Gus! Gus!" says Agnes, putting both arms around me when we were outside the parlor door; "what shall I do? Oh, what shall I do?"

Something came up into my throat, but I choked it down, and said, "See here, Agnes, I guess I can do some good, if you'll teach me too, along with them."

"Oh, you dear boy!" says Agnes. "Let you spend your holidays shut up in a school-room? No, indeed."

"Now, that's mean of you, Agnes," I said. "But we'll see."

So I went straight off to Aunt Rose and asked her, and next morning I was in the school-room.

First of all Agnes thought she'd find out what Lily knew.

"Lily," she said, "who signed the Magna Charta?"

"Floyd Ireson," says Lily, grave as a judge.

"Floyd Ireson? Lily, what do you mean?" says Agnes, not knowing whether to be angry or not.

"Well," says Lily, "doesn't it say,

> ' Floyd Ireson for his hard heart,
> Tarred and feathered and carried in a cart ' ?

"That was the Magna Charta of course. Maybe it was 'the women of Marblehead' signed it, though. I don't know."

"What can you tell me about William the Conqueror!" asks Agnes.

"He wanted people to worship his hat," says Miss Lily; "but they just all opened their windows and prayed to the yeast instead. So then he said, 'England expects every man to do his duty,' and when they wouldn't, then he let fly at at them, and his arrow hit the apple on his son's head, and then hit a tree, and flew back and struck him in the eye. So he died."

Agnes gave a kind of a sigh, and took up a geography. "What is the capital of Connecticut?" she said.

"I don't know. Wooden nutmegs, I s'pose," says Lily.

"Lily!" cried Agnes, out of all patience. There are two capitals. One is—"

"New Haven. I've been there," says Angelo, with his thumb in his mouth.

Agnes brightened right up.

"That's it," she said. "Now, Lily, what is on the bank of the Connecticut River?"

"I don't know," says Lily, slowly. "On the bank? Earth-worms, I s'pose. They most generally are. Or else crabs."

"Don't bother with her any more, Agnes," I said, too mad to hold in. "She's just trying to rile you. Then she'll yell. I know."

Didn't Lil give me a look though! I didn't care. I just went on studying like a good fellow, while Agnes put Angelo through his paces. He didn't know enough to fool. The worst and the best he could do was to put his thumb in his mouth and goggle his eyes at Agnes.

It was as good as a play to hear Aunt Rose at dinner.

"Mamma's little lammies! Have they been good, Miss May? I needn't ask, though, for they are always good. You find them pretty equally balanced. Lily is the quickest, but Angelo excels in patience. Not that he is slow, either, only not quite so brilliant as Lily, but perhaps more profound. You find it so, don't you, Miss May?"

Poor Agnes, remembering Floyd Ireson and the earth-worms, could only blush and stammer out something, I don't know what, and I guess she didn't.

Well, I can't go over that time day by day, you know. I did what I could, but it wasn't much, Lily was awful cute. Somehow it was never she that did things—spilled torpedoes about, and left pins in chairs, and such—but always Angelo, and there was no use scolding him. If Lil had put him up to it, he

never told, nor she neither. Sometimes Lil knew her lessons
and more times she didn't. When she didn't she just went on
with a lot of bosh, looking as wise as an owl and as innocent as
a rabbit all the time. Angelo never knew his lessons, and never
pretended to, but just looked stupid and put his thumb in his
mouth, and began to roar. Then Aunt Rose would come into
the room like a whirlwind, with her eyes like blue blazes, and
scold Agnes, and pity Lily (she was always yelling like mad too
about this time) and carry Angelo off.

One day things had been going contrarier than usual, and
Allice was clean tuckered out. When Agnes opened her desk an
ink-bottle upset. Of course it was nobody's fault that the bottle
had been tilted up so that the least jar would send it over. Only
Agnes was sure hadn't left it so, and I saw Lily coming out of
the school-room the night before, grinning. Lily had learned
the wrong history lesson, and Angelo hadn't learned his at all.
Then, of course, they both howled. For a wonder Aunt Rose
didn't come in, so after a while they shut up. Then Agnes set
Angelo a multiplication sum on the blackboard, and then she began to hear Lily her French. Lil could translate well enough
when she choose, but today she didn't choose. So she bungled
and stammered and made hash of it generally.

Agnes looked at her for a minute. Then she tried to speak,
but broke down, and laughed instead.

"Why, this is very strange, Angelo," said Agnes, when she
had looked at the sum. "You have the answer right, but every
figure of the working out is wrong. You must have copied the
answer?"

"Didn't," said Angelo, and that was all.

"It's a shame," says Lily, like as if she was talking to her
book. "He did it, and he got the answer, and that's all about it."

Just then Aunt Rose came in with her aunt, Mrs. Severance.
She was awful rich, Mrs. Severance was, and Aunt Rose was as
pleased as Punch to see her. I knew something as soon as I
looked at Mrs. Severance, but I kept still. She was a fat old
lady, with a crumpled up face, all dressed off in satin and lace,
with diamonds that winked and looked wicked like Lily's eyes.

"Here are my lammies," said Aunt Rose. "I have brought Mrs. Severance in to see them, Miss May. Aunt Ginevra, this is Miss May, the governess."

Mrs. Severance put up her gold eye-glasses and looked at Agnes sort of puzzled, but she didn't say anything.

"And how are the lammies getting on?" said Aunt Rose, stooping down to kiss Angelo. "What a long sum for a little puzzle-pate. Isn't he a clever darling, Aunt Ginevra? And can he do it, Miss May?"

Agnes hesitated, but Lily chipped in. "Oh, yes, he can do it fast enough. He got the answer at once, but Miss May said he must have copied it."

"Angelo copy his answer! Angelo the soul of honor!" cried Aunt Rose. "Oh, Miss May, how could you?"

"This is Gus Lawrence, from Boston, Aunt Ginevra," she said, when she thought of me. "He must have been a fellow passenger of yours upon the steamer."

Mrs. Severance put up her glasses and looked at me.

"I think I remember him," she said, slowly. "Miss May's face too, struck me as familiar, but for the moment I could not place it. Now, however—you are the young woman who navigated the steamer I think."

"Navigated the steamer? I?" said Agnes, struck all of a heap.

"Yes, my dear, certainly," said Mrs. Severance. "I saw you myself with the quadrille, or whatever you call it. I never can remember their sea terms—so unfeminine! It was you who ran us into that gale, into the very teeth of it. What possessed you to undertake such a thing?"

"I-I-" said Agnes; and then she went into a fit of laughter again; and then she said. "Oh! I beg your pardon." And then she laughed again; and then she began to cry, and just bolted out of the room.

Mrs. Severance and Aunt Rose looked at each other.

"Dear! dear! said Aunt Rose, "I am afraid that I have been mistaken in Miss May; she seemed so gentle and modest."

"Modest!" said Mrs. Severence.

"Me and Angelo don't like her," piped up Lily, in her shrill voice. "She laughed at me just like that when I made a mistake in my French this morning; and she scolds us awful when we don't say our lessons to suit her."

"Depend upon it, my dear, it's a mistake," Mrs. Severance said, nodding her head slowly. "Who sent her to you?"

"Mrs. Lovell, of Boston," said Aunt Rose. "It would never do to offend her, but—"

"A very unreliable person," said Mrs. Severance. "Philanthropic you know; always taking up with doubtful people. Why she is still hand and glove with the niece of that dreadful man, with whose story all Boston is ringing. So unfeminine to encourage that sort of thing. I have no doubt that Miss May is a mere adventurer."

Then I just blazed out. "I guess you don't know what you're talking about," I said. "If you knew she was Agnes Wyvern, you'd sing a different song." Well, they were astonished enough, but not just the way I'd meant.

"Agnes Wyvern!" squealed Mrs. Severance. "The very girl!"

"Agnes Wyvern!" squeaked Aunt Rose; "the niece of the forger, the embezzler, who would have been sent to State's prison if he hadn't cut his own throat! Ugh!"

I was scared to death, I tell you. Before I had begun to get over my scare, Agnes came back. She began to apologize for the way she had left, but nobody listened. Aunt Rose had her young ones gathered up, one in each arm, and Mrs. Severance stood up, with her eyeglasses on her nose.

"Don't try to distract our attention from the main point, if you please," she said. "The question now is whether what Gus has just told us is correct. Is your name Wyvern?"

Agnes just gave me one quick look. It wasn't a cross look, but it most broke my heart, for all that.

"Oh Agnes, I didn't mean—" I said; and then I just boo-hooed like a baby.

Agnes gave a sort of little quivery smile and said, "Never mind, Gus; it doesn't matter."

"Answer me if you please," Mrs. Severance said; and Agnes turned to her.

"I was at one time known as Agnes Wyvern," she said, "but my real name is May. When my parents died, my uncle took me, and by his wish I bore his name. By Mrs. Lovell's advice I assumed my own, after—after." Her lips quivered, and she stopped, and clasped her hands tight together.

"Of course, Miss May, you understand," said Mrs. Severance, after a pause.

"That I must go?" said Agnes. "Oh, yes! I should have gone in any case, though, for I cannot teach. I found that out on the steamer, you know, Gus," she said, turning to me with the weakest, poorest little smile, and the tears dripping fast over it.

Lily looked on, grinning her very wickedest. Angelo looked on too, till, all of a sudden, he began to roar. Now who'd a thought it? He'd got fond of Agnes, and didn't want her to go. The more Aunt Rose tried to hush him up, the louder he yelled till she was 'most wild.

"Pray go, Miss May, and end this most distressing scene," she said at last. "This convinces me that your influence has been very bad. The dear child never showed any temper before, never! Your money and your meals shall be sent to your room. It is too late for you to leave today, I suppose; but tomorrow—"

"Tomorrow morning I will leave, madam," said Agnes.

"I'm going too, you know, Agnes," I said, when we were outside. "I can't stand it here after this."

"You dear boy!" said Agnes, squeezing my hand tight. "But what would your mother say, Gus?"

"The mammy?" I said. "Why, bless your heart! she'll be too glad to see me to say anything. Say, how are you going, Agnes? By steamer?"

Agnes just stopped short. "What day of the week is this, Gus," she said.

"Friday, says I. "And, oh, jolly! why, the very steamer

we came on goes back tomorrow. Are you going by her, Agnes? Say!"

"I suppose so," says Agnes, slowly; "yes, I must. I cannot stay here, and the journey by land is so expensive; but—"

"Why, Captain Floy 'll be no end glad to see you. What's the row, Agnes?" I said, but she didn't answer.

We went off next morning, and the last thing we heard was Angelo's roars, and the last thing we saw was Lil's face grinning over the balusters. Agnes didn't talk much on the way down to the Pine Street wharf, but she kept turning red and white, and sometimes she smiled and more times the tears came into her eyes.

When the captain saw us, it was as if a great light broke all over his face like sunrise. "Are you going back with me, Gus?" he said, but he only looked at Agnes.

"Yes," I said, "were going back, Agnes and I. Aunt Rose was too many for us.

After a minute Captaid Floyd said:

"Take her aboard Gus. You can take your pick of state-rooms, for you are the only passengers this trip.

Then he pulled his cap a little further over his eyes, and went on overseeing the men.

That trip wasn't half as much fun as the other had been, for it was as still as still all the way. But Agnes was so queer. I didn't know what had come to her. First off she had to go and tell the captain she only came that way because she hadn't money enough to go by land. Of course, he thought she didn't want to go with him, and he looked awful sorry, and didn't come near us again for ever so long.

"Agnes, what makes you so queer to the captain?" I said, once.

Agnes turned all red, and she looked at me very sharp and quick. "Am I queer," she said. "How?"

"Why, you're not a bit like you used to be," I said. "You don't even look at him if you can help it, and you are so still all the time. Say, Agnes, don't you like him any longer?"

Agnes was looking down into her lap, and she didn't look up.

"Like him ? Yes, I like him," she said.

"As well as you used to ?" I asked.

But Agnes just said " Yes," and no more. So then I thought maybe he'd like to know it.

"I understand, Gus," he said, looking, oh! so kind and so sorry; "I know what she's afraid of, but she needn't be, bless her !"

I was glad enough we weren't going to be on the ship as long as we were before. We ought to get in Monday noon, the captain said ; but something happened before that. Just as we got up on deck, Monday morning, there was an awful clatter, and a clatter that you don't know what it means scares you 'most to death on shipboard. The bell began to ring ; not ting-ting, ting-ting, like it does when it strikes the half hours, but hard and fast, like it was too scared to stop. Then the sailors came flying from every part of the ship. For one minute it just rained sailors—sprouted 'em, too. The steward came up the cabin stairs in two jumps, and they all made straight for the pumps. They pumped like mad for a minute or two. Then the bell rang again, and they rushed to the boats.

"They can't put out the fire, and they're getting out the boats, Agnes," I said.

Scared ! Of course I was scared. So would you be. Fire at sea's no joke. Just then I caught sight of the captain, and I grabbed Agnes and put for him, dragging her along.

" Captain, will you take care of us ?" I said ; but the captain just began to laugh.

"What a shame !" he said. "I thought you had been warned. It is only the drill we have to go through every fort-night, so that in case of accident there will be no confusion."

"And there is no fire ?" said Agnes, very slowly, as if her lips were stiff with cold.

" None at all," said the captain.

Then Agnes just sat down on the pump, and turned so white

I thought she was going to faint. The captain caught her, for she sort of swayed over, and said, "Run for some water, Gus."

When he caught her, though, she held held herself up a little, and turned a slow sort of pink, and quivered her eyelids, so I stopped.

"Don't be afraid, Miss Agnes," said the captain, in a sort of choked voice. "I will let you go as soon as you can stand."

"I am not afraid," said Agnes, softly, while the pink kept on coming back to her cheeks.

"I remember the distance between us, which once for a moment I forgot," he said. "Believe me, I will not grieve your sweet heart in that way again."

"Won't you?" said Agnes.

That was all, but she just lifted up her eyelids and looked at the captain, and the captain started, and then looked down hard at her. Then she jumped up and covered her face with her hands and ran down the cabin stairs. The captain looked like a man in a dream. He rubbed his hands over his forehead once or twice, and then, all of a sudden, he broke into a smile that flowed all over his face, and the tears jumped into his eyes, and then he just turned on his heel and walked away.

Of course I asked Agnes what it all meant.

"The captain has been helping me to find my latitude and longitude," she said ; "or else I've been helping him. I'm afraid on the whole, that was the way of it. Dreadful, wasn't it, Gus?"

"Not if he couldn't find it without you," I said, wondering what she made such a fuss about that for.

She just laughed a happy sort of little laugh, and said, "Well, he didn't seem able."

A PHOTOGRAPH.

BY NELLIE C. T. HERBERT.

The bright sunlight falls through the pane,
  And crowns a portrait that my gaze
Rests on, and there comes to me
  A memory of other days.

The time when first we met returns,
  Again I hear old ocean's roar,
Again see sapphire waves and sky,
  And foaming breakers on the shore.

All fades, and in my hand I hold
  A photograph. Time was when I
Looked at it with a happy smile,
  But now I view it with a sigh.

The size of a man's hand, at first,
  The cloud that came between us two ;
So small 'twas scarcely visible,
  And then, ah, me ! it grew and grew.

Until it darkened everything,
  Shrouded my happiness, and left,
Me with a sharp, a sudden pain,
  As one who's suddenly bereft.

So vividly do I recall
  The grave dark eyes, the slow sweet smile,
The hair tossed from a forehead white,
  The low, clear voice that did beguile.

Oh, fondly cherished portrait, you
  Are all that's left me of that time—
You, and a feeling that I might
  The name Regret to it assign.

THE NEW MOON.

BY N. C. T. HERBERT.

Outlined against the darkling blue,
  The little silver crescent hung;
Upon the serene summer air
  The flowers their fragrance flung.

" Now make a wish," said Lillian.
  " For know you not, whatever boon
That of the new moon you may ask,
  It will be granted soon ?

" O'er my right shoulder, I can see
  The silver gleam; good-luck be mine,
My wish I'll make quite secretly,
  That you may not divine."

He smiled upon her, as they stood
  Beside the casement opened wide.
" I've made my wish," said he; " it is
  That you may be my bride."

Lifting up her fair sweet face,
  She looked at him with mock surprise.
" Why, that is what I wished ! " she said,
  The love-light in her eyes.

Ah, little moon—'twas thus you brought
  Together loving hearts and true.
They might have drifted far apart,
  Had it not been for you.

SEVEN TIMES TEN.

To My Mother on Her Seventieth Birthday.

BY M. EMMA SIDNEY HERBERT.

CONTENTMENT.

The dew still sparkles on daisies and clover,
  There's a rainbow in heaven ;
I've lived my seven times, over and over,
  Today I am ten times seven.

You bells in the steeple have rung out your changes,
  Some sad, and some joyous to me ;
And in the evening of life, I am listening,
  Your echoes come over the lea.

Too faint, and too fleeting ; and yet, O what pleasure ;
  To list to the music that's borne me today,
'Tis heavenly harmony, slow, soothing measure,
  And every sad cadence has stolen away.

In life's echoes, one hears,
  More of mirth than of tears,
Should one listen for aye.

Heigh-ho ! rings now the marriage bell,
  Ringing out gladness.   Yes, I am a bride,
Waiting as claimant, my one constant lover,
  Henceforth, 'till death part us, to walk side by side,
To love, and to cherish; though darkness may hover,
  Faithful, whatever betide.

O, list again, and what to hear,
  But children's voices sweet,
And once the sound of their footsteps anear,
  To make joy all complete.

To see, to meet, to know,
  To love, then me to leave ;
But can I chide, if they bestow
  The bliss I would receive?
To see, to meet, to know,
  To love, then me to leave,
'Tis ever thus that children go—
  O, heart ! why should'st thou grieve?

I pray you hear my song of home,
  For it is not long ;
You will not hear should you farther roam,
  A happier song.
A home ne'er had a prouder mother,
  Nor fairer children, nor better name ;
Content to live with no wish for other,
  Nor thinking of wealth, or fame.

And ask you what is my home to me,
  My home of love ?
'Tis all that I wish my earth home to be :
  A portal to mansions above.

Should I long to go? Nay, I fain would stay,
  And yet I am willing to answer the call ;
But the world is so bright at the close of the day,
  When the sunset glows with a glory untold,
And clouds are turned to ruby and gold,
  And the vesper hymns are the sweetest of all.

THE BURIAL OF LINCOLN.

MAY 4TH, 1865.

BY MRS. MARY RANKIN JOHNSON.

" Bear him gently to his rest "* said the people.   It is done.
We have borne him gently on toward the setting of the sun—
We have gently, sadly, laid him in his Western home to sleep,
Loving hearts and guardian angels, their watch above him keep.

O never such a funeral the whole wide world has known,
Not the greatest, or the best beloved, that sat upon a throne;
O never such a triumph did any conqueror meet,
With victory on his banner and a nation at his feet !

In a solemn march of triumph, bore we proudly on our dead,
And the people rose to meet us with a blessing on his head.
They raised triumphal arches, glorious banners, o'er our track,
The bells pealed forth a welcome, and the cannon answered
          back.

But the city's hum was hushed, the banners draped in gloom,
And o'er that grand procession fell the stillness of the tomb—
Only the bells were tolling—" Four years ! four weary years ! "
And the blessing of the people, fell in silence, with their tears.

Keep back your tears O nation—Does not a conqueror come ?
Though the busy brain is resting, the kindly lips are dumb—
Four years of weary warfare—are they not over now ?
Receive him as a hero.   In triumph crown his brow !

With a sob comes back the answer —" O we cannot ; he is dead !
Our Father, O our Father ! Our Glory and our Head !
How is our strong staff broken !   How can we joy today ?
We have nought but tears to give him—Bear him gently on his
          way."

So we bear him gently onward, mid the stillness and the gloom ;
Through the states, and o'er the rivers and mountains to the
      tomb,
Thy beauty and thy glory, O land his name shall be,
Who saved a struggling nation, who bade the oppressed go free.

We bear him gently onward, with a proud and mournful tread,
Where Illinois awaits him, her dear and honored dead,
Receive him back O Mother—not unknown as he went forth,
But the glory of our nation, the honored of the earth.

There gathered to her bosom, he sleeps his long last sleep,
God gave it His Beloved—he was weary—should we weep ?
O, God our help in trouble, our hope in years to come,
Be Thou our strength our refuge and our Eternal Home.

    * Words on one of the Arches.

SIC VITA.

BY MRS. EDMUND L. JOY.

When we snatch life's prizes—the hand is not bold
While we coin our thoughts—another's are sold
While the feast is preparing—the guests wax cold
When angels visit—our welcome is doled
As the sunshine brightens—the shadows grow bold
In our cherished plans—mistakes unfold
While pleasures are budding—the heart grows old
When wealth is garnered—we touch not the gold
For the fifth act is played—and our days are told.

LINES ON THE ALABAMA RIVER.

BY MRS. F. WOLCOTT JACKSON.

Alabama ! gentle river,
  As we rouse thee from thy rest ;
Waking many a throb and quiver
  In thy calm and placid breast ;
     Half I fancy that before
     None have passed thy waters o'er.

Playful river ! that dost wind thee
  With an air so coy and meek ;
Didst thou wish that none should find thee
  In thy game of hide and seek ?
     What caprice thou dost pursue,
     Twining, doubling still anew!

Thou hast sought the forest only,
  Sole companion thou has made ;
From thy sides in grandeur lonely
  Rise thy moss-like banks of shade.
     While the oak's and willow's daughter
     Stoops to kiss thy brazen water.

Juniper and laurel blending,
  Dread not the grim woodman's stroke ;
Mark the bay her verdure lending,
  And the deep green water-oak ;
     While beyond them dark and tall,
     Solemn cypress lifts his pall.

Here magnolia ope's her flowers ;
  Dogwood peeps with star-like eyes ;
Honeysuckles rear their bowers ;

Jes'mine sheds her fragrant sighs
    O'er the blossoms low but sweet,
    Meekly growing at her feet.

Here brown moss, with fringe-like sweepings,
    Decks the aged oak tree's face ;
Ivy moves with subtle creepings,
    And the vines, which interlace,   '
        Clinging by their scarlet hands,
        Bind the forest as in bands.

On this spot, the moon, reclining,
    With her courtly stars around,
Gazes with a tender shining,
    For she loves this fairy ground.
        And when day asserts her law,
        Sighs because she must withdraw.

Thus the Indian sighed to lose thee,
    Sweetest stream ! which, when his sight
First beheld, he straight did choose thee,
    And in accents of delight
        Named thee, with enraptured breast
        "Alabama ! here we rest."